# This Past Year

By Philip C. Mack

Based on a true story

# Prologue

Late summer in Paris and Nicola sat at a café close to the Eiffel Tower on a warm evening. She'd been living there for a few years, but the novelty of the place had not yet worn off. She wasn't sure if it ever would; she loved every sight and every sound.

An old man sat at the table next to her with a poorly folded broadsheet newspaper. His cappuccino and baguette arrived and he dutifully tore chunks off the baguette, thickly layered masses of butter on it and dipped it into the layer of froth on the top of his coffee. She lit a cigarette. She hadn't been smoking long and often wondered why on earth she started smoking in her late-twenties, but she was in Paris so it was normal. If her parents knew she smoked they'd go crazy and she'd never hear the end of it. She drew the smoke in through her soft delicate lips and the flame crawled up towards her fingers like a tiny spider along a drainpipe. A loose ribbon of smoke emerged from the end of the cigarette and rose into the evening air.

She missed her best friend back in Scotland, but they were always so close that distance didn't really matter to them. Of course, nothing could beat actually being in the same city or even the same country, but Nicola was in France enjoying herself. Her parents did not approve of her being there. They couldn't understand why she wanted to live so far away and would always give her a hard time about it. They'd always ask her if she'd had her fun yet and was bored of the place and when can they expect her home. It would always make her more belligerent with them and her stubbornness proved to make it a permanent thing. It was her life to lead and she was prepared to live it her way. No one could tell her what to do.

After school, all she wanted to do was get as far away as she could. She hated school and had a bad reputation there. People used to spread rumours about her – and truths about her – so as soon as she was able to, she got out of Scotland. She didn't want to face those kinds of people and be reminded of some of the bad choices that she'd made growing up. School was hard for her. She lived in a small secluded village and didn't have any brothers or sisters, so other than her best friend, she had no one. That only made the relocation very easy.

She had a French boyfriend who she'd been with for several years, but she had plans for them to get married. They'd been together long enough and they both loved each other. Lately, he'd been having some issues with his anger, but he'd been under a lot of stress at work so Nicola made allowances for him. She thought the perfect thing would be for him to propose and then he'd have something positive to look forward to. She'd tried planting the seed with him and dropped hints whenever she could. She had visions of him getting down on one knee at the foot of the Eiffel Tower and all the tourists and dog-walkers and cyclists and runners would see her and be jealous of what an amazing continental life she was having. He wasn't ready to propose yet, but she supposed he was still too concerned about things at work. She was happy to give him time.

Hunger rolled in her stomach like thunder and she thought about ordering some food. She was careful not to spend too much money because she was trying to save as much as she could to buy a place for her and her boyfriend, or as she hoped by that time, her fiancé. She was very excited at the prospect of them having their own place together. Her savings pot was coming along quite nicely though, so she decided to order herself a little something. Anyway, it'd be easier if she just ate there before she got home, because her boyfriend often had a peculiar attitude with her regarding food. He was always very wary of what she ate and would criticise her at times, but she supposed he was just looking out for her.

The old man coughed and looked derisively at Nicola as she finished her cigarette. His baguette-butter-froth regime had been interrupted by wayward bands of smoke from her. He asked the waiter for some extra butter and Nicola thought about telling him that his cholesterol would probably kill him much sooner than second-hand smoke might. But he was just a grumpy old man and Nicola didn't really mind. Besides, she wasn't one for confrontation. In fact, she hated it and would avoid it at all costs.

She received a text from her boyfriend asking her why she wasn't at the apartment. She replied immediately and asked for the bill before getting her things together. She'd lost track of time sitting at her table, so now she was in a rush to get home because he didn't like to be kept waiting. He'd often ask her where she was or who she was with, which became annoying at times, but Nicola knew it was only because he loved her and she meant everything to him.

Sometimes, he came across quite harsh and he'd upset her, but she'd console herself with the fact it was surely a cultural thing. She'd avoid talking about it with her best friend however, because she'd tell Nicola that actually *he* was in the wrong. Nicola supposed she would only say that because she didn't know all the facts and couldn't ever appreciate how things really were over there. No one understood the love she and Patrice had.

# Chapter One

Snow began to fall late on a January night. Wind whipped between the buildings indiscriminately coating every surface with weightless sticky snowflakes. They coalesced on Charlie's window and slid down like tears as he stared blankly at his computer screen. The falling snow was charged by the streetlights that stood far below his flat creating orange glittery arcs that hung from each lamppost. The River Clyde lay dark and broody as it ran its course past his building. He sat at his desk and flicked through pictures on his laptop getting sentimental about life and decisions made in the past. He questioned himself and wondered how things had turned out the way they had. By no means was his life wasted, he was skilled beyond skilled. But to him it all meant nothing, because he was facing another night alone.

He stood up leaving a photo on the screen and walked over to the kitchen. The flat was very modern, which wasn't immediately a concern of his; he just liked the fresh clean-cut feel of the place. He had only recently moved in and despite being in his thirtieth year, it was his first 'own place' ever. Two adjacent corners which encompassed the living area were walled only by glass. Light would flood in during the day and he commanded an excellent view across the city one way and over the hills the other. On the dining area side, one large glass panel was a sliding door which led out onto a rooftop terrace. Further in from the dining area lay the living room. It was filled with new sofas and furniture and the computer desk he'd been sitting at. Initially he had no interest in viewing the place because it seemed too fancy, but the estate agent convinced him otherwise. When he got there, he was captivated by the glass walls around the living area. He loved being able to see out and view things, but most of all he loved the connection to everything outside.

A few boxes of things lay around waiting to be shown to their final stowing place. A couple of them had his dad's scribbly writing on them: *New Flat* or *Charlie's* they read.

He opened a double cupboard to look inside but it was not what he was looking for. He was still trying to settle on his cupboard layout and had swapped things round a few times. He tried another. *Bingo*. A few bottles of whisky were nestled inside and the rest waited sleepily in the boxes. He lifted and inspected the bottles in turn, every time rejecting them, 'Nope, that's too nice.' He was a person who liked to drink the whisky he bought rather than just hoard it away in a dark cupboard for no one to see or enjoy, but he was very reluctant to waste good whisky that had to sit patiently in a cask for years, only for him to throw it down his neck. And that was all he wanted to do. They were the sort of whiskies that he wanted to share with friends or to drink in the company of people he loved and cared for. Yet, he wanted something to drown out the noise in his head and sufficiently disassociate his brain cells so that he might get some sleep.

After deciding to keep them for a better time that he convinced himself would come, he instead made a cup of tea and returned to the computer. He resumed clicking through photos and reminisced. The only recent photos all seemed to be work photos; Syria, Jordan, Iraq, Nigeria, Sierra Leone and Central America. He had very few social photos from the past few years. For that, he'd have to delve into photos that were several years old and very much out of date. They were of a life that was once good, filled with good times and with love.

Charlie Maxwell joined the army straight from school. He already had a background in the Armed Forces and accelerated up the ranks until he was selected for Special Forces. He served a few years as a Section Commander and was tasked with the widest range of operations from what he referred to as 'First-in, Last-out' warfare, to hostage rescues, to coca eradication. He was headhunted as a Close Protection Officer for high-ranking officers and eventually VIP's, including foreign dignitaries. He'd travel overseas and coordinate security details for a whole host of events. He then spent time in Counterterrorism both at home and overseas. He was decorated several times for his service and bravery. More recently he had taken a role in Private Security, but that finished suddenly after five months, at which point he crawled back to the Armed Forces Careers Office and became an Army Skills Instructor. He was on the payroll of a Contingent based in Ayrshire. He didn't know why he took that one other than it being something different (and immediately available). It was also in a new place, but it was at 'home.' It was in Scotland.

He grew up on the east coast of Scotland, east of Edinburgh, but craved a change so decided to move to Glasgow. He loved Edinburgh, but his intentions were to start living a 'normal' life. He wanted to find someone to share it with and hadn't had any luck in Edinburgh during the times that he'd been home. Glasgow was a higher population so that ought to increase the chances, he reasoned.

He tipped his mug towards the un-illuminated ceiling light and it was finished. 'What now?' he asked himself. He had the nice apartment, a nice car, some money in the bank; all things that people say they strive for in life, and still he felt like he had nothing. The past few years he was made to be invisible, and invisible he was. He missed out on all the carefree shenanigans that all his friends seemingly got up to.

He stared out over his terrace and looked upon the fresh snow as it began layering gently outside. It looked delicate and soft and inviting. The notion came for him to go out for a drive. It was always a good way for him to clear his head. He went through to the bedroom and opened the wardrobe. He was an organised person and on the far left were some outdoor and winter clothes which he threw on. The far right saw a few suits hanging which he'd break out for a special occasion. Casual and smart shirts bridged the divide in-between. He put on black tactical trousers, a t-shirt, a navy wool pullover and grabbed a jacket, hat and gloves. Before leaving the flat, he switched off all the lights except the one in the hall and headed down to the parking garage in the basement.

The garage was instantly colder and it gave him a hint of the temperature outside. It was dimly lit and not very well occupied. Most of the people that stayed in the building worked in the city and had no need for a car. Of the few cars that were slumbering there however, they were mostly expensive and prestige. These were owned by managers and executives and only ever saw the light of day on the occasional Sunday, for a first date, or any other time they felt the need to show off. His was also an expensive high-performance car but it was not for show. It was the only car there that had been properly used.

Pulling out of the garage onto the road, the snow creaked under the tyres. It was very light but still falling. He drove into the night, not knowing where he was driving to or what he'd do when he got there. The air was crisp and sharp and it began thumping in the open window as he left the city. The temperature dropped further still and he started to feel the chill surround him. His ears popped a few times from the panting air pressure through the window. It was potentially uncomfortable but he was just glad to feel something. The weather forecast didn't expect snow, so the roads had not been gritted. It got heavier and lay thicker and thicker on the deserted asphalt that led out of the city. He would pass the occasional car carving their cautious way through the freshly rested powder. Most likely they were on their way home and just got caught out, but soon they'd be in the comfort and warmth of their home with the ones that they loved. Other than that, there were seemingly no other cars around. Who else in their right mind would willingly be out in such cold and harsh conditions? Hence, he was in the same place he always found himself – where no one else would choose to be.

Charlie was lonely. The job had cost him the only relationship he'd ever had and as he thought about his new flat full of nothing, he wondered if it had all been worth it. Perhaps he'd have been better off staying at home with her, rather than trying to be someone and do something, because he couldn't cope with the desolation any more.

As he drove, he focused on the road. He concentrated on the stiffening rubber compound of the cooling tyres as they pushed through the bed of snow trying to find tarmac. They struggled for grip at times, sliding then regaining control, sliding then straightening up again. He played around with the oversteer on every corner. He'd deliberately push the throttle a little too hard and the back end would step out, causing him to use corrective steering. It felt like a while since he'd had to drive like that. He was highly trained in advanced car control, which came from his time in Close Protection. That meant he was used to driving that way sometimes whilst taking fire, or even returning fire, so he was just playing. His heart rate accelerated and adrenaline started to flow into his bloodstream as his driving became more reckless.

As his senses became keener, his speed increased. The car travelled faster and faster and he could feel the grip go completely at times. The car squirmed and wriggled. He kept it on the road but the style of driving was fast becoming incompatible with the conditions. Even in his self-destructive state however, he still considered other people and would only be reckless when he knew he was alone. *If I crash out, I don't want to take anyone else with me*, he thought.

As he was selected for Special Forces, it became increasingly difficult to sustain his relationship and as far as his family and girlfriend were concerned, he was still doing the same job as any other soldier, but it seemed all of a sudden, he didn't want to talk anymore. He wouldn't be in regular contact and he'd refuse to talk about the things that he'd done. His father had an inkling because he knew how good he was. He never intimated that to his mother however, since she worried enough as it was. Instead, he'd be forced to pacify her about why her son didn't want to talk to her anymore. As for his girlfriend, it was hard enough for her to deal with him being away before, despite relatively regular contact, but the increasingly secretive nature of his work put too much of a strain on them and they broke up after several years of being together.

They were childhood sweethearts and the couple at school that everybody envied. They seemingly had the perfect relationship, but after school he wanted to get out into the world and achieve things. He wanted to do some good and feel like he'd contributed to something somehow, whereas she was determined to just get a normal job, live a normal life in a normal house and start a family. He wanted that too, but not immediately. His aspirations drove him further and further away from her until he was too far to return. He had been devoid of real human contact in the years that followed, but was afraid to get close to anyone else whilst he still had that job. He didn't want to feel that pain again or be forced to break someone's heart either, so he threw himself into work.

He stopped loving her a long time ago and stopped pining for her, but now he craved someone – anyone – who could make him feel anything like that. He began to feel not human, as if he had turned himself into a machine; a machine capable of the most extreme tasks in the most hazardous conditions and a machine that felt no emotion. Except he did have emotions and the more he tried to deny them, the more exacerbated they became.

He was annoyed with himself. He had come full circle to the mindset he suffered sitting at his desk about an hour beforehand. *Is this it?* he thought. Is this how things would be for the rest of his life? Nothing but emptiness and self torment? He couldn't stand the feeling. He refused to return to the work. He had chosen to give it up to seek out a life for himself. He was only officially an instructor by now, but it bored him. He'd consult and assist with some domestic counter-terrorism jobs if they were related to jobs he'd done before, but that was it. He wanted a 'normal job', yet didn't know what. He had no idea how to spend his life now that he had it back.

The engine roared and whined as the supercharger surged air into it, propelling the car forward with excessive speed, and his thoughts encouraged him along. *What if I just push it too far and take the car off the road? What if I just end it here? It may even look like an accident.*

*There's no note to be found in the flat, everything's normal. Everything's normal...and I can't stand it.*

He thought about his affairs and finances and what the implications might be if he jumped off the mortal coil. He had very little debt, just a few hundred on a couple of credit cards, just to be normal. There was the mortgage on the flat, but it could easily be sold. He'd bought it with a healthy deposit anyway so it was bound to be in positive equity. Then there was some money in the bank and his savings. That would mean he'd leave money behind and none of the family would be put into financial distress by his demise – merely emotional distress. He thought about the things in his flat and if there was anything he wouldn't want his family to find but there was nothing. He'd not been there long enough to accumulate anything and everything else was new and shiny.

The road emptied and straightened out and he pushed the pedal hard. The speedometer shot up and he shut the window. His eardrums were grateful as the pounding cold air stopped bombarding them only for a frantic silence to fill the car. Seventy miles per hour; the snow turned from soft flurry to warp speed in the windscreen. Eighty miles per hour; the wheels twitched and quivered as the snow filled the treads and he started to lose grip again. Ninety miles per hour; the corner was still a distance away but he slammed on the brakes as he approached. He fought with the wheel and the car shrieked, sliding only slightly off track. The ABS clicked away under the brake pedal and the car strived for traction. He felt bad for the car and the thought crossed his mind about its unnecessary destruction. It took a lot longer than usual for the car to stop. Charlie knew exactly the distances and from what speed, but only for dry or rainy conditions, he'd hardly driven like that in the snow before. The road swept round to the right and he eventually came to a stop, dead straight, just before the corner. That was merely a test run. He was not one to be ill-prepared or do things in half measures, so he had to investigate the absolute limits first. He was fairly confident that he found them and moved off again.

He drove a few corners until the road straightened out again. The speed mounted once more. Fifty; he put the meaningless destruction of his car out of his mind. Sixty; the car changed up a gear and the wheels spun. Seventy; *TING!! TING!!* A high-pitched alert and vibration came from his centre console. It distracted him for a second until he realised it was his phone, but kept his pressure on the throttle. Eighty; he looked back up at the road. Suddenly through the haze of his speed and windscreen wipers and headlights, he saw something in front of him. A deer stood proudly in the middle of the road, uninvited to the chaos. He hit the brakes as a reaction, then a thought came to him and he shut his eyes. He blindly steered to the right in a half-attempt to avoid the deer and kept his eyes shut. He could feel the car spin and spin. He was prepared to hit him and felt bad that he might kill it, but thought it was a perfect excuse.

*It's now justified. So that's it, I'm finished. It's all over and soon there will be no more pain. People can read about the multiple decorated ex-serviceman who's taken out assassins and terrorists, only to come home and be killed by a deer on a snowy road.*

He was prepared for impact. He felt the car turn around. And turn around again. He continued to slide, keeping his eyes shut. He wondered when the impact would come and wondered how it would feel when the car eventually came off the road and wrapped itself around a tree. He continued to slide. He wondered if it would be fast. He wondered how long it would take for someone to find him. Then he wondered how horrific it might be for someone to find him like that.

The car ground to a halt. He opened his eyes. His hands were pinned to the steering wheel. Smoke rose from the front of the car and whipped up through the beam of the headlights. He wasn't sure how many times he had spun, or even if he did spin. Did he just imagine it? He got out of the car and removed the torch from his pocket. He inspected the road and sure enough, there were thick marks carved through the snow, crossing over and crossing over, stretching for a few hundred yards. He pointed his torch down the road but the deer was gone. He shone it into the woods and saw nothing. He tried the field on the other side; nothing.

His heart pounded and pounded. Snow filtered through the trees that lined the roadside and landed on his nose and cheeks, melting instantly from the heat that suddenly flushed his face. He looked back at the car and the headlights continued to shine up the road casting long low shadows from the grass verge and along the tyre tracks. The engine was still purring and the door was open, allowing a few snowflakes to gather in the door pocket. The smoke issuing from the front grille was being gently dispersed by a soothing wisp of wind. Otherwise, his car was still fully intact. He felt grateful for that, at least.

Looking further up and down the road there was no trace of anyone else. He'd gotten away with it. His heart was still racing as he experienced the same feeling he used to get from his job. He had walked away from several car wrecks and it was just part of the routine, just another day at the office. But here, it was a wreck without the wreckage. His instincts were triggered however and his strong animalistic aptitude for survival took over. He was breathing heavily and the cold black air filled his lungs. It felt clean and purifying, softly suppressing the fire that raged inside him. He felt ashamed about what he had done, or what he had tried to do and was glad that no one had to stumble across him unawares come the morning. Returning to the car, he shut the door, put the heater on and turned on the radio. The car ended up facing the way he came, exactly on the correct side of the road, so he thought he should oblige. 'Go home, Charlie,' he whispered to himself. He slowly and calmly drove off back the way he came.

On the outskirts of a town, there was a round-the-clock supermarket in plain sight from the road. It had been snowing there too, but not so heavily. It was a big supermarket and there were only a few cars parked there at that time of night, probably mostly belonging to staff. They all had a matching smattering of snow on their windscreens and roofs. He wondered why it was necessary for a shop to be open twenty-four hours a day in such a quiet place, but was relieved that it was because he needed the respite.

He parked the car unnecessarily far from the door, picked his phone up from the console and headed inside. The security guard watched him as he walked around. Of course, he was aware that he was being watched and it was a usual occurrence for him. He had a confidence and a subtle presence that some may mistake as a shop lifter. He looked shifty. Then there was the way he was dressed with all dark clothes, tactical trousers and hat and gloves, all completely appropriate for the conditions outside of course. It may have been all of that, or perhaps it was just the fact that he was seemingly the only customer in the shop. After grabbing something to drink and eat he held the receipt in plain view as he exited, intimating a nod at the security guard. He suddenly remembered his phone went off and unholstered it. He removed a glove to swipe the screen. "*Message*: Hey! How are you? Do you remember me?"

The message was from *Nicola Wallace* and the name rang a bell. He touched her picture to view it full size. 'Shit, yeah. I *do* remember you,' he exclaimed to the empty car park. It was someone he went to school with. They were never terribly close and didn't have any classes together, but he saw her around a lot and spoke with her often. Charlie remembered her as being attractive but he was never interested considering he was so in love at the time. It had been about twelve years since they last spoke. He had never heard of her or thought of her since. *I wonder why she's getting in touch,* he thought. He started to construct a reply then deleted it, deciding it would be better to reply in the morning. It was already very late at night, or early in the morning and he supposed she wouldn't be expecting a reply immediately. He got in the car and tried to recall conversations they had all the way home.


A siren tore through the serenity of the winter morning as a police car sped along the Clydeside Expressway. He woke up like a shot and checked the time: 7:43am, then laid his head back again and stared at the ceiling for a while. He thought about the previous night and how crazy he had been and made a promise to himself to never try anything like that again. It would be so unfair on his family and friends. And despite feeling like that the night before, he was glad he was unsuccessful. It's amazing how everything always seemed better in the morning. He realised that suicide wouldn't really stop the pain, it'd only pass it on to someone else. Thinking about the deer, he considered it to be an unlikely saviour and remembered the message he received.

The television showed the news as breakfast cooked. The coffee percolator sat bubbling away, spewing a heavy caffeine aroma throughout the flat as he looked out the window and to the hills beyond. They were still white, but the snow had almost already gone from the terrace. He sat down to eat and thought about his reply. He went back onto her profile and noticed that she also happened to be living in Glasgow. He added her and started his reply. "Hey, you know I was feeling pretty down last night and I was pleased to hear–" He deleted that. "Hi, I'm great thanks! Talk about blast from the past! I was just out for a drive–" he deleted that too. He drafted the message several times until he eventually sent: "I'm fine, thanks! Must be about twelve years? I see you're in Glasgow too. I don't know how busy you are these days, but it'd be nice to go for a catch up if you're able?" The message was difficult to write and he couldn't really understand why.

He looked through some of her photos. The first one was her standing outside at a coastal ruin. He recognised it because it was from home. She was leaning against a wall and the sun was setting over the sea behind her. The sky was filled with pinks and oranges, a streak of cloud ran across the picture and she looked just slightly off to the right-hand side. She wore a black waterproof jacket with bright blue zips and her dark hair fell around her shoulders onto it. She was beautiful. He always had a dormant fondness for her, one which he didn't know if he was suddenly realising. That made it worse. The night before he could have sent the message and not scrutinised it too hard, but now he had to worry about how to present himself. Charlie wasn't used to it.

He tried to reassure himself that the reply was sound. He thought maybe he'd been a bit pushy asking to meet immediately, but he was always direct. Still, a feeling of dread came into him. Maybe he should have just asked how she was and took it from there. He knew nothing about her current situation, yet his intentions were genuine and he replied merely as an old schoolmate and as a fellow Glasgow-dweller. He assumed she was married with kids despite the lack of evidence from the few pictures on her profile. Little did he know the hardship she was going through.

# Chapter Two

It was a Tuesday afternoon and Charlie waited outside the place she suggested. He glanced at his watch and wondered where she was. He wondered if he got the right day or place, or if she had changed her mind. He tried calling but it went straight to voicemail. So now she was ignoring him? For some reason, schoolboy nerves washed over him when he arrived. The sensation started to subside after a while, only for them to return little by little the longer he stood waiting. He could hardly remember the last time he'd ever felt butterflies in his stomach like that.

People went about their daily business. Cars, buses, taxis and trucks went past, people heading to or from meetings, students and mums and dads and kids buzzed along the pavement as he stood idle.

He wondered how long he ought to leave it until he went home again. He'd never been stood up before so didn't know the protocol.

He checked his phone a few times and kept it in his hand so anyone watching him would see that he was waiting for someone, instead of just being a weirdo standing around. Being someone who used to watch people covertly, he would always have a sense of displaying what he was doing, or subverting his actions to appear how he wanted them to appear, should anyone else be watching him. He knew that really, nobody was watching, but it was just how his brain was programmed from work and it was very hard to undo. He wore jeans and a nice t-shirt. It was a neater appearance than his usual one. He was in the habit of tactical trousers and boots and would feel odd if he wasn't wearing that during the day. When he started in Counterterrorism, he had to slip into everyday life without looking too conspicuous, whilst maintaining an operational readiness. He was always ready for something that might never happen.

As he got ready to leave, he dressed as normal then thought to look in the mirror. He looked utilitarian and perhaps a little intimidating, not like the kind friendly guy that Nicola would remember from school. He was still in there though. He wondered why he was even concerned about how he looked, but decided to get changed anyway. The one compromise was his jacket. It was still cold outside so he wore his softskin covert tactical jacket. There was a pocket in the back which contained his gloves. He pulled them on after he got out of the car because the chill nibbled at his fingertips and knuckles. They were his old fast-roping gloves.

He scanned up and down the street as he thought about abandoning the afternoon. A bus sat opposite for a while and when it pulled away, she appeared beyond the roar and smoke of the engine. He recognised her immediately. She wore a dark purple coat and her handbag refused to stay on her shoulder as she dashed across the road. 'Oh my gosh, I'm so sorry I'm late! There was a problem with the train, so I had to get the bus. And my phone died so I couldn't get in touch. How are you? It's really nice to see you!' She gave him a hug and kissed the air in front of his cheek. 'Have you been waiting long?'

'It's nice to see you too. I was a bit late myself, so don't worry about it.' He was lying of course but didn't want her to feel bad. His timekeeping was impeccable and he always arrived in plenty of time to anything. Unfortunately, he had arrived almost half an hour early and she was half an hour late, but he didn't mind at all now that she was there. He was aware that half an hour was much too early to arrive for a date, but then it wasn't a date it was just a catch up. Either way, he was way behind in normal social practices.

Beneath the coat she wore jeans and a check shirt under her navy blue jersey. The dark waves of her hair were slicked back over her head and tied into a tight ponytail. She was as beautiful as he remembered, or maybe even a little bit more so. 'Shall we go inside then?' he asked. 'I've never been here before.'

'Yeah, let's get in from the cold!' She rubbed at her hands and gave a quick shiver. 'I'm here fairly often, it's a favourite of mine.'

It was a gastropub which served really good food and had specialist beers and ale. The décor was quite wooden lodgey and all the tables were thick solid oak. She picked a table.

'Would you like me to hang your coat?' She looked at him inquisitively and he pointed out the coat hook next to them.

'Sure, thanks. I've never noticed that before. I don't know how long I've been coming here too!' In the first few seconds of entering, he surveyed it because it was a new place to him. He noticed the coat hooks, as well as where and what type the fire extinguishers were, how many people were inside, including how many staff, what ages and physical capability they all were and where the emergency exits were. This was another old habit of his.

'So...' she wondered where to start as she shuffled along the bench to sit opposite him, 'what have you been up to the past twelve years?' She smirked.

'Well,' he smirked back, 'just been working away. Sort of finishing up now though and looking for something new...it's been a...well...I just need a change of direction.' She tilted her head as she

listened intently to him, 'And I've just recently moved to Glasgow...'
He was a little bit lost for words. 'It hardly seems like twelve years does
it?'

She noticed he said '*I*' moved to Glasgow. She had wondered
whether or not he was still with his high school sweetheart. It seemed
not, but she wanted to be sure. 'Yeah, twelve years. Makes you feel old
doesn't it!' She took a sip of her drink. 'So...are you still with Rachel?'
She had already been through all the photos on his profile and couldn't
see any recent evidence of her.

'Oh no, that finished a long time ago. We were together for six
years in the end, but...it was hard with my job. It put too much strain on
her and we sort of drifted apart. What about you? What have you been
up to?'

'Well...I did my art, if you remember,' Charlie smiled and
nodded. 'I moved around a bit. I lived in Paris. I was there for a long
time, it was...quite good,' there was a long pause, 'but I just decided to
come home. I'm also quite new to Glasgow. I think it's amazing how
we ended up here at the same time though!'

She was right. They had both been far from home, gone through
so much and both come back. The remarkable part though, was that they
settled not at home outside Edinburgh but they both decided Glasgow

would be the best place for them to start afresh from their old lives and experiences.

'That's a shame about you and Rachel, you guys were a really sweet couple. What was your job? How come that got in the way?'

'Well, you'll remember how I was all about armed forces when I was at school, so I followed that path. I ended up as Special Forces, Close Protection and that sort of thing.' He paused as he wondered how much detail to go into. 'I was away a lot. I was often not in touch with her…because I couldn't…and…it was hard for her not knowing if I was going to come back, or come back in one piece…you know? I would promise her I would every time I went, and…' he shrugged, 'I managed to keep that promise. But it took its toll.'

'Oh God Charlie, that sounds intense!' She ran her slick ponytail through her fingers and draped it down in front of her. 'Are you still in touch with her?' He felt like she was really putting him on the spot. They'd only just met after so many years and she was intently quizzing him about a relationship that finished seven years ago.

'Erm, no. We've still got a few mutual friends though, so I hear about her now and then. She's married with two kids and I'm told another on the way. That's great…for her. She always just wanted to settle down, which I wanted too, but just not straight away. So we just didn't…fit anymore, I suppose.'

'And what about now? Are you with anyone?'

'No…completely single.' He cursed himself and thought he couldn't make himself seem any more desperate.

He thought it was too early to be talking about relationship statuses but she'd already set the precedent, 'What about you? You got a boyfriend, married?'

'No. I just broke up with my fiancé. It was a bit messy…but I'm moving on now.' *Messy* was an understatement, and *moving on* was a lie. Suddenly, a tremor of zeal ran through him. *Is this why she wanted to meet? Is she looking for someone new? I was always nice to her.* The thought nudged about inside his head as he looked at her again. Her eyes were like silky dark chocolate and they watched him keenly. The words from her mouth were sweet like birdsong on her peach lips as she continued, 'And the art thing didn't really pay off. I retrained in business and marketing…of all things. I'm currently looking for a job here, but it seems nobody's hiring.'

'Don't worry Nicola, I'm sure you'll find something soon.' He wasn't sure if he was talking about the job, or a partner.


They spent a couple of hours trying to get caught up on the previous twelve years and despite all the talking that went on, they both hid things from one another. She started checking her watch as the afternoon wore on into the early evening. She had plans with her best friend who Charlie also knew from school. Despite intending to already be at home getting ready, she was still sitting chatting with him because she was enjoying herself. He could listen in a way that no one else really did and was interested in all the things she said. That was something she remembered of him before.

He didn't probe her when she talked vaguely about things that would lead to a difficult conversation for her, one she was not yet ready to have with him. He also didn't try to steer the conversation onto him, yet things would come up about him that most people would brag about. He had the nice penthouse flat with some outside space on the riverfront. She invited herself round at some point and as she asked more about it, he felt obliged to show her a few photos. He only had the photos on his phone for his own reference after viewing the place the first time and didn't tell her about the fancy car or the other things he had because he supposed if she was meant to know about them, she'll see them in good time. He wasn't sure what her intentions were and didn't know if they'd meet again, or when.

'So, I better let you get on, have you got any plans for tonight?' he asked.

'Well, I'm meeting Claire, we're going to a comedy club. Feel free to come along.'

Claire Stewart was Nicola's best friend at school. They were always together and seemed joined at the hip. During the conversation, she told him how they were still as close and she was living in Glasgow too. That was the main reason for Nicola deciding to move there.

Charlie thought for a second, feeling a palpitation in his chest he didn't quite recognise. The time spent catching up with Nicola was nice – it was an experience unlike any others he'd had recently and he feared he might get carried away. He had to limit himself and cool off from the meeting before seeing her again. He was unsure of himself and she looked so beautiful. Her smile was so vibrant and it altered something in him.

'Erm, I'm busy tonight I'm afraid. Maybe another time?' He thought that should be good enough and that'd give him some time to reflect and they could message each other later.

'How about Thursday night? We're going to a play, you should come along.' It didn't look like she was going to let him get away without agreeing to the next rendezvous. He liked it.

'Sure, I'm free.'

He walked the long way back to his car. The empty seat on the passenger side questioned him as to why he didn't offer her a lift home or agree to go along to the comedy club. He pondered that as he drove back to his flat by himself to spend the evening on his own.

# Chapter Three

He rode the subway to the west end and walked along to a church that had been converted into a theatre. Posters hung on the railings outside advertising the play and indicating he'd made it to the right place. Other than that, the outside of the church remained the same. The Gothic building stood on the main road next to the traffic lights and he stood too, waiting for Nicola and Claire.

The play starred one of Nicola's friends and she'd arranged to pick the tickets up on arrival. Charlie wore a plain black suit from the far right of his wardrobe and a dark grey shirt from the middle. He looked smart whilst feeling a little bit naked without his tactical trousers, but supposed he had to learn to handle the feeling if he wanted to start being 'normal'. In the distance, Nicola's hair blew and whipped in front of her face and she peeled it away using her pinkie. He could see Claire and recognised her instantly, the same way he did with Nicola. They both looked the same as they had at school, the way they moved and their whole aura. They both looked as pretty and as youthful. He felt as if he was back in time, despite the fact that he never waited on them for anything ever before.

'Hey Charlie!' Nicola started waving frantically. She hugged him warmly as Claire waited to say hello.

'Charlie! Oh my God, it's been so long! You're looking really well.' Charlie had never been much into working out, only working. But his job crafted his body into a strong, robust and attractive one. He still had the kind smile that Nicola and Claire knew. His eyes were still as striking but seemed somehow deeper from all the things he'd seen, good and bad. His hair was a little longer. He decided to let it grow out and only had it 'tidied up' by the hairdresser since finishing. It was usually always kept short so he could be operational and this was the first chance he had to grow it and he really suited it.

'It's great to see you, Claire. You're looking well too. Both of you have hardly changed from school, still as beautiful as I remember.'

'You've not changed either,' Nicola claimed. It wasn't true. The years of combat and the break-up with his high-school sweetheart, followed by years of failed attempts at finding someone to love him had changed him.

Charlie's heart was too big. He had such a desire to care and guard people from all the horrible things in the world, which meant he only ever wanted to have meaningful relationships. They proved to be more and more elusive as time went on. He wasn't particularly keen on the club scene and much to the puzzlement of his friends, had turned down a lot of girls that were just looking for a casual hook-up. 'That's the perfect scenario!' they'd say. He often questioned himself about it too, but knew deep down it just wasn't his style. There were a couple of occasions where he'd convince himself just to take whoever it was home. He'd try to pick out something endearing and something unique in her and exaggerate it to a level where, in his drunken state, he could feel something rather than just the physical. But he didn't enjoy the awkwardness of the morning. Waking up to someone he knew nothing about or sleeping with someone and never seeing them again wasn't a sensation that he particularly enjoyed. He gave a lot and had a tendency to get very attached. Every girl left an impression on him, be it after six years or six hours together.

It may have been down to the fact that he had a serious relationship from school. The formative years of his life were not spent getting drunk and sleeping with random people. He was blissfully happy in a relationship with someone who he loved very much. He was aware that all his friends were doing that sort of thing, but he didn't need to. They only did that because they wanted to be having sex, but he had it regularly and didn't need to go out to find it.

'Shall we go in?' Claire asked. The play was an amateur production by a local theatre group. Charlie wasn't sure exactly what it was about. Not that he had anything against theatre but he just never had much of a chance to go before. The fact that he didn't understand it didn't make him question how good or bad it was, rather, it made him feel like he was a bit out of his depth by not being able to appreciate it. He didn't mind at all though, because it was a new activity for him and it was with Nicola and Claire.

'So…how was the play?' Nicola had a mischievous look on her face and looked to Charlie with anticipation.

'Erm…it was…good?'

'It was shit, Charlie. That's two and a half hours of my life that I'll never get back!'

He conceded. 'Yeah, well…it was a bit…out there?'

'Oh, you're far too polite!' She gripped his arm briefly. 'I'm just going to go and say hi, then how about we go for a drink?'

They took a taxi five minutes into town to a bar that was hidden away along an alleyway. It was a popular place, but one that you had to know existed otherwise you would walk past every day and still not be aware it was there at all. On the street front was a newsagent, which helped disguise it even more. They headed down the alleyway and heavy cooking smells spewed out onto the street from the restaurant on the opposite side of the alley. The meagre street lighting threw a dim light onto the industrial refuse bins standing along the wall of the restaurant. It looked like an alleyway that would only be used for deliveries during the day or a potential indiscrete urination point once the clubs were closed. And yet, there was a bouncer standing in the nook of a door with a sign suspended above his head.

They had to walk down stairs to get to the bar and Nicola pushed a door open at the bottom. It was a narrow double door and Charlie had to push the second one open to get through unhindered. Once inside, it looked like a retro mish-mash of a family home. There were small round tables and a few booths around the edges. Alcoves adorned most of the walls which held charming pieces of tat: old board games, jigsaw puzzles and cathode ray television sets that were long since dead. Retro posters hung, sometimes squintly, at random intervals. The people inside were mostly students with skinny jeans and holes in their loose jumpers and Charlie felt quite out of place. It was too hip for him.

The bar was small yet well appointed. The barman wore jeans, a white t-shirt and navy waistcoat. He had long hair tied up into a bun and looked friendly but tired of pouring vodka cranberries all night. They picked a booth and Charlie went to order some drinks. Nicola followed. 'Good evening guys, what can I get you?' Charlie looked at Nicola but she waited for him to order.

'I'll have an Old Fashioned? If you do them?' The barman looked pleased to have something different to make and wasn't offended by Charlie's inquisitive tone. Nicola was surprised. She didn't even know what an 'Old Fashioned' was.

'A vodka tonic and a gin and tonic, please,' she said.

'Right away,' said the barman with a friendly smile. He picked a short wide tumbler and lifted it up to the light to inspect it for cleanliness.

'An Old Fashioned?' she asked, as the barman started to cut away an orange peel. 'Is that your drink then?'

'It's one of the things I drink. It's whisky based though. I'm a big whisky fan.'

'Oh, bloody hell, are you always this fussy?' She nudged him and giggled playfully.

'I prefer discerning…' The barman couldn't help but overhear and chuckled to himself under his breath as the drink started to take shape.

When they returned to the table, Claire was patiently waiting. He sat opposite them and they continued their catch up. After Nicola's meeting with Charlie, a full debrief was conducted at the comedy club, so Claire was up to speed so far.

'I totally knew that you'd end up in that job. That was always your thing at school.'

'And he looked really good in the uniform too!' Nicola interjected.

'How cool is it that we've all ended up here in the same place at the same time?' Charlie was swirling his drink around in the wide glass whilst the ingredients interspersed.

'I know, Nicola and I were saying that the other day. I'm really glad to see you two again.'

Whilst the three of them talked, Nicola didn't take her eyes off Charlie. He found it incredibly useful in trying to gauge the whole situation. At school, Nicola and Claire were essentially one and the same person. They both meant the same to him and treated them the same way, which was in fact the same way he treated everyone else. Charlie was always a gentleman, perhaps not entirely of his time.

Growing up, he'd always been very close to his mum and sister and as such always held women in very high regard. After seeing Nicola again for the first time, he felt a pang of appeal towards her but couldn't understand if it was just from seeing an old acquaintance after so long and the throwback it gave him to a simpler and happier time, his mounting desperation, or if there was something more to it. He had never met up with an old school friend, particularly a beautiful female one, after twelve years, so had no way to evaluate. That was of course, until he met Claire again that evening.

Claire spoke to him with interest and they enjoyed catching up but now as he sat opposite them in a bar probably too trendy for him, drinking a drink called an Old Fashioned (funnily enough), he didn't see them the same way as he saw them at school and they were not one and the same. Claire was great and he was very happy catching up with her again but Nicola was different.

'Claire, take our photo!' Nicola handed Claire her phone and slid out of the booth to swap sides. She put her arm around Charlie and smiled as widely as she could. She sat very close and some of her hair fell onto him. He could smell her perfume and felt the slenderness of her thigh against his.

'Smile!'

When the photo was done, Nicola didn't move except to remove her arm from Charlie's shoulder. She stayed so close to him and shuffled her feet, crossed and re-crossed her legs a few times as they sat there. She often touched Charlie when doing so, but neither of them minded. They talked and laughed and she often glanced her hand onto Charlie or made excuses to touch him. She was flirting for sure.

The bar became busier as more student types filtered in through the narrow double doors. The room next door had been opened – that was the club. The booming of the speakers could just be heard through the music and drone of everyone in the bar area. He wasn't drunk enough yet to dance but was coerced into going through by Nicola and Claire. The club room was still empty but they grabbed a table. After piling their coats and handbags inconspicuously into a corner, they headed to get more drinks. The club was filled with a dense blue light and other lights flashed randomly as the speakers blared. He could feel the thumping in his chest and throughout his body. His hands trembled a little bit and he wasn't sure if it was the music, alcohol or anticipation that caused it. He often suffered a tremble in his hands. It was some kind of side effect of the job, the rough duty and the constant injury, but it was a little stronger than usual.

They continued talking, although it was much more difficult. He would have been quite happy to remain through in the other room talking peacefully with them. He often had difficulty when there was a lot of background noise. Being exposed to so much gunfire and explosions had a negative effect on his hearing. When it was quiet, he would remember that he had tinnitus and his ears would ring, but in a loud club it made communication even more difficult than it ordinarily would be. He struggled to catch everything they were saying and it frustrated him. Thankfully, Nicola sat next to him again and she would press her hands on his thigh to lean in close and talk to him. Only then would he be able to hear things properly.

A few people started to dance and so followed a few more including Nicola and Claire. 'Come on Charlie!' He may have declined had it not been for the way Nicola looked. Her hair fell about her face like ribbons of midnight silk and her smile was contagious and catching. He slinked his way onto the dance floor abandoning his empty glass at the table. He began to dance somewhat awkwardly and after persevering for a few minutes felt he needed a bit more Dutch courage. He approached the bar in the club room.

'Old Fashioned, vodka tonic and gin and tonic please.'

'Sorry mate, they only do Old Fashioned's next door. Can I get you something else instead?' He thought about heading through to the other bar but didn't want to just disappear because he could feel Nicola's eyes on him.

'Erm, rum and coke instead then. Cheers.'

Whilst the drinks were being poured, Nicola watched as Charlie was approached by a girl at the bar. They spoke for a while and she took out her phone. Charlie took out his wallet and gave her a twenty-pound note. The girl turned away, paused, turned back to give him a huge hug and then went off with her friend. She saw the whole thing unfold and demanded to know who the girl was to him and why the fuck he owed her money.

'Who was that girl? What did she want?' Her face was hard and there were creases on her pale brow.

'It was some Australian girl. She had this bullshit story about needing to borrow money for a taxi home. She was asking for a fiver and said she'd take my number and we'd go for a date and she'd pay me back, she must have thought I was born yesterday.'

'And what did you do, I saw you give her something though?'

'Yeah, I gave her twenty quid, told her to get home safe and that I'm too busy to catch her for a date.'

'What the fuck Charlie?? Why did you do that??' Swearing from Nicola's lips didn't seem right to him. It was like a big dog shit in a bed of roses. He was taken aback at her reaction.

'Well, on the outside chance that she might use it to get home, or she'll have some of it left to get her home then that's alright.'

'Why…I don't…Where did she go? I'm going to get your money back.'

Nicola filled with anger and was determined to find this girl and make her account for taking money from Charlie and taking him for a fool. She marched towards the bar and looked left and right. Charlie followed her and placed his hand on her back to turn her around. 'Nicola, forget it. It doesn't matter.' She appeared unsettled and Charlie couldn't place it. Was she drunk and overreacting? Or was it something else? Charlie thought she might have been jealous. It all helped the feeling that was starting to mount about her intentions.

'Just…you can't do that sort of thing, you know? What a bitch, just because she's pretty she thinks she can take advantage of you…I don't want to let anyone take advantage of you.'

'I had the choice Nicola. And if I told her to get lost I'd be worried all night about whether she gets home or not.'

'She's not your responsibility though.'

Claire had been looking for them and approached from behind. 'Well, maybe not, but–'

She interrupted him, 'What's going on here then? Looks like some serious talk?'

'Oh, no, it's nothing. Just Charlie being too good to people like usual.'

'Come on and dance you two losers, we're in a club!'


It didn't take long for Nicola to forget all about the girl who cleverly extorted twenty pounds from Charlie. She really couldn't have picked anyone better. As they danced, Charlie's suit jacket was unbuttoned and flapped around. She tugged at it a couple of times to bring him in closer. He liked when the space diminished between them. She could smell him and his scent was manly and powerful. There was a whiff of whisky and citrus on his breath. She felt compelled to wrap her arms around him but something in her made her refrain.

The way her eyes were lit and how her smile looked in the flashing lights of the club made him feel like he ought to try and kiss her, but he resisted. They'd met as friends and he was in no rush. It was clear to him that she enjoyed his company and he was certain that this was not the only time they'd be dancing together, or find themselves close to one another. Any other man would have probably gone in for the kiss, but Charlie was not any other man. He was happy to play the long game and where someone else would be happy to get her into bed and wouldn't care whether or not she'd call or see him again, Charlie definitely didn't want that. *There must be some reason why we've met again after all this time,* he thought.

He wasn't exactly shy but there was something unquantifiable about her that made him nervous. It gave him a vulnerability that was new to him. He was a man so collected in his thoughts and actions and would know exactly what to do in any given situation – except this one. He feared no man and nothing, yet her and her smile had some kind of power over him. He still felt the thumping in his chest from the speakers in the club, yet thought the thumping inside him may well persist long after he'd gone home.

He took a break from dancing to have a few more drinks. Perhaps more alcohol would hinder the synapses and he might not overthink the situation and just enjoy it as a good opportunity to let off some steam. It had been such a long time since he'd been out and he was having a great time with the company of two beautiful women. What else could a man want? He went through to the other bar to order another Old Fashioned from the friendly barman and there was a girl already at the bar. Not only did that bar have the better drinks, it was very quiet, so was worth the short walk through from the club. The girl at the bar was stunning. She had long blonde hair which fell in boundless curls. She was obviously a little bit drunk already and was pleasantly surprised by Charlie's presence. She wore a short red dress and leaned hard on her arms on the bar. Her luscious curls fell and stopped just short of the countertop.

'Hey you,' she opened with.

'Hi, how's it going?' She smirked and looked around the bar area before looking back at him. He felt the need to fill the silence with something. 'So…you having a good night?' he asked.

'Yeah, it's good. I don't know where my friends have gone.' She continued to stand at the bar waiting for something. Charlie wasn't sure what to say next. He wasn't used to chatting girls up in bars, not that that was what he was doing. She had no drink in front of her, so thought he might as well offer her one.

The barman tried to not come to any conclusions about the girl who Charlie was now buying a drink for and made the drinks whilst Charlie and the girl in the red dress made small talk. After paying, he thought about inviting her back through to sit with him, Nicola and Claire until her friends turned up, but remembered how Nicola had reacted with the Australian girl so thought better of it. He didn't want to rile her.

When he came back through to the club, a man was speaking to Nicola by the other bar. He had a fatuous look on his face and an ungainly posture and kept touching Nicola. She giggled and smiled at him. Charlie didn't get jealous, his mind merely whirled and spun downwardly. He thought maybe this was a point that he'd overlooked. Perhaps she was only dancing with him and out with him because she knew him from before. If they'd have been strangers in the club, she probably wouldn't have danced with him at all. Maybe he should have invited the girl in the red dress through after all. Seeing her talk to someone else gave Charlie images of her going home with him instead and this man maybe taking that kiss that he thought about earlier. He felt more stupid than the look on the man's face.

He met up with Claire at the table. 'Where's Nic?' she asked.

'She's over there talking to someone.'

'Who?'

'I don't know…some guy.' He was proud that he managed to keep his tone flat. A look of dismay flashed onto Claire's face but she wasn't going to offer the reason freely. 'Why?' Charlie probed.

She took a second to form her reply. 'Because she really needs to finish things with her fiancé before she starts meeting new guys.' Charlie hid the shock inside him. Claire was now telling him that she's still got the fiancé she said she'd broken up with. She got up from the table to find her. 'Come on, Charlie.'

Claire found Nicola and took her away which somehow left Charlie with the guy.

'Alright mate? You must be Charlie?'

He was confused. 'Yeah, what's your name?'

'Aaron. It's good to meet you man.' Aaron offered his hand to Charlie so he shook it politely. 'Can I get you a drink?' Charlie wondered how this guy knew his name and wondered what else he knew about him.

'No, I'm fine mate, thanks.' Charlie lifted his Old Fashioned to show the mostly full glass.

'Special Forces, eh? Fuck sake man, that's quality!' It seemed that she had only been talking about Charlie with him.

Nicola watched him carefully through the smoke and dark blue of the club whilst she was being given a reprimand by Claire. Charlie talked to his new friend as he continued to reveal things he knew about him. Meanwhile, the girl in the red dress had been looking for him. She closed in and draped her arm around him as she clinked her glass with his. Nicola broke away from Claire and dashed over to Charlie. 'Come on, let's go!' She merged her hand with his and led him back to the dancefloor. The sensation of their intertwined fingers was absolutely divine to him. It was such a small thing, but one that he felt was quite significant. Their hands nestled together like two perfectly aligning halves. 'Dance with me, Charlie.'

'Where are the fucking taxis? It's freezing!' Claire exclaimed as they stood at the taxi rank. A line of people had assembled along the side of the road waiting for early morning transportation home. They were weary and unsteady on their feet from the alcohol and a long night of dancing. A few girls sat shivering on the steps of a shop with their high heels haphazardly abandoned beside them. One girl was rubbing her ankles and the balls of her feet.

Claire's teeth chattered as they stood there patiently, so Charlie took his jacket off and hung it around her. It still carried his warmth and smell and kept some of the cold breeze off her. Nicola now suddenly complained, 'God, I'm really freezing! It's so freezing!' She looked at Charlie and he didn't know what else he could do. He just gave his jacket to Claire and wasn't about to take it from her, that wouldn't be fair. Nicola leaned her head on Charlie's shoulder and slipped her hand along his back, passing electricity through him. It buzzed and tingled throughout his whole body. 'You'll just have to cuddle me for warmth!' *Yeah, this'll work*, he thought. He moved her in front of him so he was not shutting Claire out, although when he wrapped his arms around Nicola it felt like they were the only two at that taxi rank, or Glasgow, or Earth. Her whole body was pushed against him eagerly and despite her complaints of feeling cold, she felt warm and soft against him. She nestled into him and stayed that way as they advanced through the queue and until a taxi arrived for them.

He removed his jacket from Claire and opened the taxi door. 'Charlie, come on! You're letting the heat out!' Nicola said.

'I'm just going to walk, you know I'm in the complete opposite direction.'

'It doesn't matter, don't be silly! Why would you wait ages for a taxi and not get in?'

It was obvious to him, 'I just wanted to wait with you two and make sure you got a taxi home alright.' The taxi driver started the meter and Charlie glanced at him, catching him red-handed. They both piled out. Claire gave him a cuddle and told him how great it was to see him again. Nicola pulled him in tight and gave him a kiss on the cheek. 'Right, in you get, your meter's already started. Text me when you get home.'

He watched them wave from the taxi as the driver impatiently pulled away from the side of the road. He started walking down the road in the cold by himself but wasn't completely by himself for the first time in years. The cold didn't bother him because he felt a lingering warmth from their presence – especially Nicola's. He rubbed at his eyes and caught a whiff of her scent on him after holding her for so long. She sent him a message: "We had a really good time tonight! You should have just got in the taxi! Let me know when you get home! Xxx"

His building came into sight. A few free taxis drove past as impatiently as their taxi did. He didn't want to get one, he enjoyed the walk. It was a clear night and the streets were quiet as he chased his condensing breath along the pavement. He looked towards the Clyde and it was completely still. The breeze had died off and it mirrored the image of the opposite bank serenely on its surface. He wrote his text back and sent it before reaching home. He didn't want to keep her up any longer, even though she didn't have work or anything in the morning.

It was a brand new apartment block and stood on the north bank of the River Clyde. His flat was on the seventh floor. He usually took the stairs as a way to keep his level of activity up, because he didn't exercise as much as he did before and now led a comparatively sedentary lifestyle to his previous one.

He rode the lift. The shoes he had on, although very smart and stylish, were nowhere near as comfortable as his boots, so his feet ached from the walk and the dancing. Once he got upstairs he could again see the River Clyde and its serenity. The flat lay still and empty. Now drenched in silence once more, his ears started to ring. That was the tinnitus. He felt as if he'd stumbled into someone else's flat, or perhaps due to how immaculate he always kept it, the showhome. It didn't look as if anyone lived there. Either way, it was his and he earned it through hard graft, some of the hardest graft on earth no less.

He'd never rented anywhere before, it was his first place from moving out. Considering he worked away so much it was never worthwhile renting or buying a place that would lie empty and need maintaining for no reason. In the early days, Rachel was still staying at home and studying. She couldn't afford to move in somewhere with him so they'd split his time home between her parent's house, his parents' house and weekends away when they could. He offered to get a place by himself and she could just live with him, but she wanted to pay her own way so that arrangement didn't sit well with her.

In the past few years, he'd come back for a few weeks, maybe go on holiday with friends then be away again for six months or more. He also believed that if he did ever meet someone else then he'd be quite happy to pay rent or buy somewhere if they both were to live together, but that never happened.

Officially living with his parents allowed him to save, and save he did. He would spend a little when he got home, but without Rachel he didn't have much to spend his money on. Everything else he earned when he was away was staunchly saved in the eventual event of him buying a house like a normal person would.

His one guilty pleasure was cars. He had a separate savings pot accumulating so he could treat himself to a nice car. He loved high performance cars and just feeling power under the right foot. Driving armoured cars for VIP's gave him a taste for it, other than just being a normal boy who grew up looking at posters of supercars and sports cars. He enjoyed the thrill and danger of rounding a corner at high speed and testing the limits of grip, knowing that if he pushed it a bit more he might end up off the road. But knowing those limits made him feel masterful and in command.

Flicking a light on, the living area was revealed. All the nice furniture and modern décor lay around in a cavernous cavity where he stayed by himself. A few friends had been to visit since he moved in but mainly the time there was spent alone. He wanted to fill it with good memories and good times. He wanted to display photos and have stains or dings on the furniture (to a certain extent) caused by nights of frivolity and drunkenness.

Another message came through: "I hope you had a good time tonight. We'll have to arrange something again soon. I had a really good night. Thanks for coming out. ☺ Sweet dreams. Xxxxxx"

The number of kisses on the text had increased suddenly and drastically. Was the alcohol kicking in? Or did she really feel like she owed him or wanted to give him that many kisses? He switched on the stereo in his bedroom to help drown out the tinnitus as he prepared for bed. Before undressing, he caught himself in the mirror. His suit still looked sharp, his face did not look wearied in the same way the rest of the taxi crowd did. He almost didn't recognise himself.

# Chapter Four

'I'm just saying Nicola, you need to watch what you're doing. I think you need to clear things up with Patrice once and for all.'

Nicola swirled the remnants of her latte around the bottom of her coffee cup. A few wayward coffee grits churned around and held her gaze. At least, she'd rather look there than directly at Claire.

'Are you listening?'

She eventually lifted her head with defiance. 'Yes. Yes I know.'

'And by clear things up, I mean get rid of him permanently. He's not just going to go away. You have to be clear that it's over.'

'It's not like I'm getting involved with anyone else anyway, so I don't even know why you're bringing it up.' Claire thought about some of the guys she'd flirted with when they'd been out. Okay, flirting was just flirting she conceded, but then she thought about Charlie. She knew they'd been meeting up for coffees, dinner and movies just the two of them. That was the real reason she brought it up.

'Even if you're not, it doesn't matter. He probably thinks you're still just visiting home or something. What if he...we've been here so many times before Nic Nac. You have to let him know that you're not going back.' It was tough love from Claire. As always, she had Nicola's best interests at heart but Nicola was avoiding the situation altogether hoping that it would just work itself out.

On one hand, Claire could understand. She'd tried to tell Patrice that things were over for good but he would manipulate her into flying over to see him until returning to true form and she'd run home again. Claire would be there every time but it was beginning to take its toll. There were only so many times that she could encourage Nicola to finish things properly and be ignored without it starting to bother her.

'You know...' Claire exhaled sharply, 'I can't stand this shit much more. And neither should you.'

Nicola sighed and finished the last dregs of her coffee which had already gone cold. Claire checked her watch. 'I need to get back to work, but please…you can't just keep ignoring it.'

She sat in the coffee shop for a while after Claire left and looked through some messages from Patrice.

"I miss you cherie. Come back soon. Je t'aime. Xxx"

"You can't leave me. You are my fiancée, you made a commitment. What will everybody think if you change your mind now? Everybody will know that you are wrong."

"If you leave me I'll kill myself and you will have to explain to my parents and my brother and his family. They will know it is all your fault."

"Last night was the best. I'm very happy that you are back in Paris where you belong. Don't be stupid and run away again, I'm sick of making excuses for you. Je t'aime. Xxx"

"You are a fucking idiot! You think you can run out on me you stupid bitch! I will fucking come to Scotland to get you if you will not come back to me! Don't make me fucking come there!!"

"When will you come back to Paris? I hope you're not fucking other guys there. Remember you belong to me."

She stopped reading and let herself crumble a little more inside. She knew what she had to do but for the very life of her could not muster the energy to do it. He would complain about trying to sort things out over the phone. 'It's not the proper way,' he'd say. She'd then feel obliged to spend her rapidly depleting savings on flights to Paris. Then when she was face-to-face with him, she would struggle to find the words and it would just be easier to let him have sex with her. At least then he wouldn't be angry, but then after a while, the sex wasn't enough. Patrice was abusing her physically and mentally. The physical was only every now and then, but the emotional abuse was constant, hurt her the most and left the deepest scars.

He came to Scotland once and stayed with her at Claire's flat. All he did was complain about how shit everything was and how much better she'd be in France. When she got her own place, he stayed over and told her he'd never come back because why should he 'make all the effort?'

She did a quick search for flight prices on her phone using the free Wi-Fi in the coffee shop. A young girl came to clear the table and the rattling of the cups and saucers suddenly broke her chain of thought. Charlie entered her mind and whilst her phone was still in her hand, she wrote a text.

"Hey Mr Handsome, how are you today? What you up to? Just wondering if you're free some time and we can go do something? X"

Claire had left some money for the coffee and once Nicola paid, she headed out and into the bustling lunchtime buzz of Glasgow's West End. It was a cold clear day. The sky was clear blue except from a few smatterings of white fluffy cloud around.

"Hey, good thanks. I'm just in Ayrshire at the moment, just a half-days training. Waste of time really, but I'll be back up by early evening. If you've got anything in particular in mind just let me know, because I can pretty much schedule my work at the moment. X" *Mr Handsome*, he thought. *That's a great sign.*

She thought about Patrice as she approached her flat and wondered what to do about the whole situation. She didn't know how to break things off with him and doubted that she ever would. *Maybe I should just fuck Charlie and tell him I've done that*, she thought. *Or maybe I don't even need to fuck him, just tell him I did?* She knew though, that Patrice would never accept that one way or another and rather than repel him, it would give him something else to have a handle over her.

"You free tonight then? Xx" she texted back.

Charlie picked her up from town. She'd been at the gym striving hard to maintain her gorgeous figure. On his way home he stopped off to buy some ingredients to cook her dinner and prepared a pot of curry before heading to pick her up. He wanted to make something that showed how good a cook he was and how 'domesticated' he was, but was concerned about making something too fancy. He didn't want her to know how much he was trying to impress her. The gym was not so far from Charlie's flat. In fact, it was closer to his flat than to hers. It was located next to a constantly busy bus stop and she emerged with her gym bag and handbag thrown over her shoulder. Charlie was sitting in the car on the opposite side of the road and saw her pull out her phone to call or text him. Her hair was freshly washed and fell around her beautiful face with sheer refinement. She thought about washing it that morning but couldn't be bothered. Now that she was meeting Charlie, she knew she had to. She wanted to look good and feel good for him. He got out and beckoned her across. She examined the car as she approached.

'Hey, Charlie...is this your car?'

'Well, yeah…' he shrugged. Its large wheels were wrapped with slick black low-profile tyres. It sat with poise and menace in the middle of the city. It was the type of car that she'd imagine only footballers or top executives would drive. She was very surprised that Charlie could afford a car like that. As it happened, how he ended up with the car was a very fortunate turn of events indeed.

Through a contact of his, he landed a Private Security gig for an old actress in London. Gertrude Khan lived by herself in a big house on the edge of Hampstead Heath. Her husband was a doctor to the stars but had died many years ago from cancer. Since then she'd been an alcoholic. She had a daughter who was mostly estranged from her, except from the times she'd come calling for money. It was her daughter who put the position out to tender and as it turned out, it wasn't so much of a Close Protection or even a Residential Security job, it was a babysitting job. Gertrude was essentially lonely. She was massively eccentric and lived constantly in the past. She had been a successful actress in her younger years but now she was washed up and had nothing much going for her. She was incredibly wealthy with her and her late husbands' estates but her needs were simple – vodka on a daily basis.

Charlie lived in a wing of the house, which was obviously included in the job, but he had no need to protect her from anything other than herself. He would wake her up in the morning and cook for her as well as doing her shopping and running errands. After a month or so of encouragement from Charlie, she began to venture beyond the house and garden. Charlie would drive her in his car and she disliked it. The car was just so normal and did not offer her the amount of luxury for the actress that she still was in her head. He was still saving for his nice car and the pot was growing healthily. Since she started venturing further afield, she asked him to find a car for them to drive around in and he came back to her with suggestions. He was so excited to be able to go car shopping – money no object – and he'd get to drive it everyday. Eventually, she bought a powerful luxury estate car. Charlie thought she'd prefer a saloon but what he didn't know was that it was the same type of car her late husband had, albeit the brand new model. She would sit in the back with a pashmina wrapped around her head and dark glasses on. The back windows were heavily tinted, that being her sole specification requirement. She didn't want to be seen or recognised by anyone, not that there was much hope of that anymore.

Gertrude admired Charlie. He was a handsome young man with a wonderful smile and she enjoyed his company a lot. She tried to encourage her daughter to come round and had ideas about matchmaking them, but Charlie couldn't stand her. She did nothing for her mother and whilst Gertrude couldn't see it, was only ever interested in how much money she could sponge from her.

Despite growing an attachment to her, Charlie became bored very quickly as a babysitter. He felt sorry for how her life had turned out and so always showed her kindness. He wanted to try and bring something bright to each of her days but she was long gone and there was no bringing her back.

With the lack of challenge, Charlie would find things to do around the house. It was a huge old house which had gradually fallen into disrepair. There were rooms full of clutter and mess that had been abandoned for years. After some coercion, he persuaded her to get the house in order and under her direction, he did it. She had a double garage which was occupied by her old film reels on one side. They were stacked haphazardly from the floor up in their original cans and had been there for a very long time. Damp had ruined the first few layers but he managed to salvage the rest and store them in a newly cleared out cupboard in a spare bedroom. He found an old film projector upstairs during the clear-out and after a little tinkering and research online, managed to get it going. They sat one evening and watched one of her old films. Gertrude really was beautiful when she was younger, he thought. It gave her so much pleasure to watch her old film in original format – the whirring of the projector, the heat from the bulb and the flicker of the picture on the white sheet Charlie suspended in her living room.

After a few months, Charlie had sorted her whole house into excellent order. His days were mostly filled with nothing and as he drove her around, she could tell that he was becoming absent. She knew that was not how a handsome charismatic young man should be spending his days, despite the good money and benefits – not to mention the lack of threat from gunshots or explosions, of course. Eventually she spoke to him about it. 'I know you're not happy here anymore, darling.'

'No…I'm quite happy.'

'Come on, Charlie, you don't fool me. Why would you want to waste away with an old bat like me?'

'You're not an old bat.'

'Forgive the colloquialism, but my life's already down the shitter, darling. There's no need for yours to be too.' She adjusted her pashmina. 'I'll speak to Riya…but I think we may no longer require your services.' Charlie's face dropped, he had just been sacked after all. She realised how bashful she had been and it was not at all what she intended. She wanted to 'free' Charlie and let him get on with his life. 'Don't worry though. Of course, you'll receive a severance package…I'm not just going to throw you out on your ear, darling.'

Gertrude convinced her daughter Riya that she didn't need babysitting anymore. The few times she did call, Riya had certainly noticed a difference in her with Charlie in her life and the house wasn't a wreck anymore. Plus, that would save on the inheritance anyway. Despite only being there five months in total, Gertrude wanted to give him a years' wages. After negotiation, she and Riya settled on five additional months' wages. Behind Riya's back however, Gertrude had a bonus for him. She let him keep the car. 'Well, it's not like I have a use for it do I, darling?' It was true. Never mind the fact that she was constantly drunk, Gertrude didn't know how to drive.

He opened the door for Nicola and took her gym bag, placing it in the boot. She slithered into the car and its bucket seat enveloped around her. The velvety suede and nubuck caressed her freshly exercised and showered body. She sank deep into the car and was surrounded by carbon fibre and brushed metal. The windscreen seemed like a giant letterbox in front of her and a large screen equipped the dashboard with a plethora of functions. Charlie sat down behind the wheel and pulled the door shut. All the sounds and smells of the street disappeared. It was just them in their comfortable little haven.

The car vanished from the city streets into the underground parking of his building and trickled into his allotted parking bay. 'Do you need your gym bag?' She pondered for a second. She had spare underwear, shampoo and conditioner and make up along with her sweaty gym clothes. She wouldn't be washing her hair again but thought a little more about the spare underwear before batting a rash decision from head. 'No. Thanks.'

They took the lift to the seventh floor and were greeted by the scent of automatic air-freshener. He opened the door to his flat. 'Welcome.' He was so glad to have her there. He felt a sense of pride being able to show her an undoubtedly nice flat and not some grotty shit-hole. He'd worked hard for it and hoped that she'd approve. Charlie had stayed in some really poor accommodation over the years and around the world, so he thought he deserved a bit of comfort and luxury now.

She stood at the full-length windows looking out over the River Clyde, the city, and the hills in the distance as the rice cooked. It was an amazing vantage point that Charlie had. He clinked plates, cutlery and glasses as he laid them out on the glass topped dining table.

Charlie was in the kitchen when Nicola's phone rang and she went through to the hall to answer it. *Is this him calling?* he thought. There was no way he'd be able to hear her from the kitchen without stopping cooking and switching off the stereo, which would have made it far too obvious. He tried to anticipate how she might feel when she came back through. Might she be upset, or try to lie about things again? She emerged from the hallway with a big smile on her face. 'Hey…' He didn't want to be demanding but continued, 'who was that?'

'Job interview. I thought they weren't going to call back. But it's tomorrow at 2pm.'

'Oh, nice!'


Nicola had worked in art circles before. After a couple of years working in an art gallery in Paris, she was given the job of managing it. She then applied for a junior curator post elsewhere but was told she didn't have enough experience. She gradually came to the conclusion that art had no future because most of her artwork ended up pro bono. She spent a lot of time promoting herself and put herself forward for things with no real results.

The art gallery was quite high profile and she was paid reasonably well for it. She enjoyed seeing different pieces and particularly new and upcoming artists. She thought that being in that culture, she might be able to pick up a few chances herself, but nothing ever came to fruition. Then she ran from Paris.

She handed in her notice with immediate effect and didn't even meet the boss. She quoted 'personal reasons' and left the letter at the gallery. Her eye was black at the time and she didn't want to let anyone know about it. She wore a lot of concealer and oversized sunglasses despite it being late autumn when she dropped the letter off with the receptionist. Patrice went home to his parent's house for a long weekend and Claire went to Paris with only hand luggage, she'd only be there for a night. Nicola bought two suitcases so that she could pack them with as many of her possessions that she thought would survive the flight. They flew back to Scotland and Nicola crashed in Claire's place for a while.

Claire's flat was small and much too cramped for the two of them but they had to make it work. It was a big invasion of Claire's life but she didn't mind. She let Nicola know that she was always welcome and could stay there forever if she needed to, rather than ever go back to Paris. Nicola picked up a few jobs here and there, mainly temping for offices. In Paris, she was saving to buy an apartment with Patrice and like Charlie, was starting to accumulate a decent amount before she ran. After two months at Claire's however, she had to find her own place and started to dip into her savings to pay for rent.

She had retrained through a scheme at the jobcentre and had 'new skills' which she could use to apply for jobs in Glasgow. She had looked at what vacancies there were in anything that she could possibly see herself doing for a while and had decided that business and marketing would suit her well. She had been running the gallery quite successfully and did well to promote new artists (except herself), so thought that would follow on quite nicely.

'Shit, Charlie! I'm nervous now.'

'You'll be fine, don't worry about it. So…do you have to prep for this tomorrow?' Charlie eyed the bottle of wine that he'd just opened as it sat longingly on the dining room table and he knew he had to try and recap it somehow.

'Well, I've already read up about this company but that was a while ago. I'll probably just reread and do a bit of prep tonight.'

All of Charlie's plans were thrown out of the window. He had an image of sitting out on the terrace to finish the bottle of wine with her. Perhaps the sun could have gone down over the hills and scattered some amazing colours into the sky. Perhaps she'd have been so impressed by him and his cooking that he might have been able to get that kiss that he'd been craving. He knew there would be no chance of that now. 'It smells delicious,' Nicola said. 'Can we eat now though, please? Because I'll need to go home soon.'

'Sure.'


Charlie woke up early and wandered through to the living room. The bottle of wine stood full on the kitchen counter with the cork inverted and stuffed back into the neck. Crystals of red wine shone like tiny rubies on the end of the cork. The emptiness that filled the big flat was somehow diminished with her presence there the previous night. Even though she had to leave shortly after dinner, there was a sense of her that remained.

The company was a well-known, successful one and it seemed like a great opportunity for her. Nicola became so timid in the car on the way back to her flat but Charlie could tell it wasn't simply nerves. She was lacking in self-confidence. It was an important event for her and when she was with Patrice, he would never offer her support. He would make her feel that if she achieved anything it was down to luck, or being in the right place at the right time. She felt that she had no worth and going for the job interview brought back a lot of bad memories for her. The real reason she didn't excel in her art was not due to a lack of talent. It also certainly wasn't due to a lack of connections; it was her inherent fear of humiliation and depreciation that she always felt because of him.

Charlie pottered around all morning and browsed for jobs online but without a clear objective. He resisted calling too early fearing that he would disturb her should she be getting a good long sleep before the interview. By the late morning he thought she should be awake so called to check how she was and wish her good luck, 'Hey, how's it going? How are you feeling?'

'Morning, Charlie. Oh, it's a disaster so far! I should have checked my suit last night, there's a big rip in the trouser leg. I totally forgot about it. I'm so stupid. I don't know what I'm going to do!' She paced around her bedroom with her suit laid out on the bed. 'I don't have any other trousers or skirts here that would be suitable and I've not got time to get the train in and out of town to go shopping. I'm a disaster, I don't deserve this job. This just shows it.'

Charlie listened to her self-deprecation and it felt like someone was pushing a knife into him. 'You're not stupid Nicola. It's not your fault they gave you less than twenty-four hours notice.' He continued, 'I'll come and pick you up and we'll go into town and find something, alright? And where is the interview?'

'It's in the city centre. No, I'll just have to find something here. I was going to call Claire and I'll just borrow something from her.'

'But she's at work though, isn't she?'

Nicola paused. 'Shit, I'll just phone and cancel, I'm not going to go there and make a fool of myself. They might be able to reschedule.'

'Erm…I don't know if they'd be able to reschedule.' He didn't want to make her feel like she was a last resort for them but had to point out: 'That was a late call last night, so they'd probably just be looking to fill the interview for today.'

'Oh, God, what am I going to do? I just won't go. That's it.'

'Listen, just take it easy, I'll come and get you, we'll run into town and you can get something appropriate. Just take a deep breath, get everything else that you need and I'll be there in about twenty minutes.'

'Charlie, are you sure?'

'Absolutely sure.'


She came out to the car wearing jeans, pumps and a smart white blouse. She had a large black handbag and her suit jacket was folded over her arm. Charlie took her jacket and hung it on a hook above the back seats whilst she got in the passenger side. She forgot how the bucket seats caressed her and she seemed to calm down a little. She was with Charlie now and she somehow felt comfort around him. Her anxiety that had steadily mounted through the morning was starting to abate. They drove quickly into town. He used his 'scanning and planning' techniques and whilst abiding by the speed limits (more or less), he made good lane selections and predicted the traffic flow to maximise progress.

They parked on a quiet side street close to George Square and walked through to the shops. She was flustered as she tried on a few pairs of trousers and was overly concerned about how it looked. 'Nicola, it doesn't need to be exactly perfect, just reasonably presentable for the interview. And then when you get the job, you'll have time to shop properly before you start.' She didn't agree. She was fast running out of money and still had the low self-worth which meant she doubted she would get the job at all. These trousers had to match her suit jacket colour *and* be a perfect shape and fit otherwise she wouldn't feel comfortable. They had to be suitable for the other job interviews that she was sure she'd have to attend. A new suit is supposed to make you feel a million dollars, it's supposed to inflate the ego enough to make you feel like you were something, and in her case, that she was worthy of the job. If she felt frumpy then she just wouldn't turn up. The only problem was that she was running out of time.

Eventually she found a pair that were perfect but didn't match the colour of her jacket. She looked at the price tag and her heart sank.

The trousers were quite expensive and she'd have to buy the trousers *and* the jacket. There was no way she could afford it, unless of course, she could guarantee she'd get the job. 'They look great.' He tried not to look too hard at her curves in the trousers.

She fumbled the price tag again. 'They don't match the jacket though, but I could maybe just leave the jacket out.' It was still the tail end of winter in Scotland, so there was no way she'd get away with just a blouse. She had a rain coat which wasn't particularly smart but would pass as an outer winter layer, but without the suit jacket it wouldn't look right at all.

Charlie had a look at the price tag. 'You need the jacket as well, Nicola.' They'd already been to a few shops so he knew what size to grab and made her try it on. She pulled it on and the tag whirred round blurring the numbers as her hand pushed out through the sleeve. She looked smart. She looked beautiful. She looked vulnerable and unsure. 'Right, we'll just get that. Trousers and jacket.'

'Charlie, no. I… I can't afford it.' She felt ashamed to admit it. She didn't want to admit any weakness towards him and she didn't know why. He had no concern over how much money she had and was already sure that given how long she'd been looking for a job, she wouldn't be exactly flush with cash. 'I'll buy you them.'

'No. I can't let you…'

'What else are you going to do?' He checked his watch and tapped the face. 'You've got about forty-five minutes, there's no point trying anywhere else, we're just wasting time.' He removed his wallet and picked a card out to make swiping motions with it against his wallet, even though they stopped swiping cards a long time ago. 'It's now or never.' He grinned and wiggled his eyebrows up and down trying to lighten the mood.

'Okay.'

He caught the scent of her as he removed the jacket to take to the till. She returned to the changing room to put her jeans back on. 'Do you not just want to keep them on and they can ring through the tags? We'll just explain to them it's a wardrobe emergency.' Nicola called through *no* as she drew the curtain shut around the corner. She didn't want anyone else to know how hopeless she'd been. She came back out from the changing room in her jeans, carrying the trousers. Charlie was perched on a plinth between some manikins and stood up as she approached. Her arms came around him and her head sunk into his chest.

'I'll pay you back, Charlie. Are you sure though?'

'Absolutely sure.'

She smiled and let him go eventually. 'So…where are you going to get changed?' He tried to think of places where she might change, but there were only toilets and even though there were some 'decent' ones in the city centre, he still couldn't imagine her preparing for a job interview in a public toilet. He'd expected her to just leave them on from the shop as he suggested.

'I'll just change in your car.' He looked at her. 'I mean…if that's okay?' The thought of her removing her clothes in his car was utterly tantalising. His main aim of course was to preserve her modesty but the back windows of the car were heavily tinted thanks to Gertrude, so it was possible.

'Yeah, well, it's up to you.' As soon as they left the shop, Nicola suddenly noticed what a beautiful day it was. It was cold but clear and the sun was out. She carried her bags like a child who was just bought that toy they'd been promised so long as they behaved themselves. She felt special.

They walked back to the car and he unlocked it for her. As a reprieve, he spotted a coffee shop close-by and went there to buy some coffee and food for them both. He thought about standing guard, but that in itself would draw attention to what was happening in his car. He also feared so much succumbing to the desire to catch a glimpse of her as she peeled her jeans off and slid them down the nubuck and suede before pulling on her smart suit trousers that he just bought for her, so he had to put some distance between them.

He bought a couple of sandwiches which he poked gently but securely into his jacket pockets and carried two coffees back to the car. As he approached, she opened the car door and got out. She pulled on the jacket and stood back trying to catch her full-length reflection from the car. 'Here – latte, one sugar, right?'

'Yes, you remembered.' She smiled and sighed a breath of relief. He sat his coffee on the roof of the car and pulled out the sandwiches. 'Roast chicken salad or pastrami and edam?'

'Chicken please.' That was what he suspected and he preferred the pastrami and edam anyway. They had just under half an hour left and her interview was only a few minutes away, so they had just enough time for her to refuel and enjoy her latte. She stood outside the car because she was concerned about getting crumbs not just on her suit but in Charlie's shiny car. He took a bottle of water out of the boot and gave it to her. 'You've fixed everything Charlie. You're so...' she considered what word to use: amazing, thoughtful, incredible, '...practical.' It carried less weight and wasn't as sincere or warm as she intended but it was already said. There was no doubt that he was practical, he was the master of practical. 'I mean...like...' she wanted to rephrase it somehow, 'you can just sort everything out like it's no hassle. Nothing's ever a bother.'

He kept an eye on the time for her and suggested they make their way to the building. She had demolished the sandwich like a ravenous animal without leaving any marks on her suit. She'd been so worried that morning she forgot, or more, she chose not to eat anything. 'You're going to ace this interview Nicola.'

'I hope so.' She didn't sound convinced.

'How are you feeling?'

'A bit sick.'

'That's just the sandwich. I think you took a lot of air down with it,' he smirked. She forgot herself for a second and a smile lit up her face as she struck him playfully. Patrice would never joke with her about food. He used to make her feel guilty whenever she ate. 'You're eating again?' he'd say. It got to the point where she'd hide food and eating had to be a surreptitious affair. The times where she had to sneak sandwich ingredients into the bathroom, assemble and eat it there whilst the shower ran for no reason were the absolute worst.

'Did you have anything to eat before that today?' Nicola shook her head. 'You should be eating breakfast every day Nicola. The most important meal of the day, that's what they say. Am I going to have to come round and make you breakfast every day and make sure you eat?' He was trying to flirt but her mind was elsewhere.

'I'm just not sure why they'd want me.'

Charlie sighed noiselessly next to her as she plummeted once more. 'Well, how about you concentrate on why they *would* want you? You need to project how smart and capable a young woman you are. But first you've got to believe it yourself.' He kept his eyes on the road. 'And there's no reason for you to doubt yourself. If you want the job, it's yours for the taking. It's really simple.' He smiled still looking towards the road.

'It's just, I've never actually worked in this field at all. I've not got any experience.'

'Okay, but the person that will interview you today will have been in your exact same position at one point. Experience is one thing, but they're looking for potential too. You're smart Nicola, and a quick learner, adaptable, right?' She nodded. 'Those are qualities every employer wants, doesn't matter what it is. But you need to believe in yourself. It's so important.' She faced exactly front. 'And half of the people you'll be going up against have probably never been much outside of Glasgow. You've seen the world, you've got a lot of experience actually. You ran an art gallery...in Paris. Compare that to all the other people that'll be there today.' He managed a quick glance and a smile towards her. 'I believe in you. Otherwise, I wouldn't have rushed across town to help you buy that suit if I didn't think you were going to get it.'

She was pacified. Over the length of a few city streets he'd made her feel like a person again. He merely called to check how she was and discovered all the things that were in the way of her and a successful interview and with calculated composure came and fixed everything for her.

They pulled up outside the building with a comfortable amount of time left. 'Open the glovebox,' he instructed her. Her hands felt around the carbon fibre as she struggled to locate the handle. 'May I..? ' His hand delved slowly for it and he reached forward and between her legs. *Pop!* The glovebox opened and he pulled out a couple of granola bars for her. 'Put them in your bag, it's probably going to be a long afternoon.'

'Charlie, you're too good!'

'Do you need picked up? I could wait for you, or come back?'

'No, really, you've already done so much. I'll make my own way back.'

'Well, let me know how it goes, of course. And good luck. Not that you need luck. Remember, if you want it, it's yours.'

She leaned over and hugged him. He smelt fresh and clean. 'Thanks for everything, Charlie. I don't know where I'd be without you.' The words just seemed to flow naturally from her mouth without any conscious decision to say them. 'Probably sitting in your flat in pyjamas?' He made light of the situation but didn't miss the true sincerity of what she said.

He waited for her to disappear into the building before swinging the car round into a gap in the traffic. He wanted to just stay and wait for her. He wanted to steal another hug from her when she came out, whether it was in celebration or consolation. But he was quite happy with how he'd been able to help her, so that'd have to be enough for the time being. The only problem was that the more time he spent with her and the more he did for her, the more he craved her, to the point he thought that maybe he'd never be able to get enough of her ever.

Charlie received a text from Claire: "Hey Charlie, have you heard from Nic? I haven't heard from her since yesterday afternoon. Tried phoning today at lunch but it went straight to voicemail." This may not have seemed like a big deal to most people, but it was out of character for Nicola when it came to Claire.

He wrote back, "She's in a job interview. I'm not sure what time she'll be out."

"Oh, okay. She never mentioned anything about a job interview."

"Oh, I thought she'd have told you. They just called when she was round last night. It was maybe a cancellation or something. How are you anyway?"

"Yeah fine thanks ☺ I'll catch her later then."

Claire was a little surprised. How did Charlie know about her interview before her? And why didn't she tell her that she was going round to Charlie's for dinner? Claire was always the first to know about anything that Nicola was doing. They had no secrets at all. She wasn't upset with Charlie. There was no one knew Nicola better and the only reason she'd secretly spend time with Charlie was because she was up to something.

Charlie sat in the pub where he first met up with Nicola a few weeks earlier. He waited for Nicola and Claire but this time he didn't feel so awkward. He didn't arrive half an hour early either. There was still uncertainty but of a different nature altogether, yet Charlie felt he was making ground towards her. He just had to help her get her life back on track enough so that he could reach her. He didn't want to force it though because if it was going to happen it'd have to be perfect.

After sitting for a few minutes, the door swung open with a creek and the blast from a bus turbocharger whooshed in with them.

'Charlie!' He got up to greet them and gave them both hugs. Nicola sat next to him on the bench and Claire sat opposite on a chair.

She got a call two days after the interview with the job offer. The company had just undergone a merger and as such was going through a major expansion, taking on a large number of new staff. The only drawback was that it didn't start for a while, until all the other rounds of interviews were complete, but Nicola figured she could temp again in the meantime if she needed to. Now that she had a start date at least she could budget what remained of her money until then.

The interview saw her take part in group activities and discussions as well as an individual interview. A couple of the group activities included a lot of moving around the room and role playing in some kind of corporate bullshit teambuilding nonsense way and Nicola was so tremendously glad that she had on a great new trouser suit that fitted her well. She had received a few compliments on it after arriving. That elation that Charlie provided made her sail through the whole afternoon with an air of confidence which didn't go unnoticed by the selection team. In her interview it was explained that she was indeed a cancellation and the lady interviewer said to Nicola that she 'knew it was short notice' and was 'very glad she could make it'.

'It's such a great opportunity. I'll be based in the Glasgow office, but the parent company has offices all over the world and I might get a chance to go abroad again. I'm really excited!'

'That's great. I knew all along you'd get it,' Charlie said, whilst hoping that she didn't have to go anywhere abroad at all.

'My mum and dad are really pleased. They're glad I've got a job here and that I'm…staying,' she paused, 'and I've got a favour to ask you Charlie.' He looked quickly across to Claire trying to look for a clue but she didn't know either.

'Oh, God, not another one!' he joked.

'My mum and dad gave me some money for a car. I don't really need to travel much for work, but I might be at the Edinburgh office now and then. And there's also a lot of networking that I'll need to do, and that'll be late night finishes. So, I was wondering if you'd be able to help me find a car?'

'Sure. I'd love to.'

## Chapter Five

Nicola had printed out a list of potential cars that she'd found online and she shuffled the sheets in Charlie's passenger seat. 'I just want to find out where all the garages are so we're not doubling back on ourselves unnecessarily,' he said.

'Yeah, okay.' She pulled the back page of each result out and handed them to Charlie. He sifted through and drew a route in his head, taking into account potential places to stop for some lunch if they got hungry.

'My mum wanted to come along but it's a long way for her to come through and then go trailing about garages all day. And I didn't know if you'd have minded or not.'

'Why would I mind? I'd like to meet your mum.'

'She's been asking a lot about you, actually. She wants to meet you too.'

They arrived at the first garage and Nicola got out of the car. She didn't know anything about cars and didn't know where to start. She passed her test when she was eighteen, but had hardly driven since. She didn't have money or a great need for a car before and then when she moved to France, she didn't have confidence to drive on the opposite side of the road. Besides, she lived in the city so could access everything she needed to by the Metro.

Cars were Charlie's thing and he was also quite cunning in the buying and selling of them. He had a good technical ability and was able to discern whether a car was good, or whether it was a lemon. Growing up, he had always helped his dad as he worked on their cars. His dad was an engineer and a particular amount of that ability had certainly been passed hereditarily to Charlie. If he hadn't got involved with the Armed Forces, he expected that he'd have become an engineer for sure.

She wandered round dozens of cars with a wide smile on her face. She peered into a few windows and stroked a few car bonnets as if that might be able to give her a clue of the condition. 'Can I help yous at all there folks?' A young man with a massive amount of hair gel cementing his quiff in place slinked a well-trodden path between the tightly parked cars. He was closer to Nicola and closed in some more.

'We're just having a wee browse, mate. Well, there was a car that you found online wasn't there?' She pulled out the pieces of paper from her handbag and found it.

'This one here, do you have it somewhere?' she asked.

The salesman perused the print-out, 'Yeah, just over here folks.' He led them through the labyrinth of cars until they reached the one she had seen. It was, as all the other ones were, tightly packed into the forecourt. 'I'll just get the keys.'

Nicola and Charlie inspected the car and waited for the man to return. Charlie popped the bonnet and had a look. He opened the oil filler cap on the engine and there was a yellow gunky build up on the inside of it. He poked at it with his finger and the salesman looked at him, puzzled. 'The oil's emulsified. So there's water getting into the engine somehow,' Charlie determined. He looked towards Nicola shaking his head. 'It's not a good sign.'

'Obviously, before the cars go out, they get a full service and valet.'

'But how long has the oil been like this? The damage is probably already done. And unless you find and fix the problem, you can change

85

the oil and it'll emulsify again immediately. The head gasket's gone or something.'

'Well, I'm not a mechanic, so I couldn't say. But as I say, they get a thorough check over by our service department.'

Nicola watched and listened carefully to Charlie as he talked about things she and the salesman had no comprehension of. 'Okay, buddy. Thanks for showing us. We'll have a think about it.' The salesman insisted that Charlie wait for a business card so he could phone if he had questions and in the meantime he'd get someone to have a look at the oil, but Charlie and Nicola wouldn't be back.

The sun was already starting to set and Charlie was getting very hungry. They'd looked around a few garages and nothing really took her fancy. They didn't get a chance to stop for something to eat. They both wanted to get around all the garages that day. Well, she did at least, and he wanted to give her what she wanted. He wouldn't have minded spending another day or two trawling around garages with her. The last garage of the day was on the edge of Glasgow.

'Oh, Charlie, I love it. I really, really want it! It's a grand too expensive though. It's so typical!' She sighed deeply. As she sat behind the wheel in the forecourt, Charlie sat next to her in the passenger seat. It was a nice car. It was definitely the kind of car he could imagine her in and it was nice to sit on the passenger side with her behind the wheel. It altered the dynamic and made him feel somehow closer to her. Somewhere in the back of his head he imagined her picking him up in that car and them driving to go and meet her parents or going out to places together, just the two of them. It felt somehow even more special than when she was in his car. If she bought it, she wouldn't have had anyone else in it before him. He wanted to be her first passenger. He wanted to be her only passenger, except perhaps for Claire of course.

She sat stroking the steering wheel before he interrupted her daydreaming, 'So are you going to take it for a test drive or what?'

'Erm...can I? But...I haven't driven for ages. Is it alright?'

'Rule number one – never buy a car without test driving it.' She bit her lip and stared intently ahead out of the windscreen before turning to Charlie.

'I don't think I can. But...could you Charlie? Could you test drive it for me? I wouldn't even know what to do on a test drive. Will the man be with us?'

'I don't know, sometimes they do come, it just depends. Here, probably not, because my car is sitting out the front, so they know I'll be back for it.'

'Can you drive it for me, please?'

'Yeah, sure.'

It drove quietly and smoothly. There were no extraneous knocks or bumps and all the buttons worked. The gearbox seemed smooth and the engine was sprightly enough for what she'd need. He turned into a quiet street in an industrial estate. The road was wide and empty. 'Right, you're turn.'

'What? No, it's okay. Just you drive it.'

'Nicola, you might hate it. Then what? Just have a go.' She became nervous and he knew she hadn't driven for several years but considering she was about to buy a car, it was already time to get back into it. 'I'll be right here. I'll help you through it.'

They swapped seats and Charlie was quite shocked at how deficient her driving skills had become over the years. She struggled to reach the pedals after Charlie had sat there and she couldn't see what she was supposed to in the mirrors. He prompted her, 'So…adjust your seat…then your mirrors.' He had to talk her through the whole thing; it was like lesson number one. Thankfully she could remember which pedals were which. 'Now…slowly up with the clutch until the tone changes. Then hold the clutch still.' The car jerked a little as she brought the clutch up and down a couple of times, above and below the biting point. 'It's clear, so now the handbrake.' She looked down and fumbled the button, Charlie had put it on too firmly for her to remove.

When he reached to help, her hand was still there underneath his as the handbrake dropped. He felt that electricity again.

They drove around the block a few times and he made her reverse too just to get familiar enough before heading out onto the public roads. They made it safely back to the garage but she began to panic as the parked cars left very little margin for her to manoeuvre. She stopped the car at a haphazard angle in the middle. 'Can you park it for me?' He thought it would be fine if her reversing was that bad that she'd have to take him everywhere just so that he could park up for her. She stood to the side as Charlie backed the car neatly into a space, got out and showed her how to lock it.

'So, what do you think then?' he asked.

'I love it. It sucks so much though…'

'What?'

'I can't afford it. It's a thousand pounds over my budget. It's not fair! I should never have looked at it.'

'Well, let's speak to the guy and we'll see if we can get him down at all. But the most important thing is don't let him see that you're too excited about it otherwise he'll know he's got you. If it appears that you need some convincing then he might move on the price.'

'How did you get on then?' the salesman asked. Nicola waited for Charlie to answer.

'Yeah, it's a nice car. We've seen a few others that were quite nice though, so we'll have to think about it because this one's a bit more expensive…unless there's something you can do on the price?'

'I'm afraid the prices are set centrally, we don't have much control over that. But it's already at the best price, it's a lot of car for the money, you've driven it yourself now. Obviously, it's not in the ball-park of your car, but it's perfect for a first car and I think it'll suit your lady very well.'

Nicola giggled and they looked at one another. Charlie opened his mouth to correct him but then didn't say anything. What was the point in trying to explain everything to this salesman? Never mind the fact that Charlie didn't know exactly how to describe their relationship anyway. Nicola wasn't bothered by his assumption. She was quite pleased to be called Charlie's 'lady'. When she was with Patrice she was never referred to as a lady. In fact, she was hardly a woman.

'Can I get you two a coffee or something? And I'll speak to my boss and see if we can do anything at all.'

'That'd be good. Black, no sugar for me, thanks.' Charlie said.

'Milk and one sugar, please. Do you have a bathroom?' As Nicola got up, Charlie tugged her arm gently, pulling her in close to have a quick strategy meeting as the man walked away from the desk.

'What's the story then? Do you want this?'

'Yes, I really do. I love it Charlie.' Her eyes flicked up to the salesman as he waited patiently and respectfully out of earshot. 'I love it even more after driving it. I'm glad you made me drive it. But it's too expensive.'

'Well, we'll see what price they come up with.'

The man showed her the way to the toilet as he headed for the coffee, leaving Charlie sitting at the desk by himself. It looked like an old school teacher's desk that they'd either bought from a scrappy or found at the side of the road. There was a small stack of business cards on the table for a man that had a different name to the one they were speaking to. There was a pile of leaflets in an acrylic stand about service plans and something called 'Supacoat' which Charlie could glean was to do with paint protection. The computer looked new but the monitor looked like it was from the early nineties and had a few greasy fingerprints on it.

Nicola freshened up in the toilet. The bathroom was a unisex one but was separate from the staff toilet which she was very glad about. The mirror was small but she still managed to check how she looked in it. She took her bobble out and re-tied her hair, tucking the few shorter strands that don't go in the bobble behind her ear. She touched up her lip gloss. It was a pale discreet colour which made her lips look succulent. She took out her phone and thought about texting Claire, purely by habit, but then she thought she'd just wait until later and she could tell her everything about how Charlie got her to drive for the first time in years and about how disappointed she was that she couldn't afford the car.

The man came back to the old teacher's desk with two dispenser machine coffees and put them down, one in front of Charlie and one in front of Nicola's empty seat. The man didn't wait for Nicola before revealing his news. 'Right, so I've spoken to the boss and even though we can't change the prices seeing as they're set centrally, we could put a dealer contribution of two hundred and fifty pounds towards it.' Charlie picked up one of the service plan leaflets and had a quick read.

'Okay…' He waited for Nicola to come back and thought about how to play it. She loved the car. Charlie loved the car. 'This service plan here…' Charlie pointed, 'basic service for three years. That's three hundred, right?'

'That's right.' Charlie checked over his shoulder for any signs of Nicola.

'How about instead of your contribution, you give us the service plan? I'll give you a thousand pounds deposit and she'll give you the rest. Then you get your full screen price.' The man pondered hard. Was Charlie trying to do him here? It was a bit of a switch-up and really, he ought to speak to the boss again but he didn't want to go running, he wanted to be a big boy and make the decision himself. He wanted to close the deal there and then.

'We're not even trading in a car or anything towards this. It's a straight sale for you. Full screen price.' Those words again rang like bells in the salesman's ears.

'Okay, we'll give you the service deal instead.'

'There's just one more thing...' Charlie added. 'If she goes for it, I'll give you the thousand pounds, but give me a separate receipt for that and put it on hers as 'deposit.' Just tell her that's a dealer deposit like you mentioned. I don't want her to know I've put the money in, she'll not let me. Then add the service plan and when we come to pick the car up, she'll pay the balance.'

The man thought again if this was all some kind of con, but it wouldn't be. The only deception was to Nicola about where the deposit came from. 'Alright, that's fine.'

'But she's not to know I've paid the first grand okay?'

'Alright, got it. God, I wish you were my boyfriend!' the salesman joked.

Nicola returned to the table and her ponytail swept side-to-side as she sat down in the seat next to Charlie. She lifted the beige plastic cup to her mouth and blew swirls of steam and ripples over the surface with her freshly glossed lips. The man looked towards Charlie to bring her up to speed because he was a little nervous about saying the wrong thing to give it all away. 'So, what they're willing to do is make a dealer contribution of a thousand pounds and they're also going to throw in a three-year service plan. So that's your servicing taken care of as well for the next three years. You'll just need to buy tyres and stuff if you need it.'

Nicola's heart sang. She could get the car at the budget she had *and* have her servicing paid for?? How amazing was that?? She looked at the salesman just to check it was true and Charlie wasn't pulling her leg. 'Yeah that's right. So, the dealer deposit effectively reduces the cost of the car by one thousand, I managed to talk my boss round. And we'll give you the three years basic service as well. It is your first car after all, so we thought we would give you the best deal we could. It's more than we would usually do.' *That's plenty*, thought Charlie. Nicola wanted to jump up and down but managed to contain herself.

'Erm, can we have a moment to discuss it please?' she asked, with as much decorum as she could.

'Of course, take as much time as you need.' As he left the teachers desk, the salesman knew it was done. Although she did very well, he could read the excitement in Nicola and he sensed that Charlie would have done anything to get the car for her if that's the one she wanted.

'Charlie, oh my God! I think I'll buy it!' She grabbed his hands in excitement. 'Do you think I should buy it?'

'Well, if you like it so much, then yes. I really like it. It's a great wee car. And you've got your services included too. So are you going to go for it?'

'Yes. I think so. Should I wait and let my parents see it though?'

'I don't think there's any need, you don't want to wait and then it ends up being sold. It's a good deal, so I'd just go for it. It's up to you though.'

'Okay…I think I'll just go for it. So, what do we do now?'

'Well, they'll prep it and we'll come and pick it up as soon as they've got it ready. It's usually about a week. You'll just need to sign for it and pay the balance when we pick it up. And I'll help you get all your insurance and everything sorted in the meantime as well.'

'You mean I don't have to pay anything today?'

'Not a bean.' Charlie beckoned him over.

'So, what's the verdict then?' He already knew the answer.

'Yes, we'll go for it,' Nicola said. *We*, Charlie thought. *Nice.*

'Excellent.' They shook hands and then the man turned to Charlie.

'We've just got a new line of car-care products in. Maybe something you'd be interested in for your car, if you'd like to take a look. They're all in the office there.' The man was getting in on the subversion. 'I'll take you out and you can have another look at the car whilst he's looking there.'

Charlie headed to the office, not to look at car care products, but to hand over a thousand pounds deposit for Nicola's car as she practically skipped outside to see it again. He put the deposit on his credit card. *Why have a big limit and not use it?* he thought. Then it hit like an atomic bomb – the realisation of what he was doing for her and about his feelings for her. He knew it was far too early to do something like that but he didn't care. But it was certainly not the kind of thing you do for just a friend.

Her budget came from her parents. It was a big expenditure for them, especially since her dad was retired, but they felt that buying her a car would provide her with a great tie to Scotland and they'd do whatever they could to prevent her from returning to Paris. The salesman had already explained to the office about the deposit that

Charlie would give and they wrote up a quick headed letter to say that the deposit was indeed paid for by Charlie.

In the end, he was glad that he did not correct the salesman about them not being together, because how the hell could he explain handing over that amount of money to someone who he wasn't even with?

# Chapter Six

Clouds gathered over the town on a Thursday night. Charlie picked up his schoolbag and hefted it onto his shoulder. It had two straps but he only wore the right strap despite it continually trying to make a break for freedom. But at high school it was seen as decidedly un-cool to carry a bag as it was actually designed.

He turned right out of the school gates and the light was starting to ebb out of the sky. It was just after 6 p.m. and he had been volunteering at the After School Club. He was approached by the Deputy Head at the start of the year because he had a reputation of being responsible and diligent, despite the fact that two years earlier, he had been responsible for the worst fight the school had ever seen.

Charlie was an outsider, he lived in the next town and none of his friends at school he'd known from nursery, as the rest of the kids at school seemed to. He was a mystery and therefore a threat to the delicate hierarchal system of a high school. He did have good friends and much to his preference, they were completely unlike the popular pupils, which were mainly made up of thugs, idiots and cowards, sticking together like some disillusioned band of brothers with inflated egos and sense of worth, finding immortality in numbers.

It was something petty. David Christian saw himself as a leader and an all-round hardman. He blatantly pushed Charlie for no reason as they passed in the corridor. He did that to most kids, but none of the other kids would ever push back. Charlie did, and hard. David Christian was knocked almost off his feet. It was only the proximity of the lockers he fell against which stopped him from hitting the floor. Surrounded by the force field of his motley crew he told Charlie that he was *dead*, to which Charlie simply extended his middle finger as he walked off.

Over the few weeks that followed, David Christian – known as Chris to his pals – antagonised Charlie relentlessly. Charlie chose to ignore him but would never forget a single word he said and instead, piled the hostility up in a box which would soon overflow.

'Here he is, Charlie Cuntbag.' He looked around to his friends for approval, extorting a few laughs here and there.

'Just because your last name's Christian, it doesn't mean you're Jesus, you dick.'

Charlie had worked on that retort for a while and delivered it with perfect timing in front of a full playground. It took Chris a few seconds longer than it should have to figure out, but looking round he could see everybody was laughing at him and he was enraged.

He lurched towards Charlie hastily. Charlie ducked, took a step to his right and delivered a devastating blow to Chris's face. Blood, snot and spit exploded from his nose and mouth. He couldn't tell properly where Charlie was since his dumb brain was still rattling around in his skull, yet he tried to lash out towards him. Charlie delivered two precise and deadly jabs at his kidneys and then another across the face. Chris hit the deck. The conspicuous circle of pupils that suddenly formed on the tarmac between two school buildings alerted teachers to a fight – it could mean nothing else. Charlie had opened the box of pent up aggression with volatile accuracy, except he only got to use up part of it and he really struggled to put the lid back on. Now, the remainder of it passed through his body, coursing like a thousand galloping horses, pumping his chest in and out, in and out, blood rushed like a torrent, pounding through his ears. His fists were clenched and he was slightly squat. His teeth were gritted together so hard he felt like he could chew bricks.

Charlie wanted to stamp on Chris. He wanted him to suffer. He wanted to teach him a lesson for all the indignities he'd shown everyone else at school. He felt exhilarated whilst cursing himself for not doing something about him before. *Why did I let this guy get away with this for so long? I could have saved a lot of people a lot of anguish. I sat back and let him get away with it. I should have done something before.* Charlie felt a spike of guilt about not being more proactive. Now, he felt, was time to make up for it. He didn't want to stamp on his back because it was as important to damage his ego and reputation as much as his body, so grabbed him and tossed him over. Chris flopped over like a rag doll and faced inertly towards the sky. Charlie was ready to do some more damage.

A hole formed in the crowd, then another. Two teachers charged within the ring of spectators. The weight shifted onto his left leg as he prepared to use his right to do the stamping. 'Charlie! Don't you dare!!' screeched from one teacher's dry throat.

'Stop, Charlie! Bloody hell!' from another. The sound of teachers' voices made him desist immediately. Maybe it was because one of them swore in front of pupils, albeit not strongly, but it was a sweary word nonetheless. Or maybe Charlie knew it was too much and was just waiting, hoping that someone would be there in time to stop him. It certainly wasn't going to be one of the other kids.

The first teacher was a young female biology teacher. It was her first year teaching and despite knowing of him she'd never had Charlie in any of her classes. She was horrified by the scene in front of her. A pupil lay in an insensible state on the gravelled tarmac with blood seeping from the openings in his face. The second teacher was Mr Reader who Charlie had for geography. He was also relatively young but had been teaching for a few years. He approached Charlie but was unsure how to deal with him. Charlie was well built with broad shoulders even at that age. Mr Reader felt a compulsion to grab him so he couldn't do any more damage but at the same time felt a prick of fear. They got on well and Charlie was always attentive and contributory in class. They often enjoyed making jokes about things and sometimes each other to a certain, professional extent.

To Mr Reader, this wasn't the Charlie he was used to, it was a completely other side of him. 'Charlie?' Turning towards his teacher, Charlie's rage immediately withdrew from his face because he had no issue with him. The now aptly named Mr Reader could tell that he didn't pose a threat to him, or to anyone else other than Chris. 'Come on, let's go.' He put a hand confidently on his shoulder and without a further word or any resistance led him to the headmaster's office.

The police arrived about twenty minutes later and started to gather statements and evidence. In those days, schools were not furnished with CCTV, but it was clear what had happened. The reputation of both boys involved was well known throughout the school. Charlie's for being an (up until then) model pupil. He volunteered some lunchtimes to the Access Scheme, which was the school's programme for special needs pupils. He was always well turned out in school uniform. He was polite and respectful and as such was widely liked by the teachers. The only times he'd been at the headmaster's office was to receive some kind of congratulations. Chris on the other hand was a known troublemaker. He disrupted classes, bullied people and smoked on the school grounds. He would vandalise school property and write profanities about the teachers on whatever surface his permanent marker would take to. They'd suspended him several times and tried to expel him.

Once the police gave the all clear, the paramedics scooped Chris up, ferrying him to hospital. The school pleaded with the police to handle it themselves, not only to avoid any superfluous attention, but also because they knew the full story and didn't want Charlie to be unfairly or harshly judged. They had to repeat the same plea to Mr and Mrs Christian when they arrived at school the next day, citing 'Chris's' bad behaviour to their advantage. Thankfully for Charlie, both pleas were successful, the latter one, eventually and grudgingly.

He got a big slap on the wrists but nothing more. They hoped that 'Chris' might return as a much calmer and well-behaved, or at least, better-behaved pupil after being kicked off his top-spot. Perhaps the humiliation was too much, or he was so shook up that he'd forever feel in fear, but either way David Christian never set foot in that school again.

Charlie continued down the road away from school. His bus stop was on a main road that led the opposite way out of town. It was about a ten-minute walk but he used a bus stop deliberately further away. The town centre bus stop was a magnet for the David Christians of the world and despite knowing he could handle himself, it's that very knowledge that gave him fear. He was capable of causing some serious damage to people and that was not a quality he liked to encourage. He gained the nickname of 'bully-killer' and sometimes recalled the fight and thought about not being able to limit himself. Charlie was part pacifist, part vigilante. The vigilante part was borne from the fact that he spent a lot of time being respectful and thoughtful to people and he believed everyone should be like that, as idealistic as it was. Frustration would mount when people were heinous to one another, especially for no reason. Ultimately, he didn't want any trouble, so the town centre bus stop was somewhere he'd avoid.

He adjusted his backpack as it slipped unnecessarily down his shoulder. He was approaching the end of the road, a few hundred yards from the school. That was where the rural service and catchment area school buses dropped pupils off and picked them up again at the end of the day. One of the bus stops hid under the bridged canopy of two old oak trees. The trees stood in a small grassy patch with a low dry-stone dyke around the periphery. He continued walking as he was, on the opposite side of the road, then he spotted a familiar figure. A girl from his year was sitting on the wall texting on her phone. She had a big black shoulder bag which lay dilapidated on the ground at her feet. She wore black trousers, a white blouse, black jumper and a black cotton blazer. As he drew closer, she looked up quickly, checking up and down the road as if something had startled her. He could see her face. *Nicola.* Her gaze left the road and she waved as she spotted Charlie. He returned the wave, checking for traffic before crossing towards her.

'Hiya, Charlie.'

'Hi, Nicola, what you up to?'

He recognised her bus stop but it was a little over two hours after school had finished. She took one of the local buses to and from school, one that ran a sparse service throughout the day to some of the more secluded villages that surrounded the town.

'I've just missed my bus, the next ones not for aaaages.'

'How come you're so late?'

'Oh, I was with…er…some friends.'

She mirrored the question. 'I do that after school club thing. I'm just going to get my bus too, when's your next one?'

'Bloody hour and a half!'

'Can you not just phone for a lift home?'

She hesitated a little, 'I don't…erm, my mum and dad are both busy,' she came up with.

They talked a little more. He liked listening to her but wasn't really concerned with the juicy gossip she had. He just somehow enjoyed hearing the tone of her voice; the cadences up and down and the tunefulness of it. She'd laugh at some of the things she'd mentioned and tender creases formed around the corners of her lips. Charlie and Nicola were not at all close friends, they didn't even have any classes together, but just talked because of the proximity they often found themselves to one another. Through the big oak trees he could feel a few spits of rain touch down on his cheeks and forehead. He waited for a polite break in the conversation to check his watch.

'I better go, Nicola, if I want to catch my bus.'

'Alright, I'll see you later.'

She smiled as he left for his bus stop. He thought he'd probably have to pick up the pace to make it on time. He'd let the conversation go on longer than he wanted, but he didn't want to be rude and interrupt her. The closer he got to his bus stop, the more the rain seemed to increase in intensity. Reaching the retail complex, the bus stop was in plain sight, but still some several hundred yards away, even if he cut through the car park. The complex itself was not much; a supermarket, a petrol station and a couple of takeaway places. The wind picked up a little and brought with it not only a chill but the mingled smells of each takeaway place combined in some kind of culinary cacophony. The scents hit the pit of his stomach and it grumbled. Sometimes they would cook at the club but somehow they would never know until the actual time. As such, he told his mum to not bother cooking food on a Thursday night because often the dinner she'd make for him would go to waste. That night they cooked nothing of course.

The rain was starting to fall and a soft fresh aqueous fragrance mixed with the food smell. He checked his watch, *four minutes to go*, and determined there was insufficient time to stop for food. At that very moment, the bus hauled around the mini roundabout. He still had a couple of hundred yards to go but started to bolt. The bag that rested uneasily on his shoulder began to flail around at the sudden increase in motion. The bus accelerated. He checked the bus stop and it was empty. He had to hope that someone was going to get off and tried to scan for anyone onboard standing up to push the 'stop' button. No one did. He waved his arm as he chased the bus, but it closed in on and sailed right past the bus stop. 'Shite.' He consulted his watch again, *three minutes*. He didn't think his watch was slow, in fact, if anything it was a few minutes fast because he didn't like to be late for things. 'What a bastard.' He was convinced the bus driver was at fault because they were quite bad for doing it on that service. There had been many a time where the bus was early and he'd be grateful for it because he'd been waiting a while. The frequency of his buses wasn't much better than Nicola's and to top it off it was starting to rain properly now. The bus stop was just a pole in the ground, no bus shelter, no way to hide from the rain as he thought about how to fill the next rainy hour.

The grumble in his stomach beckoned him to go and get some food, so he bought some chips from the chip shop. As he walked back to the bus stop, he had to figure out how to eat them in the cool rain without ruining them. The thought of Nicola also waiting in the rain entered his head. He turned round towards the supermarket checking how much money he had left and decided to buy a cheap umbrella. His mum used to tell him to carry an umbrella, but he always found it took up unnecessary room in his schoolbag. Even when it rained, he hated using one anyway. It seemed like quite a hassle to carry and battle the wind, not to mention that people would give him a hard time – a teenage boy using an umbrella? As a man, it was maybe only acceptable to use an umbrella if you were in a smart suit, or of course, in the company of a lovely lady.

The wind picked up by the time he exited the supermarket and it chilled him through. Despite the rain, he put the umbrella in his bag. He still wasn't in a suit or the company of a lovely lady yet and headed back towards school and to Nicola's bus stop. He concentrated on keeping the bag of chips as dry as possible. He sent a quick text to his mum to inform her of the delay.

"Hi mum, sorry, forgot to say this finishes late tonight xxx"

He lied, but it was a white lie. He didn't want to have to explain to his mum because she wouldn't understand why he'd want to walk back to school and wait with someone else until they got their bus. It would invite an unnecessary line of questioning. He walked fast and the usual ten-minute walk didn't take so long. He crossed the junction at the lights and that took him back onto the road where Nicola was. She was still sitting there. Her eyes were squinting from the wind and rain as she held a purple ring binder to protect her hair, obviously that was more important than whatever schoolwork she had in it. She looked upset and miserable – abandoned even. But then he supposed that most people wouldn't be happy about the prospect of over an hours' wait in the rain for the next bus.

'Hello?' he called. She looked round with surprise.

'Hey, what you doing?' She looked at him and he was already wet.

'Missed my bus too! It was bloody early again. They're always doing that.' He took his schoolbag off, revealing a dry patch on his back and placed it on the ground. 'Want some chips?' She looked at the paper bag and politely declined. 'Is it okay if I wait with you?' He removed the umbrella from his bag and popped it open as the lovely lady criteria had been fulfilled.

'Sure.' He held the umbrella over her and she stuffed her folder away before taking hold of it. 'You're a lifesaver! Oh my God. It's just typical that it'd rain. But look at you, prepared with your umbrella and everything.' The rain was slightly abbreviated by the oak trees, which made much less frequent but fatter drops fall over the bus stop.

'There's no shelter over at Sanderson's, so I thought I'd come back and wait with you if that was alright.' He opened the bag of chips and despite the bag being wet on the outside, the chips were still appetisingly fresh inside. They shared the cover of the umbrella as he began to eat. The smell of the sauce vaporised, hitting the pit of her stomach and she could no longer deny to herself that she was hungry. She still didn't take any.

They talked and passed the time. Cars went past in the rain and the sky grew darker by the minute. Car headlights came on which energised the splashes of rain on the road and the street. Puddles grew and reflected the humming streetlights that had been switched on and were warming up.

'So what's your plans for when you leave school?' Nicola took a second to ponder it, although she had it mostly figured out.

'I'm doing art. I've got an offer at Edinburgh and in Glasgow, but I fancy moving abroad to get away from this place.' He sensed something in her tone when she said *this place*. 'What about you?'

'Well, I'll probably just continue with the army thing. I've got a few regiments that have invited me to the careers office. I don't know exactly what I'll do but I want to do something specialist, something quite niche, but it'll probably take me a while to work up towards that. My parents aren't keen though, they want me to go to uni. My dad says it's a waste of my brain. And my mum just says she doesn't want me to go too far away. More like she doesn't want me in harm's way.' He poked around and grabbed a chip before quickly eating it. 'And Rachel's really not keen either. I've tried to talk about it but she just sort of closes up and gets upset, so I change the subject. Sort of running out of time though.'

At school he was in the cadets and excelled in everything that he did there. He enjoyed the training and had an aptitude for it beyond any of his peers. He was the senior NCO of his contingent and had been put forward to represent them in all sorts of competitions against other contingents. He won every time. He knew that moving up to the regular army would be something completely different, but who else had a better grounding than him? It seemed a waste to not use the talent and skills he'd developed over the six years at school. Regiments had tried to recruit him as soon as he turned sixteen but he was determined to finish school – for whatever reason. Now they were offering him potential fast track promotions and a reduced return of service by his reputation and accomplishments so far.

'It must be quite hard. I know I wouldn't like to have that conversation. How long have you been going out now?'

Charlie swallowed another mouthful. 'Eight months. Next week.' He smiled as he thought of his girlfriend. Rachel and Charlie were very close and trusted each other completely. So much so that it never even entered his head about someone seeing him sit with Nicola in the rain having bought an umbrella specifically for that and getting the wrong impression. He didn't come back to see Nicola for anything other than to help keep her dry, keep her company and share his chips until her bus came. When he came back and saw the look in her squinting eyes, he thought that maybe he was right to do so.

'That's quite a long time…for school anyway. You guys are a really cute couple though.' Nicola was right. Rachel would tell her friends about all the things he did for her and that would spread to all the girls in sixth year. They were all jealous.

'Thanks. Yeah, she's great, I love her very much. You're suuuuure you don't want a chip?' Nicola had been eyeing the package of saucy starchy, carb-tastic chips with envy every time Charlie picked one up, which hadn't been missed by him.

'Umm, just a few, then.' She took the chips and tried not to scoff them too eagerly. Like most girls her age, she was self-conscious about her looks and her weight so chips were a big no-no. But it was late and Charlie guessed that she'd probably not had much to eat during the day.

'You need energy for the bus ride home anyway, you're out in the sticks, aren't you?' he smiled. Nicola nodded back as she ate. Producing a bunch of napkins he grabbed from the chip shop counter, he wiped the sauce off his hands and kept enough for Nicola to do the same when she was done. 'Just finish them if you want, I'm kind of full anyway.' It didn't occur to her that as a young man, half a bag of chips would not be enough to fill him up, but it was sufficient to tide him over until he got home.

They continued to talk and the rain seemed to run out as the time went. Her bus turned onto the road and kicked up some spray from the asphalt as it approached. Nicola quickly lifted her bag onto her shoulder and thrust her hand out onto the road waving it franticly to make sure the driver didn't miss her. The driver signalled to stop. 'Well, Charlie, thanks for keeping me company and thanks for the chips.' She swept a loose clump of her hair behind her ear and tried hard not to blush too much. 'You're really sweet.' She thought about giving him a hug but became suddenly too aware that he belonged to someone else. At that age, any physical contact with a member of the opposite sex was still intriguing and she didn't want to do anything out of order because he'd been a perfect gentleman to her.

'Yeah, no problem. Get home safe.'

'You too.' The bus door hissed open and Charlie gathered his things as she got on. He hefted his bag onto his shoulder once again and she waved from the back window of the bus as it pulled away. The engine strained in anticipation of the winding roads ahead and emitted stinky diesel fumes which tickled the inside of his nose as he turned to walk back towards his bus stop.

The bus was empty except from one little old lady that sat in the first seat with a huge handbag across her lap. It was a small bus. Small enough to negotiate all the old, narrow and tight country roads and – except during the school run – big enough to seat anyone who needed to travel there several times over. She undid her hair bobble and pulled her hair down shaking it out to relieve what stress she could. She rubbed her hands on her scalp and sighed deeply. Her hair fell around her pretty young face as she thought about Charlie. She thought about how kind he'd been to come and keep her company and how genuine he was. He really wasn't there to pull any moves on her or had vulgar intentions, unlike the boys she spent time with after school who said they'd drive her home and instead left her to wait in the rain. *Rachel's so lucky to have him.*

# Chapter Seven

'If you pick me up about eleven, that'll be fine.'

'Okay, well, have a nice time. I'll see you then.'

Charlie hung up the phone as he approached the car. They struggled a little to hear one another because he'd been out for a walk with an old friend along Gullane bents. The wind was strong and the chill had whipped around him. 'Was that her then?'

'Yeah, she's been at her parents and she's meeting a few friends for drinks tonight. Then we'll drive back to Glasgow.'

Charlie had been getting his friend, Grant, caught up on the recent events. He had done a stint as No.2 RCO (Range Commanding

Officer) at Catterick Garrison and Grant was in the Armoury. They became friends and after realising they were from the same area, had stayed good friends ever since. Had he been a school friend however, he'd have perhaps warned him off because of her reputation or at the very least questioned her intentions with him. 'So what you got planned for her birthday then?'

'I'll drop her off at her friend Claire's tonight and I've arranged for them to go to a spa in Glasgow tomorrow, then we're all going out tomorrow night. I was talking to Claire about maybe going to Loch Lomond or something as well on the Sunday.'

'Is she not having a party? It is her thirtieth after all.'

'No, she just wanted to keep it low-key, just me and Claire.'

'Oh aye…just her two favourite people then?' Charlie smirked at the realisation.

'Well, maybe…hopefully.'

'Sounds good mate. You gonna seal the deal then?' Grant laughed and made a rude gesture with his hands.

'Well, we'll just see. I can't rush her though, I'm happy playing the long game anyway.'

'Just make sure it's not too long though, because…' Grant paused.

'Because what…?'

'It's the other 'F-word'…friend!'

Charlie finished dinner at his parent's house and the glass of wine his dad poured him was left untouched. It was a feeble attempt to render him over the drink-drive limit so he'd have to stay over and subsequently spend a bit more time with his mum. She missed Charlie a lot and since he was continually in the same country they felt that he should be spending more time with them. His dad missed him too whilst understanding that he had his own life to lead, but they still knew as little about it as they did before. He didn't mention Nicola. He didn't tell them it was her birthday that weekend. He only intimated that he had to go back through to Glasgow because he had plans with friends. That was true of course, it wasn't that he would lie to his parents, but at the same time he didn't want to divulge any more information than was absolutely necessary.

They watched television for a while and Skyped his sister in London. It was rare to have all the family 'together', even if Skype was involved, but it was something. He and his sister were always close but their lives in the recent years seemed divergent. She was seven years older than him and Charlie missed her a lot. They would always plan to spend more time together but somehow their plans would never come to fruition. He wanted to show her the flat. She knew the car, because he'd visit her regularly when he worked for Gertrude. That was very convenient. But since he left London he hardly ever saw her.

*It's just off Leith Walk,* he remembered her saying, but had never heard of the place before and her instructions were quite vague. He stopped the car and got out awaiting her phone call. Eleven o'clock came and went, but he didn't expect her to be exactly on time. She eventually called.

'Charlie, where are you?'

'I'm just on Leith Walk, close to the Chinese Shop, which pub was it again?'

'Oh, I'm just up the road. I walked my friend home, I'm on Iona Street.' Her tone was shaky, her nose sounded stuffy and her breaths were short and gasping. He wasn't sure, but he thought she might be crying.

'Okay, I'll be there in a minute.'

He swung the car round and raced back up Leith Walk. When he rounded the corner, he could see her standing by the side of the road at a crossing point. It wasn't really a great place to stop the car but he didn't care, she was wiping tears away for sure. Bags of presents sat on the ground next to her and the bunch of flowers she held in one hand were pointing towards the ground. 'Just get in, I'll get your stuff.' He opened the boot and quickly gathered her things. He couldn't let her help because he was trying to conceal her present in there. It was a big green box and whilst he supposed she wouldn't be able to determine what was inside, he still didn't want to give her the opportunity.

Charlie joined her in the car and pushed the radio off, 'What's wrong?' No reply came. They were dazzled by a van that flashed its lights angrily as it was forced over onto the other side of the road to pass them. He reached into his door pocket and pulled out a packet of tissues. 'Nicola, what's happened?'

'Nothing, just drive…please.' She took the tissues.

He paused for a second before putting the car into gear and sliding off along the road. He caught glimpses of her beautiful but darkened eyes as the car pitched back and forth over the speed-bumps like a rickety boat in the harsh sea. Flashes of light caught her from lampposts and other traffic and she didn't say a word to Charlie. It drove him crazy. 'Will you tell me what's going on?'

'It's nothing.' She took another tissue out of the pack and he switched the radio back on but kept it low as he drove through the lonely city streets towards the bypass.

They reached the edge of Edinburgh and the lights that flashed on her face became dimmer and less frequent. He wanted to just talk with her, but didn't want to press her, 'Are you hungry?' She sniffed. 'Nicola?'

'Yeah…' She stared out of the car vacantly, 'I could probably eat.'

He thought about what options he had between them and Glasgow and wished he had thought of asking before they actually left Edinburgh. 'McDonalds okay?'

She nodded her head and placed her hand on top of Charlie's, 'Just the drive-thru though. Please.'


They arrived at Claire's and mercifully there was ample parking for a change. It was just supposed to be a drop off but he parked up right outside her door. Nicola headed round to the boot to retrieve her things. 'Erm, just go ring the bell, I'll bring everything up.' Nicola did as commanded and didn't give it another thought, her head was elsewhere anyway.

'Hey, Nic Nac! Hey Charlie!' Claire had been patiently waiting for their arrival. She noticed the bags and flowers that Charlie carried for her. 'Someone's popular!'

Nicola hugged Claire and headed straight for the toilet. 'Can I get you a cup of tea or something, Charlie?'

'Erm, yeah, actually. That'd be nice.' They went through the hall door and entered the living area. Charlie's voice went low, 'Just so you know…she's been crying the whole way here. From the moment I picked her up, till about five minutes ago. We stopped for some food and she cried the whole time eating that as well. Not that she ate much of it, mind you.'

'What's wrong with her?'

'I don't know. She wouldn't tell me.' Claire pondered as she filled the kettle with water.

'Why wouldn't she tell you?'

'Don't know that either.' She clicked the kettle on to boil and they took a seat on the sofa. Through the hall door they heard her come out of the bathroom and her phone began to ring. She went into Claire's bedroom and firmly shut the door.

'But…I don't know why she wouldn't tell you. It must be to do with Patrice, but I don't know why she doesn't talk to you about it. It's not like she doesn't trust you or anything.' A loud laugh came through from Claire's bedroom. Who the hell was she talking to that made her laugh out loud? She giggled and was suddenly much livelier than she was during the car journey. Claire turned the television down but they still couldn't make out what she was saying. The thought entered her head as to whether or not she should have muted the television in case she said something about Charlie.

The kettle began to boil and steam poured out the spout dancing along the underside of Claire's kitchen cabinets. More laughs came from Claire's bedroom. 'Who's she on the phone to now anyway?' Charlie shrugged and shook his head. Claire went through to offer her some tea and Nicola dismissed the offer whilst not interrupting the conversation. She tried to figure out who it was on the other end but she couldn't.

The cups of tea were sipped as Claire and Charlie discussed the plans for the weekend. 'So, I'll come round tomorrow about ten with breakfast, then I'll take you in to town for the spa.'

'Did you tell her yet?'

'No. I didn't really get a chance on the way, you know? You can tell her in the morning. And are we still on for Loch Lomond for Sunday?'

'Yeah! Oh, it sounds so great. I've not been up there for so long.' Claire smiled warmly at him.

'I'll make a picnic and everything to take up. Any special requests?' he asked.

'No. Just anything, Charlie. I know you'll make it special.' The door opened and Nicola came through as if nothing was the matter. Apart from the blotchiness in her cheeks and the puffiness of her eyes, you'd never be able to tell that she'd spent the whole hour and a half in the car crying her eyes out. It must have been something big. He burned to know.

Charlie sat outside on his terrace for a while as the day began and the city started to wake. After readying himself, he readied her gift. She had mentioned that Sweet Peas were her favourite flower so he spent a lot of time on the internet and the phone contacting various florists around the UK to find someone who could supply him with thirty-five sweet pea flowers. Hedging his bets as always, he allowed for a few of them to be damaged in transit, or for some to not be perfect. In actual fact all thirty-five arrived intact and bloomed flawlessly. He had thought a lot about what to get her and it was difficult. He'd have spent hundreds of pounds on her without batting an eye, but he felt he had to not be too extravagant. He didn't want to seem like he was trying to buy her affection, so it had to be understated yet thoughtful.

He also knew that she dreamed of owning a chocolate brown cocker spaniel, so he trawled the internet for a soft toy version. He also bought a small piece of pink gingham ribbon and sowed it into a collar for the dog before placing it into a shoebox with holes poked in it.

124

He removed five of the flowers and placed them in a tall tumbler with water and stood it in the centre of his dining room table. It brightened the place up a little and softened all the manly edges in the flat. It was like a touch of Nicola in there.

He arranged to get the flowers sent to his parent's house. That was mainly because he knew that either his parents or someone next door would be there to take the delivery as he might be out running around for Nicola somewhere. He used that as an excuse to visit his parents, as well as the fact that he was through to drive her back to Glasgow anyway.

The parking situation outside Claire's hadn't changed much from when he delivered a weepy Nicola to her, so he parked right outside again. He had borrowed one large and one small hamper from his parents (another good reason to visit home), and brought some fruit, juice, muesli, croissants and other nice pastries with him. They were piled neatly into the small hamper. It sat on the tailgate as he collected the flowers. It was almost ten o'clock and Nicola looked out of the window anticipating his arrival. 'Charlie!' she shouted from the window. 'Do you need a hand?'

'No, it's okay, but...can you get away from the window please?'

She could see that he was struggling with something and didn't have difficulty in realising it was something for her. She happily obliged.

She buzzed him up and opened the door for him. She looked fresh faced. Her hair was slicked back over her head in a tight ponytail. He liked when she wore it like that. He liked when she wore it any way actually. From the bottom of her jeans he could see odd socks, one pink and one orange. He assumed she had another pair at her flat exactly the same. She wore a black strappy vest which revealed the definition in her sweet shoulders and the curve along her neck ached for him to place his best kisses on it. 'Happy Birthday!'

He produced the huge bouquet of flowers. 'Oh my God! Sweet peas!' She looked round for Claire but she was in the bathroom with the door closed. 'How…how did you know they're my favourite?'

'You mentioned it before.'

'Did I? I can't even remember.'

'There's thirty. One for each year.'

'Oh my God, Charlie, I LOVE them! That's so amazing. It's the best and sweetest present ever!'

He handed her the shoe box. 'Be very careful with this one...'
She took it from him, noticed the holes in the box and looked at him
with terror in her eyes.

'Charlie, what is this??'

'You'll just have to open it. Go on, she doesn't bite.'

'She??' Nicola carefully peeled the lid off the shoebox and relief
washed over her.

'Oh my God! It's a cocker spaniel!' She laughed realising she'd
talked incessantly about owning a chocolate brown cocker spaniel, and
lifted her out to take a closer look. 'Charlie, you gave me such a fright,
when I saw the holes in the box, I didn't know what to expect!'

'Well, how else could she breathe?'

'Oh, she's so cute! Look at her little pink collar!'

'Yeah, customised...I made the collar for her. Now she just
needs a mummy.'

'Oh, I love her Charlie. I'll call her...pinky.'

He reached down for the hamper. 'And what's that?'

'That's your breakfast.'

Claire appeared from the bathroom. 'Oh, Charlie, I haven't got my face on yet!'

She seemed a little embarrassed but as they were all getting closer, she supposed that she would be seen without make-up on at some point. Her eyes seemed smaller than Charlie recalled. 'Still beautiful you two anyway,' he said. He then realised that Nicola hadn't put her 'face' on yet either, but there was a vitality in her skin, an energy that buzzed from her features.

'Have you told Nicola about our surprise yet?' Claire asked. Her face lit up and she seemed to jump up and down although it was more a rocking onto her tip-toes and back.

'What surprise??' Charlie smiled and wanted to let her hang on a little longer because she loved the anticipation.

'Don't you want to tell her, Claire?' She still shied a little from her lack of make-up when Charlie would look at her, but was slowly growing accustomed to letting him see her like that.

'Charlie, you tell her, it was all your idea.'

Nicola grabbed his closest forearm and tugged at it pleading to find out. 'It's nothing much, just a spa treatment in town. But it'll be nice.'

'Oh, that's so nice. Thank you.' He shut the door behind him as she led him through to the living area carrying the flowers and her puppy. 'I could really do with a de-stress, so I'll probably do it soon.'

'Well, I hope so…because erm, it's today. I hope that's okay?'

'Oh, yeah, well…that should be fine.' Her tone was still bright but she sounded a little disappointed, 'It's just I was planning to go shopping with Claire, but I suppose we can shop any time.'

'Well, you'll still have plenty time after you two get out.'

'Oh, so Claire's coming too?? Oh, that's perfect!' Finally, the penny dropped. 'God, Charlie, you really do think of everything!' She put her gifts down on the sofa so she could pull him in close. He wrapped his wanting arms around her locking her inside his forcefield. 'You're so kind. Thank you so much.' She let him go. 'For all of it I mean…it's so amazing. You've made this such a great birthday already. And I was so worried about turning thirty.'

'You're welcome. And…' he thought about not asking, but he had to. Perhaps she'd tell him why she was crying the night before, '…how come you were worried about turning thirty?'

'Oh, just…well, my birthdays the past few years have always been pretty dreadful, so…' she smoothed her hair back unnecessarily. '…but you've made me a happy girl.'

'Well, so long as you're happy, that's all that matters.'

A pure smile came to her face and washed out the darkness in him. 'I *am* happy. And it's all down to you.'

# Chapter Eight

Claire stayed at Nicola's after their night out and Charlie headed home by himself. When he got back to the flat, nothing but five sweet pea flowers were there to keep him company and he longed for her. He wondered whether he was doing the right thing by taking care of her the way he did. It was an awful lot of time they spent together and they would always become very close, but still he felt that there was an impassable gulf that stood between them. He still needed the affection and love that he so badly craved but since meeting up with Nicola again, he wanted it only from her. Yet, he still spent his nights alone.

He'd talked to a few girls when they were out the previous night but Nicola always seemed to appear at the wrong time and gave them the wrong impression. With the obvious chemistry between them, it appeared as if they were together, the way she hung onto him and touched him. But they weren't. Nicola watched him all night and didn't like how many girls would approach him. They were always quite scheming, she thought. They'd never approach him directly like the way she just messaged him and met up with him. They'd hang around him, or bump into him and Charlie would be polite and talk to them, but she knew what tricks and tactics they were trying. She hated the thought of Charlie with someone else. He was hers to do with as she pleased.

He arrived at Nicola's with breakfast once again, but it wasn't fruits and muesli like the day before, it was eggs, bacon, cheese and bagels. They all needed a wholesome breakfast after the night of drinking. Charlie wasn't hung-over, he had some kind of ability to not get hung-over despite the fact that he would certainly drink, and drink a lot. He made them his famous New York bagels and it was seemingly the best breakfast both of them had ever had.

'Oh, God. Where did you get the recipe for these?' Nicola asked through a full mouth.

'When I was in New York, I sometimes ordered a breakfast bagel, and I sort of had to recreate it when I got home.' She said that she didn't like fried eggs but he encouraged her to try his 'flat egg' and she certainly approved. 'It's kind of legendary, eh?' he laughed.

'So…can we stop somewhere on the way?' Nicola asked. 'Like, just for some supplies…'

By supplies, she meant more alcohol. She was looking forward to her day with Claire and Charlie up at Loch Lomond. 'Yeah, well, I need to stop for some petrol anyway, so you can get your 'supplies' at the same time.'

It was a pure day in late spring. The sun shone and the sky was clear. It was warm and Charlie drove with the window open most of the way. Nicola and Claire both sat in the back with a bottle of gin, a couple of bottles of tonic and some snacks, getting chauffeur driven along the country roads. They pulled in to a few places to stop for photos but Charlie had a spot in mind for lunch. He stopped just past Rowardennan Lodge and parked the car up. On the banks of the Loch Lomond the wind was a little stronger and Nicola felt a bit of a chill. 'God, I'm freezing, I think the alcohol's made my blood too thin!'

Charlie was in the boot preparing the picnic basket; the large size hamper that he borrowed from his parents. 'Do you want an extra layer? I've got some here if you want.

'Oh, yeah, that'd be good.' Along with his large ammo box of survival equipment and the two 'bug-out' bags he had fastened to the bulkhead he would usually have the choice of a jacket, hoody or a fleece

133

appropriate to the prevailing conditions outside. He lifted them out to let her see.

'Which one do you want?'

'The fleece will be perfect, thanks.'

She took off her coat to wear it underneath. As she reached up to slip it on, Charlie could see the slenderness of her body and the shape of her curves accentuate through her stretching. He wanted to pull her in close as she pulled the fleece down over herself, cruelly terminating his wonderful view. 'Hey, it's not bad. I thought it'd be baggier actually. Maybe I'm putting on the beef!' she joked. 'It's those bagels of yours!' *Or maybe all of my things fit you perfectly,* he thought. She gathered the collar in and took a deep breath, feeling the caress of the microfibre. 'Oh, God, Charlie it smells of you!'

'It smells of man!' Claire added.

'Well, I hope it's a good smell?' he chuckled, as he picked up the hamper and revelled in the fact she was familiar with his scent.

They found a spot on a small patch of sand. It was a small corner of beach with rocks either side and they had it all to themselves. Charlie spread out a blanket and they all sat down. Nicola started to take a few photos of the place and a few photos of Charlie as he began to unpack the picnic. He pulled Tupperware boxes out one by one. 'So, there's sweet chilli chicken...cream cheese and smoked salmon...cheese and salami...and tuna.' Charlie had also packed a cake and as they ate, he discreetly plunged thirty candles into the icing. They all went for a late lunch after the spa and shopping the day before, but they didn't officially have dinner and they didn't officially have a cake, so Charlie brought one along.

'Ready for the next course?' He lit the candles inside the hamper and the cake emerged triumphantly from within. He started to sing happy birthday and Claire joined in.

'Now, make a wish...' Nicola hesitated. *A wish,* she thought, *what do I wish for...?* She closed her eyes and blew all the candles out in one go. The breeze along their private stretch of beach helped a little. A family of ducks approached as Charlie began to slice the cake. They must have wondered what all the noise was about. Nicola fed her crusts to them and they hung around to join the party.

'Oh, man I am stuffed!' Claire said.

'Me too.' Nicola lay back on the blanket and stared up at the sky and Claire joined her. Charlie felt decidedly awkward and perhaps a little left out. He thought about maybe just going for a walk and that somehow he was intruding on them, or intruding on her, because he watched her snuggling into his fleece as she lay back on the edge of the loch. He tidied some of the picnic away back into the hamper so the ducks couldn't help themselves.

'Are you not going to join us?' asked Nicola. 'Come on, there's a space here.' There certainly was a space there, right next to her on the blanket, although he'd have quite happily laid on razor blades or fire just to lie next to her.

'Okay.'

He lay back and she shuffled a little until they were touching. He loved it. The sensation that she sent through his body chased away all the demons and misgivings he had about himself. A tremendous rush filled him and he somehow felt his senses heightened. 'So, Charlie…'

'Yes?'

'Have you been in any relationships since Rachel?'

'No.' He had to try and think ahead about what he was going to say, this was a chance for him to pitch himself. 'I mean, it was hard with the job. And the thing was, I didn't want to get into that position again. I didn't want to hurt someone by me being away all the time, and I didn't want to hurt myself by having to break up with someone that I…you know, loved. But then as time goes on, you think about whether it's worth it. Sure, I did really well and I'm…celebrated…or whatever, but

I've not got anyone to share it with, so it sort of doesn't mean much to me.'

'Yeah, I suppose you don't ever see any women in that line of work either, do you? I bet you're like an animal when you come back into the real world and see a woman for the first time!' Nicola's blood-alcohol level was elevated and she was feeling a little cheeky towards him.

Claire came to his defence, 'Charlie, an animal? I don't think it's possible Nic Nac.'

'Yeah, but going for months and months without even seeing a woman...'

'Well...it's not like you never *see* women...'

'Oh yeah? Sounds like a story there,' she said.

It wasn't really a path he wanted to go down, but he did nonetheless, just to satisfy Nicola's curiosity. Talking about his job was something he never did, so this also seemed like a good opportunity to do so. 'Okay, so there was one hostage situation I had. She was a Dutch journalist captured by Boko Haram in West Africa... I really cared for her, but she was married anyway. It's just because we ended up really close and everything, but it was more situational than anything.'

'So what happened? You rescued her?'

'Yeah. Romy, her name is.'

'Am I going to have to drag it out of you? Tell me all about it.'

He had to formulate the words in his head first and was worried about how much detail to go into. 'She was reporting on the kidnappings of girls in that area and Boko Haram caught wind of it so kidnapped her too. They'd raped her and strapped a bomb to her for two days and that's all she had on, not knowing if it was going to go off or not. Most likely it was a dud, but it's just…mind games, you know. So, I was sent in with a team.' The ducks walked past them where they lay once they realised they were getting no more crusts or cake. 'We tracked her down and she was blindfolded with gaffa tape and naked when we found her. She had a dirty sock in her mouth with tape over it. She was in a state,' Charlie paused, 'I'll never get that image out of my mind. How people can treat other humans like that. And that's not even the worst one – not by far. But one of my team got shot, it was just a graze thank fu–, I mean, thank God.'

'And then...? You got her out?'

'Yeah. But after my team were stood down and went home, I stayed with her for a couple of weeks until she was better, just fetching stuff and talking to her. I got quite attached to her, but it was just because of the situation. She had been through a lot and just needed someone to look after her.'

'And did you see her after?'

'Well, no. But she's married. The Dutch foreign office didn't let her husband travel to see her there though, so that's why I stayed to take care of her. She needed someone there and she seemed to respond well to me. She still writes to me regularly.'

'Was she beautiful?'

Charlie recalled the image of her. From the pictures he was given of her during the briefing to the recollection of when he picked her up naked off the floor and how close to death's door she seemed, to the brightness in her eyes as he wished her luck at the airport. 'Yeah...stunning actually.'

'Oh God, I bet she loved you though. I mean, if someone rescued me like that, I'd be totally gushing for them...'

'Oh, Nicola, that's gross!' Claire barked.

Charlie lifted his wrist and pointed out a bracelet he wore. It was actually a necklace, but he preferred to wrap it a couple times round his wrist. It was a small plain wooden crucifix on a thin cord. 'She gave me this. It was hanging in her room when I went to pick her up some clothes. I thought she'd want it because that would be a time when she needed faith the most. And then she gave it to me at the airport. I've worn it ever since then.' Nicola turned onto her side facing Charlie to inspect it closely.

'That's really nice, Charlie. You were her hero.'

'Oh, I don't know about hero, it's about being human. You don't do these things for glory, you do them to help. That's where I get my reward.'

'I bet she thinks about you all the time though.' Nicola returned to her supine position next to him. 'I can't even imagine a situation like that.' She sighed deeply. 'All my stories are pretty boring in comparison…but…oh I don't know…'

'So what about Patrice?' Claire interjected. She wanted to bring him up when they were in front of Charlie. She knew Nicola didn't want to mention him to Charlie and just wanted to gauge her reaction.

'Well, that's just…oh it's a load of shit Charlie…Anyway, it's over between us. But I sort of don't want to get involved with anyone just yet. I don't think I'm ready. I'm just happy being me at the moment.' Claire recognised that whilst things were over between her and Patrice, she still hadn't made it clear to him. She had been through it so many times and even though Nicola was getting much more involved with things in Scotland, she felt Patrice was still very much on the scene. But she didn't want to call her on it in front of Charlie, she just wanted to check.

'I just need a bit of time to chill and then…I'll be ready. And it'll be so much better.' Charlie took that as a clear message. He had doubts mounting about her and the way he craved her was becoming ridiculous. Now there was hope. She said with her own soft gorgeous lips that she needed time.

'I think it's such a great thing though Charlie, to have saved her life…but other than that, you've not had any girlfriends since Rachel?' She'd brought the conversation round to his love-life again, so she was certainly interested in it for some reason and probed not-so-delicately about it.

'Yeah, no girlfriends. And I don't really get much from you know…casual encounters.' Charlie continued to state his case whilst he had the chance. 'I'd like something meaningful, I suppose. I'd rather stay in and cuddle someone I love than sleep with a stranger. And I don't need to sleep around to prove myself either. I've got a hundred stories like that rescue. It's that sort of stuff that makes me a real man, not how many notches there are on my bed post.'

'I think that's a great way to be Charlie, especially these days. There are no more gentlemen like you. Everyone is so cruel and selfish. And they're only interested in what they can get from something…or someone.' Nicola sighed deeply. 'So, like…tell me more about your work. What other places and things have you done?'

It was the most Charlie had ever talked about it and he felt so good being able to share it with Nicola (and Claire), whilst sparing her all the harrowing details. 'Well, I was recommended for special task forces several times. I did some pretty specialist stuff, like coca eradication in Central and South America. That was pretty extreme. I had to learn Spanish for that as well actually.'

'What's coca?'

'It's what they make cocaine from.'

'Oh. Wow. Serious stuff. That's cool that you speak Spanish from it though.'

'Well, Spanglish maybe!'

'Do you speak any other languages?'

'Yeah…so Spanish, some Arabic, some Russian…' he thought on…

'French!' Nicola helped. That was the language taught to everyone at their school, and of course, the foreign language she was fluent in.

'Yeah, a wee bit, but I've never really used it…erm, some Mandarin, and a bit Japanese from my close protection work.'

'That's amazing! I was going to learn Spanish actually, but never got round to it. Give me your best line then.'

Since Charlie was lying back on the sand staring up, he thought of a phrase. 'Quiero mirar el cielo.'

'And what does that mean?'

'It means, *I want to gaze at the sky.*'

'Oh, God Charlie, you could charm the pants off anyone with that!'


After lying for a while, they packed the remainder of the picnic things up. Claire found a few more scraps for the ducks but they were long gone. Despite not being properly dressed for it, they wanted to go for a walk. Charlie was in his 'day order' however, which meant tactical trousers and boots and was more prepared for the sand and muck of the tracks there. He did think about jeans, but he'd been smart the rest of the weekend and he knew they were going out in the 'sort of' wilderness so he had justified it to himself. Nicola and Claire walked behind him as he led the way. His boots left gentle impressions in the ground as he forged a safe and suitable path for them, testing where the hardest and driest ground was.

Nicola watched him. His gait was firm, yet laced with sensitivity. He didn't yield to the path, only to the things around him. He touched the foliage, stared into the trees and watched the wildlife and flowers around him. He took in all the sights and smells and the beauty of the place. It was so endearing to her. He was obviously capable of so much in so many extreme conditions, but watching him do something as simple and soft and as ordinary as walking around there, he brought a sense of ease in his surroundings. He was quiet yet powerful. She took some photos of him as she walked behind him. She switched her phone onto silent first however because she wanted to capture him like that without him knowing he was being watched and being admired.

An old tree had fallen and departed from the path to lean on the beach. He walked out along it and his balance was impeccable. He didn't reach his hands out to steady himself, he was steadfast and strong. He gazed out onto the loch and watched as a pleasure boat passed two kayakers. The blue shimmered all the way across to the other side where the lush green hills ascended to touch the sky. She took a photo of him out there too.

'So, I don't think there's much more along there other than muddy tracks and I don't want you two to be sitting in my car with muddy bums, seeing as your shoes are…not really compatible.'

'But they're stylish!' Claire said as she pointed her toe into the ground.

'I'm not denying that!'

Nicola had warmed up by the time they got back to the car so she took her coat off but left Charlie's fleece on. She found it so comfortable. They became less and less chatty as the miles increased from Loch Lomond. Nicola thought a little more about her wish. *I wish this year will change things for the better.* She snuck glances of Charlie as he concentrated on the road ahead and she thought if he might be the key to it. He was literally the perfect man.

Before long, Charlie could hear the soft elongated breaths of two tipsy girls fast asleep, warm and safe in the back of his car. He checked them both in his rear-view mirror every now and then. He was happy. He cared for them very much and they were sleeping sweetly on the way home after having a lovely day out. If he could speak to his seventeen-year-old self, he would never believe that he'd have taken Nicola Wallace and Claire Stewart to Loch Lomond on Nicola's thirtieth birthday weekend and he'd never believe that he'd be falling in love with Nicola now. And if he could speak to himself at the very start of the year, he'd never believe how things were about to get better.

He arrived back at his flat after dropping them both off, whilst the fatigue of the weekend's activities started to dawn on him. He poured a large whisky for himself and put the television on for some company and to drown out the tinnitus. A message came through from Nicola: "Charlie, me and Claire are so happy to have you in our lives, you are truly an amazing person. You need to know how much we both love spending time with you. You made my weekend 100%. Thanks again…XXX"

"You're very welcome and that's nice of you to say ☺ I'm just chilling with a whisky now, and it'll be bed soon! I'm really glad you enjoyed your weekend. Goodnight. XXX"

He put the phone back down and poured another whisky when another text came through.

"I totally forgot to say, I'm going to be house-sitting soon just for a week. It's back through home for family friends and I was just wondering if you wanted to house-sit with me? We're still a few weeks away so I hope you've got time to shuffle things around. Don't worry if you're busy though, I just thought it could be fun! ☺ X"

"I'd love to. X"

# Chapter Nine

'It's this one, on the corner, to the left.' The early summertime sun was already starting to set as they approached. The road they drove was very familiar to him. On one high-speed corner, the driveway led up a quarter mile to the country house. He'd driven the road and driven past the driveway entrance perhaps a thousand times before.

'The house is up there? I thought it was just a farm access or something?

'No farm, just the house,' she said.

They turned neatly off the road, threading the car between the thick short tree trunks that sat either side of the entrance. They had red bike reflectors screwed into them which allowed the driveway to be identified more easily in the dark. The road turned from tarmac to gravel and muck. It was tightly surrounded by trees for the first hundred yards or so before opening out the further along they got. A few birds darted across the car windscreen and disappeared again through the trees.

The house came into sight and it was old and rustic. Although there were some signs of maintenance, it looked like it could have done with a lot more. Some places had new fresh paint and others were in desperate need of it. He supposed that maintaining a house like that was a proverbial never-ending task. Individual dormer windows shot out from the top floor demanding a superior view of the countryside around.

It was more or less in two symmetrical halves, except from an extra vestibule, a conservatory and a couple of parked cars on the left-hand side. A small lean-to for wooden logs was well stocked and the logs still clung on to some of the previous night's rain. He slid his car into a gap alongside the other two cars and in front of the lean-to. She looked at him with a sense of excitement and the full weight of the circumstances suddenly came bearing down on him. 'Here we are!'

*Here we are indeed*, he thought. But what did it mean? They'd be alone there the whole week, but was it going to be awkward silence and distance between them? Or did she want to wait until then for something to happen? 'Yip,' came his reply.

He stepped from the car feeling the fluctuations of the gravel and stones under his feet. She went straight up to the house forgetting all about the bags so he retrieved them from the boot himself. He watched her as she approached the house and fished the keys out her handbag trying to remember which order she'd been told to use them in. She still couldn't fully remember. Although she'd been at the house many times, it was obvious that this was the first time that she'd been left in full charge of it.

'Have you house-sat here before?' he enquired.

'Yeah. Well, my mum has, and I've helped.' He wondered what stopped her mum from house-sitting this time and just as he drew breath to ask, thought perhaps that would reveal how she had orchestrated the whole week. He didn't want to put her on the spot, or especially, he didn't want to be proved wrong.

After a couple of minutes, she figured the keys out and opened the door. The burglar alarm started to sound and thankfully she had no problem in disarming it. He had a holdall of hers on one shoulder and his rucksack on the other. He carried shopping in his left hand and found himself much too wide to fit through the narrow country door in his current load-out. 'Let me take the shopping…'

He followed her along a dimly lit hall and tried to decipher the photos and paintings that hung along it. The wall was thickly painted brick in a muted cream colour. At the end of the hall were three thick wooden doors. She swung the middle one open to reveal the massive country kitchen. He watched her enter and take a seat at the table. Pulling her hair bobble off, she shook her hair down with a sigh. She ran her fingers hard along her scalp and he craved that he was doing it instead. *This week is going to be torture*, he thought, as he stood awkwardly in the kitchen with their bags on his back.

'Well, come in then, grab a seat. You want something to drink? I'll put dinner on in a bit.'

He put the bags down close to the door and walked to the kitchen table. It was massive. He counted ten chairs around it, but guessed you could seat another ten quite comfortably at it. The two chairs closest to the Aga didn't match. They were probably replacements for the ones sat in most often over the years by the mister and misses he could see in some of the photos around the place. He sat opposite her and she tilted her head to the side, scratching behind her ear like a puppy. Her hair cascaded as if it were the flow of an unseen waterfall somewhere deep in the rainforest where no one had ever set foot before. She awaited his reply. 'Erm, yeah, whatever you're having?' She rolled her eyes and smirked as she got up. Her waterfall of hair swung forward before settling around her shoulders. He continued to look around the kitchen in a deliberate attempt to not watch her. She looked in the fridge and crouched to reach what was at the bottom.

'Beer?'

'Yeah, that's fine. We don't need to go out anywhere else tonight do we?' She stood up and peered from around the open fridge door with two bottles of beer in her hand. The lights she'd put on in the kitchen made her eyes twinkle with intensity.

'No, we're staying in.'


She gave him a tour of the house. The rooms were extensive and quirky. Bedrooms were located on half-landings and mezzanines, en-suites were tucked randomly in rooms not big enough to warrant one, he thought. There were several lounges and drawing rooms, all of which looked locked in time, like they'd hastened upon an uninhabited deserted house, but somehow he could imagine each room filled with joy and laughter when the whole family was there. A baby grand piano sat in the bay window of one sitting room. It had a thick cover over it with a thin layer of dust on it. Properly upholstered sofas sat around rosewood furniture with thick black wrought iron studwork, probably all bespoke and handmade. Those rooms of the house were to lay dormant that week and Charlie and Nicola would make good use of the kitchen and conservatory.

The conservatory was probably the cosiest room in the house and was just along a short hallway from the kitchen. It had two upholstered sofas similar to those around the rest of the house and they more or less filled the room. The covers had been replaced, much like the two kitchen chairs, and the Persian rug that sat in front of the fire was becoming threadbare in a few places. A large tartan wingback chair sat closest to the fire. It had a plain green cashmere throw and a few cushions on it. A television was mounted on the wall just to the side of the flue from the fireplace. Charlie sat there, trying to figure out how to operate it, which seemed somehow impossible. There were six remote controls that were originally sitting on the armchair and he tried to match the brand to the television. Nicola shouted through something about switching the tuner box on first. He investigated.

She appeared in the doorway of the conservatory wiping her hands with a tea towel, 'Dinner in about half an hour.' She smiled as she saw him struggle with the mish-mash of technology in front of him. He looked at her for help. 'I've no idea either Charlie! Could you maybe get the fire going? There's some logs in the hamper,' she pointed to the corner of the room, 'and there's more outside next to the car. Do you know how to light it?'

Charlie didn't have much experience with those types of fires since he grew up in a modern house, but he thought he could manage. He recalled his bushcraft training and the first time he ever lit a fire by flint and good preparation. 'Yeah, I should be fine.'

After dinner they sat in the conservatory. He wished he'd been first in, because he'd had the decision of choosing to sit next to her, or on the other sofa. He sat on the other one, which he regretted as soon as his backside hit the foam-covered springs. The only positive from there though was that the view was magnificent. She had tied her hair back up to cook dinner, but that only revealed better her beautiful face. One lamp was on in the corner and some light crept through from the hallway. Outside, the black of the night sapped the light through the windows. He could see nothing beyond the glass panes in their flaky green painted wooden frames. He sat gracelessly on the sofa holding a beer. The sofas were so deep that his legs shot straight out and dangled like a child's legs sitting in daddy's seat. She folded one leg under herself and the other lay with poise. The slender shape of her leg in her jeans was utterly tantalising. She rested an elbow on the top of a cushion, crushing it out of shape, with a glass of something in her hand. She played with a tassel that had come loose on the corner of the cushion. It looked repairable, but the more she played with it, the less repairable it became.

She was quiet and distant, trying to look out of the opaque conservatory windows. He wanted to make an excuse to go and sit next to her. He wanted some reason to be next to her and put his arm around her. The pulsing glow of the fire deepened the beauty of her features and the flicker in her eye stole pieces of his heart unapologetically. Her mind was elsewhere. She thought about a life that she'd left behind and

153

wondered how she ended up in this position with Charlie now. Was she doing the right thing? Was this some kind of rebound? Would he just turn out to be the same as the rest of them? *Why didn't he come to sit right next to me?* she thought. After a few minutes of silence and daydreaming by both of them he tried to reach her. 'Nicola, are you alright?'

She clambered back into the room with a crash. 'Yeah, I'm fine. I was just…miles away.' She forced a smile.

'What do you want to do tomorrow? You said something about the river?'

'Yeah…no, I don't want to go there…we'll do something. Figure it out in the morning?' she offered.

'Sure, okay.' Silence prevailed, with some partial respite provided by the television.

Charlie wondered what they might do to fill the night. They couldn't go anywhere in the car because he'd had a few beers. It was densely dark outside, so a walk seemed a bit extreme and before he got a chance to ask for suggestions, she said, 'I've got quite a sore head. I think I'm just going to call it a night. I'm really tired.'

*Well, which is it?* he thought, *you've got a sore head or you're tired?* He was much too polite to ask. You could be both he surmised, but he knew she was neither. They both got up in unison. She walked

154

towards him and he couldn't read her at all. What she really needed was to be held and comforted, not that she could figure that out and not that she gave Charlie a chance. She knew she needed Charlie and that she wanted him to be there with her, but she wasn't ready for anything to happen. She wished him goodnight and Charlie sat back down, deflated. He was left alone in a strange house, with no idea of how to fill the evening.

He looked at his watch and it was still early. He was frustrated that he couldn't go for a drive despite not feeling drunk in the slightest. It had felt like a long time since he'd driven around those home roads. They always gave him comfort and reassurance. Anyway, he didn't know how to lock and unlock the house, so the fear of setting the alarm off and being discovered by the police in a house that was not his nor his companions didn't seem appealing. He could have just left it unlocked he supposed, it's not like there was anyone around and no one knew they were there. But the thought of leaving her there alone in an empty house, unlocked for anyone to intrude on her did not agree with him in the slightest.

He wrote out a message: "Can I get you anything? ☺", he then rewrote and sent: "Just let me know if I can get you anything ☺" Not that he knew where anything was, but he had to let her know that she wasn't by herself in that big house. It was the two of them together, isolated and alone. There came no reply all night and as he lay by himself in some strangers' bed, he felt the loneliest he'd ever felt in a long time.

He pulled the car up in front of the lean-to. A gap had developed from the logs they'd expended over the few days they'd been there. She got out as he popped the boot open and started to gather the shopping, leaving the heavy bags for him. 'So they arrive about six, but we don't need to have dinner ready for then, just whenever.' Her mum and dad were coming round for dinner and she seemed slightly nervous about it. She usually avoided visiting whenever she was in Scotland and hardly talked about her parents. In fact, she usually dodged the subject when it came up.

After the first awkward night, they had enjoyed the rest of the time they'd spent at the house. They went for walks and tended the chickens and pigs – the main reason the house needed watched when the owners were away. Charlie had learned the secret to locking and unlocking the door successfully and was now in charge of this when they came and went. He even started fixing small things around the house such as door latches, dodgy floorboards, the kitchen cupboard that didn't ever shut and the wobble in the chest freezer through in the larder. He didn't think the owners would mind, mainly because they probably were not aware of specific items that needed fixing. But he felt that if he was staying there, he ought to contribute somehow.

The house reminded him of Gertrude's big house in London. He sometimes wondered how she was – whether she was still drinking or even living. He almost felt the same sort of atmosphere between him and Nicola as he did then. As the days passed, he was more in charge of the house than she was and he was babysitting her. Not to mention how he was trying to make her live and enjoy each day again. But he was spectating a version of his life that he knew would not last forever. He ran around for Nicola as if he was some kind of footman, but Gertrude looked out for him too and he'd forever be grateful to her for gifting him the car. He thought about what it was Nicola did for him. Other than enjoying being the object of his affections, he couldn't think of much.

They spent evenings in front of the television or out revisiting some of their local but separate stomping grounds. They drove around East Lothian and walked along beaches and up hills during the day. They'd stop for coffee or lunch and it had been special for both of them. This was the kind of comfort that Charlie craved and it did a lot to wash away some of the anguish he held in his heart. Nicola was so glad to have been spending the time with Charlie but she still felt some kind of block with him. She knew she needed him but she didn't want him.

They talked a little about school and how miserable she was there, without giving anything specific away. Charlie was aware of the stories that circulated about her and they all sounded pretty extreme and ridiculous yet she did allude to them being true. But at that time, he was happy with Rachel and had enough going on in his young life that he didn't ever concern himself with the usual schoolyard garbage and never gave any consideration to the rumours he heard.

He was glad that she would stick around in the evenings instead of making an excuse to go to bed early. On the second evening he made the transition from *other sofa*, to *same sofa*, and the move seemed completely natural. There was the occasional touch of the arm here or there, or she'd flick her hair and he'd be caught by a few frisky strands. He'd mastered the art of tucking his legs up and didn't seem as clumsy as he did before.

She unloaded the bags and separated the ingredients. Some went in the fridge, some to the chopping board. She seemed more organised than he'd ever seen her before. In the frenzy of preparation, he felt a little bit spare and decided to leave her to it after she declined his help. He sat and watched the television, which by now he was able to operate. Once everything was prepared she came through with a bottle of wine and two glasses. 'Could you open this please?' she asked, 'I'll need it to get through tonight.' Rather than being his usual analytical self, he assessed it as a throwaway comment. One that any person now in their thirties, who was still unmarried and did not own their own home might act at the impending arrival of their apparently judgemental parents. No doubt they'd also want to know what the nature of her relationship with Charlie was. So did he.

It was six o'clock on the dot when they arrived. He hadn't been nervous beforehand, but somehow the shrill ringing of an unfamiliar doorbell filled him with a sense of trepidation. Why should he be nervous if he and Nicola were merely friends? He had no reason in particular to want to impress them, except he did – he really did. Nicola led a kindly looking woman into the kitchen. 'So nice to meet you, Charlie. I'm Anna. We've heard a lot about you,' she said expectantly. She was shorter than Nicola but had the same dark hair and a warm smile.

'Oh, really? I hope it's all good?' he joked.

He shook her hand as Nicola's dad came in. He was tall and decorous. 'Charlie…finally, we get to meet.' Although perfectly polite, he didn't feel the same instant reception from her dad as he did from her mum.

Nicola took their coats and hung them on pegs adjacent to the fridge in the kitchen. They all sat around the kitchen table as a few pleasantries were exchanged and her dad investigated how exactly they met. 'James, I've told you a hundred times, they were at school together!' Anna snapped.

'Yes, but that doesn't explain the...' he did a quick calculation in his head, '...twelve years between school and now.'

'I just found him on Facebook dad and thought I'd message him because it'd been a long time.'

'That's a nice car you've got out there Charlie. What's that cost, seventy...eighty grand surely?'

'James, honestly! What's it got to do with anything??' Anna came in again.

'It's just a question...can't say a bloody word right.'

Nicola poured some drinks for her parents and then the questioning resumed.

'So, Nicola tells me you're ex-special forces?'

'Yeah, that's right.' James waited for him to elaborate. 'But I'm just looking to come closer to home now. I feel like I'm missing out on a lot with that sort of work.' Charlie felt a compulsion to look at Nicola at that moment but knew his movements were being closely scrutinised by her dad. She was the sort of thing he was missing out on. She was the thing that he wanted his life to be about now.

'I never knew military paid so well, though.'

'Dad! He's worked hard for everything he's got. It's not like he was born with a silver spoon in his mouth, just–' she hesitated for a second and then went for it, 'just a heart of gold.'

'Yeah, well some of my contracts were private, US Federal funded sort of thing – Anti-Narcotics. They were pretty big earners. And the car was actually like a bonus from another job.'

Nicola and her mum began cooking and Anna was about to suggest that Charlie and James go through to the conservatory for a seat, but didn't want to leave her husband unsupervised. Since meeting up with Charlie again, Nicola had been keeping her mum involved with all the things he would do for her as a way of avoiding visiting. Nicola wanted to reassure her mum that someone was taking good care of her, so now was convinced that they were in some kind of a relationship, otherwise why on earth would he take such good care of her if he wasn't getting something out of it himself?

Anna quickly figured Charlie out and thought that he was the kind of man that Nicola needed to be with, someone kind and caring. His smile was charming and there was a tenderness in his eyes. When he spoke, everything he said seemed thoughtful and somewhat profound. Never mind that he's got a nice car and flat, Anna had come to realise there was much more to it than that, even for her precious daughter. That was the reason why she didn't want James to scare him off somehow.

Nicola traditionally did not have a good track record at picking men, even from school. Since she'd been with Patrice, they were only too aware about the abuse she suffered at his hand, and at his tongue. She had flown home many times to her parents saying that it was over, but it would only take a few of days for him to manipulate her into going back. Despite the fact she never did anything wrong, she'd feel the need to apologise by the time she got there.

She started to hate going home though because her parents would judge her and grill her over what happened and want to know all the details when all Nicola wanted to do was bury her head in the sand. She couldn't take the lectures they'd give her about him which is why she started to simply run to Claire's instead. She had been caught up in the whole Paris culture and maybe thought it was normal, or that it was the continental style of life that she was looking for away from home. She thought it might have been something far removed from relationships and experiences she had before, except it wasn't, it was just in France instead.

Her dad, on several occasions, wanted to buy a ticket to France and break Patrice's legs, knees, back and whatever else he could, but the thing he feared the most was losing Nicola. He warned an older boy off her whilst she was at school and she ran away from home. It was winter and she could have frozen to death that night. They supposed that she must have stayed at a friend's house, but not Claire's, because they'd have known to go looking there. It took about a month after that before Nicola so much as looked at her dad again and that hurt him so much. It also hurt him so much to know of the abuse that she was suffering, but he had to not interfere so they could remain as a safe place for her, somewhere to retreat to whenever she needed. It was important that she had that and it was important for him to preserve it.

After dinner they all retired to the conservatory. It was bitterly cold because they had neglected to light the fire until then. The kitchen would always stay warm because of the Aga and they didn't notice the drop in temperature through the rest of the house. Her mum and dad sat on one sofa, so that made his choice of sofa easy again. He didn't know how comfortable to get with Nicola considering her parents were there. He had a feeling her mum would be happy with it, but still couldn't read her dad. That man was a closed book with no pictures on the cover. 'Nicola, come and help me get some drinks, will you?' James said. 'Anna, I'm going to open another bottle of wine, what would you like?'

'Anything but French,' she retorted. There was something about her tone that Charlie picked up on. *Anything but French, like Patrice.* Probably, she didn't even have anything against French wine, but it was a sly dig at Nicola. Those were the kind of comments that she couldn't stand and the reason that she'd try to limit her time spent with them.

Being an only child, when she told her parents that she wanted to move to Paris they essentially forbade her. She was all they had, so if she went to Paris they'd miss her terribly. After months of work by Nicola, she managed to convince them everything would be fine and there would be nothing to worry about. Then she met Patrice. At the start, things were great – they were perfect, perhaps. But it didn't take long for her first black eye, and she didn't even realise the psychological abuse. Because she'd gone against her parents wishes and managed to convince them that nothing bad would happen should she move to Paris it meant that she had to make it work, at all costs. Then she could prove that she hadn't been foolish and show them that they were wrong.

Nicola brought some wine through for herself and her mum, whilst her dad found some whisky and brought through two glasses. He passed one to Charlie and he tipped it towards the brightest source of light in the room to discern the colour. He spun the liquid round and watched the legs cling and run down the sides of the glass. Her dad watched him as he was now nosing the whisky and was impressed.

'It's Glenkinchie, just along the road.' James said.

Charlie scrutinised it further. 'Must be the ten year old?' James wasn't even sure. Charlie continued, 'Because it's a twelve year old they do now, it's a bit darker, finished in a sherry cask…they don't do the ten year old anymore.'

It was clear that Charlie had far superior knowledge of whisky than James, much to his surprise. He expected Charlie to not be keen at all. This was all part of the test and seemingly Charlie was the first to ever pass. 'Charlie's an even bigger fan of whisky than you are, dad.' James was glad. It meant that Charlie appreciated the finer things in life.

'I hope you didn't just open it? Because they're just going up and up in price now.' James's face dropped as he realised he did exactly that. But the family friends always said they were welcome to anything and considering they didn't drink whisky they'd have much less of an idea about it than James did. Most likely they received the whisky as a present or won it in a raffle and it laid there for years gathering dust. 'Don't worry,' Charlie chuckled. 'I'll nip up there tomorrow and get another bottle, they'll still have plenty, but now's the time to buy.'

Despite having only had half of her glass of wine, Nicola's mum started to make excuses for her and James to leave them be. It was still reasonably early and both Charlie and Nicola could tell she was trying to make herself scarce so that they could have some privacy. 'Well, we'll leave you two to it…' She gave a cheeky smile as she rose and prodded her husband to get up. 'We don't want to cramp your style…'

'Muuuummm…!' Nicola expelled through gritted teeth. James was quite annoyed to be peeled away from the television. He also wanted to stay longer and chat with Charlie. Whilst he felt a lot more relaxed about him, he still wanted to know more. Charlie intrigued him.

He seemed very knowledgeable and wise and he obviously cared for Nicola. He wanted to get to know him better because as her father, he wanted to make sure his baby girl would never come to any harm ever again.

James and Anna stayed in one of the big bedrooms on the opposite side of the house since they'd been drinking and couldn't drive home. Charlie sat next to her on the sofa, whisky in hand. 'Want some?' he placed the glass under her nose and she took a sniff before recoiling in horror.

'Ugh! How can you drink that stuff??'

'Well, really, it's quite easy,' Charlie demonstrated and took another sip. 'Voila!' he immediately wished he hadn't used French.

'My parents both really like you Charlie.'

'That's good. I like them too. So...I passed the test then?' Nicola smiled, because he had and with flying colours, but she didn't admit it.

'Even my dad!' she snorted. 'He usually gives all my boyfr–' she paused, 'everybody a hard time.'

He tried not to dwell on her slip of the tongue. 'That's fair enough if you ask me.' Charlie reached for her hand and took it in his.

'When you've got something really precious you want to look after it, don't you?'

As she sat on the sofa, she could feel the warmth of the fire on one side and the warmth of Charlie on the other. She drew breath a few times to speak but said nothing. A curl of hair fell down from Charlie's hairline but it was too light for him to feel it on his brow. She liked how he'd let it grow out in the past few months. The contours of his face added depth to him as he watched her in the low light of the conservatory. The television quietly continued on about something to do with the countryside. It showed rolling hills and beautiful views, much like the ones they'd enjoyed that week.

Charlie tried to figure out the whole evening. He didn't think that her parent's opinion had mattered with any of her boyfriends before and certainly not about Patrice, so why should she be so concerned about getting their approval now? Or was he reading into it too much? What about her slip of the tongue?

He scrutinized every last square millimetre of her face. She was infinitely beautiful. She knew he was watching her and she let him. The way Charlie adored her made her feel exonerated from everything in her past. This was a man who desired her in a pure and genuine manner. He was the first man to ever make her feel so special and to have gone so long without saying a single stupid or insensitive word. That was something that she really needed, because she still hurt so much and he

167

could tell. The remnants of Patrice still lingered and he knew he still had some pieces to put back together before anything could happen between them. He didn't know if he should try to push her there or wait patiently. She blinked and her eyelashes were like butterflies' wings in slow motion, batting hard and delicately over those huge eyes of hers. She turned to Charlie. 'Want a top-up?' She pointed to his glass.

'Yes, please.' She leaned towards him on the sofa and took the glass. The distance that diminished between them momentarily felt exquisite. It was like the lead in to a kiss, perhaps he'd have to settle for that. She came back with two glasses of whisky and a box of chocolates. 'What, you drink whisky now?'

'I just want to try,' she smiled. Nicola already started to feel the effect of the alcohol in her head.

'This is a good one to be starting on then, it's nice and light.' She dropped the box of chocolates onto the sofa, handed him his glass then slumped down next to him. Either it was the wine she'd already had, or she just misjudged it, but given the amount of space on the large sofa, she slumped herself tight up against Charlie and she didn't readjust herself. She took another sniff of the whisky and recoiled once more. She pinched her nose with one hand and downed the whisky. 'Hey, that's no way to treat that!' he protested.

'What? Just because you can't do it!' Charlie knew she was teasing but downed the whisky anyway before realising she'd poured him a much bigger one than hers. She giggled and took the two empty glasses, placing them on the side table before opening the box of chocolates.

Removing a chocolate, she lifted it up to her lips. Her tongue met the chocolate and her eyes were closed as she bit it in half. Charlie heard the chocolate part into two pieces with a dull click. She fed him the other half. He savoured it. She perused the menu to select the next chocolate. 'Are you not still full?' he asked.

'Well, I didn't have two helpings.' She jabbed him gently in the belly.

He shrugged. 'It was great food, you should be pleased!'

'So…am I not allowed?'

'No, of course you're allowed.'

Nicola regressed for a second, 'You know…he never let me eat chocolate. He said I'd get fat and that no one would ever love me if I was fat.'

Out of the blue came a confession about Patrice at last. 'I hope you know that's a load of rubbish Nicola. You can eat that whole box and…' *I'd still love you*, he had to stop himself from saying, '…you'd still be as lovable as always.'

'Thank you, Charlie. Okay, just one more….' Her finger wandered the menu. 'Praline.' She picked it up and sensually halved the chocolate making low *mmmm* noises before closing it in on Charlie. She deliberately missed his mouth and was trailing the chocolate around his lips, nose and cheeks. The chocolate had started to melt by the warmth of the fire and her fingers, which made a few smudges on him. She laughed and giggled finding it hilarious to subject Charlie to such an ordeal. Finally, he snapped his lips quickly around the chocolate and he thought her fingers lingered between his lips a few seconds longer than they needed to and their eye contact felt a little more intense than usual.

She laughed again and bowed her head forward, bumping it off his chest. When she brought her head back up, her hair was all around her face and the most natural thing for Charlie to do was sweep it behind her ears, on both sides with both hands. She returned the favour and swept the curl back up into his hair that she'd had an insane desire to do since they got to the conservatory. They both paused, the space between them dwindled and under the flicker of the fire, their lips touched. First a small connection, then after checking it was real, Charlie leaned in more and she reciprocated. He shuffled closer, pulled her body in closer and wrapped his arms around her. Smells of dark chocolate, whisky and red wine intermingled with the smoky log-burner fire. Her eyes were closed, but his were open. He wanted to memorise the moment so that he could replay it to himself in the future.

Finally her eyes opened and caught his. Her tongue and lips left his and it felt as if gravity inverted. She drew back still in his arms and he reluctantly let her go. She sat back down with a gap in-between them. The sensation of the kiss still sizzled on his lips like a hundred chilli peppers and he was already replaying it in his mind. She looked straight ahead trying to look out of the window but could only see her own grumpy reflection in it. Her arms were folded and she gave no indication as to what to do next. Charlie held out his hand towards her. She saw it but ignored it. 'Nicola? What is it?'

'We shouldn't have kissed. It was a mistake.' It seemed like it was his fault, that maybe he'd taken advantage of her in her tipsy state, never mind the fact that she was the instigator and she didn't have to kiss back.

'I'm sorry, but all this...' he looked around at the cosy fireplace, the empty wine and whisky glasses, the box of chocolates and the comfy sofas '...I thought it was what you wanted?'

'Well, you thought wrong.'

It was a massive slap in the face for Charlie. 'Well...I'm sorry. I'm sorry I'm a *mistake* to you.'

171

'Oh, don't be like that Charlie!' her voice escalated slightly, but still not to a level where her parents would hear.

His voice was pleading as panic rose in him. 'Like what exactly? I don't understand what I've done wrong. You gave me all the signals, you kissed me back too, you know.' Perhaps he was being stupid. Maybe he *was* taking advantage of the situation. After all, he was so lonely. Maybe he jumped in too early and pushed it. That was what he'd feared all along and the reason why he'd given her space and time, but after months spent together, it was just a kiss. 'What's this all about Nicola?'

'Nothing. Nothing. Just forget it.' She was volatile. Her hair fell forward obscuring her face again and eventually, he gently took her arms and lowered himself in front of her dipped head. She resisted at first, but he was delicate and reassuring.

'Nicola, I'm sorry if I've done something to upset you. I obviously misread the situation.' She swept the hair out the way of her face at last and looked at him. 'What's going on? You can tell me.'

'I'm sorry, maybe I've just had too much to drink. It was a mistake.' There was that word again. Charlie could think of a few mistakes himself; like how he'd wasted a week of his life there, how he'd shown her so much respect and gotten nothing in return, like how he replied to her message that first time and asked to meet up with her.

'I'm sorry Charlie. I think…can we just forget about it?'

*If only it were that simple,* he thought. 'If that's what you really want, then…I'll never mention it again.' He couldn't say that he'd forget about it, because that kiss would forever be burned into his memory.

He lay in bed replaying the kiss in the dark and cold of his deserted room. It was the only thing keeping him warm. The smell of her on him, the congruity of their breath and their lips, the way her soft and warm body felt as he pulled it up against his. It felt so good. It felt so right. To him the kiss was momentous. He tried to close his eyes to sleep, but they refused. He played the kiss out over and over in his mind before he fell asleep.

In the other room, Nicola had been sitting at the dressing table in her pyjamas and robe looking into the mirror. She brushed her hair pointlessly. She maybe got to about a hundred strokes or so before she stopped. She quickly took her robe off before getting into bed to minimise the time outside the covers, because her room was cold too. She couldn't sleep. She touched her lips imagining Charlie's on them once more. As far as kisses go, that was a good one. With those thick shoulders and arms and with all the power he had, he was so tender. He held her in such an affectionate way. She'd never felt that kind of raw compassion that went way beyond the kiss itself. It was like being wrapped up in a dozen soft, warm and fluffy blankets. But at the same time, it was like feeling invincible and that nothing could impinge upon her. It was a completely new sensation and it kept her up all night.

# Chapter Ten

Nicola pulled up squintly outside the building next to Charlie's and gave him a call. 'I don't know how to get into your car park bit.'

'It's a wee turn off just…where are you?'

'I'm outside you're building.'

'Hold on a second.' Charlie slid the heavy glass panel to the side and stepped outside onto the terrace. The wind whipped around him as it raced over the top of his building. He walked up to the edge and checked the road below. Nothing. He crossed to the other side and saw the top of her car. 'I've got you. You're on the wrong side, that's next door. Just stay where you are, I'll be down in a minute.'

Charlie coached Nicola along to the M8 and they joined the motorway on their way back towards the East Coast. She sat perfectly on the speed limit with her hands tightly gripping the wheel. She checked her mirrors diligently as she was passed by other cars. 'Move to this lane, or we'll end up in Stirling.' She checked her mirrors again and flicked her signal on before drifting over into the correct lane. There was no emotion on her face, only pure concentration. Charlie didn't feel nervous in any way. Sure, she was a novice driver who had passed her test more than ten years ago who was now driving on her first motorway ever, but he didn't care. It was exactly where he wanted to be.

Nicola called him the day before to ask if she could drive them somewhere. They'd already been out many times as he got her back into driving, but only locally. She wanted to go somewhere further afield. 'So where do you want to go?' he asked.

'We could go through to North Berwick? I mean, if you've got the time. If not, just stay in Glasgow again.'

Charlie and Nicola still spent all their time together. The work itself was as much or as little as he wanted it to be, and recently, he'd been sidelining it to make Nicola his priority. Up until then Nicola only had Claire with her in Glasgow, who worked during the day and the occasional late night, so she'd become infinitely bored. But it wasn't long before she started work so she was trying to make the most of her remaining free time and having Charlie there with his particular schedule was perfect for her.

'What speed is that truck going?' She peeled her eyes off the road for a second to throw a confused look at Charlie. She didn't understand the question. 'What speed are we doing?'

'Erm,' she checked, despite it not changing, 'seventy?'

'Are we going faster than the truck?'

'Yes?' she asked.

'So what are you planning to do?'

She thought about it for a few seconds. 'Pass him?'

'Yeah. So we need to check our mirrors in plenty time and move out if it's safe. If not, adjust our speed until we've got a gap. Don't wait till you're right behind him.'

Charlie bought an extra mirror and stuck it to the inside of the windscreen for his use. He wondered whether he should have bought some 'P-Plates', but considering she passed so long ago, he thought it might have been illegal or something. 'Is it safe then?' he asked. She checked carefully.

'Yeah, we're safe.' *We're safe*, because after all, they were in it together. If she fucked up, they'd both feel the force of the trucks back end, or the sideswipe of a passing car. They'd both go to hospital together and they'd maybe die together. She passed the truck and drifted safely back to the left after passing.

'See, you don't need my help.' The first smile he'd seen from her that day formed on her lips as she started to relax into it.

They rolled into North Berwick in the early afternoon. The sky was bright blue and seagulls called and circled overhead. They passed a putting green where dads introduced their young kids to golf and a bench that looked out onto the Firth of Forth was occupied by an elderly couple who sat holding hands. An old anchor embellished the green grass towards the seafront. They turned past the harbour and she pulled the car into a gap between parked cars. The car stopped in alignment to the kerb.

'I can't believe I just drove us from Glasgow to North Berwick!' Her smile beamed widely from her face. 'Thank you, Charlie.' She touched him gently on the leg and batted her eyes involuntarily. There was no way she could have pictured doing that even a month before.

'Don't mention it.' She knew that it was all down to him. Never mind the extra money that he put towards the car which she was never to find out about, but the way he'd helped her purchase the car and given her the guidance she needed to get back on the road. She had a recent aspiration to have a car of her own but wondered if she'd even have been interested at all if it hadn't been for Charlie.

They took a walk along the beach and sat down on the rocks. A sailboat tacked into the wind and the hull pushed through the cold sea, parting it either side of the bow as they sat together. Nicola looked forlorn as she gazed out to sea. 'Want to go up to the top?' he asked. At the end of the beach a single-track road ascended towards a car park which was next to a golf course. There were a few benches there in a steep but seemingly naturally terraced face that dropped back down towards the beach. The Bass Rock with its milky chalky hue was clearly visible from there, as was the rest of the seaside town. A few church spires poked up between the rooftops of expensive houses. They treaded from the road through tall grass onto well worn paths and picked a bench.

'So,' Charlie enquired, 'are you ready for work?'

'Yeah, I suppose.' Charlie waited for the explanation. 'I just...I don't know...oh, it's nothing.'

'What? It's something Nicola.' He turned his body towards her.

Nicola sighed deeply. 'Well...' she began, 'it's just...has Claire told you much about Patrice?'

*Why should Claire be the one to tell me about him?* he thought. 'Well, no…other than it's not really finished? But you told me that you'd split up with him.'

'Well, we have. But…I'm just not so sure if Patrice really knows.'

'Yeah, okay.' Charlie wondered what kind of malfunction the guy had in his head to think they were still together, considering she had a flat, a job and now a car, in a different country. But he was glad that she was talking about it with him.

'I haven't really been able to tell him. In that…I haven't told him. I mean, I said it was over, but that sort of…always happens when I leave…It's sort of what I do. But I think he's expecting me to come back.' The wind blew her hair in front of her face and she swept it aside only for it to return immediately. 'You must think I'm crazy.' Charlie shook his head softly.

'No, you're not crazy. Do you want to go back?'

'No. Not really.' She rubbed at her wrists through her jacket cuffs as a burning feeling suddenly rushed through them.

'He just makes it so hard. He never accepts it and says I can't leave him because I *belong* to him.'

'You belong to *you*, Nicola, no one else. You're not a commodity, you're a treasure. And you know, it's only foolish or greedy men that squander treasure.' Nicola reached for Charlie's hand and held it in hers. He stung inside to know the details. How could he fix things if he didn't know what was wrong? Nicola was a different person when she mentioned or thought of Patrice. She clammed up and all the colour and life seemed to drain from her face.

'I think...I need to...I need to tell him face to face. I don't want to run from him anymore. It's the only way I'll be able to draw a line under things and move on. And I can't let anyone else in until I do. I need to go to Paris and finish things once and for all.'

Charlie didn't want to pass judgement. The only thing he knew was that Claire hated him. She hadn't said much to him, but what little she did let Charlie know that Nicola was better off steering well clear and that she wasn't even safe around him. He wanted to object, but he also wanted to support her. If she had to draw a line under things, perhaps he should just let her do that and once it was done and dusted she'd finally be able to let Charlie in. 'Obviously, the decision is yours, and I know I don't know all of the details, but are you sure it's a good idea? You've got a lot going for you here now. Can you not just call him or something? You'll be starting work soon, too.'

She had thought about it a thousand times, but somehow with all the lies and deceit and falsities between her and Patrice, she felt a phone call was inadequate and that he might just put that down to the mood swings that she apparently always had and that he had to continually put up with. She turned to Charlie and her eyes screamed of pain. 'I have to do it in person.' Silence ensued for a few moments as Charlie knew that Nicola had already decided and that there would be no amount of reasoning he or Claire might be able to do to make her change her mind.

'Okay. Have you told Claire?'

'No.' He watched her as she gazed down onto the beach. 'I wish I could be more like you, Charlie.'

'What do you mean?'

'You're not afraid of anything. You can handle anything. I wish I was more like that, but it's just not who I am.'

'What makes you think I'm not afraid of anything?' She finally turned to him and her lip gloss held on to some strands of hair. 'I'm afraid of things. I'm afraid of everything I've done in the past. I can't sleep most nights thinking about the consequences of my actions and the impact I've had on people's lives.'

'So how do you do it then? How do you handle things so well? And you always know the right thing to say or do in any given situation?'

'I don't know…' He thought about it whilst being distracted by the raw emotion in her eyes and his overwhelming urge to kiss her. 'I guess it's a sink or swim kind of thing. And I've seen so much in this world that I have a certain way of looking at things…or something.' He shrugged as he turned to face the front. 'Either way, I just need to keep going.' He watched two dogs chasing each other in and out of the sea as their owners advanced slowly along the sand.

'Most of all though, I'm afraid of going through this life by myself. All of those worries go away if I have someone who loves me and someone who I can turn to when I need…comfort. When I need to be assured that I'm not a terrible person. But the way things have gone the past few years, I'm so afraid that I'll never find her. I worry that I'll live the rest of my life with this unease and hurt…or whatever it is that I feel everyday.'

'I had no idea…but…Charlie, you are *not* a terrible person. You're the exact opposite of that, believe me.' Her eyes tracked him, his masculine profile and his kind but wearied face. 'And you of all people don't have to worry about not finding someone. You're the most perfect man, and… you're so handsome and kind. I'm sure she's very close and…I don't think you'll have to wait very long.' She peeled the hair from her lips and her hand advanced towards him. She had to stop herself from caressing his face and her hand landed on his shoulder instead. His hair also seemed more sweepable every time she saw him.

'Out of everyone I know, you deserve to be happy the most. And good things come to those who wait. Everything will be alright for you. I know it.'

She leaned her head on Charlie's shoulder and he put his arm around her. 'You'll be alright too,' he said. 'You know you've got my support in anything you need to do. I promise I'll always be here for you. You just need to get through this, then you'll be where you want to be.' She wrapped her arms around him. 'Everything's going to be alright.' He placed a kiss on her head as they stared out to sea.

'For both of us,' she added.

After their day together of driving, walking and confiding, Nicola dropped Charlie back at his flat and he sat on his terrace under the setting sun. A deep burnt orange filled the sky as he received a text from Claire: "Hey Charlie, how are you? Nicola just told me that she's going to Paris to see Patrice. What are you doing tonight? I need to talk to you."

He arrived outside Claire's flat and struggled to find somewhere to park. It was evening time and everybody was home from work or shopping so all their cars were already parked and Charlie's was just a little too long to park on that street at times. Whilst he attempted to reverse into too tight a space, his phone rang. He pushed the button on his steering wheel. 'Hey.'

'Hey. Can we just go out? I just want to get out for a bit.'

'Yeah, sure. I'm just outside.' He pulled out of the space and the car was relieved it didn't need to squeeze in there any more.

Claire locked up her flat and headed down the stairs out onto the street. 'Hey, Charlie.' She sat down and pulled the door shut with a huge sigh.

'You okay?'

'Yeah, I suppose. It's Nicola I'm worried about though.' He knew that she wanted to wait until they got to whatever place they were going to before getting into it.

'So, where to?' he asked.

'I don't know really. I should probably have something to eat, but my appetite has gone. I've just been cooped up all day at work and all the paint thinner has gone to my head. And then I get that text from her.' She was so restless and distracted. 'And I've got nothing in. But I was just too tired and sick after work tonight. And I'm sick of always shopping, but I can never carry much home.'

'Well, do you want me to take you for a big shop?' She looked at him and thought it'd be quite handy to make use of Charlie's car and of course Charlie. She never shopped at the big supermarkets out of the city centre because they were too far out of her way. But the small supermarkets in the centre of Glasgow always had higher prices.

'Yeah, that'd be good.'

He drove them south to his normal supermarket. It wasn't exactly the closest one to Claire's flat, but it was the one he knew and used all the time. On the way, they talked about her shit day at work and how they never have enough ventilation when they use paint and paint thinner, and how the fumes always made her feel sick. Charlie swung the car around the mini roundabout and entered the car park. He liked to park in the same spot, or more or less the same spot. As adaptable as he was, he'd park in the same area so that it'd be easier for him to identify if something was out of place. Only, he didn't know that was why he did it, it was a subconscious habit. He picked up a pound coin that sat in his ashtray for the trolley and they headed inside.

Charlie followed Claire around as she explored the new aisles and what goods were on offer. She picked up some crafty things and put them in the trolley. She was enjoying the massive selection. 'So, Charlie…what are we going to do?' He wanted to know more about the situation. It frustrated him substantially being somewhat left in the dark. He had already told Nicola that he'd support her without considering what he might want or feel about the situation himself.

'So what's the deal with this guy then? I don't get a good impression of him from you.'

Without averting her gaze from the shelves, Claire enlightened him, 'He's a scumbag. He's an absolute waste of space. And he…he *hurts* her, Charlie. I hate him.' They had made it to the small electricals section and she fingered a few of the toasters, kettles and irons as they walked past. 'They were engaged. It was as if Nicola thought that might have changed him. He's a total psycho and she lives in constant fear of him. But she always goes running back and I don't know why. I can't remember a time when she talked to me about him the same way she talks about–' She looked at Charlie as she bit her tongue. 'All I ever hear is how badly he's been treating her and about the abuse. And that is all he's actually capable of.'

Two other shoppers angled their carts which blocked the aisle. She pushed gently past leaving a gap for Charlie and the trolley. 'It's like a pathological error that she has with him.' She looked up the next aisle, *DIY,* and decided to skip it. 'I can't tell you how many times I've had to pick up the pieces and I'm just so tired of it. I don't know how much longer I can keep doing it. But I can't just leave her, you know?' She looked round for Charlie again and he was starting down the DIY aisle.

'I didn't know it was that extreme, Claire.'

'And that's not even half of the shit he does to her. I came to Paris and we packed all her things up and flew back to mine. And she's been here ever since. I don't want her to go back because things were getting better. She got her own place, she's got a job and a car now. She's met…well…we've met up with you again, so…she's got another friend here.' Charlie picked up a pack of dust masks and put them in the trolley. 'What are they for?'

'Your paint thinner.'

'I'm afraid if she goes there that she'll not come back. He'll trap her again.' They had reached the fruit and veg section and a baby stretched his hands out at Claire and made a few gaga noises. 'It's been like this for about three or four years and I've tried to just tell her to leave him and come back, and she always agrees. But every time she came home she ended up going to Paris again. I thought this time was different though, I thought she was actually looking to stay. So why would she want to go back to see him at all?'

'I think she just wants to draw a line under things. But what can we do? I don't think it sounds like she can be convinced otherwise. I mean if you've been trying for years, what chance have I got?'

Claire stopped walking and let Charlie draw level with her. 'She listens to you Charlie. She hangs on your every word. You have to try. You have to let her know that she's already got *everything* she needs here in Scotland. Out of the two of us, you're the one with the best chance to make her see that.'

*What does she mean by that?* Charlie thought. 'Well, I'll speak to her again. We could maybe do it together?'

'Yeah, okay. We're meeting for coffee on Byre's Road tomorrow at lunchtime, you should come along.'

# Chapter Eleven

It was a rainy Tuesday morning when Charlie dropped Nicola at the airport. They were unable to convince her not to go; she didn't listen to reason. She didn't want to think about how Charlie asked her to stay and how she'd go back to see Patrice instead of spending time with him. She also knew that Claire had put him up to it. Charlie had already said he'd support her, so she knew that he wouldn't hold it against her if she went, despite the fact that he didn't want to let her out of his sight at all.

'Have a safe trip. Let me know when you get there…and…keep me updated…just so I know you're okay. Or at least let Claire know.' He retrieved her bag from the boot and pulled the handle out for her.

'I will. I'll let you know. Thanks for the lift.' Nicola hugged Charlie and placed a kiss on his cheek as he stifled an explosion in his chest. *Please come back to me*, he begged inside. He wanted her to go and come back a new person, one that was rid of this 'man'. He let her go eventually and she rolled her small case nervously away towards the terminal.

During her stay she had arranged to crash at a friends place. Severine was a former colleague of hers and stayed in a small apartment in the 18th arrondissement. The first night, Severine and Nicola went for dinner in an old haunt and had a catch up. They had worked together at the art gallery and Severine always thought Nicola was a great artist. She couldn't understand why she never had any success. She gave Nicola a set of keys that usually belonged to her mother whenever she came to visit, which meant Nicola could come and go as she pleased.

She arranged to meet Patrice on the second night, in a public place, so that he couldn't do anything to her. She sat outside at a café and waited for him. Nicola was used to stubble on him, which would just make his face look dirty. His jeans would have a few holes starting in them which may have been deliberate but she was never sure. His t-shirt would look like it needed to be washed and he would probably wear his dark grey hoody. As he approached though, Nicola almost didn't recognise him. He wore a shirt and trousers with smart shoes. His face was clean-shaven and his hair, whilst still long, was neat and tidy. He flicked his cigarette into the street as he approached.

'Cherie!' His arms were outstretched as if he was Christ the redeemer. She stood up so that she could be more ready for whatever was coming. He lifted her in a hug and kissed her. She gave a small kiss back but he didn't stop. She wriggled in his wiry arms and demanded he put her down. 'Patrice, we need to talk.'

'Je suis desolet. Of course we need to talk.'

It started off none too demanding – Nicola had to build the courage up first. It had been several months since she'd seen him and she had to get used to his presence again. During those months, she'd thought about all the things that she wanted to say to him, yet the words remained unspoken on her lips. Patrice smiled and laughed and pawed at her like nothing was wrong, as if he'd seen her that morning before he went to work and they were blissfully happy. He pulled out another cigarette and lit it. He drew the smoke into his lungs and expelled it with disregard into the Paris evening air. 'So,' smoke still issued from his face, 'are you staying this time?' The question came sort of out of the blue and even though she was expecting it, she was still not ready to answer it truthfully yet. But he always knew how to catch her off-guard.

'Well, that's what we need to talk about, actually. I was thinking of getting a job in Scotland. I just miss home and I feel I need to be closer there.'

'I don't understand, baby. You mean you don't want to live in Paris anymore?' He looked at her dead in the eye, the faux charm had gone. His hands motioned with his words and ash dropped onto the table and the street. 'So you expect me to move to Scotland?'

'No.' She started to panic inside and her hands took on a tremble. The words were on the tip of her tongue, *I want you to stay here, and I'll stay in Scotland, and we'll never see each other again,* and yet the words never came. 'I don't expect you to come to Scotland.'

'So, you want to remain long distance? I don't like this, baby. It's not good for me. There is nothing for you in Scotland. I am here, just stay in Paris, why are you thinking about stupid things?'

'It's not stupid.'

His eyes softened as he adapted to the best way to play her, it was what he was good at. He'd bombard her with questions to put her on the spot, then tone down to make it seem like he was sympathetic and caring. They usually spoke French when in France, but he would speak English whenever he tried to grovel or ask for something.

'Look, baby, I'm sorry about upsetting you before, but you have to understand, it's because I love you so much. You are my everything, so when I can't see you, when I can't be with you, I am crazy. You will never be able to find someone else like me. We are good together – the best. Everybody is jealous of us. So why do you want to stay a thousand kilometres away, what kind of relationship is that?'

'Well...I...'

'Let's just forget about everything before. You mean too much to me. I can't lose you now. If I lose you I will not be able to go on. It will destroy me, you want to destroy me? I promise, it will be different, it will be much better. Every day since you were gone, I can't get you out of my mind. When I wake up, the space in bed is too much to handle. I miss you like you wouldn't believe.' He took another drag of his cigarette and let the smoke escape as he continued delivering his well-rehearsed piece of drivel. 'I know it was my fault and I'm sorry about my temper, but it's been enough time for me to realise that I was wrong. Please come back. I love you so much. Just stay here with me. If you stay in Scotland I will miss you too much, I need you in my life every day. I can't live without you.'

He smiled warmly at her. *He does look completely different*, Nicola thought. He would never make an effort with his appearance before, but here he was, dressed smartly, well groomed for a change and seemingly pouring his heart out.

194

'Well...' Nicola thought of how to bring about her transcendence of the situation, '...I've just really been homesick, and...'

'Of course, Cherie, I understand.'

'I just need to be in Scotland, I think.' The aberrant cogs of his brain whirred.

'You met somebody else?' He didn't look at her when he said that, he merely stubbed his cigarette out in the ashtray. Nicola knew how jealous he could get.

'No! No, there's nobody else.' Charlie didn't even cross her mind. She had to come up with something to placate him. 'The truth is...erm...my dad hasn't been well...so...that's why I've been wanting to stay close to home as well.'

'Nicola, why you don't tell me these things??' He shuffled his chair closer and took both her hands in his. 'Mon cherie, you know you should tell me everything. How can we have a future if you don't tell me everything?' Nicola was confused. He was thinking about the future with her? It was always an issue they'd quarrelled over in the past. They had been in a relationship for several years and she had to pester him to propose. Eventually, it became such an issue that he proposed under duress and it ended up not being a special occasion. He had no ring, he hadn't thought anything through, but Nicola had wanted it, so he did it

195

almost just to shut her up. Yet now, he brought it up and he was looking towards a future with her, so maybe he *had* changed. She felt more at ease with him, in that, she didn't feel imminently at threat from him. That state in which she would reside between the insults and punches was what she'd mistake for love. The calm between the storms, the respite from the pain would feel so good she thought that was happiness and contentment.

'Nicola, come home. Make me complete again.' His words fell like gasoline on the fire that had started to dwindle ever since she left. *Maybe I've blown things up in my head?* she thought. *No, I have to stay strong and remember all he put me through.* 'I want to show you the apartment. I cleaned it up, it's like a new place.' She wondered if it was a good idea, but convinced herself she wasn't going to sleep with him or get anywhere near the bedroom.

When she lived there, she would always complain about the amount of hard discs and computer paraphernalia that was continually strewn around the flat. He worked in IT and was involved in some kind of computer building 'enterprise' with his flatmate who he also worked with.

She always had high hopes for the place and a vision of how she'd always wanted it to be so was intrigued to see how it turned out. *Maybe I should just see it one last time before I go, just to see how it turned out.* She lived there for six years of her life and had a lot of memories there. Her last memory was of hurriedly pulling things out of the drawers, off shelves and into suitcases with Claire. 'I can come round for a little bit, but I'm meeting Severine soon.' She wasn't, but that gave her a convenient escape and let him know she wasn't going to stay for long.

She was torn. As determined as she had been to leave him once and for all, what if there was a chance he had changed and everything could just be fine – the way it should be? She dreaded having to face up to the reality of breaking up with him from a fear of what he might do. If he'd sorted himself out then maybe she could give it another try. She did want to tell him things were over and he'd never see her again, but it was so hard for her. Ultimately, Nicola had not yet decided what she'd do. She was simply waiting for the path of least resistance to present itself.

They topped the stone spiral staircase up to their old apartment. Nicola saw a lot of familiarity. He pushed the door open, 'Et voila!' The place was clean and redecorated. It looked great. All the mess and clutter that used to contaminate the place was gone except from one small box of components that was neatly stored in the corner of the lounge. 'You see? I put a lot of work in. Everything has changed since you have been away. Also my love, it is stronger.'

Patrice said all the right things to get under her skin and she had to use all of her might to combat him. They sat down on the sofa and she noticed several photos of a happy couple young and in love, without a care in the world. They lived and worked in Paris and could take on the world together. It was Nicola and Patrice. The photos infiltrated her and she drifted back to a nicer time. The apartment was more or less the way she'd tried to make it for years and Patrice seemed to be brand new too. He never displayed photos before claiming that he didn't need a photo to remember her. He would never reveal that the real reason was in case he wanted to bring another girl back, like that secretary at his work. They'd kissed one time and it was whilst he and Nicola were together, but they were both drunk so it didn't even count. They weren't as drunk the time he *did* bring her back, but that didn't count either. Or maybe the young girl that started to work at the boulangerie, she could only have been about eighteen or nineteen years old and now he can't buy anything from there anymore.

He noticed how her gaze fell on the photos that he'd placed in frames that afternoon. 'You see, you are always here with me. But it's not the same, I miss you so much.' His hand caressed the side of her face and the feeling was very familiar to her indeed. It was a connection that she'd known for many a year and she hadn't felt it for a long time. He leaned in to kiss her again and she didn't push him off. Nicola's resolve broke and disintegrated into thin air. The familiar scent of him and the unfamiliar-because-its-improved feel of his clean-shaven face tricked her into believing him. *He's totally changed, everything's changed. This was exactly how I wanted things before and now I've got it.* 'I do this all for you.' All Nicola wanted was to be happy. She was nervous and apprehensive about starting her new job. In fact she was dreading it. Maybe she didn't need to. She could just sell the car, get rid of the flat and go back to the gallery.

After a moment's kissing, his hands advanced onto her body and started to remove her clothes. She thought it was too soon, but at the same time she hadn't had sex for so long. Besides that, there was no way she could say no, because he'd just get angry at her. Patrice removed her top before unbuttoning his shirt and standing up. 'Come on, baby. Let's go to the bedroom.'

She didn't stay over. She went back to Severine's, making an excuse about not having any of her stuff there. The next morning, she went round to see Patrice for breakfast. She brought croissants and fresh orange juice. He made some coffee as she sliced open the croissants and layered meat and cheese inside.

'So, will you bring your things back here?' Nicola wanted to take it slow, but at the same time, she didn't want to impose on Severine much more.

'I'll need to go back to Scotland and sort some things out.'

'Like what?' Patrice hid it, but he didn't want to let her go back to Scotland again, what if she was talking shit like usual and she wouldn't come back? 'You have everything here.'

'I just need to see Claire and my parents, and I'll bring some stuff.'

'You promise you won't fucking change your mind huh?'

'Patrice, please don't swear at me.'

'Sorry, baby. But you can't blame me. You have this...' he wiggled his finger around in the air, '...habit, no? I'm sorry, I just worry, you know.' It started once more, and yet Nicola still couldn't see it.

'I know. But I just need to go and clear some things up.'

'What things?' Now that she was moving back to France, she decided it wasn't a big deal about her job, so thought she'd come clean. *He'll be happy that I'm going to go home to reject it.*

'Well, I got a job, so I'll need to go and tell them I won't take it.'

'Really? A job? What job?' He tried to quash his rage as it grew in him. The bitch didn't tell him about this, she only said she was thinking about a job. She lied again.

'Oh, it's nothing. And I'll need to sell my car and get rid of the flat.' Nicola knew she had lied to him but only because she couldn't tell the truth considering how he would always react. It perpetuated the mistrust and lies between them. *Maybe I have been deceitful? I should have told him yesterday.*

'What? You have a car now also? What the fuck Nicola? Nice little setup, no?'

'It was just temporary, I need to live somewhere and I need to get about.'

'Yeah, maybe, but what about the job? That's permanent, long term.' Patrice's fury started to sublime through his skin like spilt ink through a canvass. She'd been building a life for herself out there, how dare she do such a thing without him. He stood up still holding his glass of orange juice. 'What else you have there…a boyfriend huh? I don't understand why you would lie to me. What else are you hiding from me? How many guys you've been fucking huh?'

'No, I've not. It's nothing like that.'

'It's nothing like that? So what is it like? Tell me! What you are trying to do? You found someone else??' She started to panic and the blind fear at his unpredictability came back – another familiar feeling for her. Now Charlie flared into her mind like a solitary firework in a clear night sky, glimmering and exploding into the dark silence. 'No. There's no one!'

'You're lying to me!!' He propelled his glass towards the floor at her feet and it smashed into a hundred transparent splinters. Nicola finally realised what a mistake she'd made. He hadn't changed at all and it took all of twelve hours for him to revert to his abusive ways.

'Patrice! Stop it! You said you'd changed! I can't even talk to you!'

'You can't talk to me?? You can't talk to me, huh??' He advanced towards her and gripped her arms tightly. 'What's to talk about?? How you are acting like a whore whenever I turn my back??' He shook her and her beautiful hair waved back and forth. 'You fucking someone? Who is he?? Tell me!'

'No! Patrice!' He pushed her back and paced around the kitchenette for a few seconds.

'So you won't tell me?'

He was determined that she was lying. It was the longest time she'd ever stayed in Scotland, so she must have had a boyfriend.

'Let's see how he likes you after I fuck up your face huh!' She ran for the door and managed to open it ajar before he kicked it shut. He pulled her back into the flat. 'Who is he??' Nicola thought about how stupid she'd been to put herself in that position again. She should have known better but she let him fool her the night before with the grooming and tidy apartment. But if you polish a turd, it's still a turd. *If Charlie was here, Patrice would be dead*, she thought. She felt so ashamed. Claire called it exactly and Charlie with his little appreciation of the situation gave her his support. Patrice had her tightly by the arms again. 'Who is he? Who is he?'

'Charlie! His name is Charlie, and we're in love! I don't want to be with you anymore!' She retreated into herself and just waited for it to be over. He could do whatever he wanted, like usual.

'You fucking whore!' He pushed her against the table, knocking her glass over. It rolled in a long slow arc over the edge before also smashing on the floor. Orange juice oozed slowly over the veneer of the table and dribbled down around the glass splinters. Patrice recoiled his arm and delivered a blow to Nicola's face. He hit her square in the left eye and she spun around as she fell to the ground.

A hot wet pang pounced into her hand and she realised she had fallen onto some of the broken glass. 'I don't believe you! Get out of here. I fucking hate you! You are a slut!' Nicola cradled her injured and bleeding hand and grabbed her bag.

Throwing the door open, she charged down the stairs, out of the building and onto the street. It was a narrow one-way street with cars parked either side. She ran past a few lines of scooters towards the end of the road. The piece of glass had slid into the fleshy part of her hand at the base of her thumb. It ripped a short but deep gash and stood protruding with the blood spatter, proud in her hand. She felt so out of control. She felt like running out in front of a bus and not having to deal with the pain inside, never mind the pain in her hand or her eye. *How could I have been so fucking stupid?* The blood pooled in her upturned cradled hand so she dropped it onto the street. It fell noiselessly and splattered a pattern onto the concrete as she ran away from her old apartment.

Her eye stung, she felt queasy and her throat and mouth were drier than the desert. She touched the piece of glass as she dashed towards the main road, back to where there were people. It was sunk into her hand and she didn't know what to do. Her first thought was to phone Charlie, but how could she? Even though he'd know exactly what to do, she was much too ashamed. She pulled out her phone and opened recent calls: *1) Charlie, 2) Claire Bear.* She couldn't face calling either of them. She had to deal with it alone because it was her mistake. At the end of the road she found a bench under the cover of bushy bright green trees which shaded her from the morning sun. It was at a cramped and busy intersection where cars slowly crept past the pedestrians waiting to cross and the people sitting at the café on the corner. There was some graffiti on the wall behind her which read *Libertad*. Blood continued to stream from the gash in her hand and spots of it soiled her jeans and her boots.

The glass was hard to grip. The blood had made it very slippery, but it had to come out. She clamped it as hard as she could and slowly pulled it from her hand. It was the iceberg of all glass pieces. The further she pulled it, the wider it got until finally it was out. She dropped it on the ground and it rattled as it fell between her feet. Using her one good hand she rummaged in her bag. Down there at the bottom was a spare tampon and she ripped it open with her teeth. She put it over the wound and pressed her fingers over it. The blood leeched into it like paint into a new brush. She was humiliated. There she sat on a road-side bench in Paris with a huge black eye, a deep gash in her hand and using a tampon for first aid. She cried and cried. Some people walked past and made some comments, others avoided her altogether.

Nicola was broken. She just wanted to curl up into a ball there on that bench and never move, except she knew she had to get home – home to Scotland.

She had planned to catch a few other friends whilst she was there and still had two days before her flight, but she had to leave Paris immediately. After a while, and after the bleeding had calmed down, she summoned the energy to hail a taxi and took it back to Severine's.

She headed to the bathroom cabinet to find some plasters or something to cover the canyon in her hand. She caught a glimpse of herself in the mirror. Her eye was completely swollen and her hair was a mess. The bruise was multi-coloured as her capillaries had burst and bled out under her skin. The swelling was awful. Since the wound was no longer bleeding over everything, she could use her good hand to bundle things back into her bag and get the fuck out of Paris. She wanted to leave Severine a note, but she was unable to write so thought she'd just have to text her later.

Nicola took a glass and drew some water from the tap in the kitchen. She washed away the dryness of her throat and mouth and drank so fast she choked and coughed. Water ran down from the corners of her beautiful mouth before she shakily filled the glass one more time. She noticed that the quality of the water was not as good as it was in Scotland. It seemed chalky or cloudy, it wasn't the clean crisp water she had gotten used to again back at home. She spotted word magnets on the fridge as she drank. Severine saw them one time on holiday thinking they were quirky and could help her with her English. The words were of course limited, but Nicola managed to write: going/ home/ man/ was/ bad/. She cleared a space around the words to make it more obvious for Severine to find.

In the living room she noticed an oversized pair of sunglasses sitting on the mantelpiece. She grabbed them and tried them on. They covered a large proportion of her face. She dropped her hair down and pulled it out to drape over the glasses so as to conceal the black eye as much as she could. She went back into the kitchen and searched for more words before adding: have/ you/ glasses/. She took one last look before leaving the flat and posting the keys back through the letterbox. She hailed a taxi outside. 'Charles de Gaul, si'l vous plait.'

'Oui, mademoiselle.'


Nicola kept Severine's glasses on as she approached the desk for her airline. She stood in line but it wasn't long before she was served. 'I have a flight in two days, but I was wondering whether I could change it? I need to bring it forward for as soon as possible, please.'

The woman asked for her details and what flight it was before checking. 'There are two seats left for tonight's flight,' she continued to check screens, click the mouse and type on the keyboard. 'There will be a charge to change the ticket I'm afraid. It's two-hundred and twelve pounds, eighty-six.' Nicola was devastated. It literally added insult to injury.

'Shit!' she said to herself.

'I'm sorry?'

'No, nothing, it's just...there's nothing else you can do? Because...' Nicola finally removed Severine's big glasses. '...I just need to get home.' The woman immediately understood Nicola's predicament and felt awful that she couldn't do anything.

'Oh you poor– let me check again, but I don't think there's anything I can do. Give me one moment though please.' The woman leant far back behind the desk to use the phone. She was just too far away and talked just too quietly in the background hum of the airport for Nicola to hear what she was saying. 'I'm so sorry, that's all I can do from here. Don't you have a credit card or something? Now would be a good time to use it.' Nicola's credit card was more or less maxed out. Her bank overdraft had been extended, then extended again. She was really holding on until she started her job. The flight to Paris was too much already, but she felt she needed to do it and now she was stuck there. 'Or do you have a friend who could loan you the money till get you home? I'm sure they wouldn't mind.' *Charlie.* She still didn't want to call him and admit how stupid and irresponsible she'd been, but she had to. After all, it wasn't like he would ever judge her.


Charlie was taking some *skill at arms* classroom drills for new recruits that day and showed them NSP's. That was boring enough, but he had been distracted all day thinking about how he hadn't heard from Nicola. Since they met back up, they'd talk several times a day, every day, and he didn't like the void it created in his life. They stopped for lunch and at last, a call came through from her. 'Hi.'

'Hi, Charlie…erm…'

'How's Paris going?'

'Erm…not good actually. I'm stuck at the airport.'

Charlie pondered what day it was, 'I thought you still had a couple of days?'

'Yeah…I do. But I've done everything I came here to do. I just need to come home now.'

'Is everything okay?' She wondered whether to come clean or play it down. Of course, she decided to play it down.

'Yes, I'm just not going to achieve anything more, that's it over once and for all and I just want to come home now.'

Charlie was more than happy with that news. She was coming back to him and she was finished with Patrice. 'So…how come you're stuck at the airport?'

'Well, I've tried to change the flight, but I can't. Well, not without paying over two-hundred pounds. And I just can't afford it.'

'Well, do you want my card number? Just book it and we'll sort it out later.' By sort it out later, Charlie meant *forget about it and just come back to me.*

'Charlie, is it okay? I know it's a huge favour, but I don't know what–'

'Nicola, take the number. Please.' She looked at her hand and knew she wouldn't be able to write anything down, or there would be no way she could read it at least.

'I don't have anything to write with.'

'Okay, well, just give me over to the person and I'll give them my number.'

'I'm not at the desk anymore. I'll need to get back in the queue.'

'Okay, well just stay on the phone with me then.'

'Okay.' Nicola started to feel at ease now Charlie was involved. He would fix everything. The queue moved as fast as it did before and Nicola was grateful she didn't have to find more bullshit to tell him about Severine and about how everything in Paris had changed but was still the same. He didn't want to ask her about Patrice over the phone anyway. Charlie wanted to do it face-to-face so she'd not only have his undivided attention but could fall into his arms and admit her love for him as he was hoping and fantasising.

She was second in the queue and the woman she spoke to before saw her. When she became free, she called out for her, 'Miss Wallace?' Nicola stepped up to the desk and the woman saw her holding the phone. 'Managed to reach someone then?' Nicola nodded. 'I'm so glad.' She remembered what flight she was looking for and searched for it once more. A look of sheer gloom washed over her face and she had to find the right words. 'I don't know how to tell you this, but it looks like those two seats are already gone. I'm so sorry. And that's the last flight we have out today.' Nicola was devastated but she couldn't be angry at the woman behind the desk because she seemed equally as devastated.

She lifted the phone to her ear. 'Charlie, there's no more seats left on the flight. I'll have to call you back.'

'What? Nicola?' She hung up, but he had heard her clearly enough.

'Shall I have a look at the first flights tomorrow? There's always standby for tonight as well.' Nicola's phone rang.

'Nicola? What, there's no more seats?'

'Yeah, there's none left. Probably be here until tomorrow, I'll have to spend the night at the airport. I don't want to go back into Paris.'

'Let me speak to the person.' The lady took her phone but didn't sink back behind the desk to talk this time. 'Hello?'

'Hello, sir.'

'Sorry if you're repeating yourself, but there's no flights at all?'

'There's none, I've checked. I've even checked other carriers, but there's nothing.' The woman wondered who she was talking to, probably her brother or something.

'How about first class?' Charlie asked.

'I'm afraid they don't do first class seats for that flight anyway.' *First class!* Nicola thought.

'How about the Eurostar? Do you think I could get her on that?' The woman held Nicola's phone in one hand and used the other to open the internet on her computer.

'Let me just have a look.' Nicola and Charlie waited patiently. 'I think that's probably the best bet. You'll need to allow her plenty of time to get there though. I'd say at least a couple hours at this time of day for the drive and to find the train alright. The station is quite far and the traffic might be bad. But they run right into the evening so there's no point in rushing. Looks like you can book the tickets online.'

'Okay, thank you so much. I– we really appreciate it. Can you put her back on please?' She handed the phone back and Charlie explained that he would book her tickets for the Eurostar and forward her the reservation and ticket details and to stay in the airports free Wi-Fi coverage until she got them. Nicola hung up the phone.

'So, Eurostar for you dear?'

'It looks like it.'

'Well…I'm glad that's it sorted, and I'm so sorry again that we had no more seats.'

'It's okay, you've been really helpful, thank you.'

'Erm, just wait a second, please.' She got up and left the booth completely. After a few moments she came back with a yellow slip of paper and handed it to Nicola. 'I've arranged for a car to take you to the station, I've just put it on goodwill. Just get yourself home.' Nicola couldn't believe the kindness that people were still able to show considering how terrible Patrice was. 'The car's ready when you are, just head four desks down.' She pointed to Nicola's left. 'The one with the big green sign.'

'Thank you so much. What's your name?'

The woman smiled and replied, 'Nicola.'

Charlie left Ayrshire immediately after booking the train tickets for Nicola. He ran in to see the OC and explained that he had an emergency to tend to and had to leave at once. His OC could see that there was definitely something frantic with the cool and calm Charlie. He got changed out of his combats and ran back to the car. His valiant steed headed in the opposite direction from home and it ate up the motorway miles as Charlie thought about Nicola. He thought about how happy he was to be given the opportunity to do something extraordinary for her. He thought about how she decided to come home early, so she'd obviously put this guy behind her and was ready to move on. He was glad to be the one to welcome her back home where she belonged.

His SatNav recited the directions to him as he passed motorway junctions and switched from one motorway to the next. He'd had a long morning, but he felt refreshed. He was always ready for Nicola and always felt revitalised when he thought about her. The recollection of her smile was enough to give him energy to run marathons, or move mountains. And this was it. He'd collect her and they'd go home and live happily ever after. He was excited and enthralled and brimming with enthusiasm for the long drive. He thought about the kiss he was sure to get from her at the station.

He stopped at a filling station and bought something to eat, as well as picking up a few things that he knew Nicola liked, thinking that she may well be hungry by the time she got into London. He also got her a trashy celebrity magazine so she had something to read during the car journey home if she didn't feel like sleeping.

Nicola had never been on the Eurostar before despite it being a good link from Paris. She would always opt for the flight however, because it would take her straight to Edinburgh or Glasgow. It was fast and quiet and smooth and the chair that Charlie booked for her was so comfortable. She had a look around at the other passengers to make sure no one was watching and she carefully removed her plaster. The gash was still seeping blood. It probably needed some proper medical attention but soon she'd be with Charlie and he'd take care of everything.

He parked the car and headed into St Pancras Station in London. He'd been there a few times before, including once on training and once on a job. He remembered following a man into a newsagents and then sitting watching him drinking coffee until his counterpart arrived. He then followed the counterpart all the way back up to Leeds on the motorway and found out where he was living. Mission complete. That was a few years ago. The coffee shop was no longer there since the whole station had been revamped. It had to go through a major refurbishment if it was going to be the terminus and the origin for the Paris train.

He sat on a bench underneath the board. He remembered when he was young in the Waverley station in Edinburgh and how the board would flicker and click as the letters scrolled through to the correct ones. Now a giant fancy display hung in most train stations, including this one. It was busy and he sat next a woman in her late-forties. She was quite attractive and gave Charlie a welcoming smile. He reciprocated.

The heels on Nicola's boots clicked as she advanced along the platform and despite the hordes of people, he could see her with ease. She stood out like a giant golden nugget in a pile of dirty pebbles. She wore oversized dark glasses even though it wasn't exactly bright inside the station, but they suited her, he thought. Her hair flailed around a little as gusts of wind puffed along the platform. She was wearing a long camel coloured coat and he could see dark jeans pacing, just slightly parting the bottom of the coat with each step. Her handbag was on her shoulder and she dragged her little pull-along case behind her. Charlie stood up holstering his phone and waited patiently for her. He didn't mind how long she would take. He could watch her coming back to him for ever. He left the seat next to the pretty woman and was glad to be showing her exactly who he'd been waiting for, because he knew she was watching him.

'Hey you,' he said with a smile. She heaved heavily into his arms and started to cry. Her pull-along case toppled to the ground and the hard plastic and metal handle clacked onto the stone floor and the sound seemed to reverberate around the station, punctuating her hasty return. Charlie had never seen her with dark glasses on before and just felt they were out of place. 'Nicola, what's wrong?' He lifted them up onto her head and her hair parted like waves in the night ocean. Her beautiful eye was bloodshot inside her swollen and bruised socket. 'Oh, Nicola.' He felt a freezing blinding sensation pass through him as he looked upon the damage done to her. It was a massive blow to him. Not only because it sickened him to see her like that, but because he suddenly realised she wasn't coming back early to be with him, she was just running again.

He touched the swelling tenderly in the middle of the station. She flinched and brought the glasses back down, not to hide from Charlie, but from any onlookers. The woman Charlie had been sitting next to was still watching them too. He noticed the plaster on her hand and took her wrist gently. 'What's this too?'

'Uh, I fell on some glass.'

'Or he pushed you?' She didn't answer or shake or nod her head. 'Is it bad? Let me take a look at it.'

Nicola let him remove the plaster and it peeled back revealing the deep gash in the fleshy part of her hand. Charlie's heart started to beat fast. His breathing shortened and intensified. He wanted to kill this guy. How could he do that to Nicola? How could he tarnish her with

217

wounds? How could he try to spoil such a treasure? Charlie couldn't let himself get caught up in thoughts of vengeance and retaliation however, because looking after her was his first priority. 'It's going to need stitches.' Charlie pulled out a clean tissue from the pack in his pocket. 'Pinch it there. Let's get back to the car.'


Charlie sat patiently in the waiting room at A&E whilst Nicola had her hand stitched up. He had flushed out the wound with a sterile pod and put some closure strips on it when they got back to the car. Nicola insisted that she didn't need or want to go to A&E but Charlie was driving after all, so she didn't have much choice.

It was a Thursday night and the waiting room was full of all manner of people. Some sat patiently like Charlie and some paced around only to aggravate their own impatience. The receptionist tapped away at her keyboard and spoke as politely as she could to the patients that were walking in from the street. One man held his arm in a cast and started to raise his voice at her. She kept her calm as Charlie was giving the guy a further ten seconds to start behaving himself before he'd intervene. He was in no mood. The man walked out and back onto the darkened hospital grounds.

He checked his watch. It was getting late. He'd been up since 5 am because he wanted to have a cooked breakfast and take the coast road down and it'd just be him and the open road.

He stared blankly ahead and tried to picture the events that unfolded in Paris. He tried to imagine Patrice's face and pull up an image of him from nowhere. He wanted to get Nicola home and then fly to Paris and track this 'man' down. He could do it. If anyone could do it, Charlie could. Maybe Claire had a picture of him somewhere. She certainly would have known where they lived in Paris, but Charlie wondered if it was the same place. Anyway, he could start from there. He didn't have many contacts in France, but he knew people that definitely did. The further into his plotting he went, the further from the waiting room he became, until he was interrupted by a tap on the shoulder. 'All done,' Nicola said. She lifted her hand up to show how it had been patched up in a gesture that looked like she was asking for a high-five. 'Only four stitches.' She had cheered up a lot since she'd been to get her hand sewn up. Now it was Charlie's face that was solemn and glum.

'Okay.'

He didn't have anything to say to Nicola as they walked back to the car and she began to worry that she'd pissed him off with calling him and disturbing his whole day. She had no idea of the rage mounting in him against Patrice. *If you've got nothing nice to say, then say nothing at all,* was an old adage that his parents taught him, that's why he stayed quiet. The car was parked on top of a mini double storey car park in the hospital. 'I'll...I'll pay you back, Charlie.'

'I don't care about the money, Nicola.' He went to the boot to fetch the food, juice, water and magazine he'd bought for her. He cracked the bottles open and lightly closed them so she would be able to open them with her injury. He turned round one of his rucksacks, unzipped the main compartment and felt around in one of the pockets. He produced a microfiber blanket, shook it out and rubbed a bit of heat into it before giving it to her. 'Something to eat and drink, and read. And you should try and get some sleep, we've got a long drive ahead of us.' His tone was not stern, but neither was he his usual warm self. There was something very cold about him which Nicola was picking up on. He felt guilty for letting her go. It wasn't Nicola's fault and it maybe wasn't even Patrice's fault, because after all, everyone knew what he was. Charlie told her he supported her and even drove her to the airport. He should have protested or insisted she stay, but he made it too easy for her and he put her in harm's way. He'd never do that again.

The car rumbled into life and the lights flicked on and shone over the railing, levelling out onto the first floor of the building in front. 'I'm sorry, Charlie. About all of this.'

He stared straight ahead at the letters on the building *Cardiology*. 'No, Nicola, I'm sorry.'

They approached Scotch Corner service station and Charlie wanted to stop for a while. After leaving the hospital Nicola ate half of her sandwich and had a sip of orange juice before leafing through the magazine for a while. As soon as they hit the motorway the streetlights finished and she fell asleep. She curled up facing outwards with her hands tucked neatly in-between her legs. She groaned a few times and shuffled into the bucket seat underneath her blanket. The miles fell away and the day expired into the next one. On quiet stretches Charlie opened up the car a little and the speed mounted.

It rained hard after leaving London and the raindrops hit the windscreen like the crackle of a roaring fire. He had turned the SatNav off so as not to disturb her and just relied on himself for directions, it was easy enough a road. They climbed the off-ramp and streetlights returned by the time they got to the roundabout at the top. Nicola stirred a little as the motorway smoothness ebbed away and light glanced off her wounded face. He pulled into the car park, stopping the car and nudging her gently. He didn't want to wake her, but he also didn't want to make another stop on the way up if he could help it. She smacked her lips a couple of times before removing the blanket. 'You okay, Charlie?'

'Yeah, I'm fine. I just need to stop for a break.'

'You're not feeling tired?'

There was a hotel at the service station and he had a vision of making out that he was too tired to continue up that night. They could stay there and share a room and he could hold her close as she slept, or *she* could hold *him* close as *he* slept. Other than his teeth feeling a little furry though, he felt okay. 'No I'm alright. And I'll be fine after I stretch my legs.'

Trees surrounded the dark car park and it was surprisingly busy for that time of night, but then again, it was a major north-south artery. It was only then that Charlie realised he'd taken the wrong road – for several hundred miles. That road headed up the east coast of the UK, which would lead them back home. Home: where they went to school together. Home: where Charlie should have just settled and lived a boring and ordinary life. Home: where he would retreat to whenever things got too much. He supposed it didn't matter, because Nicola's knowledge of the motorway network was not so great and she would fall asleep again once they were back on the motorway. He'd driven home from London so many times before so his head just went on autopilot. He was thinking about her and about how to make things right rather than where he was driving.

A jeep with a trailer straddled two parking bays in the middle of the car park close to where they had parked and a few people were gathered around it. The lights were on at the back of the jeep, but there was nothing on the trailer. Charlie walked past with Nicola in tow.

After using the toilet, Charlie bought a coffee for himself and a bottle of Lucozade whilst he waited for Nicola. In the bathroom she looked around and it was quiet. She peeled back her hair and looked closely at her black eye in the mirror. The bruise had developed and so had the swelling. It hurt to blink, like someone had put grit in her eye. She pushed it gently and a sharp pain shot through her head. When she came out, Charlie was standing with his coffee in hand and juice in the deep back pocket of his tactical trousers. 'Do you need anything else?' Everything she needed was already in the car, but she did want to look around the shop.

She bought a massively overpriced mini teddy bear. It was a little grey bear holding a heart that said *You're Wonderful* on it. 'I bought you a present.' She wanted to cheer him up or do something to reassure him that he hadn't done anything wrong and stop him from blaming himself. Plus, she felt nervous around a tense Charlie, because she'd never seen it before.

'You didn't need to do that...' She produced the teddy and Charlie smiled. It was a sweet gesture and it meant the world to him. She was looking for one that simply said *Thank You*. They didn't have any, but she thought that one was probably more appropriate anyway.

As they walked back to the car park, Charlie carefully peeled the lid off the hot coffee and allowed the night air to take cooling swipes at it. The people were still struggling with the trailer. He unlocked the car for Nicola but couldn't just get in without offering assistance. 'Do you need any help with the trailer?'

'Aye, well, we cannot get it working.' The man spoke with a Geordie accent. 'The lights are dead. But me son just brought it here and the lights were alright. I cannot chance it in the dark, if it were daytime it'd maybe be alright. I don't want to have to wait until the morning.' Charlie approached the trailer and checked the plug and socket were connected well. The tailgate of the jeep was open and there were two women inside, he presumed the man's wife and daughter.

'Right, try the brakes.' The man stood on the pedal from outside the jeep. Nothing. Charlie slipped the torch out of his pocket, removed the plug and had a look at the terminals. It looked fine. 'Do you have a screwdriver handy?' Charlie asked. The man fumbled about in a tool box, but there were only a few mismatched spanners, cable ties and a set of pliers in there.

The daughter's phone rang and she answered. 'Aye, we're at Scotch Corner still, pet. We've had a problem with the trailer, but now a Scotsman's come to rescue us.' Charlie smiled overhearing as he opened his own boot and lifted the partition. He kept some tools next to the spare wheel and found his screwdriver. He switched the head round

224

and unscrewed the plug to inspect the internal connections. He pulled a thin wire out and showed the man.

'Missing connection.' He changed the head to a small flat one, stripped the wire back a little bit, twisted it round and secured it. He checked the other connections whilst he had it open. 'Right,' he said to the man, 'try it now.' He switched the tailgate lights on and the trailer lights came to life.

'Oh, man, you're a lifesaver. Like I said, I didn't want to have to wait until the morning.'

'Now the brakes.' The trailer brake lights came on.

'Absolutely smashing mate! Thanks a million!'

Charlie checked back at Nicola and she was curled up in the seat again. She had been watching the whole thing and feigned sleep when Charlie would look round at her. 'Can I get you a coffee, pal?'

'No, I'm fine thanks.' Charlie pointed to the coffee cup that stood steaming on the top of his car. It was the perfect temperature to drink by now.

'Well, summat?'

'No, honestly, it's fine. I need to get her home.' He nodded over towards his car and the man could vaguely see Nicola hiding underneath the blanket in the passenger seat. Her head was leaning on the window.

225

She enjoyed the coolness of it because it helped take away some of the sting.

'Okay, looks like you need to get that one to bed.' *You don't know the half*, thought Charlie.

'Have a safe journey,' Charlie said.

'Aye, you an' all. And thanks a million once again.'

Charlie quickly drank the coffee and disposed of the cup before getting back in the car. When he closed the door Nicola pretended to wake up. She didn't want to appear to be awake because she'd feel obliged to go out and participate, but she didn't want to because then the people would see her black eye. She could hardly wear the sunglasses when it was pitch black outside. 'What happened there?' she asked.

'Just some trailer trouble. It's fixed now. The guy seemed pretty delighted.' Nicola thought about Charlie and his relentless thoughtfulness. Probably a hundred people or more came and went in the time they were struggling with the trailer, and not a single one thought to stop and ask if they needed help. Of course, Charlie did. The hundred people that passed by before probably didn't have the same skills and know-how as Charlie anyway, so they'd just keep their nose out and get on with their own journey.

'How did you even fix it?'

'It was just a loose connection. It was easy.'

'Everything is easy for you.' *Except seeing you like this*, he thought. 'You're always there when no one else will help. That's what I like about you the most.' Charlie pulled the teddy from his pocket so his new friend wouldn't suffocate and sat him in the corner of the dashboard.

'Shall we?' Nicola nodded and they slid slowly out of the car park. The man and the two women in the jeep waved frantically with appreciation as they left. *See how happy he makes people, even strangers*, thought Nicola. The car descended the on-ramp back onto the wrong motorway and the streetlights disappeared once more. Charlie turned the radio volume from minimum to mute. Nicola's slumbery breaths were the only soundtrack he wanted to listen to over and over again.

On the approach to Glasgow he gave Claire a call. It took her a long time to answer because of the early hour and he spoke as quietly as he could so as not to wake Nicola. 'Hey, sorry for such an early call, but I thought you'd like to know...'

'What is it, Charlie?'

'I've got Nicola in the car with me. Patrice has erm...'

'What? Oh no, don't tell me…'

'Yeah. So I'm taking her home. I had to get her from London though. I was wondering if you were able to come round and look after her?' Charlie, of course would have stayed as long as he needed to, and he wanted to be there with her like always, but he thought about Claire. Nicola hadn't even told her any of this yet and he didn't want to come between the two of them. 'We're about half an hour outside Glasgow, but I could swing by yours and then I'll drop you both at her flat.'

'What has he done to her?'

'She's got a black eye, and a big cut on her hand. She fell on some glass that he smashed.'

'Oh for fuck's sake! Right, I'll get ready. I just knew it. I fucking knew it.'

'Okay, I'll get you in just over half an hour.'

'No, just take her home, I'll get a taxi.'

It was after sunrise when they pulled up on the hill under her balcony. She was still fast asleep. Her eyes twitched under her eyelids and he wondered if it was dreams or muscular spasms from her injury.

'Wake up Nicola, we're here.'

He got out of the car and removed her bag from the back. Nicola remained in the passenger seat underneath the blanket. He opened the car door on her side. The pang of her eye and the cut in her hand suddenly became exacerbated by arriving back. She had to get on with a life that was not the one she had envisaged. She'd decided that was it. She didn't care whether Patrice thought they were still together or not, she'd never go back to see him. 'Nicola, come on.' She remained in the seat.

'How am I supposed to go on now? Look at me? How can I start work like this? I don't know what to do.'

'This is the perfect time to get on with your life now.' He peeled off the blanket and the cool morning air set about her body. 'You're rid of this guy. You've seen him for what he is, so now you need to put him behind you. You've got a life here now and if you're wondering where to go, then it's only upwards.' He started to fold the blanket up and looked at her tenderly. 'Trust me. You've got me and Claire, and our full support.' He kneeled down next to her.

'I just wish I could believe you,' she said.

'And when did I ever lie to you?'

Nicola slowly nodded her head and undid her seatbelt. 'Okay.'

'Come on, let's get you upstairs.'

She got out of the car and pulled Charlie in for a hug as the sun peeked between the Georgian houses. 'I have to say, Charlie, you're like my guardian angel. I'm so happy that you've come back into my life. I don't know what I'd do without you.'

She sat down on the sofa and he made them some tea. Charlie's phone buzzed, it was a text from Claire: "Be there in 10mins. X" They sat together and Nicola nestled her head on Charlie's broad shoulder until the flat buzzer went. Charlie had been completely un-fatigued until then. He'd been up for more than twenty-four hours, and other than the teaching and a couple hours wait in A&E, it was all spent driving. During the drive, he didn't feel tired at all. He'd have strength enough for her so long as she needed him to, but now that she was safely delivered home, the tiredness hit him like a sledgehammer.

Claire rushed in to look at Nicola. 'Fuck's sake, Nicola, didn't I tell you something like this would happen??' She didn't answer. She knew Claire was frustrated because she'd had to put up with it so many times, so she was allowed to be mad at her. Charlie brought the tea through and took a seat on the sofa whilst his eyelids started to feel like they were turning into stone. Nicola told Claire about the airport and the Eurostar and A&E and the trailer at Scotch Corner. 'I hope you know how lucky you are to have had him come and get you.'

'I know. He's my guardian angel.' She wanted Claire to know too.

'God Charlie, you've outdone yourself this time,' Claire said. They looked across at him and as much as he would have loved to have heard the *guardian angel* thing again, he was already fast asleep on the sofa.

# Chapter Twelve

She finished school that Thursday afternoon and waited outside to be picked up. She wasn't going to catch the bus home. Before leaving school, she checked how she looked in the mirror. She let her hair down and tousled it out, adjusted her bra to maximise her breasts, touched up her lip gloss and sprayed herself with body spray. She was meeting two guys that she met outside a disco in the town. One was at college doing Sports Science and the other was an apprentice car mechanic. Nicola was still young and these guys were older. They were hardly high-rollers, but they had a car and could go to the pub at the weekend, so to a naïve schoolgirl they *were* high-rollers.

Stevie the mechanic rolled up in his shitty old car that he thought was the best thing ever. Nicola got in and they drove away from the school. She loved the feeling when all the other girls in her year could see her getting picked up in a car with older boys. She was rolling in a different league. They only had schoolboys and she was with 'college boys' and 'professionals'. Her bad reputation at school started when she snogged one of the popular girl's boyfriends. The girls would then gang up on her and insult her on a daily basis and spread rumours about her – and spread truths about her. It didn't seem to matter that the boy kissed her too despite him being the one in a relationship. She was hardly a good girl, but it was all for attention. Apart from Claire, she didn't have any good friends at school, only a few acquaintances.

She sat in the front next to Stevie and Matt sat in the back seat. He didn't wear his seatbelt and leaned through the gap in the front seats so he could talk to her better. He put one hand over the seat and onto her shoulder. The other trailed forward into Nicola's lap. They drove endlessly around town, in the pointless way that young guys do to assert some kind of authority or prove that they're cool. After a while they dropped Matt off at his house but not before he could force his smoky tongue down her throat and grab a feel of her.

There was an old industrial estate on the edge of the town. It was formerly a factory of some kind, but the production had been moved to China, so the place became abandoned and disused. The car park had several hundred spaces where the staff used to park before an honest day's work, but now it lay empty except for guys like this who would come to do handbrake turns and other stuff in their car. The trees around the edge of the car park were overgrown and cast large shadows; large enough to park a car under. Stevie pulled the handbrake on and turned to Nicola. 'So, c'mon then…' Nicola started to panic inside. She'd been tempted by the lure of two older boys, but she suddenly realised that she was way out of her depth. She thought that they'd hang out and maybe snog a bit, she'd maybe be adventurous and snog both of them and get a reputation of being 'fun' with the older boys and then she'd maybe win some respect and be valued by them in some way. It seemed she underestimated their intentions. 'C'mon and get your tits out.' Stevie grabbed her top and pulled hard at it. *Maybe if I just show them, that'll be alright*, she thought. She undid her buttons and revealed her bra. Stevie's hand wandered around and pulled out her breasts before plunging his hand down into her crotch. He rubbed hard and unskilfully at her and her knees clamped together. 'Aaw, don't tell me you're fucking frigid ya wee cow!'

'No I just…'

'Just what? Get in the back.'

They moved to the back seats and Nicola wished she was sitting on the bus on the way home to the parents that she couldn't stand. This was supposed to be good, this was supposed to be fun, but she was just a set of organs for this guy. It wasn't as if this was the first time she had sex, but she'd usually wanted it before. She didn't want this. She didn't want his dirty oily hands on her. She didn't want his fat sweaty body close to hers. She repulsed him but he was a big guy, so she didn't feel she could do anything and she was the one that approached them. She didn't want to get a reputation of being frigid or a cock-tease. She had to go through with it.

She hated the feeling of him in her, but endured it for the few short and joyless minutes that it took him to do what he needed to do. 'Now get out,' he said.

'What? I thought you were going to drive me home?' He laughed at her ignorantly.

'Nae danger! I'm no' fucking driving out to the middle of naewhere, fuck that!' He collected her things and pushed them onto her. 'Get the fuck out the car!' Her blouse was still undone and her trousers were down. She quickly pulled them up and folded her blouse shut before grabbing the rest of her stuff. He got back into the driver's seat and started the car. 'Gonnae shut the fucking door??' She shut the back door to his car and he crunched it into gear before wheel-spinning away.

Nicola stood on the edge of the town in an abandoned industrial estate with her clothes dishevelled and a used condom at her feet. Completely used and feeling worthless, she realised she had to get home. She couldn't call her parents, because she'd get the third degree about how she ended up there and what she'd been doing. It was not worth the aggravation. After sorting her clothes and bag out, she decided to walk back to school and get her normal bus back home.

She walked the long walk back to school feeling cheap and dirty. She didn't get the excitement that she was looking for and she didn't feel valued in the way she expected she would. She thought about calling Claire, but she didn't. Claire would probably get her parents to drive her home then they'd explain what they could glean from the situation to her parents anyway, so that wasn't an option. She was by herself and there was no one to help.

She picked up the pace as she realised her bus would be at the bus stop soon. If she wanted to avoid a long wait for the next bus, she had to hurry. Plus, it looked like it might start to rain. Her walking was slightly affected by the discomfort between her legs so she couldn't walk as fast as she'd have liked. She approached a crossroads with traffic lights. There was a small grassy patch where a few old oak trees stood and there was a shortcut through there to the bus stop. As she entered the grassy patch, she saw her bus turn the corner onto the road. She ran, but the discomfort she felt made it difficult whilst reminding her of how stupid she'd been. The bus driver had no hope of seeing her running through the trees and motored on past.

Nicola was faced with a long wait for the next bus which she wasn't looking forward to, but it was what she deserved. She sat on a low dry-stone dyke at the bus stop and took out her phone. She wanted to text Stevie to tell him she'd missed the bus and tell him that she'd give him petrol money if he would just drive her home. She kept checking the junction to see if maybe he was still doing laps of the town, he might pass by. But then what if he did pick her up again? What else might he do to her in order for him to drive her home? Nicola didn't really care, she just wanted to get home. She certainly couldn't feel any worse about herself. She kept her phone out considering her text to Claire.

Across the road, a boy she recognised walked along the pavement. He was in her year and although they didn't have any classes together, they would always stop and speak to each other. He was handsome and quite quiet, but not in a shy way, he was sort of mysterious. He had a girlfriend though and everybody at school knew how good they were. A loud car exhaust boomed at the traffic lights and she checked whether it was Stevie or not. If it was, he went the other way. The boy across the road had noticed her so Nicola waved as he crossed the road towards her.

'Hiya, Charlie.'

'Hi, Nicola, what you up to?'

He recognised her bus stop, but it was a little over two hours after school had finished.

'I've just missed my bus, the next ones not for aaaages'.

'How come you're so late?

'Oh,        I        was        with…er…some        friends.'

# Chapter Thirteen

*Buzz Buzz!! Buzz Buzz!! Buzz Buzz!!*

Charlie woke to the vibration and flashing screen of his phone. He grabbed it in the dark and his eyes took a second to adjust. *Nicola.* He swept sleep from his eyes and checked the time quickly at the top of the screen before answering. 3.47am.

'Nicola?...Hello? Nicola?'

'Charlie! Oh Charlie, it's him!' Her voice was quiet yet frantic.

Charlie's mind whirred for a second. *It can't be...Patrice?* he thought. 'What? Him who?'

'Patrice. He's come to get me.'

239

'What's happened? Are you okay? Where are you?' Charlie suddenly became free from all weariness and sleepiness. He stood up from the bed and started to pace his bedroom.

'I'm at the flat. He broke in. My neighbour chased him off, but what about when he comes back? He's going to come back!'

'Have you phoned the police?' Charlie started pulling on trousers with one hand, holding the phone in the other.

'No, well, yeah. My neighbour did. I don't know what to do Charlie. What if he's here somewhere?'

'I'm on my way.'

Charlie finished dressing in a couple of seconds, pulled on his boots and ran all the way to the parking garage in the basement. His heart started to beat hard. He was used to a quick deployment, but he'd never had anyone so important to protect before, and at that moment, the person he had to protect her from was much closer to her than he was. He didn't know what he looked like, he could walk past him in the street and be none the wiser and he didn't like being at that disadvantage. He jumped in the car and started it. The V8 purred into life, just as ready as him, despite the early hour. The lights blinked on and ran down the wall as the beam levelled. He reversed out of his space and put his seatbelt on as he waited for the shutter to lift, which took, it seemed about an hour.

The screeching of the tyres boomed off the city buildings and the roar of the engine sailed high up into the warm night. He was bound to be disturbing people but he didn't care, everybody ought to be awake and paying attention, Nicola was in danger. He used all of his advanced driving skills to negotiate the roads and paused only momentarily for red lights, which all of them were, of course. There was not a single other car on the road, but he checked carefully for traffic cops. Given his years of tracking people and finding good places to stalk or stakeout from, he knew all the potential spots along that road to Nicola's which he'd now travelled a thousand times – even if just subliminally. Now that information hopped into the forefront of his mind because he needed it. His experience meant that even in his agitated response mode, he still knew the fastest way to get there would be to avoid a traffic stop, and he had to get there *now*. On the short straights that opened up, he pushed the throttle and the keen engine thrust the car along at high speeds, eating up the road. The exhaust boomed a heavy note through the empty city streets.

When he arrived, there was one police car there and another one just pulling up. He parked speedily and shot out of the car. He ran up to the main door where a police officer stood diligently. He explained he knew one of the residents, specifically, the one who had been broken into, and after a few minutes another police officer came to escort him upstairs. They had just finished taking her statement and she rushed towards Charlie as he appeared at the door, which eliminated the need

241

for the police officer to ascertain whether or not he was known to her. She threw her arms around him and buried her head in his chest. Her whole body trembled and Charlie held her close without saying a word until her tears abated. 'Tell me what happened.'

Nicola was awoken by a scratching sound at her bathroom window. She thought it might have been a cat or something sitting on the windowsill. The scratching stopped only to resume at her kitchen window. Her flat did not have a traditional hallway. Outside her front door was a walkway which was open to the courtyard and open to the elements. Those windows were situated directly on the walkway that led to all the flats on her floor. Her neighbour had heard some scratching too and had put clothes on, grabbed the closest blunt object and went out to investigate. When he opened his door, a man was forcing Nicola's lock. The man had just managed to successfully force it when he came out. Her neighbour shouted and the man fled the opposite way, down the other stairs and ran clear of the building. He was of slim build and wore dark jeans, a dark grey hoody and leather jacket and the hood was pulled up around his face. When he ran, her neighbour could see long hair swinging out from around the hood. That was as much of a description as he could manage.

Nicola heard the door lock burst open and froze in bed. She pulled the covers up over her head and shut her eyes tight. The next thing she knew was her neighbour, Glen, a large, middle-aged divorced man with a kindly nature, gently knocking at her door. 'Nicola? Nicola? It's me, Glen. Are you here? Are you alright?'

There was no response and Glen continued, 'I'm just going to call the police, okay? You alright?' She still gave no response. Glen made the call and kept guard at his door, casting an eye to Nicola's to make sure the man didn't come back. He knew Nicola but only very vaguely, they had passed a few times and only ever exchanged pleasantries. He didn't feel he knew her well enough to enter her flat without her giving some kind of a response first. He still wasn't sure if she was even at home, so stood by until the police arrived. Nicola called Charlie from the protection of her covers.

The police read back the description Glen gave of the man and Nicola was rocked to the core. They spoke to Charlie, 'We've had a look at the lock and it's been forced – that's for certain. There's no signs of forced entry on the main door, he probably sat and waited for someone to open it. We can arrange to get a locksmith out to secure the property. Otherwise we'll leave things in your hands so we can get on with our enquiries.' The officer flicked his notepad shut and looked back up at Charlie, 'Will you and your girlfriend be alright?'

'She's not–' Charlie looked at her and she didn't even notice what the policeman said. It was quite reasonable for him to presume they were boyfriend and girlfriend. She did call him instead of the police and she was so relieved when he arrived. It hurt Charlie having so many people presume they were together and yet he was more than aware they were not. 'Yeah, we'll be fine. I'll take care of things.'

'Okay, we'll contact the locksmith, they usually arrive within two hours. It'll be on your account, I'm afraid.' Charlie frisked himself for his wallet.

'Okay.'

He sat on the sofa with his arm around Nicola whilst they waited for the locksmith. Glen came in at one point and spoke with Charlie but Nicola paid no attention to the conversation at all. Glen pulled the door almost shut when he left, to help keep some of the outside, outside.

Eventually the buzzer went and Charlie answered and retook his position next to Nicola on the sofa. 'Locksmith.' The door pushed slowly open. A man with a toolbox and backpack stood in the doorway. His features were slightly obscured by the breaking sunrise. Nicola remained in the same absent state whilst Charlie tried to bring her round.

'Nicola, do you want to go back to bed?' She looked blank, her cheeks still damp and eyes blurry. 'You should go to bed.'

244

'How can I sleep? I'll never sleep again in this place!'

'Just go and lie down and I'll take care of the door.' He looked over towards the locksmith that stood patiently waiting. At least he knew he was at the right flat. 'Just two seconds buddy, come in.'

Charlie lifted Nicola and carried her through to the bedroom, tucking her in and giving her a kiss on the forehead. She was numb and paralysed. The locksmith began inspecting the lock when Charlie re-emerged. 'Replacement lock service, aye?' he asked.

'Yes mate.'

The locksmith opened his bag and flipped through a flyer highlighting what locks he had with him and what ones were compatible with the door. 'Whichever one's the most secure.'

The locksmith advanced a couple of pages in the flyer and pointed out the lock he'd be installing, it looked more or less the same as all the others. He determined the cost using the calculator on his phone. 'Two-hundred and thirty-five sixty...plus vat...' he did another quick calculation, 'Two-hundred and eighty-two seventy-two, that's including the call-out, obviously.' *Well, obviously*, thought Charlie.

'Sure, fit it, how long will it take?'

'No' long pal, maybe half an hour.'

Charlie stood watch in the hallway as the locksmith worked away. He offered him a cup of coffee, but he declined. Charlie supposed he could take a flight and have high tea at the Ritz with the price he was charging, but ultimately he didn't mind. He wanted to make sure it was properly fixed and thought about getting a newer more secure door for her, but for the time being that had to wait. Nicola didn't sleep a wink and just about as the locksmith had finished, Charlie could hear her alarm clock in the bedroom. He knocked and waited, then knocked again before easing the door open. 'You okay?'

'I need to get up for work.'

'You *are* joking, yeah? I think if there's a time to call in, this would be it.'

'But we've got a big client today, I've been working so hard on this one, I can't miss it. It'll be my first close. And...I don't want to be...here.'

He couldn't deny it. She probably would have been much better getting out of the place.

'Okay, pal,' came a voice from the hallway, 'that's yous all secure again.' Charlie was so glad he'd used those words just to give her some reassurance. He left the bedroom for a second and gave the guy his credit card details.

'Thanks, mate.' The sun was peering over the trees beyond the courtyard, forcing Charlie to squint his eyes as he was bathed in a primordial glow. He pulled the door shut and rattled it to check it was secure before returning to the bedroom.

'That's the door fixed.'

'What? How did you fix it?'

'Police called a locksmith.'

'Okay…well do I have to pay anything?'

Charlie pondered for a second, 'No, the police just bill the council, that's er…what you pay your taxes for.' She was in much too distracted a state to think on it anymore and that seemed plausible enough to her.

'Charlie, I need to get ready for work.'

'Are you sure?' She nodded from under the covers. 'What time's the meeting? You have to tell your boss what happened as well.'

'No way. I really don't think I could find the words anyway. The meeting's at eleven-thirty, should take a couple of hours, but I've got some prep to do beforehand.'

'I think you should tell someone, they ought to know. Even just go to the meeting?'

'Maybe, but…no, it's okay, I'll be fine.'

'What's your boss's name?'

'Erm, Neil. Why?'

'Oh…no reason.' He actually wanted his full name. 'Well, let me get breakfast in. And then I'll drive you to the station at least.'

'Charlie, you don't–'

'No arguments, lady.'

Charlie left after making extra emphasis on checking the door was locked. 'I'm not going far, so if you need me, just call me,' he assured her before he left. She got ready for work and he returned with bacon butties, egg butties, coffees and a few cakes and croissants. He brought a selection back for her. He felt she'd be picky that morning and food wouldn't be a priority, but he wanted to make sure she had a good feed before her big day and whatever she didn't eat, he would eat.

They both sat silently in the car on the way to the subway station. The car was much more refined and well-mannered than it had been overnight. It obeyed red lights, lane positions and all other traffic regulations. Nicola looked blankly out the window the whole way. 'I just can't stand this,' she said. Charlie looked at her as she turned her face towards him. 'I'm not even safe in my own place. He's always there.'

'It's probably just some jakey or ned. The police said the description matches someone they want in connection with other–'

'THE DESCRIPTION MATCHES PATRICE!!'

Charlie still hadn't seen any photos of him, but a skinny long-haired guy was probably how he'd imagine him. But then again it was Glasgow – there were plenty of skinny long-haired guys.

'You don't know that. What would be the point of him even…' Charlie stemmed his words as Nicola looked at him in fear.

'You don't–' She almost snapped, but her tone softened rapidly. 'You don't know him.' She didn't mean to take it out on Charlie.

'Everything's going to be alright. You've got me around and I'm not going anywhere soon, so whatever you think he'll do, he'll never get the chance.' A plan formulated in his head. 'I think you should stay at mine for a while…until this all blows over.'

It was a daring offer. He had a whole list of justifications about how that would be the best thing for her, ready to defend his impulsiveness, but immediately came Nicola's reply, 'Okay.'

After dropping her at the station, he sat in the car for a minute or two trying to find her bosses number. He only had her direct extension at the office. Having only a first name might have made it more difficult, but he found the number for the reception. Since he'd just dropped Nicola off, he realised the office was obviously not open yet, so he waited until after he was home.

'Hello, good morning, I was looking for Neil, I'm sorry I don't have a last name, he's a manager in–'

'One moment please.' Thankfully they only had one Neil in that office, and when he's one of the managers, he's easy enough to identify.

Charlie parked the car facing uphill next to her three-storey block of flats. Only residents could park in the courtyard so he would always pull up in the same place below her narrow balcony. The building was relatively modern but in-keeping with the affluence and Georgian architecture that encompassed it. All the flats had balconies facing the street outside and he sometimes envisaged creating some kind of ridiculous but romantic Romeo and Juliet gesture, but that was just a faraway fantasy.

Rain fell heavily whilst Charlie ran from his car to her door. He rang her buzzer and there was no answer. He remembered waiting there early that morning for the police officer to escort him up to see her. Just as he was about to try again he saw her silhouette through the frosted glass and she was heaving two bags down the stairs. She tried opening the door without putting them down until she realised that was futile. She buzzed him in and he stepped inside scrutinising the bags. 'Erm, how long did you intend on staying exactly?' He was joking of course. In fact, he'd have loved for her to be bringing her every worldly possession and despite the temporary arrangement, he'd be happy if she were to never leave.

'Well…I've got work stuff as well, and–' she made a redundant justification.

'I'm only teasing. Come on, let me take one.' The rain and wind battered them side-to-side as they ran to the car. 'Quick, jump in!'

She managed to escape a thorough soaking, but he had been less fortunate. The pause outside the flat and extra time placing bags in the boot meant he was wet through to the skin. She laughed at him and didn't make any apology for the soaking he received on her behalf. For a moment at least, she forgot the reason why she was on her way to his flat. Staying over at Charlie's felt like an escape. She had no idea what Patrice would do if he found her and the more she feared it, the more the dread would mount. That's if it was even Patrice at all. Going to Charlie's meant she'd be away from there if he tried to break in again. She'd be far from harm, she thought.

'So how was the meeting?'

'Oh, it went really well. We signed them, so that's a lot of my work finally paid off. Neil even let me go early, which is…unusual. He's a good boss, but he's a bit of a task master! And he gave me tomorrow off.' Nicola yawned and wiped at her eyes. 'Come to think of it, he asked me if I was okay and if I felt up to the meeting when I came in. He maybe saw how tired I was. That's really thoughtful of him.'

Charlie recalled the phone call he made to him first thing in the morning, discreetly explaining the situation. 'Yeah, very thoughtful of him,' he said.

It was not the first time they'd stayed under the same roof of course, but this time it was *his* roof. The country house belonged to neither of them. Now she was truly protected and under his care. He brought her in and gave her a pseudo tour of the flat despite her having been there many times before. She was familiar with the place, but for him this time it was different. He ushered her into the spare bedroom and put her bag down. The rain lifted the scent of her into the air as she slid past which filled him up and for a second, he remembered their kiss. A bolt of apprehension shot through him and he had to purge himself of those kinds of thoughts.

Charlie loved her, but if he wanted to be there for her and keep her in his life, he had to rid himself of any ideas that might have come into his head with her staying over. At the time, it seemed logical to let her stay. She could have stayed with Claire, but then again she didn't have the space. Plus, as good as she was, she couldn't ward off Patrice if he did decide to come calling. What's more, he never even knew where Charlie stayed. That's the only way Nicola could relax in any way and all three of them knew it. He spoke to Claire that day during her lunch break and his running around and she was all for the plan. He invited her over but she was working late and said she'd be really tired and it would be very late by the time she got there. Charlie had to be brave and endure Nicola's sweet presence under his roof until such a time as she felt comfortable enough to go home.

'And this is where you'll be sleeping.' He wished it was his bedroom they were standing in because he thoroughly hated sleeping alone. Even if she didn't want to make love or do normal couple things, he so badly wanted her to fall asleep next to him, he just wanted to feel the soft warmth of her body against his again. Ever since the kiss, he craved to feel that again. It was almost worse having experienced it rather than just wondering how she'd feel, because the kiss was much more powerful than the longing.

Most of the time he could handle the feeling, but the circumstances exacerbated his own response to her, close to a point of no control. Aside from the fact she was there to escape harm and have some respite for a little while, it was him that truly needed comfort the most. He was as damaged as she was and the kind of comfort he needed could only be provided by her.

The room was of course immaculate as she expected. The covers he had changed to light colours with flowers of pink and blue and yellow. Before, they were a plain light grey, very masculine and clean cut. It was similar to what he kept on his bed, but he thought he'd change it specially to make the room a bit more feminine for her. He had freshly laundered and pressed towels and they sat rolled perfectly into cylinders on the foot of the bed. The presentation was not unlike that of a top hotel. He placed a vase with a single sweet pea flower in it on her bedside table. It was almost like being on holiday for her, except there was no information pack to tell her where to find things or what numbers to call, because all the concierge she would ever need was just down the hall in the other bedroom.

The humidity of the evening had made a negative impact on the condition of her hair and she became embarrassed. She tried patting it down and smoothing it in her hands but all to no avail. Despite leaving work early, she didn't have time to make herself up nicely after work. They filled in the basics of the plan hastily during the day over text before her meeting. But she felt so uncomfortable in her own place that she daren't even remove her clothes when she got there. The only time she spent there was used to pack and vacate the place as quickly as possible.

He made his excuses and went to get freshened up. His bedroom had an en-suite bathroom and he had the intention of a hot shower there. 'Can I…take a shower, please?' she enquired.

'Of course you can. Make yourself at home. If there's anything here you want just help yourself, honestly.' *Including me.* She stood there in her trouser suit with her unruly hair and looked at him still unsure. He came back towards her in the hall and led her into the bathroom. He reached a hand over the bathtub and operated a few controls to produce an inviting warm stream of water from the giant polished steel shower head. His urge to take a shower suddenly grew much stronger and more immediate. *Stop it!* he told himself. She dragged her small bag into the bathroom and he politely left for the privacy and loneliness of his own shower. Before he got there, a knock came at his bedroom door. He quickly put his t-shirt back on and it felt horrible from the damp.

'Hey, erm. I forgot toothpaste and I really need to brush my teeth. And I forgot pyjamas, I don't suppose you have anything…'

'Sure. There's a spare toothpaste in the en-suite, top drawer,' he pointed, 'I'll find you some kind of p-j's.'

She sidled through his bedroom and unobtrusively inspected everything she could about the room. It had the same smooth velvet carpets and furniture as her room. It was nice, but it was also decidedly male, but then that was to be expected. There was something about the room however that felt very comfortable to her. It was minimalist; there was no tat like in her flat. Everything was in order and proper and beautifully presented.

She noticed a picture of him and what appeared to be his unit hanging out at some kind of camp and one with a tall thin man. The other man had jet black hair and black eyes that were set into deep sockets. Their arms were round one another and they were smiling seemingly without a care in the world. The only other one was of Charlie in his uniform. He was so handsome and whilst looking fierce and intimidating he looked caring and sensitive. The only other thing she noticed was the teddy bear she bought him at Scotch Corner. He had pride of place on the chest of drawers.

She got to the en-suite and looked around at the items there. She noticed a face wash and hair product and whilst recognising both brands, saw that they had Arabic writing on them. She was a little bit shocked. She'd never seen Arabic writing on something in front of her before. She'd only maybe seen it in movies about war or terrorism or on the news. It reminded her of the places he'd been and the things that he'd done. As she emerged from the bathroom, he had pulled out a t-shirt with *Royal Marines Commando* on the back and a pair of shorts for her. 'The shorts will probably be too big for you, but the t-shirt should work.' She accepted the t-shirt graciously whilst agreeing with him about the shorts, and left them in his possession. 'Do you not maybe want to go for a bath instead? I could run you one if you like?'

The thought of a bath was absolutely perfect to her. She yearned to wash off the strain and grime of the previous night and really needed to relax. 'Well, if it's not too much trouble?'

'It's no trouble at all. Give me five minutes.'

He headed through in his cold wet clothes to run her a bath and left it at a perfect temperature. 'Okay, that's you.'

'Thanks. Oh, I really need this.' She shut the bathroom door but couldn't figure out the lock. She wasn't sure if it did lock, but she didn't really care. If Charlie had some reason to come in, then he could, she supposed. She slipped off her clothes leaving them in a heap on the floor. Steam rose from the tub and the bubbles cracked and popped on the surface. She tested the temperature and it *was* perfect. She got in and fell into a different state immediately. With every ounce of water that soaked her gorgeous pale skin, she felt the outward worries that consumed her dissolve away into the silky bubbles. He had rolled up a towel into a cylinder and left it at the head of the bath. She found it and used it as a pillow just as he intended. She fell fast asleep.


Nicola had been in the bath for a while, but he supposed she needed a good long soak. He sat alone on his sofa as the rain continued to fall hard outside. A foreboding dark grey filled the sky as the light gradually expired. Heavy raindrops terminated violently like a cacophony of fire crackers on all the glass that surrounded him. A half-empty bottle of whisky sat in front of him on the coffee table with a heavy based Glencairn glass next to it. He stared intently out of the window with the weight of something monumental on his shoulders.

He didn't notice her as she shuffled through in grey jogging bottoms, Charlie's t-shirt and a thick well-faded pink towelling dressing gown. Her hair was up and she rolled the loose sleeves of her dressing gown up. She felt like she was interrupting him, 'Hey, what you up to?' He turned around and remembered to smile. He couldn't let himself be upset around Nicola. She was the one there for support and not the other way around. She appeared refreshed and relaxed.

'Nothing much.' She could sense that something consumed him, or he needed to get something off his chest. She realised there was no TV or stereo on. He was just sitting in silence.

'Erm…what bubble bath do you use? I've never came out the bath like this before.'

'What, a prune?'

A giggle escaped her lips. 'No, my skin…it's so soft.'

'Well that's my little secret extra ingredient.' She wanted to know, but also in a way she didn't. She wanted to keep it so that he was

258

the only one who could run her a bath as good as that. She didn't want to be tempted to recreate it and was continually impressed with the way he could take something so ordinary and turn it into something really special and unique. 'You want something to eat?' he asked. She did.

Knowing that he would go to great lengths to cook for her she suggested, 'How about we just order something? My treat, it's the least I can do.' She smiled warmly at him. It was a smile that could melt snow-caps or glaciers thousands of miles away from where she stood.

'Sure.'

After dinner, she cleared the cartons away and they moved across to the sofa. They watched television and talked for a while. It was still early and despite her nap in the bath, she still felt exhausted. She had very little sleep the night before which would have proved tiring enough without the extra stress and paranoia she was experiencing. Not to mention her big meeting that day too.

As they sat together, she adjusted herself to lean and rest her head on him. He put both of his arms around her to lock her in tight. The forearms that sat across her were honed. She examined them. They were not made in the gym with weights and supplements, they carried no tattoos. They were made through hard work, endurance and survival. She could see various scars from old shrapnel injuries and scratches and scrapes he'd collected over the years. These were arms that have helped people, and she thought, maybe killed people? But she wasn't sure. She had always been intrigued by his job. It fascinated her and terrified her at the same time. Either way, she'd grab an arm every now and then and adjust her position to lay her head against the fold between his forearm and bicep. She fitted perfectly.

He could feel her warmth against him and it thawed him out. It was dark and the rain persisted outside, but he felt tenderness strong enough to sublime away the dreariness of the night and burn all the rain away into sunshine. They snuggled and Charlie was happy. It felt so much more natural than when they were house-sitting. To him this was perfection. Nicola meanwhile enjoyed being protected in the safe haven of Charlie's arms. She loved the smell of his skin from the shower and the latent gentle power she could sense from his body.

They were both starting to drift off. He'd feel her jump in his arms or she'd feel him bobbing his head behind her. Of course he could have slept again after dropping her off and after calling her boss that morning, but he didn't. He set about making preparations for her arrival. The place was tidy, but he vacuumed the bedroom carpets and dusted anyway. He bought the new bedding, bought new softer luxury towels just for her then washed, dried and ironed them before rolling them up. He spent a couple of hours driving around Glasgow to find a florist that had a single sweet pea flower for sale. He relied on the research he'd already done for her birthday. It was more into Sweet Pea season, so it was a lot easier than before and he found one in East Kilbride. He still spent so much more on petrol and parking than the cost of the flower, but that wasn't the point. Everything had to be perfect.

'Charlie…I think it's time for bed.'

*NO!* he thought. That would break their embrace and he wondered when and if he'd ever get it back. Charlie thought that by the next night, she'd perhaps feel better and she'd not let it happen again. He tried not to feel too disappointed as he gently unfolded his arms from around her. He headed to the kitchen and she headed to the bathroom. The door clicked shut and she fumbled with the lock again. He took a bottle of water from the fridge, slid the chopping board out along the counter, selected the sweetest and juiciest looking apple from the fruit bowl and washed it. He unsheathed a large knife from the knife block and quickly cored and portioned the apple. He placed the pieces of apple in a small dish, covered it with cling film and placed a cocktail stick on the top so she didn't have to get her fingers sticky.

He made his way to the hall and checked that her bedroom door was still open and that it was unoccupied. He placed the water and slices of apple on the bedside table and turned the lamp on. As he left the room she was leaving the bathroom. 'There's some water there, and an apple if you happen to get hungry, but like I said, help yourself to everything and if you can't find something just give me a shout. I'm just next door if you need anything.' *Like, if you want to be held tight all night long.* She slid up to him and wrapped her arms around him. He pulled her in tight and when he tried to let her go she was still holding on for dear life. *This is nice,* he thought. *Maybe she just needs time. Maybe she's coming round.*

'Thanks for everything Charlie, I'm so glad I've got you.'

# Chapter Fourteen

Thunder rumbled and lightning struck throughout the night. He tossed and turned. Whenever it was stormy, the bangs and flashes would infiltrate his sub-conscience as he slept. It would bring the anxiety and stresses he had gone through during combat to the forefront of his mind. He spent a lot of energy burying those things deep inside himself. Now they were like an oil slick on the ocean; unsightly, harmful and hard to get rid of. Thunder boomed like explosions. Lightning flashed outside his window like pyrotechnics. BOOM!! BANG!! He woke up in a panic and shot straight up in bed. Sweat poured from his brow and his jaw was sore from the grinding of his teeth. His head hurt and his mouth was dryer than the desert that he so often operated in.

As the weather relentlessly pounded the air outside, he got up out of bed and made his way through to the kitchen. *A whisky will do it. She's asleep so she won't need to go anywhere until the morning.* His bedroom was closer to the kitchen than hers so he didn't need to go past where she was sleeping, but still remained quiet so as not to disturb her. When he got to the living area, he heard a soft puffing noise. Looking around he saw her sitting in the dark. She lit up with each crack of lightning, strobing on her as she sat on the sofa sobbing. 'Nicola?' She was startled and wiped tears from her face.

'I'm sorry. I didn't mean to disturb you Charlie.'

'No, no…you didn't. I was just erm…getting a drink of water.' He approached her cautiously. 'What's wrong? Can't you sleep?' He thought about how exhausted she must have been and how much she liked sleep.

'I had a bad dream,' she confessed. 'I know it seems childish…'

'It's not.' He was hardly having a good sleep himself. 'Want to talk about it?'

She took a moment to regain her composure as he joined her on the sofa. 'It's a recurring dream I've been having lately, and I just hate it. It really scares me.'

She is locked in a cold dungeon. Heavy iron shackles fasten her wrists to chains that are set deep into a thick, cold stone wall that seemed to seep rancid water. It has three stone walls and she is chained at the back. Thick black iron bars that run from the ceiling to the floor make up the other wall. One small skylight lets a dribble of moonlight in, just enough to allow her to see her dank surroundings. A figure appears. He moves smoothly as if he doesn't need to take steps to walk. He glides along the bars until he reaches a gate in the centre. He looks left and right to check that no one else is near and that no one is watching. He is wearing a heavy hooded cloak and a hand appears from within. He grabs the bolt on the gate and the metal scrapes excruciatingly as he slides it open. The figure glances again left and right before pushing the gate open into the dungeon.

He glides in and stands just inside the gate. Water, cockroaches and rats scurry along the floor, away from this figure. He keeps his distance as he inspects her. After a long time, he comes slowly closer and a flash of metal appears from inside the cloak. He edges closer and she tries to make out his face. She can't see it. Either she is paralysed with fear or the hood on the cloak just conceals too much light, but she can never make out a face. The figure appears like a spirit come to take her to the next place. She thinks about what things he might do to her. Will she be tortured? Is the metal a knife? Will she be cut and left to bleed out in chains? He gets closer still. She is numb all over but tries to scream. She tries with all her might but her mouth is mute. Breath flees her body and the vacuum leaves a crushing feeling in her chest. The figure gently raises the flash of metal towards her…and at that point she always wakes up.

Charlie moved closer to her on the sofa to take both her hands in his. 'Nicola, please don't cry. You're safe here. It's just a bad dream. I'll never let anyone harm you. Listen to me, I'll never let anyone hurt you again. So long as there is breathe in my body.' She finally looked at him. 'That's my promise to you.' He wrapped his comforting arms around her and she hid her head in his chest. That was a place she was becoming very used to and as much as Charlie wished it was for more positive reasons, he was glad to be there for her.

The crying subsided a little and she made an observation. 'Charlie, why are you sweating?' He was always warm, but his skin was cold, moist and clammy.

'No reason. It doesn't matter.' She didn't believe him. She stayed hidden in his chest for a little bit longer before letting him go. With one gentle motion of his thumb, he swept the tears from her cheek. She was sure that she never made a sound when she snuck through to the living room, so how could she have woken him up?

'Why aren't you sleeping?' she asked.

He drove a battered old jeep along barren rocky roads on the trail of a target. In the jeep with him was his partner, Jason. He was a couple of years older than Charlie and was tall with dark black eyes set into deep sockets and hid massive strength in his slim body. He was orientating a map and giving Charlie directions. 'It's left here…well I think it is. This map is absolutely shite. It's like they got to the map-makers as well.' Charlie swung left and the road led up towards the mountains. The decrepit old jeep struggled to aspirate air into the engine and heaved its weary way up the track. It got narrower as they progressed and the road surface got increasingly worse. 'This is donkey country only, mate.' Charlie agreed but persevered. The suspension rattled and shook them both until their teeth chattered inside their bobbing heads. Rocks became projectiles under the tyres as they scrambled along. A thick trail of dust started to form behind them which they grew concerned about. 'I'm leaving a fucking massive trail,' Charlie said.

'Need to keep going man. Not far now.' Jason swapped the map over for a field book with their mission details on it. So far it had been used to provide a workable surface to read the map. 'So our man should be leaving soon because he's RV-ing with our new POI in two hours.'

Charlie pondered for a second. 'Have you got a decent sniping position for me?' Jason consulted the map again and perused the options. This was not how they usually did things. Jobs were not hastily flung together on the move and they were not covering all of their tracks. But the opportunity arose and they followed a lead out there and their mission orders were clear. It was always difficult knowing what information was trustworthy. What if it was a double-bluff? What if they were leading themselves into a trap? It was not for them to second-guess the source of the information however. An order was an order.

Sniping was the best option, but they didn't know the area and that could be very dangerous. They tried to minimise the cloud of dust behind them because they were concerned that they might be compromised. The target could just lock himself in the basement and never come out. The twenty heavily armed guys with him would be very tricky to pass – very tricky indeed. Charlie seeked some confirmation, 'Have we got green lights for anyone else?' He already knew the answer but wanted to check again anyway. Jason ran his finger quickly down the page.

'Nope. Only retaliation to effective enemy fire. Nil engagement.' Jason looked flustered as he took out the binoculars. He scanned the hillsides and valleys. He checked every crack in the landscape for threats and for sniping points.

'Shit. Can we manage this? We have to do it now though, otherwise he'll disappear for another six years. We have to do it,' Charlie said.

Jason agreed without putting down the binoculars. 'Wait. Stop the car. Turn around. That track we passed about half a mile back, we need to take that up this mountain.' He pointed and scrutinised the map once again. Charlie turned the car around and headed back for the track they passed. He envisaged meeting some trucks head on full of guys with AK's and RPG's, ready to blow them into the dust. They didn't come.

He took the road up the mountain and kept the speed down. Time was against them, but a dust cloud would be too obvious and they'd blow their cover immediately. They continued up the mountain whilst Jason had second thoughts about his decision. He checked the map, looked back up, used the binoculars and checked the map in sequence. 'Maybe I've fucked up mate.' Charlie slowed down even more and tried to look at the map whilst still moving. He had a quick look and tried to find places by eye. He followed his gut and continued up the mountain. He could tell where the house was and was determined not to let the chance slip through their fingers.

'Right there, look,' said Charlie. He turned the vehicle off the track and bounced the jeep slowly over the rough ground. The mountain rose up quickly and provided excellent cover. Some rock jutted out in line of sight of the house. They reversed the vehicle up and went to the back. Inside the tailgate was a plethora of weapons dependant on the purpose: one sniper rifle, two assault rifles, two pump action shotguns, two sub-machineguns, a couple of handguns and a taser. Another box held all the ammunition and some pyrotechnics. Jason grabbed an assault rifle and slung it around his back. The ammo was already in his tac-vest which he pulled on over his sweaty shirt. He swapped the car binoculars for bigger ones so he could spot for Charlie. Meanwhile Charlie pulled out a long-barrelled sniper rifle and one magazine of ammo from the other box. It was more than he'd need.

They advanced about a hundred yards up the ridge and made it out into a sniping position. Charlie deployed the bipod, resting the heavy barrel on it. He lay in the prone position, testing and adjusting his position.  Jason lay down next to him and adjusted his binoculars. 'Eight…scratch the last. Nine hundred… Black Mercedes, 7 o'clock, twenty metres, observe wind movement in the bush. Left-to-right.' Charlie listened intently and adjusted his sights. He started to control his breathing and heart rate, which were higher than usual given the hasty developments of the mission. Jason watched and gave Charlie more information as they waited in the sun. It roasted them where they lay and they were soon soaked in their own sweat. Dust and sand blew around them on their rocky outcrop and stuck to their moist skin and clothing.

The longer they lay there, the more concerned they became that someone could come from the opposite direction and spot the jeep.

They had no means to conceal it and left themselves completely vulnerable to attack from that side.

Two and a half hours passed before anyone came out of the house. 'Target confirmed.' Jason patted Charlie on the back to confirm before whispering down the binoculars, 'Present coming for you soon.'

Sand blew into Charlie's ears as he heard blood rushing through them. He started breathing slow and deep, blinking pre-emptively against the dust and sand whilst concentrating hard not to lose position or rhythm of the target. He took up the backlash of the trigger precisely, whilst a bead of sweat carved a zigzag through the sand that was stuck to his face. The target approached the car whilst gesturing to a heavily armed man on his left, giving him a slap on the back. 'Hold,' Jason muttered. He bowed his head laughing, clasping his hands and almost doubling over. 'Hold.' Sweat lubricated the connection between Charlie's finger and the hot metal of the trigger but he remained steadfast. The target brought his head back up. 'Send it.' Charlie snapped the trigger back committedly. 'Confirmed! Confirmed! Let's get the fuck out of here!'

They slid backwards into dead ground before leaping from the rocky outcrop. The bipod swung like a pendulum until Charlie could house it on the move. The jeep was already facing the right direction and Jason opened the boot to quickly stow his rifle. Charlie leant the muzzle of the sniper rifle on the tailgate as he unloaded it and made it safe. Jason took the sniper rifle from him and secured it in the boot as Charlie headed to start the jeep.

They made their way down the mountain steadily and cautiously. Jason kept a staunch watch through the binoculars, scanning all the roads that left the house. So far, so good. They made it down off the mountain and hit the normal dirt road that took them back towards the town. They made good progress but stayed on alert, they weren't out of the woods yet.

All of a sudden, a dust cloud rose in the rear-view mirror from around the previous corner. Charlie checked his mirrors and Jason looked over his shoulder. He floored the pedal and the old jeep whined its way along the road, gradually accelerating. There was no need to minimise their dust trail now. They had to operate in a 'standard' jeep to maintain their cover. This meant a soft-skinned vehicle, with normal specifications, other than the hidden upgrade of a weapons cache in the boot. The insurgent's vehicles drew closer as Charlie concentrated on the dirt road. Jason established what they were up against: 'Two vehicles. Both pick-ups, two or three men riding the bed in each. Automatic weapons.' Jason wanted to shout, *Get a move on Charlie!* but he knew it was all down to the old shitty jeep they were in. *This is bullshit, we've got an old 2.2 diesel and they've got petrol V6's.* They were both thinking this. Jason looked in the back of the jeep and tried to assess how easily he could retrieve the assault rifle and cursed himself for not bringing it into the cab with him, but that was protocol. Charlie could sense what Jason was thinking, 'Leave it, just put your seatbelt on we're going off-road.'

They were closing in on the town, but were still a few miles away. 'I've been on standing patrol here a couple of times,' Charlie pointed out a few fields with dirt tracks that intersected them. 'We're going to cross here, there are huge trenches in this field, I'm hoping we can lose them there.' Charlie took a breath. 'And I'm hoping I can remember where they all are.'

Charlie took a sharp left and went halfway down the field before a sharp right onto it. Bullets pinged the jeep and smashed the rear corner window. He sped across the field and the first pick-up truck cut the corner straight onto the field from the road. Suddenly the front end of the truck disappeared into the ground. The three men that were stood in the load-bed of the truck were propelled onto the field, each man folding in half as they landed painfully. 'YES CHARLIE!!' The second jeep followed Charlie's path exactly and continued to close. The rough field bumped Jason and Charlie violently up and down and they both prayed that the suspension, engine and wheels would hold up. Some rifles were fired from the second jeep but the rough ground meant they could not aim at a single thing.

The field ran out and Charlie took up the road again. Charlie had in mind an American checkpoint that he was aware of and he drove desperately to reach it. Jason unholstered his sidearm and took aim at the front of the truck. He shot through the rear screen of their vehicle and let the full clip go. He hoped to hit the radiator and immobilise them, pausing only to ride out the heavier bumps in the road so as not to cause a ricochet inside the jeep. A few rounds hit them again. He reloaded and turned round in the seat again to return fire before making a bad observation. 'THEY'VE GOT AN RPG! FUCK!' Charlie looked in the mirror and a smoky grey trail left the bed of the truck and travelled high into the air. He hit the brakes. The bounce of the road made the aim too high and the RPG flew over the jeep. Charlie floored it again as the RPG came to a devastating conclusion further up the road off to the right, leaving a big crater. 'They're only going to have one or two maximum in that truck,' Charlie said reassuringly.

A long left-hand bend led downhill which would allow the jeep to pick up some speed. The American checkpoint was along that road. The increase in speed was bound to affect the guys trying to shoot from behind too. Some more effective rifle fire sprayed the jeep. It was like firecrackers going off inside the cab. Charlie checked over his shoulder as they started to round the corner and they seemed to be loading another RPG. 'Get ready Jason! They've got another.' Jason gave no response and Charlie looked over. He was bleeding out in the seat next to him. His eyes were still open and he looked profoundly at Charlie. 'FUCK! JASON! YOU'LL BE ALRIGHT, JUST HOLD ON, WE'RE NEARLY THERE!!' Jason had a gunshot wound to the upper arm and one in the neck and blood gushed out rapidly into the jeep. The truck stopped in the road. More shots hit them and just then, another grey streak left the back of the insurgent's truck and headed straight towards them.

Time went in slow motion for Charlie. He knew the RPG would hit them, there was no dodging it on the road they were on. The ground had steep banks either side so if the jeep left the road, they'd roll ten times and be dead anyway. He tried to undo Jason's seatbelt and he was sure he shouted at him to get the fuck out. As the RPG approached, Charlie opened his door and jumped out. The RPG struck the ground under the rear axle, which tossed the jeep into the air like a toy. Somewhere in the throwing of the jeep and dirt and earth and sand, Charlie was flung clear of the vehicle and slid down the bank. He rolled and rolled before he could muster enough energy to spread-eagle himself and arrest his slide. He heard the jeep smash back down. Slowly and cautiously, he edged up the bank, pressing his whole body against the ground using his hands to pull himself along. He could feel the hot dusty earth scratching between his fingers. He waited. The truck drove slowly up to his jeep as he unholstered his sidearm. They sprayed it with rifle-fire and sped off before Charlie had a chance to initiate his solo snap ambush.

He hoped Jason had got out and was determined to find him. He noticed a sharp wet pain in his shoulder and realised he'd been shot. *A clean through and through*, he thought. The smell of diesel and melted rubber and hot metal filled the air as he continued advancing up the bank. He checked the road carefully and it was deserted. *Where the fuck did they go?* He expected that they'd want to drag the bodies out so they could parade around with them later, but maybe they had bigger fish to fry. Or maybe they just wanted to go and pick up their friends too.

He hauled himself up and limped towards the jeep which now lay on its roof. The rear axle had detached itself and lay about ten metres away. He tripped up over another piece of debris and fell flat on his face. He turned himself over and faced the hot sun that screamed down on him. It was only then that he noticed his leg was hit too.

Charlie mustered all the energy he could to get back up. The motivation to find Jason was his biggest driver. He was still in the jeep and it looked like Charlie *did* manage to remove Jason's seatbelt as he lay slumped in the front. He was a mess. Charlie crawled in and checked his pulse. Nothing. 'COME ON!!' He tried again. Nothing. 'COME ON!! FUCK!!' He looked at the shell of his friend, but didn't yet have time to grieve. He just needed to get him along to the checkpoint for a medivac and he'd be okay for sure. He pulled Jason's legs down and he lay on the inside of the jeep's roof. Charlie grabbed their field book before dragging Jason clear. He still couldn't feel the pain of his wounds yet so tried to lift him but his legs collapsed under them both.

He looked back along the way they came, suddenly remembering that he might still be in danger, but he wasn't. The truck was long gone. Charlie checked the other way. Beyond the crumbled jeep and less than a kilometre away, the American checkpoint shimmered over the hot dusty road like a mirage, except he knew that it actually existed. 'Fuck's sake!' Charlie shouted towards the checkpoint wondering why there was no scout vehicle to come and take a look at the huge explosion that just happened up the road from them. He thought about spraying a rifle into the air, but knew that might be a bad idea because he could just be picked off himself. He had to make it there.

Late afternoon at a military checkpoint and an injured man carrying a folder of some sort approached. He was covered in blood, had a heavy limp and had an assault rifle slung over his back. As he reached about three hundred metres from the checkpoint, three soldiers jumped in a Humvee and raced along the dusty track that led away from the town. It swung violently across the road, coming to an abrupt stop. Two soldiers got out and pointed their weapons at him. 'Halt!' shouted the first one, 'Waqf!' the second.

'Friendly! Friendly! Fuck's sake.' Charlie held his hands up and the two soldiers approached as he dropped to his knees involuntarily. The short walk from the jeep had been the longest of his life. After ascertaining that he was indeed a 'friendly', they piled Charlie into the

Humvee and took him back to the checkpoint. He was helped to an officer. 'Lieutenant, we've got an injured friendly combatant here, and one casualty,' he pointed, 'along the road.'

Nicola began to feel comforted and started to forget about her dream. She was concerned about Charlie. Something wasn't right and she had already been in the living room for a while, so there's no way she woke him up. She had always wanted to know more about his work but never knew how to bring it up. When they talked about it on her birthday, she was a little bit drunk and only wanted to find out about girls anyway.

'Did you ever have any close calls before? Like…when you could have been shot or something?' Charlie thought he had a lot of explaining to do, but wasn't sure exactly how much to tell her.

'You could say…' She waited. 'Well, I've been shot – a couple of times, and sort of…blown up and been in several car smashes.' Nicola was shocked.

'Oh my God…like, what…' she collected her thoughts. She'd already seen some scars on his arms but wanted to know more. 'Do you have scars?' she tentatively asked. 'Sorry, I don't mean to pry, just ignore me.'

She didn't mean the retraction at all but he wasn't offended by the question. He started to feel like she maybe did feel something for

278

him and he really needed someone he could confide in. 'Yeah, I've got a nice gunshot wound through my left shoulder,' he tapped where the scar tissue was through his shirt, 'another on my leg, just a graze though,' he pushed a leg of his shorts up and showed her, 'and various shrapnel injuries and burns.' Nicola looked intently as if trying to summon x-ray vision to check his scar through the t-shirt. 'Do you want to see?' She nodded slowly. 'This one I got trying to flee some insurgents,' a heavy lump shot into his throat, 'I lost a very good friend that day. He died right next to me.'

'Oh Charlie, I'm so sorry.' Nicola could see the pain that thrived in him. He tugged at the neck of his t-shirt before realising there was no way she'd be able to see it without removing it. He began to lift his shirt as he sat next to her on the sofa. It snagged, so she helped him off with it. She took so much care as if the scars were still fresh wounds. He turned his body away from her displaying his back. A small entry wound tarnished his skin and she placed her thumb over it to compare the size. She thought of a way to speak sensitively, 'God, it's…it's not as bad as I was expecting.' She slid her thumb over the mark on his clammy skin a few times. 'How much did it hurt?' He turned his body towards her and her hand dragged along his shoulder line. She saw the exit wound. There was a haphazard pattern of scar tissue on the front of his shoulder. She gasped a little more than she would have liked when she finally saw it in the dim and flickering light of the storm. She touched it and traced the outline with her fingers. She wanted to feel the edges if she could – the boundary between old Charlie from school and this Charlie in front of her now.

'At the time I…I didn't feel it. But that's the adrenaline and the pressure of the situation. There was a lot going on and I had much bigger priorities to deal with.'

'Bigger than being shot?'

'Yes.' Her hand lingered on his chest and he could feel that electricity in it again. He could feel the tenderness of it. She could feel the beating of his poor heart.

'I don't believe there's anything more of a priority than being shot.'

'It's really hard to explain, but the decisions I made were the right ones at the time, or at least they seemed to be. It's not a job as such, it's…it's something else. But I wouldn't have done anything differently that day...' he looked away from her, 'except maybe pulling the trigger.'

'I just think it's stupid to maim yourself for life for nothing.'

'It wasn't for nothing, Nicola.' His tone was still calm, yet marginally defensive, 'Do you think that all the work I've done – it was all a waste?'

She was flustered because she realised she'd perhaps offended him, 'Charlie, I didn't mean it like that, it's just–'

'What about you?'

She looked at him, puzzled. 'What do you mean?' He reached gently for her hands, lifted them and upturned her wrists to display her scars. He really didn't want to put her on the spot in case he upset her, but he'd burned to talk about it for so long and he doubted he'd ever get a more appropriate opportunity again.

'What about these? Are these okay and mine not?'

She snapped her hands back. 'That's totally different!'

'I know it is, but please don't give me a hard time. Please don't say it's for nothing…I don't think it was, but…well…maybe I'm wrong.' Nicola presumed that all that time he never noticed the scars on her wrists, but it was only because he would never bring it up.

'No, it wasn't for nothing. I didn't mean it like that. I'm sorry.'

'And if you're mad about my scars, I'm mad about yours too.' His tone was soft as he lifted her hands again. She was reluctant, but let him. 'We've both got scars Nicola, but I'll never call you out on them. I noticed them the first time we met again, in the pub you pushed your sleeves up. I saw then and I knew something was up.'

She wanted to run. She didn't want to have that conversation with him. She'd avoided it so far over the months that they'd spent together because she never wanted to have to explain. What she didn't realise is that she didn't need to explain anything to him, he understood from the start. And as much as she wanted to run, something inside her locked her to that sofa in front of him. She didn't want to hide from him because he deserved more than that. 'You're ashamed, I can see it, but you shouldn't be.' He lifted her wrists to his lips and kissed them better. 'These are not your fault Nicola. And I'll never think any less of you because of them.' He had to bite his tongue to stop the, *I love you*, that was bursting to come out. He thought about telling her, he wanted to tell her, he burned inside to tell her.

'I really care for you, you know?' She nodded slowly. 'And I don't like to think about how badly you were treated that your best option was to slit your wrists. Not that I'm judging you. I understand.' He kissed them again because he felt he could still get away with it. 'You…you mean the world to me. I just wish I could undo everything he's ever done to you.'

Lightning continued to crack around them. The rumble of thunder resonated around the city streets and the rain kept pelting the windows. The River Clyde seemed to fizz as the rain drops lashed down and wind rippled across its surface. She let Charlie keep hold of her arms. Now that it was out in the open she felt so much relief. She thought so much of him to not bring it up even though he'd known for months. He wiped tears from her face and let his hand linger. 'You're an amazing person Charlie, you really are.' She closed her eyes and held his hand in place on her face for a while only to remove it to kiss the inside of it. She cracked a wry smile, 'I don't know how the fuck you're always right all the time. I don't know how you do it.'

'Well, when it comes to you, I want to make sure things are right from now on. I can't change your past any more than I can change mine.' He took a breath. 'But I can make things better for you from now on if you'll let me. I think you need me Nicola, and I need you. I need you so much.' He thought he'd overstepped that imaginary line in the sand he'd drawn for himself the previous evening.

'Charlie, I just…What I really…' She exhaled sharply. Her hands advanced onto his clammy skin. The lightning glanced off his body. It accentuated the fine honing on it that she'd found earlier in his arms. The sensation of her hands on his ribcage ignited him and suddenly all the clamminess burned away. She slid her arms around to his strong back and pulled him closer. Her head tilted discreetly, drawing him towards her. He could taste the sticky residue of apple on her lips. The kiss was even more perfect than the first one.

When the kiss stopped, somehow gravity didn't fall away this time. She didn't realise how much she wanted it too, or how she needed it even more. She felt her heartbeat race and forgot about all of her worries. Being with Charlie was like nothing else she'd ever experienced. The way he genuinely cared for her and would do anything to make her happy, filled her with an essence that was totally new and unknown. She sat back down on the sofa, shuffled side to side as she removed her underwear, leaving Charlie's t-shirt and gaze the only things on her. She'd been so comfortable in the t-shirt all night, feeling like an extended hug from him. It was freshly laundered but she could still pick out his scent from it. She stretched her leg over his lap and continued to kiss him. She pulled down his shorts without breaking the kiss and guided him in. The feeling was utterly instinctive.

He could feel her. Every bounding beat of her heart, every tremble, every quiver of her lips. Her tousled hair fell onto him tenderly touching his chest and shoulders. Their lips connected with synchronicity. Her body moved rhythmically, mimicking the throb of the rain on the windows. She pulled the t-shirt up to her neck so she could press her body against his. She needed the full body contact – as much skin to skin as she could get. She wanted as much of him as possible. His wearied but intrepid hands traced her illustrious contours. His chest rose and fell with hers. He could smell the scent of her recently shampooed hair. His eyes penetrated her, calling out to her to let go and let her heart be free, pleading for her to forever crave the tenderness she had with him in that moment. He reciprocated her motions but urged to slow it down. He wanted to take it slowly. He wanted to prolong it as much as he could.

There were no screams, no clichéd or vulgar remarks, only them, only purity. The kissing stopped for a moment but they kept deep captivating eye contact as their bodies shuddered with a release they'd needed for so long.

It was a tragic realisation of two lost souls in the world that for whatever reason found themselves together at that point in time and the universe. Lost perhaps, but lost together. He'd never felt so connected and close to anyone for years, whilst being terrified at the same time.

A hint of melancholy flashed through her eyes. *Was this a mistake too?* he thought. *Please don't say it, it'll destroy me. This was all your doing.*

Once her hips ceased motion she remained there on top of Charlie. She didn't feel she could move and knew her legs had gone to jelly. He let the back of the t-shirt fall down so she wouldn't get cold, but kept the front up as he cocooned her in his arms.

They both fell asleep on the sofa; physically, mentally and emotionally exhausted. Charlie woke up after a while and Nicola was still fast asleep with her head nestled into him. Her eyes twitched under her eyelids and he listened to her breathing deeply. He wondered where she might be or who she was dreaming of. Might it finally be him? He thought about just staying there and holding her, but he knew she was tired and deserved to go to bed and get some proper sleep. He leaned her back to pull the t-shirt down at the front. His shorts snagged at his ankles as he stood up with her in his arms, so he kicked them off before carrying her through to her room like a lost child.

The covers were still off the bed where she got up from her bad dream. The dish lay with the cling film peeled back and half the apple was gone. The cocktail stick stood perfectly vertical, stuck into a drying slice. When he placed her lovingly in bed, her hair fanned out onto the pillow and some in front of her face and he became completely aware that he was on top of her in bed. He swept the hair off her face and desire rose in him. Perhaps he could wake her and they could make love another time? What if he'd never have another chance, so why shouldn't he try for it again? Why should it always be at her say-so? They only kissed and now made love when *she* needed it and wanted it. *She* had all the control and he had none whatsoever. Should he perhaps at least just climb into bed next to her and they could sleep sweetly together? Or even just stay and hold her for a while? All the time he was there trying to figure out what to do, he was stroking her brow soothingly and placing kisses on it.

As her sleep deepened, he knew the right thing to do was let her be. He took a last intimate look at her before pulling the covers over. The t-shirt she wore had been used on exercise and around base. It had been in warzones and worn when Charlie was fresh from the theatre of combat. How it appeared on her couldn't be anything further from what it had seen before. He kissed her gently and silently on the lips and whispered that he loved her. He wasn't sure if he wanted her to hear it, but he just had to tell her somehow.

He wasn't ready to leave yet because he knew as soon as he vacated the room his loneliness would return and consume him. He retrieved and put his shorts back on before returning to guard her in the chair by the bed, ensuring nothing could touch her – including him.

Nicola woke up in an unfamiliar bed with a faint ache in her head. She sat up and looked around the room. Clean lined furniture sat on warm caramel carpets. The sweet pea flower on the bedside table reminded her she was at Charlie's.

She couldn't remember the last time she'd slept so deeply and so well. She felt the freedom of no underwear and the caress of Charlie's t-shirt around her. More importantly and more significantly, she felt a sense of peace and assurance that she hadn't felt for such a long time. After crawling out of bed, she rifled through her bag for a pair of pants and shorts, put them on and checked herself in the mirror. She didn't like what she saw but emerged from the room regardless. The flat was silent. No TV. No cooking. No music. No snoring. 'Charlie?' She slid along to his room. The door was wide open and the bed was already made. When she tiptoed through to the kitchen, her warm feet left misty outlines on the cool wood floor. A note lay on the kitchen counter:

*Hey,*

> *Just gone out to run a few errands. Be back about 12:30. There's croissants in the bread basket, if you want to heat them check the cooker for instructions. And you know where the fridge is – help yourself. Pots and pans are to the left of the cooker if you want to cook something. Call me if you need anything.*

She looked into the kitchen and as promised, two mini post-it notes were stuck to dials demonstrating exactly how to operate the oven. A final note was on an opaque black glass fronted drawer on the left of the cooker. *Pots and pans in here* ☺

She looked over to the sofa and remembered taking her underwear off there. *Oh God*, she thought. She placed Charlie's note down and walked across. They were still in the exact place that she discarded them. Had it been any other item of hers, it would have been returned to her by Charlie. Even any other piece of clothing would have been brought back to her, probably not until it had been washed, ironed and folded perfectly, of course. But Charlie didn't want to touch them. He couldn't.

He woke up in the bedside chair of his spare bedroom as soon as the first crack of sunlight fell onto his face. The previous night was like a dream to him. He had to convince himself that it happened, but then looking across to a deeply sleeping Goddess and the woman of his dreams, he realised it all did. His first thought was about how he'd probably outstayed his welcome. He somehow felt hastily estranged from her once more – emotionally banished by her impulsive fluctuations. He noiselessly crept out of the room and grudgingly went for a shower despite not wanting to ever wash Nicola from him.

He wrote a note, picked up his keys and left the flat. He thought about driving home to the East Coast. He craved the comfort of his old roads, the places he used to drive with friends, or with Rachel. He would drive and stop at various places to have lunch, drinks, walks and good times all along the coast. He wanted that again and he wanted it with Nicola. He wanted to just have someone who would be happy to be with him. It wasn't enough of Nicola to tell him all the time how perfect he was and how amazing he was. She never showed him by her actions and that hurt him the most. He enjoyed spending time with her more than he should have done, because it was always torture. It was always a guarded Nicola, she was never free. No matter how good Charlie was to her, she remained trapped in the past.

Despite craving the drive home, of course he put Nicola first so he stayed local just in case. He drove what seemed a hundred times round Glasgow on different roads. He loved the city, but after an hour of driving the buildings got a bit old. It wasn't home. There was no comfort there. It was a 'new chapter' of his life, but one that was not going like he'd hoped it would and it simply reminded him of that.

Most of all, he went out so that he could avoid Nicola for a couple of hours – for both their benefits. He wanted to swim in the bittersweet ecstasy of the previous night for a few hours longer before she brought him crashing back to earth with the inevitable rejection. He also wanted to give her a chance to get ready without feeling self-conscious and to give her a chance to retrieve her underwear from the living room. Therefore, he lied about the errands, but in the way he would only ever lie to her, to help protect her. He had nothing to do that morning.

## Chapter Fifteen


Charlie returned to the flat with shopping and a few things for her. She was already dressed and had made him some lunch for the time he got back. She knew if he said twelve-thirty, he'd be back at twelve-thirty. 'So Claire's going to come about half-six. She's planning to finish on time tonight.'

'Okay, cool. Shall I cook something?'

'Oh, yeah Charlie, that'd be great!' Nicola had been enjoying the lion's share of Charlie's cooking and there was nothing that she'd rather do for dinner than eat his food in his flat with him and Claire. He slipped off his boots and put them in the cupboard by the door before coming through to the kitchen. 'I've made you a sandwich. Salami, cheese and lettuce. And salad cream, not mayo, yeah?' Charlie was pleasantly surprised. It was nice that she was doing something for him and that she got it perfectly correct. She had toiled with herself all morning and the thought of sleeping with him again was completely out of the question, despite it being the best and most satisfying sex of her life.

Not that she could really place it, but with Patrice, she used to use sex as a weapon to pacify his aggression and make him be nice to her for a while, but with Charlie she didn't need to do that because he was perfect all the time, so how on earth would she be able to influence him? She felt that she just got carried away with the serious talk and with the break-in. She ached at that time for Charlie because it was the first and only time she'd seen him vulnerable. To her, it seemed like he'd momentarily fallen from his Godly pedestal to walk around with all the other humans who had troubles and worries and fears and issues.

'Did you get all your errands done?'

'Err...yeah.' He expected her to say that she would move back after what happened but she didn't. She was quite happy staying there with Charlie and had no intentions of leaving yet. It put him out of kilter and there was a sense of discomfort in him. The look in her eyes immediately after they finished making love told him everything he needed to know. He wished he'd had his eyes shut at that point so he'd have missed it, but he didn't. He could read her like a book and understood her completely. If he hadn't seen that, he could have fooled himself into thinking this new approach of hers was because she wanted it to work between them, but he knew it was merely to make it up to him for leading him on.

They sat together and watched television in the afternoon. Charlie felt like he wanted to leave the flat again. He asked if she wanted to go out and do something but she didn't, she just wanted to stay in with him. He loved the place but it still felt very temporary, like staying in a nice hotel. With her there it started to get more of a homely feel, but as her essence started to penetrate the walls and all around the rooms, he felt more like he was *her* guest. The spot on the sofa where they made love stood there like some kind of hallowed ground or shrine for him and he had to forever revere it because it would be the closest he'd ever get to her.

Nicola let Claire into the flat and met her at the lift. 'Nic Nac! How are you now?'

'Oh, I'm okay.' She averted her gaze just for a split second and Claire knew that was a sign she was up to something. 'We've made lasagne, I hope you're hungry!'

She led Claire into the flat, through to where Charlie was sitting. 'Look what the cat dragged in!'

Claire took a seat on the sofa next to Charlie as he opened a bottle of wine and Nicola put the garlic bread in the oven. The post-it notes were left on, so she knew exactly how to operate it. Claire spoke to Charlie as she tinkered in the kitchen.

'How's it going Charlie, how's she been today? Has she said if he's been in touch at all?'

'No, she didn't mention. But I sort of don't think she would have said anything to me anyway, she never really tells me about him.' They still didn't know for sure whether it was Patrice that tried to break in or not.

Nicola came over with three empty wine glasses. 'The garlic bread will be about twelve minutes. Should be enough time a glass first!'

She'd been upbeat and cheery all day and Charlie couldn't align with it. That was part of the reason he started to feel alienated in his own flat. She seemed to be more relaxed and at ease with everything, as if she just worked in that place. He thought he should just go back to his old work and leave her to live there and maybe she could live the life that he wasn't.

She took a sip of wine before slipping off to the toilet. 'It looks like she's set up in here, eh Charlie?' He took a second to reply and his tone was heavy and weary.

'Yeah.'

Claire could sense that something was amiss. When Charlie called her the day before to tell her what had happened and formulate the plan, it made perfect sense for Nicola to go and stay over for a while. But Claire knew there was a chemistry between them. Nicola always seemed so excited when they talked of him and Claire knew her well enough to tell that when they were all together, she was much closer to Charlie than she was to any other male friends. But unlike other men Nicola had dated and particularly Patrice, she didn't feel like Charlie would ever come between them because he was the one that was seemingly trying to involve Claire more in what Nicola was doing. Ultimately, she was used to playing second fiddle at times if Nicola had some new thing to play with, but she also knew that she was the one constant in her life so would never worry. She supposed Charlie would be delighted to have Nicola there. It was a perfect excuse for him to have her close and spend more time with her, so she wondered why he seemed sullen.

'Is...everything okay?' she asked.

'What do you mean?'

'Between you and Nic?'

He knew she was on to him but didn't know what to say. 'Yeah, everything's...well...it's same as usual.'

After dinner everybody was stuffed and satisfied and Nicola got up to clear the plates. 'Right, I'll just do the dishes, you two relax.'

'It's alright, Nicola. I'll get them later.'

'No, I may as well do them now and then they're done.' Charlie watched her as she took over the place and filled the kitchen again with her graceful motion. His eyes tracked her longingly and distressfully and Claire saw it all.

'Charlie?' He looked at Claire. 'What's going on?' Nicola stood with her back to them in the kitchen. She ran water and clattered dishes and cutlery about. The television was still on which provided enough background noise to enable a private conversation. She was only in eyeshot, not earshot.

Nicola shouted from the kitchen, 'Charlie do you want another drink?'

'Erm...I'll get a whisky. In a while though, I'll wait till you're done. And I'll make you two something as well.'

'Oh, please, your French Martinis!'

She returned to the dishes. Claire's expectant looked pierced Charlie and he wanted to tell her, but barely had the words to explain it to himself, let alone Claire. 'Well...something happened last night. But...she's not mentioned it since, and I feel I can't mention it.' His eyes returned to Nicola whilst he still spoke to Claire. 'Suddenly she's doing all this and helping out around the place and I can't figure it out. She says that she doesn't want to be with anyone right now, so I have to respect that. I just want her to be happy. I want her to have what she wants.'

'Charlie, half the time, she doesn't know what she wants.' His eyes returned to her. 'So did you kiss?'

'More.'

The look in Charlie's eyes told her exactly how much more. Claire wanted to fix it so that Charlie could be happy and Nicola could finally be with someone who could treat her so well. 'And what about what *you* want?' she asked.

'It doesn't matter what I want.'

'Of course it does.'

'But if I want to be with her and she doesn't want to be with anyone, then there's no chance, so…whether or not I have feelings for her is inconsequential.'

'Well, that's a shit way to look at it.'

'It might be. Well, it is, but it's the only way I can look at it.' He finished the last of his wine. 'But, I care for her very much and I've been helping her out a lot…and if I can just keep doing that, then that'll

297

have to do. Until she's in a place where she can be with someone again, I can wait for her…' he shrugged. 'What else can I do?'

Claire knew historically about Nicola's impulsiveness and feared that if there wouldn't be anything more happen soon then she'd be on to the next thing without looking back. Charlie was prepared to wait for her, but was unaware that he potentially had an expiry which may well have been fast approaching. Claire hoped she was wrong so didn't admit it to him, because after all, Charlie was not like any other man they'd ever known. But she wanted to sort it out before one or more of the most important people in her life got seriously hurt. She had to know exactly what was at stake too. 'Do you love her?'

'Yes. With every fibre of my being.'


'I was thinking about going home for a bit.' Nicola tucked her hair behind her ear as she kicked her shoes off after work. 'I've got some time off and I'm just going to go home and recharge.' She used to always complain about how much her parents would do her head in, so how could she be going there to recharge? Charlie thought. She quickly added a qualifier: 'Not that I haven't been doing that here, but you know…'

'That's alright, you don't need to explain yourself, you can do what you like.' He hated having to say that because he felt that would be the start of the end of their false 'home' thing they'd been playing. But whether it was false or not, they'd certainly been cohabiting his place and he'd treasured every moment.

He knew exactly what she was going to say next, 'And when I come back I think I'll move back to mine.' She avoided eye contact with him when she said it. 'But I just really want to thank you for letting me stay, but everything's okay now. I think it's time to get back to normal.' *Just let this be your normal*, he thought.

Nicola had already spent over two weeks at Charlie's and Claire had been trying to monitor things closely. She had to be very careful when talking to Nicola about it. They met as usual and she'd try to ascertain how things were developing and wanted to point out how perfect a match Charlie was for her whilst knowing only too well that if she was pushed towards something it would always act as a detractor. Nicola would have to come to the conclusion by herself. That didn't just apply for Charlie, it applied for everything. 'So how are things with him? How has it been living at his?'

'Yeah, good. It's such a nice place he's got. I love sitting outside if it's a nice morning. He's usually up early and made coffee by the time I'm up for work and I'll go and sit with him for a bit.'

'And..?'

'And what..?'

'Nothing.'

'Sometimes I get him to make me one of his bagels, or he'll make me something else. But he's always got plenty of stuff in. It's great to have a good choice, there's always something I want. I'm in the habit of breakfast now.'

It had all been part of Charlie's protective plan, brewing coffee early in the morning to gently lull her into the day, rather than waking up to the shrill shriek of her alarm clock. It also played to his fantasy. The first couple of mornings he'd hear her alarm through the wall and be reminded of how she slept in the other room. By getting up and making coffee and breakfast, she'd meander through in his Commando's t-shirt and a pair of shorts or joggers and her grubby white ankle socks to come and sit with him. It was easier that way to make believe that she'd crawled out of *his* bed, or *their* bed. A freshly risen Nicola was a sight that he adored. For some reason she felt comfortable letting him see her that way. She always felt at total ease around him. She could truly be herself and she didn't feel he judged her on how she looked, or what she said for that matter.

Nicola's admission about developing a habit for breakfast was not the kind of revelation that Claire was looking for. 'Has err…anything happened...?' Claire finally pried.

'Like what?'

'Like…you know…I mean, do you not fancy him a bit? I know you liked him at school.' Nicola caught an image of his body under hers and pushed it from her mind.

'No. We're just friends.'

'So, you mean you've been staying there for a couple weeks and nothing's happened at all?'

'No. Nothing. I don't think he's interested in me that way anyway. He's just a really nice guy. Like…a genuine guy.'

'Well…has he been out much? Is he dating or anything?'

'What is that supposed to mean? I don't even know what you're talking about just now.' Nicola's phone beeped and lit up with a message. She snatched it quickly from the table so Claire couldn't see and forgot all about the line of questioning, so dropped her defensive tone. 'Sorry, I just need to answer this.' Claire watched as Nicola replied with a mischievous and eager look across her face. She stifled giggles as she replied. 'So, yeah. It's been good staying at his, but I think I'm ready to go back to mine now.'

'And did you decide about home? I still think it's nuts you've got holidays to take already.'

'Yeah, I'll go home for a bit, maybe catch a few people and then move back to my own place when I come back.'

By no accident or coincidence, Charlie also went home when Nicola did and his parents were very excited at the prospect. He talked with them, but not really to any depth. Regarding his sister, they always knew every uncomfortable detail, yet Charlie remained a mystery. He was never shy to show them affection and would help them financially, but in terms of his personal life, he had gotten into the habit of not revealing much and it proved to be a hard habit to break. His parents wanted to hear more about what he was doing and who he was doing it with, but he was so measured that he'd only reveal something if it was of some consequence, or if it might have some impact on their lives. They were sure he was dating or something, but he hadn't introduced or even talked about a girl to them for such a long time. As much as Nicola meant to him, he'd never mentioned her yet. They were not together anyway and now that she was moving back to her flat, he felt like he was going backwards with her.

She sent him a text: "Hey, how's your weekend going? I forgot how quiet it is out here, there's totally nothing happening!"

"Yeah, but then that's perfect if you want to recharge! XX"

"I know, but I want to go out and meet my friends. It's really hard with the bus service here. Or the lack of buses! I'm supposed to be going out tonight, I was thinking of driving, but I'd like to have a drink. I should have just stayed in Glasgow!"

*Yes, you should have*, he thought, *at my place*. "Where you off to tonight? I could drive you? X"

"Just Edinburgh. No you don't have to. You're always driving me. I don't want to be a burden. I'll figure something out. ☺"

"It's up to you, but it's no hassle. Just let me know what you decide. ☺"



He stayed home and helped to cook the dinner. 'So, you staying here tonight, son?'

'Yeah, I've nothing on in Glasgow, so I'll stay over.' His dad had plans for a whisky night and started to go through the bottles in the cupboard eagerly. He pulled them out as his mum chopped some vegetables and Charlie had to try and find the words to tell him that he'd not be able to participate. 'I've erm…I might be meeting someone later though, so I better not drink.'

His dad was disappointed, but wanted to know more. 'Who you meeting?'

'Well, I might not meet her…just depends what she's up to.' The *her* was mildly incendiary and his parents waited, so Charlie

303

obliged. 'It's a girl that I know from school. We've just sort of met up again. She's in Glasgow just now as well.' That was the first detail he'd given about his love life to his parents since he was going out with Rachel and they felt it was reasonably momentous. They wanted him to be happy and to be able to share his accomplishments and his worries with someone. They knew the young boy that aged seemingly ten years after every tour and they could tell he was hiding the memory of some dark experiences.

He'd always been a caring and affectionate boy and as he grew up they knew he just wanted to care for people. They also knew how much having someone close to him helped him. When he was with Rachel they could appreciate how he went through a lot because of work, but they knew that with her, his soul was never occluded and he never carried those things into his heart because she filled it up and had the power to displace all the heinous things and travesties of humanity he was often witness to.

His mother became excited. 'Who is she?' Charlie knew he'd opened a can of worms, but he didn't do it lightly, his parents needed it too.

'Her name's Nicola.' His answer was quite closed and his parents could tell that was as much as he was comfortable revealing at that time. They didn't want to push him and they were happy with that – it was a start. His dad returned the bottles back to their slumbering place to be savoured another day and hoped they could talk more about this *Nicola* then too.

"Hey, how's your transport plans coming along? X" As much as he wanted to have a whisky with his dad, Charlie decided to remain available, just in case. As he sat with his parents however, he couldn't stand not being in her company. During the two preceding weeks, they'd sit together in his flat and watch her programs on the television, but they'd do it together.

"Hey! I'm really struggling for buses, in that there are none. I could get my mum to drive me, but she doesn't like driving at night anymore."

"Well we can't have your mum driving at night if she doesn't like to. I'll give you a lift."

Nicola thought very hard about it. She wasn't sure if she wanted Charlie to come along with her that night, but on the other hand it would make it so convenient. It's not like he'd find out what she was really doing. Plus, he'd be there to keep her safe and he'd be able to drive her home if it all went wrong. She somehow wanted him to be close after the suggestion. "Okay, but I'm just going to meet some friends. It's all girls, so I'm sorry, no boys allowed!"

"That's alright, I wasn't trying to wangle an invite! ;) I've got quite the social calendar anyway. I'm watching a crappy movie with the parents right now. Haha. :P"

"Haha, well if you can tear yourself away, then you can give me a lift just to Elm Row? Xx" She supposed that was a good place to get dropped off. It wasn't her place of rendezvous, but it was close to where she was picked up before and he knew a couple of her friends lived in that area, so it made perfect sense.

Charlie dropped her off and she walked into town to meet a guy that she found online. They'd been talking for a few days and it was just a few drinks then *see where it goes but hopefully back to his* sort of thing. He was an accountant at the Gyle and was a couple of years older than her. When they met, he was immediately showing her photos of his car and his flat as if he was the best thing ever. Charlie's car and flat were much nicer and newer and she only knew about the car when he picked her up from the gym that time. He also didn't mention his flat at all until she brought it up and after living there for more than two weeks, she almost couldn't understand it. She loved it so much that she had to stop herself from blurting out things about it at work. She didn't want to enter a conversation about why she was staying at her 'friend's' place instead of hers.

During drinks, Nicola's new friend talked about sex and was vulgar. She didn't respond positively, but then she didn't respond negatively either. He was fairly attractive but perhaps a little overweight. That didn't really bother her too much, but he was rude to the bar staff and felt like he had some kind of entitlement.

'More drinks here, a bit quicker this time, thanks.'

'Why do you talk like that?'

'Like what?'

'Is it not a bit rude?'

'I don't think so. I said 'thanks', didn't I?' He raised his eyebrows at her in an almightily patronising way. 'The thing is, there's an order. You see, I've got quite a stressful job, so I'm allowed to blow off a bit of steam once in a while. If these people were capable of doing better then they'd do it. They'd be in a job like mine, but they can't, so they aren't.' There was almost a partial logic to it, *almost*, she thought, but she didn't like any time he opened his mouth. It occurred to Nicola though, that if there really was a direct correlation between the stress of your job and how you treated people, then why was Charlie not absolutely obnoxious to everyone all the time?

He made a big deal about getting the bill and made sure everyone knew that he'd paid for both of their drinks for the evening and left a miserly tip.

They took a taxi back to his place.

Afterwards, Nicola pulled on her clothes as he fell asleep triumphantly. She sneaked through to the toilet to call Charlie. 'Hey, are you still up? Well, obviously you're still up.'

'Yeah, how's it going?'

'I was going to get a taxi home, but none of the drivers will take me all the way out there.' That had legitimately happened to her several times before, but she hadn't even tried that evening. She just wanted to get the fuck out of there as soon as possible and didn't want to bump into anyone on the street or any of the guys neighbours. She was repulsed by the man sleeping bollock naked on the bed she just snuck out of and she certainly didn't want to be associated with him. He truly was a piece of shit, but still, Nicola went through with it. Since she'd gone to all the trouble of meeting him it'd be another failed plan of hers if she bailed out.

'Sure, I'll come get you, where are you?'

Nicola thought about how far she was from Elm Row, there was no way she could manage to walk there. She could get a taxi, or she could just say they went to a different place across town, which was quite a normal thing. 'Erm, I'm in Dalry at my friend's flat. I could meet you at the Haymarket?'

'Yeah, sure, I'll be about half an hour.'

Charlie rose and got dressed. His dad woke up at the stirring because he often didn't sleep so deeply. The unintentional naps he had during the day and the weakening of his bladder with age were a big contributor to that. He came along the hall towards the toilet in his vest and pants to see Charlie fully clothed. 'What's going on now?'

'Oh, I'm just going to pick her up. She's been out with some friends. She can't get a taxi, so…'

'Oh, alright…erm, you coming back?'

'Yeah, I'll just go get her and I'll be back after I drop her home.'

Nicola gazed out of the open passenger window as they drove home. Charlie usually always drove with it open when he was in the car by himself. He liked to feel the fresh air. He particularly liked the Scottish air. He'd been in so many places that had sandy or smoggy atmospheres that he really appreciated the clean air when he was home. Whenever Nicola was in the car however, he would close it because she'd get too cold, but this time *she* opened the window.

It was a warm summer night, so he assumed she was feeling warm from dancing or drinking, but she wanted the clean and fresh air to cleanse her of the disgusting act she went through with for no reason.

She thought she'd feel better, just a bit of a 'release', but she felt worse – regardless of the fact she was nowhere close to finishing with that guy. At least she managed to sneak out without disturbing her new friend. She put that down to a bad choice and thought if she could have gone back she'd have just left him at the bar. Hindsight was a wonderful thing. *The next one will be better*, she thought.

'Everything okay?' Nicola's absence had not gone unnoticed by Charlie. She was so glad that he was home and close, so he could collect her like usual.

'Yeah, everything's alright.'

Charlie could sense something, but didn't want to push her. She couldn't even bring herself to look at him, so he gave her a get-out card just to alleviate the tension that filled the car. 'You a bit drunk?'

'Yeah.'

Charlie reached down into his door pocket as he drove and produced a small bottle of water which he handed to her. Some of her hair flicked out of the window and some swirled suspended in the car like a gathering of angry serpents and she didn't seem to want to tie it back or close the window at all. The temperature outside was still mild, but the car was starting to cool by the action of the passing air. She felt so cold but persevered, there was no way she was going to shut the window. Charlie turned up the heat anyway.

Despite suggesting that they meet for lunch or coffee or a drive or a walk, they hardly met at all when they were home. Charlie was used to her messages in the morning or late at night wishing him 'sweet dreams' or to 'sleep tight.' Those types of messages stopped when she stayed at his because she could say it in person, but now their absence felt like a great rift in him. She hardly spoke to him anymore and she'd only text if she had 'plans' of an evening. She wouldn't message because she missed him or craved his attention in some way, only because she needed to put in place an escape plan for her nights of wanton shamefulness.

He hadn't been back to Glasgow much since she went back home, which pleased his parents. He did check on the flat one day on the way back from Ayrshire and it felt terrible being back without her. The sense of her was leaving the place. They met just the one time for coffee but she was very guarded around him. She was not as warm as she used to be and he could feel her slipping away not just from the flat, but from him, and he didn't know what he could do to get her back again. Perhaps it was all just a bit overwhelming staying together and playing house. Maybe she just needed some space and time to come round, he thought – ever hopeful as he was.

"I'm going out again tonight and I was wondering if I could get a lift? So long as you're not busy. X"

Recollections of conversations he'd had endless times flashed through his mind: *'Don't be so easily available,' 'play a bit hard to get,' 'don't just go running when she calls.'* All sound advice from friends, colleagues, strangers, and of course he would ignore them all. *But she needs me and with her is the only place I want to be.* "Yeah, sure…Who's all out tonight then?" Nicola had been careless and didn't think far enough ahead. Those kinds of rendezvous had become so common for her that she would no longer give them a second thought.

She had to come up with an excuse, she couldn't just say a 'friend' again, that was always such a cop out and she didn't want Charlie to get suspicious. "Claire's coming through with a few girls."

Each time he'd picked her up to 'meet friends' she had more make-up on and dressed more provocatively whilst being more aloof with Charlie. 'Okay, well, have a good time. Say hi to Claire for me.'

'Yeah I will. And I'll get you back here about one, yeah?'

'Yeah, see you then.'

The car glided away along George Street in Edinburgh and he turned left at St Andrew's Square. He didn't head home. He felt uneasy, so went for a drive instead. He drove the country roads down to the borders. It was quiet that night and he pushed the car a little. The rubber of the tyres interfaced well with the warm road surface and the car sped round the corners as they fell hard and fast one after the other. Charlie's eyes narrowed as his brain processed the road surface and conditions as well as taking in all the information necessary to keep his drive safe. He watched for other cars and police cars, but there was no one around. He optimised his road position with each bend and hurled the car around each one with expert execution. He slowed down for towns and he passed a lot of them. Random places that he was vaguely familiar with lay dormant. No one stirred, except for the occasional taxi or person double parked as they ran in for a fish supper.

The roads led him all the way back to Edinburgh in the end. He turned around at a wide t-junction to a scheme of new houses on the edge of one of the towns. He arrived at her pick-up point just before one o'clock and waited patiently. One o'clock came and went. He did think it was an early pick up considering the clubs were usually open until three, but that's the time she said. At half past one he sent a text: "Hey, I'm just here whenever you're ready." Quarter to two and he decided to phone.

Nicola lay asleep in a stranger's bed. He was a nice guy and she'd enjoyed her night with him, but it was not her intention to fall asleep, however. She was awoken by her phone. It buzzed and flashed in the dark of the room. The band of light shone up out of her handbag and she woke abruptly. She realised she'd fallen asleep and knew Charlie would be waiting for her. She missed the call and he tried again whilst she ran as silently as she could through to the hall. 'Hey, Charlie.'

'Hi, where are you?'

'Oh, I'm er…already home. Did you not get my text?' She had to make something up on the spot.

'No…'

'Oh, I'm sorry. I just got the train home, I wasn't feeling very well so I just went home early. You're not waiting for me are you?'

'Well, I am actually.'

'Oh, I'm so sorry.'

'What train did you get?'

'Erm, it was an early one, and then I just got my mum to pick me up from the station, I didn't want to bother you.'

'Oh, okay.'

'I better go, I don't want to wake my parents.'

'Alright, well, I'll speak to you later then?'

She hung up the phone without replying, crept back into the bedroom and back into bed with the guy. She didn't want Charlie to see her or pick her up after that one and she thought the guy was alright so didn't want to run out like she had with all the others. *That's what sluts do*, she thought.

Charlie was left stranded in the middle of Edinburgh. His whole evening had been dedicated to her safe and timely delivery to and from town and it had been spoiled. He didn't get to drive her home and he knew something was wrong. He sat in the car for a while before growing concerned about her. What if something had happened that caused her to go home early? What if it was something else?

Despite his suspicions, he always tried to give her the benefit of the doubt because he believed she would never really lie to him. He decided to call Claire to find out what happened and check what her plans were for getting home. He knew Claire still had a lot of friends in Edinburgh and supposed she would be crashing at someone's place. The phone rang and rang. Eventually she picked up and he could hear music in the background, so presumed she was still out. 'Hey, Charlie. Is everything okay?' Claire was concerned as to what would warrant a call from him at such an early hour. She knew he'd stayed at home to be close to Nicola.

'Hey. Is Nicola alright?' he asked. 'What happened to her tonight?'

'What do you mean…?' Claire thought on and very quickly realised what Nicola had been up to and where she would have been. 'You're not still driving her about, are you?'

'Yeah, but not tonight. Well, I dropped her off earlier. She said she went home early though and I was just wanting to check if everything was alright? She said she wasn't feeling well?'

Claire knew he was given duff information, or at least led to believe something other than what Nicola was up to. Claire was out, but with her workmates in Glasgow. She thought about covering for Nicola, but respected Charlie too much to lie to him. She didn't want to break it to him over the phone, or be the bearer of such bad news at all, but she also didn't want him to be driving her around to sleep with other men when she knew how he felt about her.

'Charlie, I'm out in Glasgow, I wasn't with Nicola tonight.'

'Oh…'

'Listen, do you want to just come through and we'll go out?'

She didn't appreciate what time it was. 'It's way too late Claire, by the time I get through everywhere will be shut.' She really wanted him to come through so she could convince him to stop driving Nicola around for her debaucherous activities. She also really didn't want him to be alone, because if he hadn't already figured it out, he would soon.

316

'Charlie, just come through, there's a few of us here, we'll do something. Anyway, I'm going to need a lift home.' Claire knew exactly how to pander to Charlie's protective nature.

'Okay, I'm on my way.'

When he came off the M8, he had to dodge the revellers that lost all sense of the green cross code as he made his way along the busy road at kicking out time. He found a space along Sauchiehall Street and pulled into it. After a while, Claire appeared with a few friends. She was with two girls and one guy that she worked with. They were talking rubbish as drunk people do, but Claire didn't seem so drunk. 'Who is this hunk?' one of her friends asked.

'Everyone, this is my good friend Charlie. Charlie, this is Amelia, Jenny and Richard.'

'And where the fuck have you been hiding him?' Claire's friend Jenny approached him with a wide smile. She was beautiful and Charlie caught her eye immediately. 'Is this your car?'

'Yeah.'

'Are you a drug dealer?' Claire rolled her eyes and Charlie chuckled.

'No, I'm not a drug dealer.'

317

'That's a shame, because I'm up for partying tonight.'

'Well, I'm very sorry to disappoint you…'

'Who says I'm disappointed…?' She pawed at Charlie and continued drunken small talk with him. She wore a short flowery green dress and had swooping golden hair. Charlie felt a little disenchanted at her advances because he was upset about Nicola. He had figured it out. He perhaps figured it out after the first time; the way she hung her head out the window, the despondent look on her face and the way she evaded him. Still, he wanted to drive her because he wanted to look after her. He wanted to be there in case the guy was a total creep and she could come running to him and then she'd realise that Charlie was the right man for her. But that night she'd crossed the line.

They started to say their goodbyes to some other revellers, which took a long time because of the alcohol. Jenny hung around Charlie and leaned on him a lot. He liked the way she smelled and it was nice to have someone who was seemingly interested and who was upfront about it. He tried to get Nicola out of his mind and his eyes fell upon Jenny as a potential diversion. She was drunk, but she seemed quite fun and her smile was nice. Charlie whispered to Claire, 'I've got loads of booze at the flat, if you still want to drink some more.' She pictured him going home alone as the alternative and didn't much fancy it.

'Okay, party at Charlie's everyone!' She counted the people with her and checked the car to make sure everyone would fit. 'Right, get in!' Jenny ran to the front seat to be next to Charlie, despite him expecting that to be Claire's seat.

'Fucking hell, this is such a nice car! Oh my God!'

When they got back to the flat they filled it with noise and a bit of life. Charlie put some music on at a reasonable level and got some drinks out. He slid the glass door open to the terrace and Jenny and Amelia ran through it so they could dance outside. 'Just please, stay away from the edge.' It would take a considerable effort to fall accidentally from the terrace, but he didn't know them and Jenny at least seemed quite unpredictable. Charlie felt very much on the back foot and there was no way he'd be able to catch up to their blood-alcohol levels.

'So, what happened tonight then, Charlie?'

'Well, I'm not sure. She said she sent me a text to say she was heading home, but...I don't know, I just don't believe her. But I hope she's alright.' He imagined her lying in the arms of some stranger who didn't know her and it tore him up – someone who didn't know what she liked to eat, what her favourite drink was and how to make it exactly to her liking, or what kind of music or movies or anything she liked. *How could she?* he thought.

'I don't think you should be driving her about anymore. She's a big girl, she can manage herself.' She wished she hadn't worded it like that because it made it sound like she was going to keep on sleeping with strangers and that she'd now do it without involving him. As bad as it was to be driving her around to do it, it somehow seemed even worse to him that she might do it without his knowledge at all. But he simply couldn't do it anymore.

'I won't.'

Jenny came back in after her rooftop dancing. 'Fucking hell, this place is great…erm,' she had to rack her memory hard, '…Charlie.'

She took a sip from her glass and spilled it as she put it back down on the dining table. She came in close to him. 'So do you have a girlfriend?'

'Well, no…but,' he wondered how to word it with Claire in earshot until he realised it wouldn't make any difference if she was there or not, 'there is someone who I love very much.'

'Well, where the fuck is she tonight? And is she okay with you having hot drunk girls in your flat when she's not around??' She tugged at Charlie's t-shirt and stretched it out of shape. *Good questions*, he thought. He headed to the kitchen and poured himself a large whisky and downed it fast. The amber liquid warmed him up from the inside and he felt a throb from within. It may or may not have been the whisky, he wasn't sure. 'Well, she's a lucky fucker!' Jenny continued. Claire could tell that he was growing weary of Jenny's relentless and shameless advances.

'Jenny, come and pick some music.' He was glad to take a breather from her until Nicola pounded in his head again.

'Can I get you another drink, Claire?'

'No, I'm alright, thanks. I think I'll need to go home soon. I'm pretty beat.'

'Well, you can all crash here. The spare beds made up, you can kip in there, unless Jenny beats you to it!'

Claire laughed. 'No, I think she's got plans for the other bed, to be honest.' Claire gestured towards Charlie's bedroom.

'I don't think so.'

'Why not, Charlie?' He looked over at her as she browsed Charlie's iPod. She was leaned over at the computer desk and her backside wiggled as she flicked through tunes. It was certainly a lovely backside, Charlie thought. 'Okay, she's a bit drunk tonight and maybe not given you a great impression but she's a nice girl.' Charlie was surprised at Claire's endorsement of Jenny but the truth was, she wanted Charlie to have some enjoyment and not just dedicate himself to Nicola, especially not when she was behaving like that.

'I'm sure she is. Well, yeah, she's gorgeous, if not a little erm…forward?'

'Sometimes it's good to have someone who's straightforward with you though, Charlie.'

They listened to some more music and it wasn't long before people started to fall asleep. Richard was the first. He was already too drunk and tired when he arrived so just sat quietly at the dining room table the whole time, enjoying the cool breeze from the terrace, sipping water and holding his head in his hands. Amelia then fell asleep on the couch and was soon followed by Jenny. Charlie covered them with blankets and hoped that no one vomited in the night. He left a few clean glasses out by the sink so they didn't need to route through all of his cupboards should they need a drink in the night. He showed Claire to the spare room and gave her a hug. 'Goodnight Charlie. Thanks for tonight. And I'm so sorry about…' she wanted to say Nicola, '…Jenny.'

'No – thank *you*. Thanks for the distraction. And she's nice, she's funny. But you know who I want.'

'I do. I just…well, goodnight.'


At the other side of the central belt, Nicola lay wide awake ever since Charlie called. She couldn't think about anyone or anything else and had almost forgotten she was in bed with somebody, because he'd came to so little consequence for her. Nicola writhed with thoughts. She couldn't reconcile why she was so happy to sleep with any other man, and yet when it was over, all she wanted was to be tucked up next to Charlie.

Charlie left his door ajar so he could keep an ear out for his guests. He had developed a keen sense of hearing, despite his tinnitus, but he was good at figuring out people's movements by their sounds and he knew all the noises each particular part of his flat made.

He wasn't long in bed before he got a text from Nicola: "I'm really sorry about tonight. I never meant to muck you about. I should have been clearer with you. It won't happen again. xxx" Charlie read it a few times and tried to figure out whether she was talking about the lift or her sleeping with strangers.

# Chapter Sixteen

Claire waited for Nicola to call when she was ready to go out. They were meeting a few friends to go to the comedy club that night. She asked Nicola if Charlie was coming but she said that he was working nights and couldn't make it. Although he'd explained he was merely instructing, his job still seemed a mystery enough to both of them and that made Nicola's lie a very easy one to believe.

He had been teaching that day but certainly was not working that night. He sat home by himself trying to enjoy his own company. It was a clear night and he'd already been out for a walk through the centre of Glasgow. He walked about seven or eight miles. He'd try to keep active but hated the gym. It wasn't the exercise that put him off though; it was more the cock-measuring of the insecure egotistical guys that continuously occupied the weights area. These guys could probably squat or bench more than Charlie, but he'd run rings round them at anything in the real world. At home on the east coast he'd go up hills, take his mountain bike out on the old railway tracks that were now bridleways or he'd walk along the beach. The closest beach was a reasonable distance away and that was one drawback he felt from living in Glasgow. So he'd walk. It was a low impact form of exercise, but since he'd spent so much of his life in high impact, high stress and high-risk activities, walking was nice.

It was getting late so Claire decided to get in a taxi and make her way to the club. She was meeting everybody else there. She sent Nicola a text: "Nic Nac, where are you? I'm leaving now, just meet us there. Give me a call or text when you get this! XXX"

Claire would experience it at times. Nicola would drain the battery of her phone with constant texting and Facebooking and tweeting, so the occasional few hours where she hadn't heard from her were usually because she didn't have her charger with her. Or maybe she just got stuck at work or something.

They all met in a pub around the corner from the comedy club and people asked where Nicola was. One man, Tommy seemed especially interested. 'I thought Nicola was coming?' Claire wondered how he knew because she certainly hadn't told him.

'Yeah, she's maybe just running late or something.'

She tried to save Nicola a seat, but the place was packed. They watched the acts but Claire didn't laugh at a single one. Another hour passed and she became increasingly concerned about her whereabouts. *It's not like her to be stuck this late*, Claire thought, *surely she'd have made it to a charger by now*. At a break between acts she got up to call her again. It went straight to voicemail. *Maybe Charlie's heard from her*. She wasn't sure if he'd be able to pick up if he was at work, or if she'd be calling at a really inappropriate time, but she was sure that Charlie was smart enough not to have his phone on loud when he's hiding in someone's cupboard gathering information on them – or whatever it was he did. As he sat watching television, his phone began to ring. 'Hey, Charlie. I'm really sorry to disturb you at work but–'

'I'm not at work. I'm at the flat.'

'Oh, I thought…Nic said you were working nights just now.' *Something's not right here*, Claire thought. 'Have you heard from her at all? She was supposed to be meeting…' Claire looked back in towards the group of friends she was with, 'me, but I haven't heard from her all night.'

'Her phone's probably just dead again. When was the last time you heard from her?'

'I know, I thought that too, but I haven't heard from her since lunch time. I'm getting a bit worried, she's supposed to be out now.'

'I'm sure she's fine Claire.' Charlie thought about what to do. Should he go round to her flat and check on her? Should he just stay there in front of the television? What if she was home and with someone else? What if she was just home alone and didn't appreciate Charlie's unannounced arrival? But what if there was something wrong and he did nothing about it?

He supposed he could live with going round and making a fool of himself over missing if something was wrong. Besides, it's not like it would be the first time he'd been made a fool of by her. 'Do you want me to go round and check on her?' Charlie heard rapturous laughter as the next act had already began his set. 'Where are you?'

'The Stand.'

Charlie was a little hurt. That was something that they all did together, the three of them. He could appreciate however, if they wanted to spend a little time together just the two of them. He tried not to think about it too much, despite the fact that he didn't know there was a whole group of them and how he wasn't invited. 'Okay, I'll go and swing by and give you a call back.'

'Charlie?'

'Yeah?'

'Can you come and get me please? I'm not enjoying myself anyway. I dunno, I just want to see her and make sure she's okay. Do you mind?'

'No, of course not. I'll be about twenty minutes.'

Claire made her excuses to the rest of the group and stood outside waiting for Charlie to come. The summer night air turned chillier than expected and she didn't feel she was dressed appropriately anymore. She wore a sparkly sequined top over a couple of black tops, dark blue jeans and silver pumps and wished that she had brought a jacket with her. A bright beam of light swept round the roundabout and illuminated the street in a vibrant glow as Charlie pulled up to where she was standing.

He tried calling a couple of times from the car and could understand how Claire was beginning to get concerned about her. There was something very disconcerting about having her phone go straight to voicemail constantly, but at least it was only a further five minutes' drive from the club to Nicola's flat.

He looked up at her balcony, scanning for the milestones that he'd locked into his memory for his fantasy. The dreamcatcher with chimes which hung from a black hanging basket bracket and her bright blue highly glossed plant pot that stood proud but empty overlooking the street. He confirmed her balcony but saw no movement.

They pressed her buzzer and there was no response. 'Think we should try Glen?' Charlie asked.

'Yeah.'

Charlie pushed Glen's buzzer as he was taking control of the situation.

'Hello?'

'Hi, Glen. I'm really sorry to disturb you. It's Charlie, Nicola's friend. I was just wondering if you've heard from her or seen her, because we've not heard from her and she was supposed to be out tonight.'

'Oh, I dunno. No, I haven't seen her. I'll buzz you in, just come up.'

Glen was standing at his door as they approached and Charlie scanned along to Nicola's door. 'Sorry for disturbing you, we just wanted to check...you know.' Glen understood perfectly considering the break-in and a recollection of that evening entered his mind. He recognised Claire and smiled at her. He'd seen her come and go many times, but never had any occasion to talk to her. Charlie approached her door and knocked loudly. He knocked again and called her name in his assertive instructor voice. It boomed off her door and around the courtyard. Maybe he could try that balcony thing after all and gain access that way, or at least see if she was there?

'You have her spare key with you?' Charlie asked. Claire routed around her bag and handed her keys to him. They were so often at each other's place that they both had keys just for normal day-to-day, not just for emergencies. This was starting to qualify as an emergency though.

Charlie edged the door open and called her name again. Still no response. Claire threw him an anxious look before following him into the flat. All the lights and the television were still on as if she was at home. Glen stood at the doorway as they walked through into the living room. In the kitchen there was a pan with water and pasta in it sitting on the kitchen counter. The bag of pasta was scattered all over the floor and a large kitchen knife lay stricken amongst the pile of pale uncooked shells.

He wanted to hide the discovery from Claire but she had already seen it and a bolt of fear shot through her. Charlie's senses became suddenly heightened. He became acutely aware of everything in the vicinity. He scanned the kitchen again and found nothing more out of order. The living room: her keys sat on the coffee table. He recognised them and the Eiffel Tower key ring which dangled from them, as well as the shiny golden key that he bought from the locksmith and Claire's spare key too. It was bad news. 'Fuck…what if it's him?' Claire said.

'What are the chances, though? You really think so?'

'He's a psycho, Charlie.'

'Well, I'll find him. And I'll find her.' Glen slowly walked into the flat and looked at the pasta and saw Charlie with keys in his hand. 'Are those…*her* keys?' he asked.

'Yeah.'

'But she's not here?'

Claire came out of the bedroom. 'Her phone and handbag are in there. Phone's dead.'

'Charlie, I think…I might have heard something earlier…' He felt a little frightened to say anything because as much as he liked Charlie and they got along, he was a little bit intimidated by him. Glen always found Charlie very fearless and direct, much unlike himself.

'What did you hear? How long ago, try to be as exact as you can.'

'Well, I'm not sure, but…' he checked Nicola's clock on the wall, 'maybe a couple hours or so. Then there was some shouting.'

He drew a situational map in his head and tried to think where she could be, but didn't know a thing about Patrice so had no idea how to determine his movements.

'I thought it was you Charlie. There was a big car parked outside, I thought it was yours. It was the same colour.' Glen nervously scratched at his receding hairline. 'I thought it was just a...you know...tiff, so I didn't pay any attention because I thought it was you.'

'Shit. What else about the car? What kind of car was it? Or could you hear what they were saying?'

'No, I couldn't make anything out, but then the car went speeding off. I don't know what type it was, I'm not good with cars. But it was sort of big like yours but maybe it wasn't an estate, you know? But it was the same colour.' Guilt started to buzz inside Glen's head and his peaceful night suddenly disintegrated around him. 'Actually, maybe there was a scream outside before the car left. I thought it was just kids mucking about or something, but now that I think of it...' Charlie's mind whirred with almost blind panic. He had to fall back on his training and experience to remove his heart from the situation, even though it was beating hard and fast and frenziedly.

He addressed Claire. 'Where else does he know in Glasgow?'

'Erm, nowhere really. Just my flat.'

'Right, let's go.'

Charlie ripped along the quieting city streets towards Claire's flat. There was no sign of forced entry, there was nothing amiss, they hadn't been there. She received a text from a number she didn't recognise, in fact it looked foreign. "Claire, I need help. Patrice came.

I'm at the big blue crane off Dumbarton Road." She showed it to Charlie.

'She's at the Titan Crane. Clydebank.'

Claire tried to keep up with Charlie as he ran back to the car. He weaved in and out the sparse traffic. The speed was outrageous. He topped much higher speeds than the night of the break-in. He exceeded a hundred miles per hour on some of the open urban stretches that led to Clydebank. Claire envisaged all manner of ghastly scenarios in her head. *He always said he'd come here to find her, and now he's done it*, she thought. *What the fuck was the knife for?*

Nicola got home from work and was getting ready for a night out with Claire and her friends. It was going to be a night of drinking so she thought she ought to line her stomach with some food. Tommy was going to be there too, so she had to make sure she was looking nice for him. She looked in her cupboards and found some pasta and a pasta sauce. She ran some water into a pan and poured a handful of pasta in whilst there was a knock at the door. She didn't buzz anyone up, so it must have been Glen. They had become a lot friendlier and talked much more often after the botched break-in. Nicola wondered what it was that he might want.

A foot came into the door jamb and when she opened it fully, she could see it was a very unwelcome guest. 'Patrice! What the fuck are you doing here?' She tried to slam the door shut but his foot prevented her. He pushed the door open again and forced his way into the flat slamming the door shut behind him. Nicola walked back through to the kitchen seemingly unaffected by his presence, but inside she was panicking. She tried to make out that he didn't have any control over her any more. She decided not to cower away and tried to resume making dinner. At the same time, she knew that her phone was in the bedroom, so she couldn't call Claire very easily. She didn't want to go into the bedroom whilst he was there. 'Patrice, I don't know what you're doing here.'

He stormed around the flat, in and out of the rooms, looking for something or somebody. 'So where is he, you slut?' Nicola stood close to her knife block and eyed the precise location of her big knife, just in case he tried something.

'Patrice, I don't know what you think you'll achieve. Being here just makes things worse. I thought you'd changed, but you're just the same…I think you should go.' She tried to pick up the pasta to put it away in the cupboard. He slammed it out of her hand.

'No! Where is your new boyfriend, huh?' The pasta scattered like a bag of marbles all around the kitchen floor. Nicola was now standing facing the knife block and the appeal of the big handle in front of her grew.

'He's out, but he'll be back soon, so you should go.'

'I think I will wait for him, no?' He bared down on her as she stood in the kitchen and she felt trapped. She grabbed the knife from the block.

'Patrice! Just fuck off! You're nothing to me anymore! There's nothing between you and me! Get the fuck out!' The intention was just to threaten him. She didn't think she had it in her to actually stab him.

He laughed, 'What, you will kill me huh? In your flat? With all your things here? Why you're acting crazy? I've come all the way from France to see you.'

'But I don't want to see you! I never want to see you again! Please…just go!'

She wielded the knife unsteadily with both hands. He grabbed her scarred wrists quickly and shook violently until her limp grip gave way. The knife clattered onto the tile floor. He pulled her by the hair through to the living room, threw her onto the sofa and climbed on top of her so she couldn't move. He kissed her forcefully and held her arms down. She struggled to scream because her mouth was covered by his. He got up abruptly and sat down on the coffee table. 'You see? You think you can run away, but you can't leave me, Nicola. You love me too much.' She thought about screaming again, maybe Glen could come and intervene, but when he was off her she tried to regain control and remain calm and show him that she wasn't bothered by him.

'I don't love you anymore Patrice.'

'Don't tell me lies. I know you're just pretending.' He took his pack of cigarettes out from the pouch on the front of his hoody. Nicola sat up on the sofa straightening herself out as he lit up.

'Could you not smoke in here please?'

He smiled. 'You still care about me, no? Because you still try to tell me what to do.' He exhaled and cast smoke around her living room. 'So, what we are going to do now? If you are really so against Paris, then I could move here…but…I hope you know how much I'm doing for you.'

Nicola thought about how to escape. She couldn't take it anymore. She was finally telling him clearly that it was over but he didn't believe her. She couldn't call Claire because her phone was still in the other room. She was even thinking about calling the police now too. Patrice was delusional. Nicola thought the only way would be to make a clean break from him somehow, but to do it properly. Her mistake was letting him come and visit, so he knew where she stayed, and where Claire stayed. Maybe if she just moved home for a while, he wouldn't be able to reach her there. Or maybe she could go back to

Charlie's and then look into getting a new flat. Even then, she'd still be looking over her shoulder all the time, wondering if he was somewhere around. She had to convince him, or do something that made Patrice never want to come back. 'Look, can we just talk?' Nicola asked.

'Okay, what you want to talk about?' Patrice tried to kill time until her 'boyfriend' came back. He wanted to maybe beat him up, or even just be there when he got back so that he'd wonder why there was another man in her flat, then this new boyfriend would surely leave her.

Nicola went back in time and spoke to Patrice about how good things were at the start, but this time she held on to the present. The scar on her hand reminded her of what he was capable of doing. The embarrassment of starting work with a black eye made sure she'd never forget. She was thankful at least that everybody believed her story about being hit by a rugby ball in Glasgow Green and subsequently falling on some glass. But despite saving face, she knew the real reason and she wouldn't let it leave her as they talked this time.

After a while, Patrice started to get agitated as he knew that he'd lost his control over her. She was no longer his puppet and had her own ideas and her own aims and ambitions in life. She'd never had that before and seemed to speak different words to him, as if she *had* really moved on from him.

'So…where is your boyfriend? He's been a long time already.' Nicola prickled at the thought of him not being able to leave until he saw her 'boyfriend'. When she was in Paris, she told Patrice that she was in love with someone called Charlie, but it had just been a ruse to get him off her case. Now she said that her boyfriend was on his way, except she knew no one was coming.

She realised she'd done herself a real disservice by distancing herself from Charlie, because she really wished he would just turn up at her door. 'I'll just go and phone him.' She stood up to fetch her phone hoping that there was still some battery left; she knew she still needed to plug it in to charge. 'No no no no no. I don't think so. I think you're lying again. There's nobody. You know, I don't know what kind of life you want to live if you only tell lies to people. You're always lying Nicola, you're mouth…it is so full of shit, huh?'

'Fuck off Patrice! Just leave me alone, for once in your fucking life! Get the hell out of here!' She lifted a small stone elephant ornament and made a fist around it. She hurled her hand towards his head. He blocked her. She took another swing and he blocked again, but not so well. The ornament connected with his head. He tackled her onto the sofa again and the ornament tumbled onto her biscuit coloured carpet. She curled her arms around her face and prepared for the blows. He shook her violently on the sofa.

'If I can't have you, no one will! You understand? You understand?' She kicked out and struck him between the legs strong enough for him to fall off onto the floor, but it didn't stop him for long. 'Come on!' He grabbed her hair to pull her off the sofa. He'd discovered long ago that was the easiest way to get her to move, unless she wanted all of her hair pulled out of course. He pushed her along the hall and stifled her mouth as he shoved her all the way to the car. 'Get in!'

'No Patrice!'

'I will not tell you again!'

Escaping his hold, she tried to run but he grabbed her and lifted her back to the car. She let out a scream before he had a chance to cover her mouth again, but nobody seemed to hear her or be paying attention. He slapped her and opened the boot of his hire car. He pushed her in as she struggled and quickly shut it behind her. She screamed and screamed and she could feel her screams reverberate closely around her in the boot. She became concerned about a lack of oxygen, not knowing if it was a real threat, but it was enough of a fear to shut her up and Patrice was glad. The sounds of her screams drove him crazy. She would scream at him when he hit her but it would only make him feel angrier.

He had hired the car from the airport after arriving earlier that day and he went for a drive around Glasgow. He wanted to find somewhere to take her that might be romantic so that he could talk nicely to her and convince her to come back to Paris with him the same way that he was always able to before.

He drove further west from the west end and tried a few places along the river. He didn't know Glasgow and didn't know that he was heading into the industrial part. He found a few colleges, a hospital and a big blue crane before he gave up and drove back into the city. He thought it was bullshit. There were so many nice romantic spots in Paris and you didn't have to try so hard to find them.

He now drove with Nicola in the boot and was feeling like he was losing the plot. He didn't want to lose her. He was marred with the thought of her being with another man and having a life of her own. He just wanted her to go back and for them to be how it was before. He wanted her there to cook and clean and make love like they used to and be his punch bag emotionally and literally. He drove endlessly around the city. Eventually, he stumbled upon the same road out west from her flat that he found earlier that day. He decided to follow it – it was the only one he knew after all. He felt guilty about having her in the boot, but it was her fault. *Why did she try to hit me with that ornament*, he thought. *Why did she have to run?*

He turned left off the Dumbarton Road so that he could let Nicola out somewhere quiet and they could talk about things and they'd go home, and she could sit in the front instead. There was a college next to the Titan Crane in Clydebank. Considering it was late at night, the car park was deserted as he drove past. The road came to a dead end near some railings and there was a small path which led to the edge of the quay. He got out of the car and headed to the boot. 'Nicola, I'm sorry. I just want to talk, okay?'

There was no response. He thought maybe she couldn't hear him in there. She could hear him fine well in fact and prepared herself. He popped the boot open. Nicola launched at him with a tyre wrench and this time he had no chance to block. Maybe it was after spending so much time with Charlie that she'd become a lot more resourceful. During the car journey she managed to wriggle around the boot and feel under the partition next to the spare wheel for the tool. She had no idea those things were under there until Charlie showed her it all when she got her car. She struck him hard on the side of the head, splitting it open, but he was still able to stand.

He dragged her out of the boot and threw her onto the ground. Stones poked uncomfortably into her hands and her hair cascaded down wildly as she propped herself up. Patrice touched his head and found blood on his hands. *Why has she done this? I need to teach her a lesson.* He jerked her to her feet and she started to flail her arms at him. 'You fucking bitch! I said I wanted to talk!' Her punches didn't affect him because she couldn't get enough leverage from the way he held her. She kneed him a few times in the stomach, but struggled to keep her balance as he dragged her over to the railing. She tripped backwards over the kerb but Patrice still had hold of her so she didn't fall. He put her head over the top of the railing, wrapped his thin fingers round her neck and began to squeeze.

Nicola tried as hard as she could to knock his arms away but she couldn't. She tried and tried, but she was fast running out of energy as the breaths were not coming anymore. The dark night became even darker as she squirmed and squeaked and the light started to leave her eyes. Patrice's hands were cold and bony. She tried to breathe. She tried to fall to her feet, but she was trapped with the back of her neck on the railing. She tried to breathe.

Patrice started to kiss her, making it even more difficult to gasp for air. All her power seemed to diminish to nothing and she stopped struggling suddenly. He let go of his grip. Her neck burned hot and she coughed heavily as she fell to the ground. The night sky was clear and she could see the crescent moon and a few stars in the sky above her as she lay stricken on her back. *Quiero mirar el cielo*, she thought. It was the Spanish phrase Charlie taught her on her birthday. She could feel the cold of the night air set about her chest and legs as Patrice started to remove her clothes.

Her neck still blazed, but she didn't care anymore. She closed her eyes and waited to die. She closed her eyes and hoped that she would die. That may as well be it. She'd never be free from him. She had no life anymore, so what was the point of living?

Patrice sped off after 'making love' to her under the stars for the last time. His heart raced. He knew what he'd done was wrong but he just couldn't help it. She lay there so helpless and didn't resist. She remained there for a while in the dark with her underwear and jeans round her ankles and her t-shirt and jumper were bundled up around her neck.

Since she wasn't yet dead, she decided to pull her jeans up and her tops back down. She was starting to get the feeling back into her body and realised she was shivering. She propped herself up against the railing that she'd been strangled against and looked up the road.

She thought about what to do next. She didn't have anything with her, so she couldn't call a taxi or call anyone. She could hear the cars on Dumbarton Road pass by. Maybe she could flag one down and catch a lift. Or maybe she could just walk home, because it was all she felt she deserved. As she waited for some energy to manifest, she noticed a couple of items on the road in front of her. The tyre wrench lay next to Patrice's cigarettes and his mobile phone. They had fallen out of the pouch on his hoody as she tried to knee him in the guts. Whilst it didn't stop him, at least that was some consolation. She wrote a short text to Claire and sat back down. Claire's and her mum and dad's phone numbers she'd known forever. The only other number she knew off by heart was Charlie's because of her work phone, when she used to constantly call him at least. She pulled a cigarette out of the pack and placed it between her dry lips before realising she had nothing to light it with. She spat it out and it tumbled down her body and hit the ground before blowing away.

'It's one of these turn-offs. Just keep your eyes peeled!' Charlie and Claire sped along the road. He jumped all the red lights and forced his way through the traffic. He didn't care about cutting people off or getting followed by police. He had no intention of stopping. In fact, he'd rather the police were with him when he confronted that scumbag Patrice. 'Titan Crane! This one!' She bashed his arm to emphasise it. He turned the corner and the tyres smoked and squealed as the car launched down the empty side-street. Nicola heard screeching tyres and saw some lights approach around the corner. Here was Patrice come for round two, or to apologise, or just to get his phone and cigarettes and leave her sitting there in the cold. The car zoomed past the empty college car park directly in front of where Nicola was propped up. She was dazzled by the lights at the height she was sitting at on the ground so closed her eyes again, but she heard more than one car door open.

'Nic! Oh my God, Nic!' Claire rushed towards her whilst Charlie looked around. Despite there being no other car there, he was expecting Patrice to still be there and he wanted him to be there. He hadn't even checked on Nicola yet, but she had Claire to tend to her. He didn't even know what harm he'd caused her, but to leave her there in the dead of night was out of order. His heart thumped hard and his teeth ground together so hard that his gums wanted to bleed. He rushed over to the railing and looked into the water somehow hoping to see Patrice there struggling in it. No such luck. He ran around the vicinity but there was no sign of him, he was long gone. Claire cradled Nicola in her arms as she seemed to be falling asleep or losing consciousness.

'Nicola,' Charlie knelt down next to them, 'we need to get you to the hospital.' She looked at Claire and shook her head.

'Charlie, she doesn't want to go to hospital.'

'You should…well, I'll call the police.' Nicola shook her head again at Claire. He pulled out his phone and Nicola put her hand on it. She'd stopped crying but he could see the tracks of her tears like silver streaks down her cheeks, glistening in the moonlight.

'No police. Please. I don't want to go through any more.'

He looked towards Claire for her opinion and she said, 'Let's get you home then.'

Claire sat in the back next to Nicola and Charlie made his way back into Glasgow. He watched her continuously in the rear-view mirror. 'We should go to the police, you know?' Nicola was looking straight out of the window when she refused again. 'Well, you're not going back to your flat. You two can stay at mine tonight.'

'There's no need for that,' said Nicola contemptuously.

'No. You will both stay at my flat tonight.'


Charlie swung by Claire's place quickly and she ran in to change and pack a few essentials. 'What did he do to you?'

'Nothing. Just forget about it. Please.'

'What kind of car is he driving?' She couldn't bring herself to speak to him any more. She hated letting him see her like that and could no longer look back at him even through the rear-view mirror. She truly wished that Charlie had been the boyfriend that was due to come back. Then none of that would have happened.

Charlie opened his flat and held the door open whilst Claire hobbled in with her. Nicola knew well where everything was around his flat and how to operate everything. Claire had been a few times but he gave her a quick brief anyway, because she'd be the one left in charge. Nicola sat down in the living room and Charlie poured her some water. He went through to the spare bedroom and started to pump up the air bed for Claire, repositioned the chair so it would fit and made up some sheets whilst it filled.

He went back through to the living room where they both sat. 'Right, I've made up the air bed in there. Just help yourselves to anything you need.' He plonked a set of keys on the coffee table in front of them both. He knew Nicola still had his spare set from when she stayed over but she didn't even have her own keys at that time. 'These are for you two. The fob unlocks the outside door.' Of course Nicola still knew, that was for Claire's benefit. 'They're mine though, so you'll have to buzz me back in when I get back.' He checked Nicola quickly before addressing Claire again. 'Will you be okay?'

'What, Charlie, where are you going?' she asked.

'I'm working nights, remember?' He replied to Claire but was looking at Nicola.

Charlie headed back out into the cool night with vengeance on his mind. When he got to the car he pulled on his old fast-roping gloves with the double palm, good for fast-roping, and good for smothering people. He drove to Nicola's flat and parked up on the hill opposite, a block away. A dogwalker went by with a huge shaggy dog and they didn't see Charlie sitting in the car or notice the ticking of the exhaust as it cooled. A couple of cars drove past him, or drove past the junction in front of him. Charlie waited patiently.

Almost three hours had passed since he arrived and there had hardly been any movement. That made it easier. It wasn't like he'd need to pick him out from a crowd. A car turned off the road and bumped the kerb before stopping next to her building. The lights went off but no one got out. It was a fairly big car, a saloon, and it was the same colour as Charlie's. *This is him*, Charlie thought.

Charlie got out of the car and stuck to the shadows as he walked down the hill. The thick hedges that lined the big houses provided excellent cover. Charlie froze as another car drove through the small junction. After a few seconds he resumed his covert advance towards the recently parked car. He could see the interior light was on inside as the occupant fidgeted inside. He stealthily crossed the road and clung to the front of the building, round the corner from the car. He waited and listened.

Patrice wanted to call Nicola but he couldn't find his mobile phone anywhere. He wanted to see her and wanted to know that she got home after leaving her. If he didn't get a response from her flat then he thought that he'd go and look for her and bring her home. The car door opened and Patrice stepped out. Charlie waited and could hardly breathe. Pressure built up inside him like a bomb – one that was about to explode. Patrice looked up towards her balcony and Charlie watched him patiently. He didn't know the same milestones that Charlie did. He didn't know which one was hers.

Patrice started up the hill towards the door and Charlie emerged from the wall. He walked noiselessly behind him as if he was out on a lovely evening stroll. He gained on him and as he got closer, he spoke, 'Patrice?' He looked round at this stranger. 'Oui?' Charlie punched him hard in the face. Black eye. Patrice was startled and confused. He had no idea what was happening. He'd been drinking before he went round earlier that night and he'd been drinking after leaving Nicola, which didn't help him. Charlie punched him hard in the torso and winded him badly. He doubled over and Charlie brought his fist down hard on the back of his head. Patrice fell to his knees. Concussion. He struggled for breath almost as badly as he had made Nicola struggle. His head span like a whirligig. Charlie kicked him in the torso. Broken ribs. He pulled him up and dragged him back to his car before slamming his head into it. Broken jaw. Patrice fell flat on his back and Charlie stamped on his shoulder. Broken collarbone. He pulled him up again as he started to beg for mercy.

'Please, no more, no more. Please!' Patrice reached for his wallet and pulled it from his jeans. 'Please, just take it!' Charlie took the wallet from him.

'This isn't a fucking mugging you piece of shit,' It's also highly unusual that a random mugger might know your name, Charlie thought. '…this is for Nicola.'

He pulled the cards out of the wallet, scattering them on the ground hoping that some jakey would find them and max them out. He found the photo section of the wallet and ripped it out. 'And you certainly don't deserve to have this.'

He popped what remained of his wallet into the post-box before returning to hit him hard again in the mouth. Broken tooth. It hurt considerably more because of the broken jaw that preceded it. Patrice begged some more and fell to his knees in front of Charlie, tugging pitifully at him. The rage that had mounted over months started to seep out of Charlie, but even he knew he had to stop. It was very hard for him to put the lid back on the box of rage when he could picture Nicola slumped against the railing like she was. He knew he'd raped her. But it wasn't just about what he'd done that night. Why could Patrice do as he pleased with her, when Charlie had treated her like royalty and gotten nowhere?

'Please, stop! Who are you?'

'I'm…' he thought about it, '…Nicola's guardian angel. And if you ever hurt her, threaten her, or even try to speak to her again I'll come to Paris and I'll fucking finish you. You will never see her again, do you understand?'

'You are Charlie?'

*What the fuck?* Charlie thought. *He knows my name.* 'Do you understand??' He raised his fist.

'Oui! Oui! Je comprends! I understand!' Charlie struck him on the side of the head and finally Patrice passed out.


Nicola was at the office. She had a photo of her and Claire, one of all three of them and a photo of Paris in spring pinned to her cubicle wall. She had settled in very well and sometimes thought back to the day of her interview, and how she was about to cancel over her ripped trousers. Her mobile phone rang and she didn't recognise the number. It was French though, so she decided not to answer. There was a message left on her voicemail which she picked up during a quiet spell. It was from a woman, she spoke in French: "Hello, Nicola. I just thought I'd give you a call. I want to know if you know anything about what happened to Patrice? He is in the hospital in Glasgow and he's been beaten up very badly. I don't know if you're still talking to him or not, but I was just wondering if you could go and check on him before I arrive tomorrow. I hope you're well." It was Patrice's mother.

'Shit!' Nicola stopped her work for a second and tried to think about what might have happened. How the hell did he end up in hospital? A glimmer of sympathy flashed through her and she didn't know why. She couldn't concentrate on anything else that day after the message and just watched the clock tick round until five o'clock came and she left the office like a shot. She got changed at her flat and got the train to the other side of the city. She wasn't sure how to get there by car and felt too rushed to check it out. She walked up Glasgow's High Street, past the student flats, past the cathedral and on to the hospital.

She inquired at the desk about him and was asked what her relation was to him. 'I'm his…girlfriend.' She couldn't say sister or cousin or something because she wasn't French and maybe they might not have let her see him if she was just a friend. She carried his mobile phone in her handbag. It was two days since that night he came to her flat unannounced so the phone battery was a long time dead. She came out the lift and checked the signs looking for his ward. She took a few wrong turns and doubled back on herself before finding the right place. She waited patiently at the ward desk to speak to the nurse there. 'Hi,

I'm looking for Patrice Paget.' There were multiple scrawls on a whiteboard and despite the information being in plain sight it was only really the nurses who could decipher it. 'Aw yeah, the French guy? He's in room eight.'

'Thank you.'

'Erm…are you a relative?'

'I'm er…' she had to tell the uncomfortable lie again, 'his girlfriend.'

'Well…' The nurse came round from the desk. 'He's in a bad way…he's been really badly beaten. I'll take you there.' Nicola didn't know what to expect or whether to be glad it had happened. Was this karma getting back at him? The nurse stopped outside the room and looked to Nicola as she asked her more.

'When did he come in?'

'It was…' the nurse thought back, 'early on Wednesday morning.' Nicola realised that was the same night he came to 'see' her. 'Apparently he'd split up with his…girlfriend…?' she gestured towards Nicola. 'And he went out and got really drunk and ended up in a fight with a guy, and then all the guys friends jumped in.'

'How bad is he?'

'They really did him over. There must have been a lot of them.' The nurse tried to gauge Nicola's reaction. 'The funny thing was, they dropped him off at the hospital. He had a hire car and he was found just outside the ambulance parking bay. But there's no way he drove. He was unconscious on the back seats.'

Nicola's mind raced. There's no way that he bumped into a group of neds, who after beating him up would drive him to the hospital. To the hospital staff it must have just been a small wonder, but one which was inconsequential to them.

It wasn't possible, Nicola thought, and it was not a random thing. Charlie said before leaving that he was working nights, but Nicola knew he wasn't. They supposed that he just wanted to get out and clear his head after bringing them home.

It had to be him. There's no one else who was capable and there's no one else who'd take him to hospital after. The hospital called the police as they were obliged to do, but Patrice was still out cold. They told the nurses to call once he came round but Patrice insisted on not getting police involved.

The nurse opened the door as there potentially some discomfort and doubt as to whether or not she his girlfriend, although she was sure Nicola was at some point. She paused outside the room and looked through the open door at him. He seemed unconscious and had a few tubes in him as well as casts and bandages. His jaw had some kind of wire contraption fitted to it. Despite her distance she could see him clearly enough. The nurse came back out of the room. 'Do you want to go in?'

'No. No, I…Can you just give him this please?' She rummaged in her bag for his phone and gave it to the nurse.

'Okay, is there anything else?'

'No. Thank you.' The nurse smiled and walked swiftly away to resume her many other duties. Nicola stood there for a little while longer. She didn't want to go in the room. Even in his degenerated state, she was still frightened of him. She could feel the burn of his hands and strain around her neck and still had an ache at the back of her head where she'd been pressed against the railings. She'd been wearing a scarf at work those past few days in order to cover up the bruising. Then there was the way he forced himself on her.

She took no joy in seeing him like that though. That wasn't supposed to ever happen, she'd never ever expected to see him that way. They were supposed to be happy and living in Paris and she'd be selling her paintings and they'd be living a good life together. She was infinitely frustrated that she couldn't have that and never would.

As she walked back to the station, she placed a call. 'Hi Claire.'

'Hey, Nic. How's it going?'

'Well…I don't know where to start actually. I got a call from Patrice's mum saying that he was in the infirmary here because he'd been beaten up.' *Good*, thought Claire. 'I've just been to see him.'

'Oh, Nicola, I hope you're fucking joking? You go and visit him after what he did to you?'

'No, well. I didn't see him. I didn't go in.' Claire didn't care about what had happened to him, how it came about or how badly he'd been beaten – the worse the better in her opinion. 'The nurse said that he'd been out and got drunk and beat up, but–'

'Well good! It's no more than he deserves!'

'It was the same night he came round.'

'So, if he's been out and got drunk because of what he did to you, he's brought it on himself. I hope you're not feeling sorry for him. I'm serious.'

'I think it was Charlie.' There was silence on the phone and Claire determined how undeniably possible it was.

'So, what? Just let it be, he's done you a favour.'

'Done me a favour? How can you say that? Patrice is fucked up in there!'

Claire bit her tongue as she wanted to explain how happy she was to hear that Charlie had done this to Patrice. It was a long time coming. 'Just let it be then Nicola. What's done is done.'

Charlie was in Ayrshire going through the Six Section Battle Drills when he got a text from Nicola: "Hey, what you up to tomorrow evening? Can I come round?" She was pissed off at him but didn't carry any of that through in the text, because he'd see it and be on guard. She wanted to put him on the spot about what he did.

A text came back over an hour later saying, "Sure. I've got a short day tomorrow, so I'll be back late afternoon. Just pop round when you like."

Nicola drove to Charlie's flat after work and she'd learned where the visitor parking was by now so parked neatly in a bay. Charlie buzzed her in and left the door ajar. He was half way through washing up the crockery, pans and cutlery. 'Charlie?'

'I'm through in the kitchen.' She closed the door and headed along the hall. He wore shorts and a plain dark grey t-shirt. The darkening early autumn twilight seeped in through the many glass panels in the room and she could see the accentuations of his strong body as he dried a plate. The big glass door was slid open and the fresh

357

breeze diluted the cooking smell from the flat. She couldn't identify the smell, but whatever it was it smelt delicious. 'Hey.' He smiled in ignorance of what was on her mind. 'How are you? You want a drink or something?'

'No, Charlie. I need to talk to you.' He was intrigued. Had she finally reached a place in her life following the events of the other night that she could forget about this guy and move on? Had she *finally* had enough time to reflect on all the support and things he'd done for her over the past several months and at last willing to show some proper appreciation?

'I got a call yesterday.' She stood in the doorway to the hall and didn't come into the living area. She kept her bag on her shoulder and her jacket on. It didn't look like she was going to stay for long. 'It was from Patrice's mum. She said he'd been beat up really badly. I went to the hospital to see him and…and…' she looked around the living room then back at him, '…was it you?'

'Was it me, what?'

'Come on, Charlie! Did you assault him?' She sounded more like a police officer than Nicola. He put down the towel and stopped drying dishes once he realised it was serious talk. 'No. Why? Is he bad?'

'Yes, he's fucking bad!'

'Did you see him?'

'I know it was you! Just admit it!'

'So, what if I did?' Nicola marched in and slammed her hands on the breakfast bar that was between the two of them. Her bag fell off her shoulder so she dropped it to the floor. 'Why did you do it?'

'Do you really need me to answer that question??'

'I don't believe you! Why do you feel the need to stick your fucking nose in other people's business??'

'Oh, so I stick my nose in your business now? It's fine when I'm looking after you, you know I've always got you best interests at heart, so what is this? Why are you so upset about this anyway?' Charlie stopped short of saying he thought she'd be happy; that's not what he expected or wanted. He really wanted her just to never find out about it and for Patrice to disappear out of her life for good. He didn't want to seem as if he was trying to be her hero.

'I'm upset because…you're always interfering!'

'Helping…interfering, whatever you want to call it.'

'Oh don't be so fucking righteous! You think you've always got the answers and you're so smart! Well, I'm fine by myself. I can manage fine without you!' Charlie tried not to take to heart what she was saying, he knew she was upset. Forever making excuses and allowances for her, he thought maybe she just needed to get it all out in the open and purge herself, so he was ready to ride the wave until it crashed onto the shore and then she'd fall into his arms and everything would be okay.

'Alright, you can manage fine, but…things have been better with me around haven't they?'

'No! I wish I never got back in touch with you! I'd be better off without you actually!' Nicola was panicking and lashed out. She struck out with her words and landed heavy, heavy blows on Charlie.

'Well, I'm sorry if I've 'interfered', I'm sorry if I ever cared for you so much.' They'd never argued before, he'd never seen her upset like that before. How could it be that the man that treated her like shit and oppressed her, insulted her and beat her, had her running back to him all the time and could never do any wrong? And all Charlie had done was care for her and look out for her, showed her thoughtfulness and kindness and tried to find ways to try and improve her days even slightly, yet he was supposedly wrecking her life? It was so insulting to him.

'Why did you do this? You didn't have to do this,' she said.

'Of course I had to. *You're* the one that said no police. So this is how I deal with things.'

'Really? So now I know you. I can't believe this.' She shook her head and sniffed as she started to choke up. 'You're a dangerous man. I'm going to go and see him. We should never have met again.' She picked up her bag. 'I don't want you to call me or message me any more. Just stay away from me.' She turned without looking at him again and stormed out of the flat. The door slammed shut.

Charlie picked up his half-empty glass and serenely walked through the open glass wall out to the terrace. He looked over the edge and found her car. It wasn't long before Nicola was leaving the building and did a sort of half walk–half jog to the car. He watched as she pulled out of the car park and out of his life. Charlie screamed out into the cool evening air for all of Glasgow to hear and hurled his glass towards the ground, smashing it into smithereens. The juice crept slowly in all directions between the tiles of the terrace.

She had no intention of seeing Patrice again, she just wanted to make Charlie feel bad – and that she did. He'd done something to protect her and she was seemingly going to run back into Patrice's arms. He couldn't comprehend it.

Tears streamed down her face as she drove back to her flat. She struggled to concentrate on her driving and mistimed a few red lights and bungled some lane changes, but mercifully without any consequence.

Did she really just say all of those things to Charlie? Why was she so upset that Patrice was badly hurt? She did want to see him in some pain and for there to be some repercussion for him, but not to that extent. She herself had threatened him with a knife and hit him with her ornament *and* the tyre wrench. If Charlie had stopped after the first few blows, then he'd not be in such a bad way. He certainly would have been able to just fly back to Paris and never return. There would have been no phone call to Nicola from his mother.

Charlie was never one for half measures however and felt the need to drive the point home, not to mention how he took out some of the frustration he felt about Nicola on him. With the way Patrice had hurt Nicola over the years though, Charlie still felt he didn't hurt him as much as he deserved. He wanted to get rid of Patrice altogether. He was certainly successful, but it seemed at too high a price.

## Chapter Seventeen

Charlie woke up early in the morning. The naked woman next to him in bed was still fast asleep. The covers were just over the curves of her slim body protecting her modesty, but Charlie had already seen and felt every curve anyway. He walked through to the kitchen to pour himself some water. Outside it was raining and he wondered what Nicola was doing. Was she up yet? There was no way to tell. He still missed those messages from her in the morning as soon as she woke up just to say hello and wish him a good day. Glancing at his watch, he supposed she was waking up about that time too, but then what difference would it make?

He switched the television on for some company and kept it low so as not to disturb his guest. An empty bottle of wine stood on the coffee table in front of him with an empty glass and half a glass with impressions of lipstick on the rim. He sat in the place where he and Nicola made love, to try and feel something more – to find that feeling that was missing from the night before.

Jess, who lay in his bed, met him at a petrol station. She had her manual out and was feeling around the bonnet. Charlie, being ever helpful approached her. 'You alright there?' She had slyly clocked what car Charlie was coming from.

'I'm just trying to get the bonnet open.' The fact that she was a young and beautiful damsel seemingly in middling distress didn't even factor into it for him, he'd have helped regardless of who it was.

'Engine troubles?' Charlie thought if she wasn't able to open the bonnet that she'd struggle to fix an actual problem. Plus, it was quite a new car, so he doubted engine trouble anyway.

'No...I need to fill my water up.' It was autumn and the fields were being harvested which left a lot of dust in the air. She held a bottle of mineral water that she'd bought in the service station.

'Well, were you going to fill it up with that?'

'Why? Is it bad for the car?'

'No, but there's water over there. Your car doesn't need Evian, you know? It'll drink tap water, it's not too fussy.' He smiled and gestured over to the side of the forecourt where the machine was. 'You finished filling up?'

'Yeah. I just need to pay though.'

'Okay, go and pay then move your car over there, I'll show you.' Charlie moved his car over to the service bay and waited for her to do the same. She made sure Charlie wasn't looking and had a quick check of herself in her mirror before getting out of the car. 'Okay, so...can you pop the bonnet?' She looked at Charlie expectantly. He slid past her and opened the car door. He felt around for the catch, popped it open and rested it on the arm. 'How long have you had the car?'

She thought about it. 'A few weeks, it's my first car. Well, the first that I've bought and it's all mine.' *Just like Nicola's*, he thought.

'That's your water there.' He tapped the blue cap at the side of the engine bay and flipped it open. 'Pull that nozzle over.' She touched the one on the machine that said 'water' and wondered how it could possibly reach over. 'It pulls out.' He came across and showed her as he found a twenty pence piece from his pocket to put in the slot. It buzzed into life and he filled the reservoir with water adding a little screen-wash from the back of his own car. She raked in her purse to reimburse him. 'It's okay. It's only twenty pee,' he smiled. With a car like that she supposed he wouldn't really miss twenty pence or even twenty pounds. He dropped the bonnet shut and snapped his hand back. 'Ouch!'

'Oh! What is it?'

'I broke a nail.' He shook his hand and blew on his fingertips as she laughed. Her smile was fresh and bright. He wasn't flirting as such – she seemed nervous about the car and he just wanted to make her feel at ease. He was also trying to inject humour into his day as a way to distract himself from the misery. But he remembered when he used to do those types of things for Nicola and felt distress rise in him. He wanted to get home straight away so he could suffer in silence and solitude. 'Well, happy motoring.' He turned back towards his car and made it to the door before she spoke.

'Thanks so much. Erm…I was just wondering,' she pursed her lips a little, 'what if I need to top up the oil or something? I should maybe take your number?' She was beautiful, but Charlie was hurting so much that he didn't feel he was able to do anything about it. He certainly wasn't going to chase after her. But she'd asked for it so cunningly that he thought it would almost be rude to refuse. Maybe she did this sort of thing all the time and he'd just be another guy on her list. As it happened, she'd never asked a guy for his number before, but she sensed something about Charlie that was different. He had no intentions of chatting her up, he only wanted to help. Plus he was handsome, had kind eyes and a nice smile. It was only his phone number, he supposed, it wasn't like he was obliged to do anything.

They exchanged numbers. 'It's Charlie Maxwell.'

'And I'm Jess Stephenson.'

'Well, it's a pleasure to make your acquaintance, Miss Jess Stephenson.' He rubbed a little of the engine bay grime off his hands onto his t-shirt and shook her hand. 'It is *Miss* isn't it?'

'Yes, it is.' A glimmer flashed through her eyes.

Charlie drove away from the service station and wondered what had happened. Why did a pretty girl want to give him her number? She must have seen something in him that she found appealing, but he felt so low about himself that he couldn't find what it was. Maybe it was the car, he supposed. Women perhaps don't always admit it, but they prefer a man with a nice car than one with an old banger. Either way, he didn't expect to hear from her again. It was good practice though, he thought. If he maybe one day wanted to try and find someone again, that little exchange may come in handy. But Charlie thought that day would be far away if it ever even came.

Two days went past and Jess could wait no longer to text him: "Hey. I need to top up my oil, but I can't get the bonnet open." Charlie took his time writing the reply. He needed to not be serious or full-on like he always was. Nicola still consumed him, but he regarded it as training.

"Well, I can recommend a good garage."

"See that's the thing, it's so hard to find a mechanic you can trust these days. I like the ones that you find in petrol stations lol."

The to and fro went on for a few days and Charlie started to become tired of it. He didn't really care whether he got to see her again so just thought he'd ride it out until she got bored. Most people love the thrill of the chase, but not Charlie. He only got a thrill from realising affection.

"What you doing this weekend?" she finally asked.

He moved off the sofa leaving the television down low. He realised he didn't know what Jess's preferences were for breakfast. Was she a croissant type of girl like Nicola, or was she a cereal, or an eggs and bacon type of girl? In fact, there was a lot he didn't know about her and he really feared getting to know her.

She was young and smart and beautiful. She taught at a school in Glasgow and was well travelled. She took two gap years to travel and work around the world teaching English as a foreign language. She'd spent time volunteering in West Africa in a place close to where Charlie had also been. Their jobs could not have been more different however.

Through in the bedroom, she lay there delicately. Her head reeled with the perfection of the previous night and the perfection of Charlie. He was hunky and handsome, he had an amazing flat and car, he was great in the kitchen *and* the bedroom and he was respectful and thoughtful to her.

He cooked for her the previous night and they sat up talking and drinking wine until late. Charlie didn't make a move on her and she wasn't used to that. He was happy to talk to her. She liked it. She would get advances all the time from men, or inappropriate remarks directed towards her but she felt he wasn't capable of any of that. She didn't have any doubt about whether Charlie found her attractive or not, he'd said as much when they met again.

She stirred in bed as Charlie entered the room. The soft feel of the duvet was nice against her bare body, but she craved to feel Charlie close to her. 'Come back to bed.' He slipped under the covers and lay next to her and she clambered onto his chest. He wrapped his arms around her and kissed her tenderly on the head. Her hair smelled of coconuts.

'What kind of stuff do you like for breakfast?'

'Oh, I'm not fussy. There's only one thing I'm hungry for just now though.'


Charlie still taught, but was becoming very disillusioned by it. There was a certain emptiness that the training gave him and being crestfallen as he was, he wanted a clean break from anything military. After all, he was already dangerous as a young man and the skills that he perfected over the years were only meant to cause harm to people – or beat the living shit out of possessive and abusive ex-fiancés – and look where that got him. Jess hated his early starts when he'd drive down to Ayrshire and as the days passed, he'd start to leave later and later and take the motorway instead of the coast road. As much as possible, he tried to limit his teaching to days when he knew Jess would be busy.

She would always rush round as quickly as she could after work. She'd float on a cloud all day long, picturing Charlie's face and the sensation of his thick yet gentle shoulders tingle through her fingers. She'd recall the tenderness of his lips on her soft neck and wished every second away until she could experience him again.

As it approached the October break, she was so excited to spend every waking moment with him, as well as every non-waking one. Charlie suggested that they should go away somewhere and asked her to come up with some ideas. She didn't care where they went, just so long as they were together. He wanted to take her away for her, but he also wanted to get away from Glasgow for a while. Every room of his flat still screamed of Nicola but he hoped that after a little time away with Jess, that might dissipate. If it didn't, he didn't know what he would do.

Jess came round and Charlie had dinner ready. It rained again, but the sky was still bright. She parked in the visitor parking and took the lift up to the flat leaping onto him as he opened the door. Between the kisses she managed to utter, 'I've missed you.' He loved the affection she gave him because it was exactly what he needed. She was the mortar to repair the falling walls of his heart. Most guys would be put off by a girl who's too much, but it was the only thing that could ever start to repair Charlie. Jess was good for him and he knew it, but there was still something in him that didn't ever let it sit perfectly, like a faulty weevil trying to right itself over and over. Although, it wasn't even so much as the weevil being faulty, it was more that the ground it was on was continuously unsteady.

'So,' he piled some chicken onto his fork, 'have you decided where you want to go?' She'd perused the quandary all week and had a few ideas. She sought advice from her friends and colleagues and didn't want to be too extravagant or demanding of Charlie. He said he'd take her anywhere she wanted, but because they hadn't been together for very long, she didn't want to push things. She thought about going somewhere up in the highlands or islands of Scotland, but thought she may have had an opportunity to go further afield. He did say *anywhere*.

'How about Paris?' Of all the places that she could have picked, of course she had to go for that. It was an obvious choice for a romantic getaway though.

'Paris is a bit…' he searched for the right word, 'clichéd, isn't it?' She looked a little dejected. 'How about New York or something?'

Her face lit up and the dejection disappeared. 'New York?? Really??'

'Why not?' She put down her knife and fork.

'Oh my God, I've always wanted to go!! Are you sure??'

'Absolutely sure. So, you're alright with that over Paris?'

'YES!' She came round to his side of the table and threw her arms around him.

'Charlie, thank you, thank you, thank you! You're just so amazing!'

'So, we'll get it booked then.'

'Okay.' She stood next to him at the table waiting for him to get up. She was so excited.

'After dinner though, if that's okay?' He laughed at her hyper-activity and it gave him so much joy to see her so happy.

'Oh, of course. Yeah.'


The Friday before she finished up for October break, he drove her into school. They met in town for dinner the previous night before going back to his. She'd stayed so often that she already had a lot of her own things there. It was moving fast, but they were both enjoying themselves. Charlie thought very highly of her and he just couldn't stand being alone in the flat, especially at night, so was happy for her to come round all the time. Jess was falling in love with him. She was only in her mid-twenties but she'd grown so sick of sleaze-balls and creeps. Charlie was a breath of fresh air for her.

He dropped her off in the school car park early. There were no pupils around, but the teachers were arriving. They wondered who the hell was rolling up in such a fancy car. Jess didn't want to rub it in other people's faces, but she felt so proud to arrive in Charlie's car and kiss him slowly before going to work. 'This day can't go fast enough, babe.'

'I know. I'll get you back here then. Have a nice day.'

She wandered to the door slowly so she could watch Charlie drive out of the car park and squeeze in another wave as her colleagues gathered around to question her about the mystery man. She'd told a few of her good friends about him already, but it wasn't common knowledge because it hadn't been a long time yet.

During break time a few teachers came into her room to quiz her. It was amazing how quickly gossip spread around school and the teachers were often worse than the pupils. Since it was the last day before the holiday, the lessons were very light and there were no assignments handed out. She didn't feel it was fair to give her pupils work to do when she was going to New York to have the time of her life.

Charlie arrived back at the school a little early and parked up on the road outside. He checked the hotel's address and had a look at it again on the map through his phone as he waited for 3pm to tick around. He'd worked in New York before as Coordinator for a Close Protection Detail, but that was just a short contract. He had to look after some VIP's that were attending a UN conference and he was put up in a nice hotel in midtown. His role was split fifty-fifty with another Coordinator, so he more or less had as much time off as he spent working. That meant he could wander around, but he never liked to go too far, just in case. It would be good to go back and not have work to think about. He could just go somewhere and be a tourist.

The school bell rang and brought Charlie's head back to Glasgow. Pupils started to stream out like confetti in the wind and he slowly slid the car along the now densely pedestrianised car park. *I maybe should have just parked straight in here*, he thought. The pupils all looked at his car and wondered who it could be. It wasn't one of the teachers, that was for sure. He remembered that it was a point of interest when he was at school for the kids to know what car each teacher had. Not only was it important should the need arise to egg a teacher's car, but also to figure out what sort of street-cred they had. He also remembered having to get away from school sharp otherwise he'd never make the bus on time and have to wait for the one at five past five at night.

He stopped the car as a girl headed straight towards him. She was texting on her phone or Facebooking or tweeting and the rest of the world didn't exist. She still headed towards him as Charlie thought that he should have *definitely* parked up before the bell rang. But the car park lay completely still when he arrived and he felt he'd be just too conspicuous parking actually in the car park.

She came closer still and Charlie turned his radio up. He didn't want to blast the horn at her and give everyone a fright. It worked and she looked straight up, startled by Charlie's presence. She altered her course to come along the driver's side of the car and he turned the radio back down. She was a very pretty girl, probably in her last year at school. She had yielding dark hair and unsullied pure hazel eyes. Her smile was warm and he was reminded of Nicola. She didn't look exactly like her, but she satisfied Charlie's lingering fixation with her. She stopped momentarily and said *sorry* through his open window. He wanted to say *sorry* or *it's okay* back, but nothing came from his mouth. She smiled at him and went on her merry way. He was taken aback by her and thought about Nicola at school. He'd never have thought that any of that could have happened. He never thought about her after school, they were never significant to one another, so what cruel trick of fate had brought their paths together once again only for things to turn out how they did?

Jess came out with a few of her friends and they talked for a few minutes. He wondered what to do. Should he get out and be introduced to her friends? She kept looking over at the car but gave no signals. The young girl flashed through his mind and so did the memory of Nicola, so Charlie opened the door and got out. She'd been waiting for him and beckoned him over. He put his hand on her hip and gave her a small kiss on the side of the head to greet her. 'Everybody, this is…' she thought about adding 'my boyfriend' but instead ploughed on through '…Charlie. Charlie this is Gillian, Isobel and Beth.'

'So, we hear you're taking young Jess to New York?' Gillian said.

'Yeah, that's right,' he looked at Jess and smiled. 'I can't wait.'

'I've been on at my Brian to take me for twelve years, and still no sign of it!' Beth added.

They exchanged a few more pleasantries before Jess wished them all a good break. She felt so special by the time she got in the car. 'I'm so lucky to have you and I really appreciate you taking me to New York, it's like a dream of mine.' She shook her head and chortled.

'What is it?' he asked.

'Nothing, just…you're so good to me.' A part of her thought he was too good to be true and what if this was some kind of scam or something? Yet then again, he didn't even ask for her number, everything came from her. After only a short time he was taking her to New York, and Beth's husband had been promising for twelve years and they still hadn't been. But there was still a niggling thought in the back of her head that there may be something about him that would turn out to be a deal-breaker, but she tried not to think about that.

'Well, you deserve it. You make me happy, so I want you to be happy.'

She leaned her head on his shoulder as Charlie pulled out of the car park. There was no sign of any school children and there was no sign of the girl that reminded him of Nicola, unless of course she was at the end of the street waiting for the bus, or maybe she'd been picked up by some older boys. He couldn't bear the thought and had to pacify himself not to trawl around the nearest abandoned industrial estates to find her and drive her home before she was taken advantage of. Looking back, he was fully aware of Nicola's reputation. He knew the things she got up to but chose to ignore it all. He felt foolish thinking that she was any different from then.

They drove through the west end. It was a grey dreary day but there was no rain. The air was somehow thick and unseasonably warm however. As Charlie drove, he would always scan the whole area in front and behind. It was a thing that he'd done for years, his situational awareness was incredible and he would never miss a thing. They turned left at a mini roundabout and he spotted a familiar figure. He pulled the car in quickly to the side of the road. 'That's my friend, I'm just going to say hi.' Jess appraised the pavement occupants and there was an old man with a grey bonnet carrying a plastic shopping bag, a middle-aged woman walking a small dog, a teenage boy with a backwards facing cap carrying a skateboard and a young woman with a rucksack on her back. She couldn't see any potential peers of his. He hopped out the car and jogged round to the pavement. 'Claire!' She was walking in a world of her own until Charlie startled her.

'Charlie, hey.' She tugged out her earphones, saw the car and heard the engine still running.

'How are you?' he asked.

'Yeah, I'm fine.'

'How's Nicola?'

'Well, she's alright, but–' The passenger door popped open and Claire saw Jess emerge from the car. *Who the hell is this?* Claire thought.

'Claire, this is Jess. Jess, my very good friend, Claire.' It seemed it was a day for meeting friends.

'It's been a while Charlie. I'm sort of running home though, I've got an appointment later.' She wanted to bring Charlie up to speed with Nicola. She felt guilty about not keeping him informed and she could tell that he was bursting to know about her, but it was not the time. 'We should meet for a catch up,' she said. Claire looked weary from work and life and he didn't want to keep her any longer.

'Yeah…' Charlie realised all too well that Nicola would hear about the attractive young woman who got out of the car. '…erm.'

'This week is jam packed, but how about next week?'

'We're going to be in New York,' Jess blurted out.

'Oh, okay, well give me a call when you get back and we'll organise something.'

Claire could sense the interrogation she was going to get and it wasn't as if she'd be able to keep it from Nicola. She wanted to ask if they were an item but by the wary look in Jess's eyes could tell that they were. 'Have a nice time in New York.'

'Thanks Claire, I'll give you a shout when we're back. Take care.' She didn't know whether she should give Charlie a hug like they usually would, but went for it anyway. The only thing to hide from Jess was Nicola. Claire missed Charlie. And that strong manly and platonic embrace was always comforting. He really knew how to hold a woman. She could understand why Nicola would run to there all the time. Jess was opening the car door as Claire spoke to her, 'Nice to meet you.'

'Likewise,' came Jess's bogus reply.


They resumed the drive to Charlie's flat and Jess was silent the rest of the way. She didn't rest her head on his shoulder and she didn't rant and rave about New York. When he saw Claire, the two options passed through his mind in a split second. He could have driven past and Jess would be none the wiser. Claire most likely wouldn't have spotted Charlie's car anyway. Or he could stop and speak to her and see how she and Nicola were. He didn't feel he needed to conceal the fact he knew Claire from Jess, there was nothing going on between them. Had it been Nicola, he'd have driven painfully past for sure.

He kept sneaking glances at Jess as she sat quietly. 'You okay?' He touched her on the hand and she withdrew it.

'Yes, I'm fine.'

'You're about to fly to New York with a dashing gentleman for a romantic getaway and you're 'fine'?'

'Yes.'

Charlie knew that seeing Claire had bothered her. Jess thought that was it. That was how he was too good to be true. He was obviously a player. He must have a hundred women in his little black book and that was another one. How can he drive for ten minutes and randomly spot a 'very good friend'? She hugged him when they said goodbye as well so she must be an old flame of his, one which he's still close to and that wouldn't do at all. 'Are you being a silly Jess right now?' His tone was light as he tried to get through to her, but she continued to provide one-word answers.

'No.'

'I think you are...' She scowled at him. 'Claire,' he began, 'is an old friend of mine. We were at school together and we're now in Glasgow just by coincidence.' He scanned the road and slowed down for a pedestrian to finish crossing.

'What do you mean *very* good friend?'

*Is she really doing this?* he thought. 'I mean, I've known her a long time and we're good friends. Do you think if there was something between me and her that I'd have stopped with you in the car so you could see each other?' He omitted the twelve years that he hadn't heard from or spoke to her, but technically he had known her a long time.

'So…you've never gone out with her?' He brought the car to a stop at a red light.

'No.'

'Have you slept with her?'

'No, never. I'm telling you Jess, she's a friend. She's sort of…more like a sister.' Charlie realised it as he said it. He did love Claire and always looked out for her as much as Nicola, he'd do anything for her, but there was just never any romantic connection. He missed her a lot though.

'But she's beautiful. You promise there's nothing between you?' He thought about it and decided to cunningly rephrase it, because he'd never want to lie to her. There was definitely something between them – that being Nicola.

'I promise to you, Jess Stephenson, that I have never had any romantic liaisons with Claire nor shall I ever. I love her to pieces but as a friend, and that's it.'

'Okay.' She was sort of convinced and a rush of adrenaline filled her. She hoped that she hadn't pissed Charlie off, and she hoped that he wasn't lying. The red light changed and he moved off.

'You know…you're really cute when you're jealous. Your wee button nose goes all crinkly.'

'What?' Her lips started to curl upwards and she tried not to laugh. She slapped his leg.

'You're crazy to think I'd see someone else behind your back, Jess. You have to know that. That's not me at all.'

'I'm sorry, Charlie. It's just–'

'Jess, it's alright.' He grabbed her hand and kissed it as he scanned and drove the road. 'How many flights to New York do you think I can afford anyway?' he joked. *Probably a lot*, she thought, but she believed him. 'How about I take you shopping tomorrow for some new clothes for our holidays?' A smile started to return as she was reminded of lucky she was again. There's not a lot of guys would think about how a woman wants new clothes to go on holiday.

'Yeah, that'd be good.'

'That's if you still want to go to New York with me.' His tender smile melted away all the ill-feeling in her.

'Of course.'

'I mean, if I'm going to be seen with you in public, you'll have to get some…' he wagged his finger at her school teacher attire, 'decent clothes anyway.'

'Hey!' The humour worked well and Jess was back to normal. Charlie was so important to her and she didn't want anything to get in the way of it. No other woman, no nothing. She rested her head back on his shoulder, but remained quiet for the rest of the journey home.

Nicola parked her car outside Claire's flat and had to think back to Charlie's instructions. *When the wing mirror is in line with the pillar give it a full turn to the left, until the car is at forty-five degrees…* She had been terrible at parallel parking but now she could do it without any problem, so long as she remembered Charlie's instructions. She brought a pizza for her and Claire and they were going to watch a movie. Claire wondered whether to tell Nicola about seeing Charlie, but it prickled in her like an unscratchable itch. Nicola was sometimes economical with the truth but Claire rarely kept anything from her. Now for the first time she was thinking about not being fully honest.

'I bumped into Charlie today.'

'Uh-huh…' Nicola tried to make out as if it was something insignificant.

'He's looking well.'

'That's good.' Nicola opened the pizza box and slid a knife through the plastic.

'He's going to New York next week…' Claire was working up towards it, '…and he was with a girl…' Nicola stuffed the plastic back into the box and folded it in an attempt to fit into Claire's bin. It was too big and poked out the top.

'Which one is the oven again?' There were no post-it notes to direct her. Claire came over and switched the cooker on and set the temperature.

'…and they're going to New York together…'

'That'll be nice for them.'

'Nicola!'

Claire was stunned by her nonchalance. She seemingly didn't care what Charlie was doing or who he was with, except she burned inside to know who she was, how they'd met and what she looked like.

'What? That's good for him.'

'So what's the deal with you and Tommy?' Tommy was Claire's friend that Nicola met one night at the comedy club. He and Nicola had started to spend a lot of time together and she hadn't really been keeping Claire in the loop.

385

'He's nice. He's really funny, he makes me laugh.' *Is that it?* Claire thought. Claire liked Tommy. They were at college together and she'd known him for a several years, but he was not a patch on Charlie.

'Are you two an item?'

'Well…I suppose so.'


They ate the pizza and put the movie on. Claire hardly watched it despite it being one of her all-time favourites. She couldn't help but think about how Nicola had so easily disgorged Charlie from her life after all he had done for her. She was so glad when she heard about Patrice and felt such a sense of satisfaction. Charlie had done right by her as he always did, yet Nicola took Patrice's side, or seemingly did by not taking Charlie's.

For Claire, there was a big personal loss too. Charlie was a very valuable and loyal friend. He'd helped her out with a hundred small things in her life and was always there to rely on. It was good for her to have a big strong man with his skills and resources who she shared a purely platonic connection with. He was always kind to her and many of the things he did for Nicola he'd do for them both so that they could be together. Not to mention the weight he helped to bear with Nicola's issues. That was ruined now. Without him, Claire would now have to rely on an ex-boyfriend or someone else who was trying to get into her

386

pants, or her big brother who would complain endlessly about driving all the way through to Glasgow to do something for her, and tell her how it was 'about time she grew up'.

Nicola sat munching chocolate, seemingly oblivious to the fallout of her actions. Her phone lay on the sofa next to her and it lit up as the credits started to roll. 'It's Tommy,' she said with a smile on her face. 'I'm going round to his after this.' It was unusual for them. If Nicola would come round, or if Claire went to hers, they'd stay up until early the next morning and talk rubbish and just hang out and be friends together. Now it seemed like she was being squeezed in before she went round to Tommy's for the 'main event' of the evening. Claire didn't like it.

'What about Charlie?' Nicola looked at her.

'What *about* Charlie?'

Claire didn't want to fall out with Nicola, but the whole situation was antagonising her. 'I think you should apologise to him.'

'Oh, for what, Claire? I've not done anything wrong.'

'But you have and you refuse to see it. You shut him out after what he did to Patrice, but I'd have done that to him if I was able to.'

'Yeah right. There's no way you'd have done that to him.' Nicola knew exactly what Claire was getting at, but rather than admit she was wrong, she'd just try to palm her off. 'There's nothing to apologise for.'

'Yes, there is, and I would have, Nicola, a thousand times over! How many times have I had to pick up the fucking pieces with you?? And I do it because I love you, and I'll always do it. And I would have done that to him in a heartbeat because when you've got someone that you love, you'll do anything you can to protect them. You've made a big mistake with Charlie. And you're mucking around with Tommy.'

'What difference does it make? Anyway, he's with some other girl now, so it doesn't matter. Everything's turned out fine.' Claire remembered the frantic look on cool calm and collected Charlie's face as he was desperate to ask about Nicola before Jess got out of the car.

'Everything's *not* fine, and it matters to me. He's the best thing that's ever happened to you…and to us. And you've fucked it all up. What's Tommy done for you?'

Nicola collected her handbag, threw on her trainers and jacket. 'Claire, you're way off on this. I'll come back when you've stopped talking rubbish.' She kept her tone calm as she tried to retain her nonchalant façade and opened the door quickly to escape before Claire could see her resolve break.

Claire returned to the sofa and cried. She cried for losing Charlie and she cried for what'd happened to her friendship with Nicola. They'd only ever argued once before and not only was that about something trivial, it was over fourteen years ago. She got up wiping her face and switched the television from DVD back to TV. Over at the window she could see Nicola's car still parked across the road. There was a small light in her lap – it was her mobile phone. Claire supposed she was texting Tommy to see if she could come over early.

Charlie was already in bed with Jess. Her hands roamed his strong back as he was on top of her. His phone flashed as he received a message but neither of them noticed. They were in a world of their own. "Hey, Charlie! Claire said she saw you today, we should have a catch up, it's been a while. Hope you're well. Xx ☺"

Nicola drove away from Claire's and arrived at Tommy's. He'd been out for a few beers with some of his workmates and was feeling amorous by the time she arrived. She was upset about the argument with Claire and wanted to talk about it, not that she'd tell him what the argument was about exactly, of course. His hands were all over her and he started to kiss her. 'I've been wanting this all day,' he said.

'Tommy, Tommy. Just er, stop a second. I don't feel well tonight.'

'Oh, I know what will make you feel better.' He started to undo his belt and trousers.

'Sorry, I think I'm just going to go home. You should sleep this off.'

'Oh, don't go. I'm sorry, I'm just a bit drunk. Just stay, I'll behave.'

'Alright.'

He sat down to watch television and Nicola made herself a cup of tea and a strong coffee for Tommy. By the time she came through he was already fast asleep. She let herself out and drove home on her own.

Charlie didn't read her message until the next morning. Jess was in the shower and she sang – badly – but she sang nonetheless. Charlie had put happiness in her life, so why shouldn't she sing? He used the other bathroom to shower and started to prepare breakfast. He could tell by the particular slaps of foamy suds on the shower floor that she was washing her hair, so he knew he had plenty of time. It was a croissant type of breakfast. The percolator gurgled and the smell of warm croissants and coffee filled the air.

It was a nice day so they decided to walk into town. They stopped in a few shops and she tried clothes on. She went into the same place he bought Nicola's suit. He never did get the money back for that. He didn't want it back anyway – not then and certainly not now. Jess looked mainly at dresses and tried a few more on. Charlie waited patiently and thought about texting Nicola back. He sat on the same plinth as he did when he waited for Nicola to try on her suit. If he did text her what would he say? He didn't want to open a line of communication with her because he was with Jess and he cared too much for her. But Nicola still eroded him inside.

Jess was the only thing that let him get on with his life. She was a Godsend and a saviour to him. He held his phone in his hand the whole time Jess was trying on her dresses and put it away just before she came out. 'I really liked this one, but I don't like the slit up the leg, it's a bit slutty. And that one doesn't fit very well.' She returned the two unsuitable ones to the attendant. 'This one's so nice though.'

'Why didn't you come out to let me see?'

'Oh. I didn't think you'd be bothered.'

'Of course I am. But, I suppose, this way will be better. I'll get to see them in New York, and you can take my breath away there.' Her heart glowed.

'Oh, Charlie.' She kissed him and made her way to the counter to pay. Charlie took his wallet out and Jess asked him what he was doing.

'Well, I said I'd take you shopping, didn't I?'

'Yeah, but I can pay. You've already paid for the holiday.'

'I know you can pay, but it was my idea, so it's my fault that you're having to buy new clothes. You wouldn't be buying these if we weren't going to New York would you?'

'Well, no. But–'

'There you go then. Plus, I want to pay so that way, when I see you in it, I'll know that I've bought it for you and it'll mean more to me.'

Jess couldn't argue there. She wanted to mean as much as she could to him. She wanted to be his one and only, above all others. The 'scare' with Claire the previous day had given her a fright, so she gladly conceded. She knew that he wasn't patronising her by paying for everything, he just wanted to show kindness in droves, it was just his way.

'Don't worry though, I'm keeping tabs. Starting with the twenty pee for water at the petrol station.'

He had high hopes for New York. He wanted it to be perfect and he wanted to fall in love with her in some movie-looking location and everything would be perfect and Nicola wouldn't even cross his mind anymore.

Tommy called Nicola the next day. 'Nicky, I'm so sorry about last night. And I'm sorry if I was out of order. I was steaming.'

'It's okay.'

'So, what you doing today?'

She was supposed to be going for lunch with Claire but she hadn't heard from her at all. They weren't talking. 'Nothing. You want to meet up? I'm really bored anyway.'

'Yeah, I'm still in bed.' It was already the afternoon. 'I'll probably need a couple more hours though, I'm absolutely burst.'

'Okay. Well…just call me when you get up.'

She'd never have to wait for Charlie. He was the one always ready and waiting, morning, noon or night. He would drink, but always remained a gentleman and the next morning he'd never be wiped out by a hangover. He's the one that would come round and make them breakfast and bring it to them whilst they were still pretty much in bed. But Tommy was nice. He was just a normal guy and guys go out on a Friday night and get drunk. Never mind that Saturday is almost gone by the time he's ready to do something.

Without Claire to help fill her day, it was a long wait until Tommy called again, in fact it was after dinnertime. Nicola hadn't eaten anything because she was going to suggest they go out somewhere for a bite to eat. She tried to call him but he was obviously still fast asleep. She stayed in her flat and watched a few movies by herself. She played with Pinky, her little cocker spaniel that Charlie got her on her birthday. The vase that her sweet peas came in lay empty next to the TV. The sweet peas were long gone, as was Charlie. He hadn't text her back despite his colossal longing to do so. Nicola felt infinitely empty. *Maybe Claire was right*, she finally admitted to herself.

# Chapter Eighteen

They left the hotel early and headed through Manhattan to reach the Ferry Terminal. Charlie wore his tactical trousers and Jess was in jeans. He never managed to get to the Statue of Liberty when he was there before because it was a little too far away – or more, it was difficult to get back from in a hurry. But now he was free to do as he pleased. They waited in line to pass the security checkpoint. Charlie knew how important they were, but he also knew how much of an overreaction they were too. The main fallout after the terrorist attacks meant that travelling and now even sightseeing had become a bit of a nightmare. He was tired of having to remove his watch and boots and undo his belt and empty his pockets and take his jacket on and off. He also liked to have a bag with him wherever he went abroad, his *EDC* or *Everyday*

*Carry*. It contained a lot of essentials and first aid equipment. It meant he was ready for anything, which was something that he liked to be. He hated getting it scrutinised by 'Security' and them trying to figure out how much of a threat he was. If only they knew that anywhere around the vicinity of Charlie was generally a safer place to be. Jess noticed a patch on the bag, 'What flag is that?'

'It's actually the nautical code flag for *C* or *Charlie*. It means *yes*,' he smirked.

'I thought it was a country flag.'

'Well it's more or less the same as the Thailand flag, except the red and blue are the other way round. But it was my insignia on all my kit before. Everybody recognised me by that.'

'Oh, okay.' Her mind wandered again. 'Have you ever been?' He looked at her quizzically. 'To Thailand, I mean? You don't have a Thai girl or something do you?' She was half joking. Only half though.

Charlie laughed, 'No, I've never been. Next holiday, okay?'

After security they boarded the ferry *Miss Liberty*. It was windy out in New York harbour and Jess clung to Charlie as they sailed away from Manhattan. The skyline started to look more postcardy with every minute that passed. There was only so much of Manhattan you can see when you're *in* Manhattan. They wandered around the island and took a lot of pictures. The sun was shining but the wind still blew. A man was directing his daughter to hold her fingers in an open pinch as he tried to line up the Empire State Building between them in his camera.

'Oh, it's just so lovely here.' Jess wandered up to a telescope and put a few quarters in to make it work. She had a look at Manhattan and found the Empire State Building, the Chrysler Building and the new tower they were building where two stood before. She came back to Charlie. 'You know,' she said looking up at the Statue of Liberty, 'it's a lot smaller than I was expecting.'

'I hope it's the statue you're talking about, yeah?'

After exhausting all activities on the island, they boarded the ferry again. 'So what do you want to do when we get back?' she asked.

'I don't mind.' He took her hand. 'I'm very happy that you're here with me Jess.' He was. If it was not for her, he couldn't imagine where he'd be, but he was thinking more gutter than New York.


They went out for dinner that night and Jess put on one of her new dresses. Charlie got ready first and went down to the bar in the lobby to have a drink whilst she finished dressing and doing her hair and make-up. He'd booked a table at a fancy Italian restaurant. He wore a charcoal suit and a smart white shirt and looked very handsome indeed. He sat in the lobby bar drinking an Old Fashioned and watched people go by as he waited.

It was reminiscent of his work, just sitting and watching people. There was a man in a tweed suit leaning on his umbrella in the lobby. He had a head of snow white hair and a perfectly groomed goatee beard. He adjusted his circular-framed tortoiseshell glasses and checked his watch. A young middle-eastern man came in wearing jeans and a leather jacket and walked past the tweed suit man. His face was stubbly and he talked loudly on his phone all the way to the lift before pushing the button impatiently.

A message came through on Charlie's phone. "Hey, Charlie. Claire and I were wondering if you were free next week for a catch up?" He still felt the need to reply but just couldn't do it. He wished he could just use the fact he was in New York as an excuse to not reply and say that he had no internet signal or something. He wondered why the hell it mattered what she thought. He didn't owe her anything, so why should he have to reply if he was busy? She was the one that said not to message or call, yet she persisted in messaging him despite not getting any replies. He did wonder however why he got a message from her after 7 p.m. in New York, because that meant it was getting late in the UK and she should be in bed sleeping – or not sleeping as the case was.

The elevator pinged and there emerged Jess. The doors opened like the parting of the Red Sea to reveal his exodus. Her velvety dark chocolate dress was accented with a deep red shawl which draped over her gorgeous pale shoulders. Men stopped and looked at her. Women stopped and looked at her. And she was Charlie's. Maybe she wasn't Nicola, but maybe that was for the best. She shuffled coyly towards him. 'So…do I scrub up alright?'

'I should say so. Jess…you look…' he couldn't find a word to describe her.

'Good enough to be seen in public with you?'

'Erm, definitely.'


Nicola lied a little in her message. Claire still hadn't spoken to her and was waiting for an apology – or at the very least an admission. She thought if she managed to get Charlie to agree to meet for a catch up then she could tell Claire and they'd all meet and everything would be fine again. She was at work all week but her days were boring and meaningless. She'd meet Tommy most nights and they'd spend some time together but she never stayed over. She really missed Claire. Without her, she only had Tommy in her life and whilst he was nice and he tried his best, he just didn't understand her the way that Claire or Charlie did. And in everything that he tried to do, he'd always come up short of Charlie's efforts.

By all counts, he was a good boyfriend, but there was definitely something missing. She lacked the euphoric feeling that she'd get from spending time with Charlie and the way he always made everything special, but because she was so determined to make things work with Tommy she wouldn't ever realise it. She always took for granted everything that Charlie did and that was why she didn't know exactly what was missing. But now in Glasgow she was alone. She'd perhaps be fine without anyone in the world except for Claire. She called her one day during lunch and Claire said, 'Sorry, I'm just in the middle of something, I'll give you a call back.' She didn't call back.

With their bellies full and their heads swimming a little in alcohol, Charlie and Jess left the restaurant. 'Of course, I wear a white shirt when I'm eating spaghetti!' There were a few spots of tomato sauce on his shirt and he spent a little time blotting it with his handkerchief in the bathroom. Most of it came off, but he knew it was still there and tried to pull his suit jacket further shut to hide it.

'So, what do you want to do now?' he asked. Jess was thinking *straight back to the hotel please.*

'I dunno, I'm a little sleepy...'

'Oh, come on. It's the city that never sleeps! We'll get to the hotel in the end, don't worry about that. Let's go down to Pier 17. Anyway, I want to show you off some more before you turn back into a pumpkin,' he joked. He was reasonably well-acquainted with the subway system and used it a lot the last time he was in New York. He didn't feel that she belonged on the subway with the way she looked that night, despite the fact that everybody from all walks of life would ride it. He hailed a cab. 'I should really be getting you a limo or something, but you know, I'm just not very good.' He shrugged and smiled at her before stealing another kiss as she got in.

'Well, Charlie, you must try harder.' She had a teaseful look on her face.

'Pier 17, please.'

They took a table outside at a bar opposite an old lighthouse ship that was permanently docked there. The Brooklyn Bridge stood proud and prevailing over the river. They sat for a while and watched the people go by. They were a beautiful couple and it had been a beautiful night. Jess was full of pasta and wine but mostly with adoration. She felt like a movie star in her amazing dress that he bought her and the wonderful dinner she'd had. Now she sat with her kind, thoughtful and handsome consort in a place she had always dreamed of being. She loved Charlie and loved him deeply. 'Charlie?'

'Yes, my Jess?'

'Do you know what the best thing I've ever done in my life is?'

Charlie thought about it. 'You're volunteering work?'

'No, no. Nothing like that.'

'Then what?'

'It was trying to put Evian in my car.'

Charlie chuckled. 'Is that right?'

'I'm so glad you helped me that day. And all because of that, we're here now.'

'Well, I just like to help people, it's what I do. I'm just glad that this time I've been able to help someone and not have it backfire on me.' *Oh, shit! What did I say that for?* Charlie scolded himself and hoped that she wouldn't ask what he meant. She didn't.

Jess wanted to tell him that she loved him but she feared it may still be too early. If she put him on the spot and he lied about loving her, or if he didn't say he loved her at all, then the whole evening would be ruined. She didn't take it any further because she couldn't risk spoiling the most perfect of evenings.

'You know, Jess. I've had a lot of hard times in my life. I've had to trawl through a lot of shit, but I've finally found my treasure.' Charlie got his wallet out as he caught the waiter's attention. 'I think it's about time we got back to the hotel, don't you?'

Jess woke up early with a thumping headache and an unrelenting dryness in her mouth. She hadn't slept much the previous night, not just because of the love-making but because Charlie was snoring loudly. He usually snored, but never that loud. She put it down to the drink and food and perhaps the physical exertion when they got back. Charlie was enjoying the deepest sleep he'd had in so many years. The demons that chased him regarding work and the life decisions he'd made usually plagued him. The loneliness was always the worst however. With Nicola it only got worse. The closer he got to her, the lonelier he'd feel. But with Jess, there was contentment and he could fully relax and sleep deeply. Nicola still hung around in his head at times but he was so keen on Jess and the night they'd spent together was amazing.

She went to the fridge in the room and took out a bottle of water. Her pallet felt waterproof as the water trickled down her throat. It took a while to get some moisture back. After using the toilet she went back to bed to snuggle into Charlie. He was still fast asleep and snoring loudly, but she didn't mind. She began to dose a little but was woken by Charlie murmuring something. It was three syllables, but she couldn't make it out. He murmured again. The murmuring eventually stopped and the snoring resumed as Charlie continued to sleep. Jess could finally get some more sleep curled into the man she loved.


Claire's week was going slowly. She'd taken a call from Nicola at work and said that she'd call her back but she didn't. She met up with a few of her friends for a drink mid week and Tommy wasn't there. He was probably with Nicola as they continued her misguided attempts of moving on. It started to become common knowledge amongst that group of friends however and people were saying, 'Oh yeah, they're a lovely couple'.

She eventually called Nicola, which was exactly as she said – just it was three days later already. 'Hi Nic. How are you?'

'Yeah, I'm fine. You?'

'Yeah, I'm fine.'

'Heard from Charlie?' Nicola asked.

'No, he'll still be in New York.'

'With his girlfriend.'

'Jess, her name is.'

'Is erm…what are you doing tonight? Want to go for a drink?'

'Sure.'


It came to Charlie and Jess's last full day in New York. He wanted to walk the Brooklyn Bridge, so after breakfast they took the subway from Grand Central Station. On the train there was a man with a portable PA system who was beat boxing. Apparently his name was 'Verbal Ace'.

Charlie's ears popped from the change in pressure as the train descended under the water and left Manhattan for Brooklyn. 'That's us under the river now,' he said. 'We're not getting off at this station though, it's the next one.' They emerged onto the street and Charlie had lost his bearings momentarily. 'That's the thing about the subway, there are no landmarks to follow and you don't know when you're turning.'

'Shall we ask someone?'

'No it's okay, if we just walk a bit we'll probably be able to see it.'

They walked along the block following Charlie's gut and there was a wide road which led to the bridge. 'There it is,' he said. He found some signs to confirm it and they followed them until they found the pedestrian entry. They took their time walking along the bridge and stopped in several places to take photographs, or just to sit. There were a lot of other couples and families and friends from all over the world. They eventually ambled back into Manhattan and they looked around the City Hall area. There were a lot of street vendors and they bought some souvenirs and presents to take back home.

They stumbled upon a memorial for fallen fire-fighters from September 11. Photos and messages and flowers occupied a wall and sidewalk and Charlie was stopped in his tracks. He looked at the faces of some of the fire-fighters and read their names and the messages from family and friends. Jess paused to wait for Charlie but had been looking the other way, not realising what they'd stumbled upon. There was a photo of one firefighter with a dog-ear and he tried to straighten it out. 'Charlie, are you okay?'

'Oh, yeah. It's just…this took me a bit by surprise. All these guys, dying in the line of duty. Just trying to help and protect people. And especially when they leave families behind, it's just…' pain and emotion rose in him, 'it's not fair.' Jess felt bad but she had no conception of that kind of loss. It was of a thing so far removed from her life, but she could appreciate the parallels between that and the job that he used to do and the friends that he had lost. He didn't cry as such, yet a tear rolled silently down his cheek and she wrapped her arms around him and comforted him. She was there when he really needed her. That was something Nicola never ever was.

Before dinner they had to pack because their flight was early in the morning. 'Oh, up at four a.m.? Why did you have to book it for so early?' she asked him.

'I'm sorry, but that's just the flight times. Just drink lots of water tonight. Then when the alarm goes, you'll have to get up because you need the toilet.'

'What??' She threw him a bemused look.

'It's true! It's how the apaches' used to launch their dawn raids. They didn't have any alarm clocks at all, did they?'

'Erm…okay.' She knew he had a peculiar knowledge about those kinds of things so she was sure he wasn't trying to wind her up. 'I'll try it. How much should I drink?'

'I dunno, about a pint or so? Just make sure it's after…' he made a thrusting motion with his hips, '…you know. We don't want any accidents!'

'That's if there is any!'

'Oh, so you think you can resist me now?' He took her in his arms and swung her around in the hotel room.

'I might be too tired, you know, before the flight. I should just rest up.' She teased him.

'Don't worry, it's me that does all the hard work anyway!'

They went to bed shortly after dinner and Jess drank a pint and a half of water before going to sleep. Charlie's trick worked, but perhaps a little too well. It was 2 a.m. and Jess's bladder was swollen. She got up quietly and checked the clock. She thought about waking Charlie too, but decided to wait until morning to give him a hard time about it. He stirred when she flushed the toilet. There was no way to do that quietly. *If he wakes up, he wakes up*, she thought, *this is his bloody fault.* When she came back through, he was still sleeping, but had started to murmur again. She'd never noticed that about him before, but then he was usually always last to sleep and first to get up. She snuggled back into him and shut her eyes laughing at his random utterances. He continued to murmur and she listened carefully to try and make out what he was saying. Again, it was three syllables. She jabbed him gently in the ribs. 'Nicola,' he said. 'Nicola.' He said it again. 'Nicola.' Jess turned over in bed and he said it clearly for a fourth time. *Who the fuck is Nicola?* She tried not to panic or get mad, it could have been anyone, or it could have been no one. It could just be random rubbish that the brain develops during sleep. She lay in bed facing away from him and stared at the curtained window until the alarm clock went off.

'Oh, good morning Jess. You're awake, so I don't need to throw water all over you? I'm very disappointed!'

'No, I think I had enough water last night, thanks very much. I was up at bloody 2 a.m! Some idea that was.'

'Oh, I'm sorry. I suppose that much water is about right for me. But you won't be able to fit as much in your wee belly.' He poked at her stomach gently with his index fingers and she jumped because she was ticklish there.

She had spent the previous two hours thinking about *Nicola* and who she might be. She convinced herself that it was nothing to worry about. The week had been the best week of her life. She tried to think back as to whether Charlie had been on his phone to someone else and he hadn't been. It must just be a random thing. He'd treated Jess so well and the week had been so perfect. He'd spent so much on the holiday as a whole, there was surely no way that he'd do that if he had something else going on.

They settled into their seats on the flight. Jess was a slightly nervous flyer, but only showed it during take-off and landing, and of course if there was any turbulence. On the way there, she tensed up in her seat and Charlie felt it. He tried to pacify her by telling her how it was the safest mode of transport.

The flight attendant stopped and talked to Charlie and Jess as everyone else boarded, but Jess knew she only wanted to speak to Charlie as that's where the majority of her conversation was directed. She got really close to him as she stretched up to shut the overhead compartment in super slow motion. Charlie was too handsome. He must have had a hundred girls on the go at one time. She thought about how she herself had asked for his number, something that she'd never done before and wondered how many more have done the same. *Who is Nicola?*

The pilot throttled up to 'take-off, go-around' or 'TOGA' as Charlie explained to her, but she didn't tense that time. It was such an insignificant thing now compared to the thought of there being someone else. If they died on take-off then that would just be fine. At least she'd be by his side and wouldn't have her heart broken by finding out something she dreaded. Jess desperately wanted to bring it up but she couldn't. When she didn't tense up as he was expecting, he checked on her. 'You okay, my little apache warrior? Comfortable?'

'Yes.' She took his hand and squeezed it hard as the plane started thundering along the runway. Tears began to roll down her cheek and she wiped them away with her free hand. 'I love you, Charlie. I love you so much. You're everything to me.'

'Jess, what's wrong?'

'Oh, it's just...I don't want to go home. I just want to stay in New York with you. Normal life can never compare to that.' He pulled her head in close to his chest as the other passenger at the window seat tried not to look or get involved with the emotions unravelling next to her.

'It can. It's not the place, Jess, it's us. It's you and me. Why are you crying you silly billy?' He held her as tightly as he could in the restricted space of the airline seat. 'And for the record...' he turned her face towards his.

'Uh-huh?'

'I              love              you              too.'

# Chapter Nineteen

Nicola and Claire had made up. They went out for a few drinks and as mad as Claire was with her, she would never have been able to stay mad at her for too long. She remained stand-offish with Nicola though until she agreed that she'd overreacted and that she owed Charlie an apology. 'I know Claire. I just suppose I got a fright more than anything else.' She continued, 'I know what he used to do for a living, but I just don't see him as someone that can do that kind of harm. It was just overwhelming for me. And to find out from Patrice's mum…it was all just a shock.'

'Well, so long as you put it right, Nic Nac, because, well…we need him back in our lives. I miss him.'

'Yeah,' Nicola agreed, sweeping hair behind her ears and rubbing her wearied eyes, 'I miss him too.'

Nicola and Claire arrived early at the restaurant and Charlie was running a little late. Jess got roped into helping with the after school club and that was one of the nights, so Charlie was free. He had been busy updating his CV as it was coming to a time where he ought to just get a 'regular job' and start living a 'regular life' – one with Jess. As such, he'd lost track of time. Listing his past credentials triggered thoughts and made him recount previous missions, especially if someone had been injured or lost their life. He wasn't so haunted by them now because of Jess, but he certainly would recount things into the fine detail. That proved to delay him in writing about his previous employment. Also, he wasn't sure how much of it he could put in because a lot of his work was still covered by Her Majesty's Secrets Act.

He struggled to find a space close to the restaurant and had to park several streets away from Byre's Road. Rain fell steadily and he jogged along the road, having to pause for the traffic lights. Tyres from the passing cars splashed and flicked up spray from the cold road as he waited for a gap to cross.

'Hey, Charlie! Not like you to be late!'

'I know, I know, sorry. Just lost track of time.' They had been huddling under Claire's umbrella and she collapsed it as Nicola pushed the door open into the restaurant.

The Maitre D' approached them, 'Table for three?'

'Yes,' Nicola replied, 'I made a reservation, name of Charlie Maxwell.'

Claire kicked off the conversation, 'So, how was New York?'

'Yeah, it was great. I got to see a lot more this time.' He thought about Jess and remembered that night she took his breath away when she emerged from the lift. He felt awkward to bring her up in front of Nicola, but he had to. 'We had a really great time.' They ordered some drinks and browsed the menu. 'What about you two, what have you been up to?'

'Oh, not much, just working away.' Claire didn't mention the fact that she and Nicola had a falling out. It wouldn't make any difference anyway. She was taking charge of the conversation which would allow Nicola some time to build up the courage that she needed to apologise. She knew she was working up to it.

'What about you, Nicola? How have you been? How's work and everything going?' The look in his eyes pierced her deeply and she felt a quivering weakness which rocked her whole body. It felt like such a long time since she'd seen him.

'Yeah, fine. Just the same, working away too. I've not had the chance to swan off to New York or anything.' *Fuck sake*, Claire thought, *you're going about this apology some way.* Charlie knew about Tommy and as much as he still burned for her, he wanted her to talk about him. He wanted her to give him reason to drive a wedge and separate his emotions from her, but she didn't bring him up by herself, he had to coerce it out of her.

'So what about you and Tommy? How's that going?'

'Yeah…fine.' *Only fine?* he thought. 'He makes me laugh, and he's a nice guy.' Nicola dipped a piece of bread in balsamic vinegar and olive oil and tore a chunk off with her teeth. Still chewing, she said, 'You know, he wanted to ask me out ages ago, but he was frightened to. He thought we were going out and didn't want to get on the wrong side of you, can you believe it?? How ridiculous!!' Claire tried to kick Nicola under the table, but couldn't get past the table leg. The glass bottled condiments shook in their wire holders instead and Charlie felt downtrodden.

Although he was happy with Jess, it was more of a learned love, a love by rote. By many measures it was perfect, but there wasn't that same unquantifiable dynamic that he found with Nicola. Rather, it was a relationship built on mutual attraction, affection and respect. But it wasn't like Nicola where he'd fallen hard and smashed into a million pieces only to pick every piece up and hand them back to her time and time again. To Charlie, Jess was an angel, but Nicola was a Goddess and he still worshipped her blindly. He never had to try hard for things to work with Jess, they just did. His logical side would tell him day in, day out, how Jess was the one for him. But logic aside, it wasn't ever an intellectual or conscious decision to fall for Nicola.

Despite her flaws and her callous nature, Charlie knew it was all a front. She had to try and laugh it off, the fact that Tommy thought they were together, because it was her that brought about their downfall and she couldn't handle that.

Claire pushed her chair back. 'Come on, Nicola, I'm going to the toilet.' Nicola didn't need the toilet, in fact, neither did Claire, it was for a quiet word. 'Back in a sec, Charlie.'

Whilst they were away from the table, Charlie checked his phone. There was a text from Jess. "Hey you. This is diiiire. I'm covered in paint! I wish you were here, or I wish I was where you were." *No you don't*, he thought. "See you later. I love you. Xxx"

They got to the toilet and Nicola knew she was in trouble. 'What the hell are you playing at Nicola? I thought you were here to apologise?' Claire only tended to use the full *Nicola* when she was in trouble.

'Well…what? I'm just waiting for the right time. I'll get there.'

'Yeah, and in the meantime you'll talk down to him like he's a piece of shit? He loves…' she paused, '…he loved you! I know he's with Jess now, but I bet if you ask him who he'd have rather taken to New York it'd have been you.'

Nicola tried to keep her front up. She tried with all her might but she could do nothing to stop the tears filling her eyes. Claire was right. The way that Charlie looked at her made her feel weak and strong at the same time. He made her feel like there could be no more sadness in the world. She was always safe and secure around him. She missed him like crazy and craved him and his body again. Tommy was alright, but nowhere near as good as Charlie. She often thought about that night at Charlie's whenever she was struggling to get there with Tommy and she'd have to bite her tongue not to say the wrong name. It was like Tommy had to really try hard to please her, but Charlie seemed effortless – in everything. She thought about the number of nights she'd lay awake thinking about Charlie and what he might be doing.

He sent a quick text back to Jess. "Well I'll have to find a way to clean that paint off, make sure you get it all over yourself, okay! ;)"

'So…what do I do now, Claire?'

'You can start by apologising. That's what you came here for in the first place. Then we'll take it from there.'

'I…I can't. What about Jess? He should be with her, it sounds like she deserves him. He deserves the best. He shouldn't have to put up with all my bullshit. It's not fair on either of them. I can't.'

Nicola ran out into the restaurant past all the other diners whilst tears rolled down her soft cheeks. She didn't stop for her bag or her jacket even though it was still raining outside. Claire ran out closely behind her and Charlie got up from the table. She signalled for him to wait as Nicola burst out onto the street filled with despair. Her head span with guilt and her heart was racked with regret. Her fluffy pink jumper delicately sucked at the soft drops of rain that landed on her as she stood out on the street wondering where to go and what to do. She thought about just running, or getting a cab back to her flat, but she'd left her purse and everything inside. He wanted desperately to go outside to her. He supposed she'd be crying and wanted to wrap his arms around her because that always made her feel better.

He wasn't so much of a fool to think that everything was great between them. He knew all too well that she treated him so badly, but good and bad he missed it all. He missed her having his undivided attention and her being the sole object of his affection.

He felt bad for Jess, but if he had to explain it any way, he'd say that he felt more that he was cheating on Nicola by being with Jess, than it being the other way around. That was the block that he had with her.

But it had to stop. At that moment he decided that he had to cut ties with her. He knew it would be hard, but he had to do it.

Claire came back to the table. 'Charlie, I'm really sorry.' She collected Nicola's things. 'Nicola's going to have to go. I'll be back in a minute though.' He did expect her to say that they'd both be going, but at least Claire wasn't leaving him too. He was concerned about Nicola leaving upset and by herself, but maybe it was for the best. As he watched them through the window, he saw Nicola put her jacket on and hang her bag on her shoulder before promptly walking off without exchanging a hug with Claire.

'What's wrong, Claire?'

'Nothing, she's just…I don't know.'

'Will she be okay? Maybe I should drive her home?'

'Really, Charlie. Just let her be, it's her own fault she gets like this. She'll just have to cope by herself for the twenty minutes it'll take her to get home. Don't waste any more of your energy on her.'

The food arrived for all three of them and Charlie had to explain that one of them had to leave. The waitress apologised and explained that she couldn't cancel the food because it was already made.

'So how are things with you and Jess?'

'They're great. She's great. And we're getting on really well. I was erm…maybe thinking about asking her to move in, actually.' Claire seemed to swallow a little hard.

'Really? Well, that's nice. Quite serious now then?'

'Well…' Claire watched him as he looked over her shoulder at the spot outside where Nicola stood moments before, willing her to come back and just be nice to him. 'She stays over so often, and when she doesn't, I really can't stand the emptiness of the place.' He chose not to admit about how when Jess wasn't there, Nicola started to leach from the walls and he'd pay attention to the reminders around the place of her former presence there.

'I just want you to be happy Charlie, because you deserve it.'

'Well, I am mostly happy.'

'Why only mostly?'

'I just feel I need to clear the air with Nicola. Other than that, this evening the last thing she said to me was that I was a dangerous man and that I was to stay away from her. And then…with her running out tonight, I just don't know what to make of it.'

'The thing is, it's never something you've done. I think she's still a little mixed up…and…well, the whole purpose of tonight was for her to apologise to you. If I'd have been able to, I'd have done the same to Patrice. I told her that. Except from driving him to the hospital of course. I'd have left him in the gutter where he belongs. That's what makes you different, Charlie. It's what makes you an outstanding person.'

Claire lost her appetite all of a sudden. Her neck seemed to turn weak and she had to use her hands to keep her head up out of the plate. 'And I really, really wanted to see you two together. I know the way you look at her, and I know you're happy with Jess, but I think you still love Nic. And she needs you. I think deep down she might…well…you *do* mean a lot to her. She never stops talking about you and asking about you. I just hope that we can still be friends…because you mean a lot to me too.'

'I know, Claire, and of course we would still stay friends, it won't make any difference to me if I'm not speaking to her. I care for you as well, you know? It's not just because of Nicola.'

'I know, but…it'd really bother her.' She flicked a piece of pasta over a few times and thought about eating it. 'Do you still love her?' Charlie thought about it, and as much as he didn't want to admit it, he did. The time that elapsed for the reply gave Claire her answer. 'Don't worry. You don't have to answer.'

Charlie walked back to his car and called Jess. 'Hey, that's me finished my dinner, I'm on my way. You want to come round to mine tonight?'

'Oh, at last…what were you doing? I've just been pining for you all evening you know…'

'That's a good girl!' He chuckled down the phone, 'I'll be round soon. You need anything?'

'Other than you, maybe a bottle of wine or something? And do you not just want to stay here? I don't want to go out again tonight, I'm all cosy.'

'Okay. See you soon.'


When Jess got in, she washed the last remnants of paint from her hands and arms. She got a few spots on her blouse and hoped it would come out in the wash, but it was water-based paint anyway. She took a bath and preened herself nicely for Charlie. It was the first week back after the school holidays and everyone was asking about her trip to New York. She took great pleasure in telling them about it and about Charlie. She showed a few photos of them and all her colleagues commented on how handsome he was. She loved it and despised it at the same time. She didn't want any other women to admire him, because he was to be hers alone.

'Where did all the paint go, then? I was hoping to sponge you down or something.'

'Well, you still can...' She kissed him long and tenderly. He pulled her in close and a flash of Nicola came across his mind. He had a hug stored up for her like a bullet in the breach for when they left all friendly after the meal, but it didn't happen. *I wonder if she's okay.* He'd thought about texting her but instead instructed Claire to check on her and let him know.

He remembered where he was and let Jess go suddenly. 'What's wrong?' she asked.

'Oh, nothing, I just want to get some wine. I maybe shouldn't have taken the car so I could've had a drink, but...never mind. I'll have one now. Got a taste for it after the meal.'

'How was it? Where did you go?'

'It was good. It was the new place on Byre's Road. I'll take you one day.'

Jess paused as she thought about the repercussions of her next question, but she couldn't *not* ask. 'Who were you with? You said it was with friends, right?'

'Yeah, remember Claire? We bumped into her before New York,' Jess nodded her head, 'and my other friend Nicola.'

Terror erupted in Jess and she felt a smack in the back of her throat. *Nicola.* Charlie obviously had no idea that he'd been muttering her name in his sleep. He had no idea that Jess had the knowledge of her name and thought he could say it innocently. He could have made up any other name or used the name of one of Claire's friends that he met before. Amelia or even Jenny could have been said and there would be no ramifications whatsoever. But he didn't like to lie to Jess. And if pushed he could say that he knew her from school too and that would be that.

'So this Nicola? How long have you known her?'

'Same as Claire, we were all at school together.'

'Oh yeah?' Jess's tone had changed and Charlie could sense it. But unlike before, where he knew she was being silly and overreacting about bumping into Claire, he knew something was up by her tone.

'Yeah, we're all old friends.'

'Okay.' Jess couldn't take it any further. She was trembling inside and she feared that if she pushed him that she might not like the answer. Most likely things were over between them, Jess supposed. Charlie really didn't seem like the type of person who would cheat. But then why would he be going for dinner with them? That was the thing that threw doubt into her head. What if he just went to dinner with this *Nicola* and Claire was not with them at all? She wasn't sure what time

423

they were supposed to have met, but she'd been at school all day. What if he'd been with her the whole day already? Why wasn't he just like other men and had male friends? Why did it have to be other women?

*Maybe if I try and get close with him now, I'll see how he responds.* Charlie felt awkward having Nicola so much in his mind when he was with Jess. He was still so full of anxiety and it ate away at his peace of mind. He didn't feel right. He thought about telling her, but then what was there to tell? Why should he volunteer information about a woman he'd fallen in love with but who continually rejected him?

Jess moved in close and started to kiss him. She undid the top few buttons of his shirt. 'I'll just pour some wine, shall I?' he said. Jess got the response she didn't want, despite jumping to the wrong conclusion about it.

Paranoia started to set in to her mind. She tried very hard to get over it but she couldn't. She had to speak to Charlie about it, but wasn't ready yet. She had to think it through very carefully before blurting anything out, just in case she might be wrong and blew it with him. Something was definitely the matter with him though. He was always so affectionate to her and never ever backed down from a kiss, or from holding her close to his big strong body.

She did very well to continue with the evening as normal. She wanted to see how he was, and how he'd act around her. Maybe it was nothing. After a short while in Jess's company, she managed to take up the forefront of his mind, but Nicola would still reside like a dark corner where no one would ever dare set foot and it cast a long shadow into his light.

'More wine?' Charlie asked.

'Yes, please.'

He smiled at her and it was warm and genuine. Jess tried to calm herself down and not get too carried away, but she watched him and wondered about him. What other things might he have to hide? She knew he had to operate clandestinely before, so an affair would probably be a very easy thing for him to pull off. He reached out for her hand as the movie played. She tentatively responded and he lifted it up to his lips and placed a kiss on it. *Or maybe I should just enjoy this and enjoy him, before it all blows up?* she thought. She slid along the sofa in her robe, closed her eyes and snuggled into him. She didn't care about missing the movie because she could put the DVD on any time and watch it whenever she liked. She wasn't so sure she could do that with Charlie now.

The clock ticked over to the next day and they were both ready to go to sleep. When Jess came into the room Charlie was already in bed. She shed her robe and climbed on top of him. She was feeling desperate. She felt that she ought to make love to him to see if it was different. But if his affair with Nicola had been going on for a while, Jess wondered how she'd be able to tell any difference anyway. A small part of her felt like shunning Charlie, but she craved him so badly and the thought of him not in her life was too much to bear. She had to do everything to be his number one and to keep what they had. As they kissed, he was tender and if anything, more tender and loving towards her. He felt like he had to make it up to Jess so tried to immerse himself in her.

Jess's head lay on his chest and she could hear his heart beating. *Why did Nicola just run off like that?* he wondered. Jess's hands wandered the definition of his muscles and tracked paths across his skin. *I hope she's alright.*

He never did get a text from Claire to say that she'd checked on her and that she was okay. He wasn't too worried about it though, because he knew if there really was something wrong he'd know by now. He supposed no news was good news. Anyway, he didn't want to be faced with having to text back or explain to Jess who had sent him a text, because she'd already been a bit edgy that evening. She hadn't spoken for a while, but her fingers still tracked him tenderly, so he knew she was still awake. 'Jess?' he said softly in the dark of her bedroom, 'I was wondering…and you don't have to answer me now…but I was wondering if you wanted to move in with me?' She turned her head up so that she could look at him. 'I mean, I know it's maybe fast, but the amount of time we spend together and everything…I just think it makes sense. But if you still want your own space that's alright, just tell me.'

A single apprehension flew into her head. What if it fell to pieces and she'd already moved out her flat and doesn't have her own place? But then, if they were under the same roof he'd not be bringing anyone else home, and aside from that, it was a big gesture and one that made her very happy.

She had to try it. If she had to find somewhere else in the end then she would just have to deal with that. 'Yes. I'd love to move in.' As soon as the words left her mouth the apprehension grew and consumed her. She should have thought about it a bit longer to weigh everything up and not said yes whilst lying with him after making love. It was perhaps not the best time to be making big life decisions, especially with all the things that were hanging over her. But she'd do practically anything that Charlie wished, just so long as she could stay with him.

Jess hardly slept. She thought about everything. Most of all, she wanted to be awake to hear if Charlie said Nicola's name again. He fell asleep and with the delicacy of Jess lying on him he was comforted. He didn't dream of Nicola or say her name at all that night and Jess was witness to it.

Charlie woke up first. Jess eventually fell asleep only a couple of hours or so beforehand but it was almost time for her to get up and go to work. They both hadn't moved a single inch since falling asleep, she was in the exact same position she was the night before. They'd slept (Jess eventually) in such synchronicity and it felt incredible to Charlie.

When her alarm started to chirp she was overwhelmed with a grogginess from the short sleep that she'd had. She felt somewhat placated about the whole Nicola thing and was very glad that he'd asked her to move in. Surely she was the only one, because it's hard to be a player when you've got a girlfriend living in your flat with you. Yet she still worried about leaving her place and not having anywhere to run to, just in case things went completely wrong.

They left the flat and made their way to Jess's car. She looked so pretty and refined in her skirt and blouse. 'So what you got planned for today?' she asked him. She thought about whether he was going to spend the day with Nicola perhaps and wanted to see if he'd lie.

'Oh, nothing really. Might just do a few scenarios for an exercise we've got coming up…Finish my CV…' She hated how free he was. Sure, it was great that he could run about and do so much with her, but with her being at school the whole day it also meant he was able to do whatever he wanted, or *whoever* he wanted. That thought suddenly flew into her head and started to erode the reassurance that she'd built up for herself overnight.

'Are you going to see your friends?'

Charlie was a little confused and sensed something about her ill-placed question. *She must mean Claire and Nicola?*

'Erm, don't have plans to. Probably not though, I just saw them last night.'

He stood close to her and she writhed with insecurity. The breeze rippled across his t-shirt and she could see his flat stomach and his front curl of hair bounced around a little. Jess couldn't just let him go without clearing the air. She wouldn't be able to settle at all until she knew everything. *Even if I just bring it up again so he'll get wary and won't go and see her*, she thought. 'So, who is Nicola, then?'

'I told you, she's a friend.'

'But who is she *really*??'

'I don't know what you mean. She's an old school friend, and we've just sort of caught up again recently, because it just so happens that we're living in Glasgow.'

She was in Glasgow. She was close. Jess had presumed that she was from back home if they were at school together. But she was there in Glasgow as well, so he could go and see her at a moment's notice, like any time his girlfriend was at work. 'What are you looking for Jess?'

'I don't know Charlie. Why don't you tell me? I mean…why would you say her name in your sleep?'

*Oh, shit!* He supposed he must have been thinking so much about her the night before that he said her name in his sleep. 'I want to move in with you and everything, but you…you have to be honest with me. Is there something going on?'

'No, there's not. Jess…'

'Well, I don't know why you'd be saying her name, and you're out to dinner with her. It's not very honest of you. I'm not sure about moving in now.' The words burned like acid as they left her mouth, but she had to be strong, she was taking affirmative action that she could no longer avoid. It hurt Charlie that she thought he wasn't being honest, and perhaps, he may have been lying by omission. He thought about coming clean but decided there was nothing to tell, there would be no reconciliation between him and Nicola. They'd missed their chance and he was sure of it.

'Jess, please. There's nothing going on.' He took a gentle hold of her hands as she stood by her car door. She tore her hands away.

'Please don't fuck with me!' Her eyes glazed over and a tear escaped and rolled down her cheek.

'Well, what do you want me to say? I've kissed her in the past, but it came to nothing, we were never actually together. I promise I'm not seeing her behind your back or anything.' Jess moved to wipe her tears but Charlie beat her to it. 'And if it came to nothing when I was single, it sure as hell isn't going to happen now I'm with you. And she's got a boyfriend too.'

'Did you sleep with her?' Charlie thought about it for a second, but now was a time to be honest. And it was months ago anyway. 'Once.'

'Well, I'm sorry, but I still don't know why you'd be saying her name in your sleep, and going out for dinner with her. It doesn't make sense to me.' She opened her car door. 'If there was nothing between you why would you see her at all?'

'Because we're friends. But that's it.'

Charlie had been completely honest, but the more honest he'd been with Jess, the worse her imagination ran away with her. Her experience with men, either past relationships she or her friends have had would tell her that a man reveals the first ten percent of what's actually going on when he's being 'honest'. She got in the car.

'I need some time to think about this…I need some space.' Charlie held the car door open and prevented her from closing it.

'Jess, please don't drive upset okay? Whatever you think, I'm being honest and that's everything. You know me.'

'I thought I did.'

'What does that mean? I'm still me. We've all had previous...'
he tripped up over the word, '...relationships.' She tried to pull the door
shut.

'But you're with me and you say her name.'

'I can't control what happens in my subconscious.'

'I know. That's what makes it worse. If you're with me, and
you're thinking about her. Do you love her?'

'I love *you*, Jess! Have I not proved how much you mean to me?
Everything I've done for you? My whole...everything...it's all about
you!'

'I need to get to work Charlie.' She'd reached saturation point
with the conversation. She hadn't planned it at all and wasn't expecting
to have such a conversation out there in the street, in her car. It wasn't
right, none of it was.

'Jess, can you ju–'

'The door, Charlie. I need to shut the door.'

He didn't want to trap her, even more than he didn't want to let
her go. She shut the door and started the car. He stayed at the car
window and knocked on it. She thought about just driving off, but rolled

the window down instead. 'Please, don't drive whilst you're upset. I love you Jess, you're everything to me. I only want you. Please, though, just wait till you've settled down before you drive off.' She turned to look at him. 'Whatever happens, I need you to be safe. Please, give it five minutes or so. Don't drive upset.'

'Okay.' She rolled up the window.


He sat for the four-and-a-half agonising minutes it took her to move off. He was parked further down the road and was glad that she took the time to settle down before driving away. He wanted to follow her to make sure she got to school safely, but he knew the very presence of him in her rear-view mirror would be cause enough for her to crash. For that reason, and the fact he wanted to give her the space she needed, he didn't follow her. He sat in his car and felt like he was dissolving into dust. He couldn't believe how Nicola had managed to fuck that up for him too. It seemed like she hadn't done enough damage so she had to ruin things between him and Jess too – by doing nothing at all. Charlie tried to think whether or not he dreamed about her the previous night and supposed it was just because he'd been worried. Maybe if he got that text from Claire that would have been enough to tie up the loose end and for him to rest easily with Jess. He remembered how perfect it felt to wake up with her in the exact same position as they fell asleep.

He had no idea, of course, that she'd heard him say it in New York, on a couple of occasions.

# Chapter Twenty

Charlie sent Jess a couple of texts during the day. The first was, "Please let me know when you arrive at work. Xxxxx." At least she had the decency to reply to that one, but she waited to reply to the rest of them. During her morning break, she had to resist with all her might to text him. It had become a habit, or even an addiction. She *was* addicted to Charlie and she really couldn't quit him. She would always text him, even if she had nothing to say. But that day she didn't, even though there were so many things she wanted to talk about.

Finally, the school bell rang to signify the end of the day and Jess had made it to her imaginary milestone and allowed the communication to resume. "Hey. I'm going back home tonight, my sister's home because it's her birthday. But I want to talk. Maybe tomorrow night, if you're free? X"

'What the hell's wrong with me?' Claire stopped chopping her onions but still held the knife in her hand as she spoke.

'What do you mean?'

'I mean, like...with Charlie.' Acid started to vaporise from the chopping board and stung Claire's eyes.

'Well...I don't know Nic Nac, but you seem to give him a hard time for nothing.' She tried to blink away the sting. 'He does nothing but look out for you. You know you were out of order at the restaurant. I don't have to tell you that.'

'I know.' She took her phone out and stared at it as if to conjure a text from him to say that everything was okay and asking if she wanted to spend time with him, but she imagined he'd be with Jess and who knew what they were doing. 'I just...I mean, I wanted to apologise...about everything. But I don't know where it comes from sometimes.' She put her phone down. 'He's always been so good to me though...'

'To us...' Claire interjected.

'I know. Do you think he'll still accept an apology from me?' Claire resumed her chopping so as not to prolong the stinging in her eyes. Rings of onions toppled like felled trees onto the damp chopping board.

'Well, he's Charlie, so I'd think yes, but…just try not to lose it.'

She came to the end of the onion and was glad to sweep it into a bowl to be cooked later. She washed her hands and tore a square of kitchen towel off to dab her eyes. 'I think…it might be a good idea to write everything down. Write him a letter. Put everything that you're thinking and everything you want to get off your chest. Seeing as you can't tell him face to face...' Claire dropped her knife into the kitchen sink and it rattled around for a second. 'Maybe best if I deliver it though. And write it tonight, before you head off tomorrow.'

'I broke up with Tommy.' Claire rinsed the stinging acid off the chopping board under the tap.

'Oh, yeah?'

'Yeah. He just wasn't…enough. He just–'

'Wasn't Charlie?' Claire offered. There was no reply.


Claire went round to Charlie's for a chat. She took the subway from the west end and watched people going about their business. She wondered what burdens they carried and what battles they fought. She felt the weight of her letter and it dragged her bag down like a bowling bowl.

Winter was starting to set in. It was a cold evening and the air was crisp and clear. As she walked along the road to Charlie's flat, she could see the building soar into the sky. The Clyde lay brooding and foreboding as small ripples whipped across the surface. She buzzed and took the elevator up to the seventh floor.

'Hey, Charlie.'

They hugged and he was unaware of the presence of Claire's cargo. 'Hey, come in.' She shed a couple of layers, resting them over the sofa where he and Nicola had made love. 'Something to drink?'

The light ebbed from the sky, disappearing beyond the hills in one direction and the concrete, glass and church spires of Glasgow in the other. 'So, what's new? Have you asked Jess to move in yet?'

'Well, yes...' she waited, '...but we sort of had a falling out.'

'Oh, that's not good.'

'It was Nicola.' Claire was confused. Had she done or said something to Jess? 'I erm...I said Nicola's name in my sleep and Jess heard it. She obviously asked who she was. I told her everything in the end, but I told her there's nothing between us. I mean, after dinner there, I know that she can't stand me.' Claire wanted to correct him, but let him finish. 'But it's better this way. If she can't stand me and doesn't want anything to do with me, then that lets me move on.'

'What did you tell Jess?'

'I told her that we'd kissed before and slept together once, but that it came to nothing.'

'Why do you always have to tell the truth, Charlie? Sometimes things are better left unsaid.'

'I'm not about to lie to her though.'

'But you'd be protecting her too, though. Now she'll be thinking you've got someone on the side.' Charlie hadn't thought of that, nevertheless he was glad he didn't lie. 'It's just a white lie anyway. Nic never got her act together for you, so there's nothing to tell.'

'I suppose so.' Charlie looked out of the window at the fading light. 'Jess deserves more though. She's actually a perfect thing, and I'm so glad I bumped into her.'

The letter gained more weight as Claire thought about not giving it to him. She didn't know what was in it, although she obviously had a good idea. Maybe he was just a stepping stone for her. And perhaps the letter would just prolong any agony that Charlie may have felt. Or perhaps it would leave the door open. She hadn't made her decision yet.

'So…what's the situation with you and Jess now? Do you think you'll patch it up?'

'I think so. I mean, she was quite upset to be honest. But…she knows me, and she knows she's everything. I know that there's nothing between me and Nicola, I've come to terms with that now and I need to move on. It was maybe a bit of a wake-up call for me too. I can't lose Jess over this. But I've not done anything actually wrong, so I know we'll work it out.'

'Do you still love her?'

Charlie knew she meant Nicola, despite her not making it perfectly clear. 'I will always love her. But I really gave myself away and got nothing in return. I can't go on like that. She's caused me a lot of damage and if it hadn't been for Jess, I don't know where I'd be right now. And I don't want to know.'

'She went back to Paris today, you know? But she's promised she's not going to see him. And I actually believe her for the first time. She's just going to go and see some old friends. I suppose she never got the chance last time she was there. They've been asking after her, so she decided to go.'

Charlie tried not to think about it. He'd have loved to go to Paris with her and walk along the Seinne with her. He knew now that none of that would happen. He'd never have Nicola and it had to be all about Jess from then on in.

They talked a little more and Claire had another glass of wine, she had to try and drown her sorrows somehow. She had to come to terms with it too, that he and Nicola would never be. Two of the most valuable people in her life who had a chance to be together, and whether it was a misalignment of the stars or not, they never made it work.

Charlie enjoyed the chat with Claire and hoped with all his heart that it wouldn't be his last.

'Well, I better head off, it's getting late.'

'I'll give you a lift.'

'No, it's okay.'

'Please, Claire. It's so cold outside. Let me drive you.'

Claire re-adorned her layers and to Charlie, what was revealed was just a spot on the sofa once again and not the shrine of his unrequited love that it had been before. He got quickly changed into his tactical trousers for going out into the cold, pulled on his boots, jacket and gloves. They headed down to the garage in silence. As they went through the door, they both noticed how much the temperature had dropped. Claire was grateful that he'd insisted on giving her a lift and that she could sit in the comfort of his car rather than face the bitter nip of the night. He'd done it again though, he'd foreseen and protected her. How she was going to miss that.

A few spots of snow started to dust the car on the way. It was still much too light to lie and the temperature was very low. Claire had her bag in the footwell on the far side of the car from Charlie. She thought hard about the letter and as they drew closer to her flat, she knew she was running out of time. She had pulled it discreetly from her bag and kept it concealed by her side.

Charlie had spent the evening talking about how he had to move on from Nicola. But what if he didn't make it up with Jess? He had to know what Nicola really felt or at the very least he might get some closure. His phone sat in the centre console and it lit up with a message. Not that she really wanted to pry, but Claire wondered who it was from, Jess or Nicola? It was Jess. "Hey. You still up? I miss you like crazy. Call when you get this, I really want to talk to you. Love you. Xxxxxxxxx"

If she was still unsure about what to do with the letter, her mind was suddenly made up. She slipped it back down the side of her leg and as surreptitiously as she could, pushed it back into her bag. She tried to be as subtle as possible, but the darkness in the car helped to mask what she was doing and she just made out that she was adjusting her jeans.

There was a space outside Claire's and he pulled into it and switched the engine off. 'I'll walk you to the door.' Her breath danced around in front of her and the glass of wine she had at Charlie's whirled a little in her head as she rummaged in her bag. She found her keys, but didn't see the letter. She did push it hard though, so it must have been somewhere down the bottom. 'Thanks for the lift, Charlie.'

'It's my pleasure.' A brief silence filled the air harder than the chill and the dark. 'Tell Nicola I'm asking for her, okay? I really hope this isn't goodb–'

'It's not.' He took her in his arms and gave her a warming and comforting hug, just in case it was the last time he saw her. 'I'll see you soon,' she said.

'Yeah, I hope so. Take care of yourself, alright? And you know where I am, if you need anything.'

'I do. Drive safely, it's looking a bit slippy.'


Charlie called Jess back from the car. 'Hey,' he said.

'Hey, yourself.' She sounded much more upbeat.

'Everything okay?'

'Uh-huh.'

443

'How's your birthday party?'

'Yeah, it was nice. Dad was mostly asleep in his chair the whole time as usual. My niece and nephew went to bed after him! And I just stayed up talking to my sister…'

'Yeah? What erm…what you been talking about?'

'Just stuff.' Charlie pulled back onto the main road and there were very few cars around. 'I've been thinking though…maybe I jumped the gun a bit. But I need to know Charlie, if there's anything going on. You have to be honest with me, and promise me.'

'Jess, I promise you, everything I told you was the truth. Nicola is in the past. We were never together when I was trying, and I'm not trying at all now. Come on, you're my whole life now, that's why I want you to move in. I want you everywhere I look. I'm all yours Jess.' He added, 'I'm *only* yours.'

'Okay.'

'I can see how it seems though, I mean, there's history with me and her, and I still spent time with her. But it never really crossed my mind, because I wasn't like…*doing* anything with her. But don't worry, I'm not going to be hanging out with her anymore. I only need you.'

'Okay.' A wide smile beamed across her face as a ton weight seemed to leave her body.

She'd discussed it at length with her sister. She asked Jess deep down if she believed that Charlie was sleeping with someone else and she felt it was a no. 'Go with your gut, it's always right. You just have to filter out the rest of the crap your head comes up with. So what if he said someone else's name whilst he was sleeping? John talks some rubbish when he's asleep, don't overthink it,' her sister said. 'So what if he's got an ex? Everyone's got an ex. It's about how he treats you. That's how you'll know. If you're always together and he's not going off somewhere, and no way he'd ask you to move in if he's got something else going on. He didn't have to ask you, you know?'

'I'm just…I'm scared to ever lose you Charlie.' She didn't really want to have that conversation over the phone, but she lay in bed at her parents' house staring at the ceiling and sleep evaded her. She had to talk to him.

'You don't need to worry about losing me, Jess. I'm not going anywhere.' Somewhere inside her, something clicked and she believed him and she trusted him.

'So…I'll see you tomorrow?' she asked.

'Yeah. I'm dying to see you. Sleep well Jess. I love you.'

Charlie got back to the flat and as he paused to let the shutter open, felt the call of the open road. He drove off down the road leaving the shutter to close by itself and headed west out of the city. He didn't feel there were as many nice drives as there were around the east coast, but also supposed there probably was, he just didn't know where they were. He felt uneasy and restless. He knew now at least that things were going to get back to normal with Jess and had a feeling they'd be better than ever. It had been a test and if they could survive the *Nicola* test, then they were bound to make it work. He still felt some anxiety however until he could hold her in his arms and confirm it. That's why he wasn't quite ready to go home.

Most of all, that was it. For the first time since he met Nicola again at the start of the year, he was beginning to move on from her. He had to for the sake of his future. It was hard, but he felt ready at last.

The road was harsh and unforgiving. As soon as he was out of the city, the temperature dropped even more. He drove with the window open and took a few corners a little too fast, he was playing again. He could feel the wheels sliding much more easily and there were obviously patches of black ice on the road. He took a right-hand bend fast and his phone jumped from the console into the passenger footwell, but it was too far away and too dark to retrieve whilst driving. The temperature had dropped so quickly that the gritters hadn't had a chance to grit the road and they probably wouldn't until the morning.

He came across a supermarket and remembered it was the same road he drove along at the start of the year. He recalled how crazy he acted that night and about the darkness of his thoughts. But the year had turned out good despite everything that happened with Nicola. He finally had hope with Jess and a bright future with her.

He decided to stop at the supermarket for old-times sake and see if he was received with the same suspicion as he walked around the aisles. He shut the window and switched the engine off. The engine blew a last gasp out of the exhaust before silence fell in the quiet supermarket car park.

He went around the other side to retrieve his phone and with the lights now on in the car, noticed something else in the footwell. It was a letter. He picked it up to examine and it simply said *Charlie* on the envelope. He recognised Nicola's handwriting and put it on the passenger seat. *I'll read that later*, he thought. He knew that Claire must have dropped it. She did seem to be fidgeting a little when he drove her home. He wasn't really interested in anything else Nicola had to say because every time she spoke to him all she did was cause him damage.

After refuelling his body and the car, he headed back out onto the consoling road. He decided he'd just go a little further before turning back. He didn't feel tired yet, but driving at night usually allowed fatigue to set in and it was an alternative to drinking too. He got quite good at finding the perfect balance between driving far enough away but getting back in time before he was too tired to drive properly. He imagined Jess would be sleeping and he desperately wanted to see her. He couldn't wait until the next day. It was finally the start of the life he wanted which had been postponed all year.

He did give Nicola a thought, but it wasn't like before. He hoped that she was doing well, but wasn't concerned about who she might be with or what she might be doing. So what if she was in Paris? And so what if he wasn't there to walk with her? It was her life to live and she'd always do it her way anyway. Perhaps she was just practice, he thought. It'd been so long since he'd actually been someone's boyfriend, so he was bound to be rusty. Maybe Nicola came along just to help turn him back from the machine that he was into a normal person that he craved to be. And for Nicola, Charlie came along to turn her life around. He could take some comfort from that at least.

The streetlights finished and were replaced by trees as he reached the country roads. The conditions were terrible. There was no snow, but the headlights beamed far ahead of him and the ice crystals covering the road made it look like it had been sprinkled with fairy dust. He wasn't feeling quite so reckless as he did when he drove there at the start of the year. After all, he had Jess to live for now. He felt a slight heaviness in his eyelids starting to set in. *Next roundabout and I'm spinning round*, he thought.

As he progressed along the road, he saw something in front of him at the corner. He had his full beam headlights on but dipped them to see if he could make it out more clearly. He checked his mirror and there was a set of headlights but they followed very far behind him.

As he approached, he realised it was a sharp right-hand bend, but on his side of the road there was a car over the grass verge. He slowed right down to take a look and it seemed as if it had just happened. He pulled up just before the car, put his hazard lights on and got out. When Charlie stepped out, his foot slipped away from underneath him, the corner was thick with black ice and as slippery as a skating rink.

He got back up and approached the car. It had been travelling in the same direction as Charlie but he'd just came straight off the road and hit a tree. It didn't look like a high-speed impact but there was heavy damage to the car nonetheless. He looked inside and a man of a similar age to Charlie, perhaps a year or two older, sat in the driver's seat and there was a baby in the back. The driver was distressed and Charlie instructed him to sit straight. 'Don't worry mate. I'll take care of you two, okay?' The man strained round in the seat and tried to reach the baby. 'Just hold on, I'll look after him, what's his name?'

'It's Oscar.'

The lights of the other car approached and Charlie wanted to flag them down. He leaned across the back seats and uncoupled Oscars' seat after a quick examination for injuries. 'What's your name?'

'Andrew, I'm Andrew.'

'Okay Andrew, I need you to just relax and I'll sort this all out in a few minutes. It just so happens I'm good at this sort of stuff, but you have to do as I ask alright?'

Charlie spoke with confidence and reassurance. Andrew felt some ease and believed Charlie even though he had an overwhelming urge to see his baby. 'I'll just flag this car down for an extra pair of hands. Please don't move and don't take your seatbelt off.'

Charlie took the torch from his pocket and waved it side to side on the road surface as if drawing an imaginary stop line. The car slowed and stopped in the road. The occupants were an older couple. 'Oh my God, is everyone okay?' the woman asked.

'I think so, erm, can I get you across please, there's a baby, would you be able to look after him just now?' He then addressed the man, 'Could you call 999? And I've got a hi-vis jacket in the back of my car.' He flicked the torch off, flipped it round and handed it to the man. Charlie clicked the button on his key fob which opened the boot and the tailgate slowly rose. 'Right hand corner next to the lights. Can you just field any cars that come, please?'

The man headed over to Charlie's car, following his instructions, as he headed back to the crashed car.

'Okay, Oscar, we'll get you out, then we'll get your daddy out.' There wasn't a scratch on him. He didn't cry and he didn't even look upset. He was unaware of what had happened and smiled at Charlie as he lifted the whole baby seat out of the car. The woman came rushing over. 'Take your time, the road's slippy as hell here.' He met her halfway and she took Oscar to sit in the back of her own car. The man donned the jacket and fumbled for the switch on Charlie's torch for a few seconds before finding it and placing his call.

A branch had come off the tree and smashed the driver's side window and Charlie stumbled on at as he approached. 'Keep your head straight, Andrew. Oscar's okay, there's a nice lady looking after him.' Andrew was desperate to get out, but Charlie wanted to give him a quick examination first and leaned in through the window. 'Do you remember the whole thing, yeah?' Andrew nodded. 'Try not to move your neck mate, just in case.' Andrew's hand felt for the seatbelt clasp. 'Just leave it on just now. I'm going to check your pupils. Charlie took his phone and used the torch on it. He pinned one eye open and shone light into it, then the other. 'Okay, good responses there. You got any tingling sensation or anything? Are you in pain anywhere?'

'My legs…erm, my neck's a bit sore actually.'

'Okay, it's maybe just whiplash but it's best if we're cautious.'

The man had placed his phone call and urged the emergency services to arrive as soon as possible, even for the simple fact that it was freezing cold. He saw some lights come from the other direction. There was a lot of noise, so he guessed it was a truck. He made his way slowly around the corner and stepped out into the road slightly and shone the torch at the ground. The truck switched off his full beam lights as he approached.

'You on any medication, or have any medical conditions or allergies at all?' Charlie continued the examination and collected information to brief the emergency services when they arrived.

'No, nothing.'

The glass from the smashed window poked at Charlie as he leaned in and he had to be careful not to cut himself. 'Okay, well, just with the neck, I think it's best that we wait for the paramedics to arrive. I don't want to take you out by myself and cause you any further injury. You're alright where you are anyway, and Oscar's safe. You'll just have to sit tight for a wee while.'

'I just don't know what happened though! I just kept going straight! I turned the wheels, but I kept going straight!'

'Don't worry about that just now, there's a lot of black ice about. No one's seriously hurt, so it'll be alright, okay?'

The lights from the truck started to approach and flood the road. The driver saw something on the corner but just thought someone was stopped for whatever reason and that it was okay to pass. The man started to worry that he might be coming a little bit too fast. He started to wave the torch at the road, just as Charlie had done. The driver was confused and took his foot off the pedal as he tried to figure it out. 'Hey!' the man shouted.

Charlie looked round. 'Just get him to stop there.'

'He's not stopping!'

The driver switched his full beams back on and saw the scene in front of him much more clearly. The man with Charlie's hi-vis jacket now lit up like a beacon and the driver slammed on the brakes. His braking was much too harsh and the wheels slipped on the ice. The driver fought for control, but the trailer started to overtake the cab. 'HEY!!!' Charlie swung his head round and saw the man in distress and running onto the grass out of the way. Charlie could now hear the shrieking of the brakes and a rumbling and bumping of the tyres on the road. The truck was out of control and slipping on the black ice. There was no way he could stop in time. 'LOOK OUT!!'

# Chapter Twenty-One

Nicola stayed at Severine's again. She had gone back to Paris for an empowering trip. She had to return it back in her head to the place it used to be before Patrice spoiled it for her. It was all part of her healing process. She had no desire to see him at last and in fact avoided the places she thought he might be. She visited her old gallery and except from her old boss everyone else was new there. She'd been out for a few celebratory drinks with friends. She was able to catch a few more than she did the last time. She was celebrating the new chapter in her life and the new lease of life that she had.

When she got back to Severine's she drew some water into a glass and looked at the fridge. Severine had long since rearranged her message that she left for her and Nicola smiled knowing that was all behind her now. She crashed out on Severine's sofa and had a sound sleep. As she slept, she had her recurring dream.

She was back in her dungeon. The stinking water still ran across the floor with the rats and cockroaches. Before long the figure appeared and entered as eerily as before, but this time she felt no fear. She felt like she was ready and wanted to face the figure up. She looked down and the flash of metal appeared from behind the cloak once again. The figure got closer and closer. Her heartbeat increased but she was ready, the figure could not hurt her any more. She didn't wake up when she usually did and got to see the face inside the hood. It was Charlie.

He looked around so that they wouldn't get caught. The flash of metal was a key and he freed her. Once she was unchained, all the power left her body but Charlie cradled her and carried her out of the dungeon. They emerged and outside it was a beautiful day. The grass was greener than green, the birds sang sweetly and a cool fresh breeze swept away the grime from the dungeon. Charlie walked still cradling her and before long, she could no longer see the dungeon, she couldn't smell the dank and foul smell of that place. She was free.

Charlie saw from the corner of his eye, the articulated lorry jack-knifing in his direction. As he began his hasty extraction, his jacket snagged on the broken glass of the window but he used his arms to rip it open, took a last look at Andrew knowing there was nothing else he could do and leaped as far as he could. The tractor broadsided the car and the trailer slammed into the front of the car. Most of the speed was gone though, and the truck pushed the car a width further into the grass.

Nicola sat at a café with Severine. It was a bitterly cold morning but still they sat outside so Severine could smoke. Nicola wore a thick black coat with a red tartan scarf. She enjoyed a coffee and a croissant and the company. The café was at the side of the road close to the Eiffel Tower. Cars and bikes buzzed around and beeped horns. She was so glad to finally have Patrice out of her life and be there and enjoy Paris once again.

Now things were different. She felt refreshed and renewed and it was all down to Charlie. Of course, Claire had helped a lot and had always been there for her, but Patrice kept re-emerging until Charlie did what he did. Nicola realised in the end that he'd done right by her and she thought about him.

She knew that there was no way she could make up for the way she'd mistreated him, but just hoped after a while they could just go back to being friends and things would be great with her, him and Claire again. They always had a great time together. She hoped that he was happy with Jess and a part of her wanted to keep in touch and not let him get too far away, just in case he and Jess did ever part. Maybe by that point they could try again and Nicola, being in a much better place, wouldn't mess it up. She didn't want to hang on for that though, she just wanted the best for Charlie and she'd do anything for him.

Claire rang her. 'Hey Claire!'

'Hi Nicola.' Nicola wondered what she'd done now to warrant a full name use. 'Erm...you need to come home...' She was confused.

'What do you mean? You know I'm not here to see him, that's dead and buried now.'

'Nicola, please. You need to come home *now!* I don't want to do this over the phone.'

'What...? Do what over the phone?' She was starting to worry. 'Are you alright, Claire?'

'Yes, I'm alright...'

'Then, what is it? What's wrong?'

'It's...I just...'

'Come on, Claire, you're scaring me now.'

'It's Charlie. There's been an accident.' Nicola paused her hand as she lifted the cup to her lips for another sip.

'What kind of accident…?'

A pause prevailed whilst Claire assembled the words on her tongue.

'Nicola, he's dead.'

Nicola lost all control of the things she was holding. The phone dropped to the ground. Her coffee cup tumbled out of her hand and smashed onto the table. It split into three uneven pieces and the warm coffee ran over the table and spilled over onto her. She supposed it might scald her, but she couldn't feel a thing. Severine gathered some serviettes for mopping up and started to speak but Nicola couldn't hear her. Claire's sobs came from the phone on the ground. Nicola buried her head in her hands. She started to panic. She felt like all the breath had come out of her body and a crushing sensation on her chest stopped her from breathing back in. 'No, no, no, no.' Severine picked up her phone and offered it to Nicola but she didn't pay any attention so tried herself.

'Alo? It's Severine.'

'Hi, Severine.'

'What's happened?'

'It's our friend…' Claire couldn't bring herself to repeat it, but Severine could glean what had happened from what unfolded in front of her.

'Oh my God. I'm so sorry.'

'Is Nicola there?'

'Um, just a moment…' She tried to pass the phone to Nicola and waited for her to take it. 'Nicola…Nicola…the phone.' Nicola took the phone, although she wished she could unhear the words that Claire had told her, but there'd be no going back.

'I don't understand, Claire. I thought you…' Tears streamed from Nicola's face adding to the coffee already in her lap. 'Were you not just round to his last night? I don't…no, no. This can't be happening. This can't be true.'

'Nic, please. Come home.'


Charlie jumped as far as he could but it was already too late. He forgot all the about the branch at his feet and stumbled on it. Before he could get back upright again, the trailer was already too close and it struck his head before careering into the car. He was pinned between the trailer and the front of the car. Andrew could see him lying across the bonnet in front of him with blood issuing from his ears. His eyes were still open and he reached out for Andrew who now couldn't get out at all because the car was trapped against hedges on the passenger side and the tractor unit on his side. He looked towards Charlie as his eyes grew dark. The car horn blasted high up into the cold night sky, yet an eerie silence descended upon them. Andrew had to concentrate hard to make out what Charlie said. 'Tell her...tell her...not to forget about me. Tell her...I'll always love her.'

He couldn't believe that was it. He couldn't believe he wouldn't ever see Jess or Nicola or anyone else ever again. The light started to fade for him and tears tracked down his face and he could feel how cold they became on his skin. He couldn't believe that he'd survived so much and at times he didn't care about whether he'd die or not, because he had no joy in his life. Suicide had always loomed over him for many years, but he had survived it. So why now, when things finally looked good, was his life taken from him? He closed his eyes as an eternal tiredness started to set in. Soon after, he was gone.

Nicola once again packed her things in a hurry. Severine had tried to call the airline on her behalf to ask about bringing her flight forward but they advised her to get to the airport and that she could perhaps go onto standby. She called a friend of hers that had a car explaining the circumstances, so managed to arrange a lift to the airport. Severine went in to the ticket desk with her and had to handle the conversation because Nicola was just too distraught. 'I'm sorry, but there are no more flights today.' Nicola barely had the energy to stand, but she had to find the strength to get back. She didn't know what she'd do when she got there and tried not to realise that her timely return would have absolutely no impact on the outcome. But she had to get back and be somehow as close to him as she could.

'Nicola, Nicola. There are no more flights today, cherie.'

In a brief moment of clarity, Nicola knew exactly what to do. 'Eurostar…' she said.

Claire met her at Central Station in Glasgow. They flew into one another's arms and felt strength in seeing each other again. 'Nic, I'm so sorry.'

Nicola nodded through her tears. 'Me too.'

They headed outside to catch a taxi back to Nicola's. She didn't feel weary. Obviously, the extra train journey made travelling back to Glasgow a much more arduous one, but Nicola had to be strong to get back to Charlie. She had to find a way to manage without him now. By the time she pulled in to St Pancras Station she'd had time on the train to gather the ability that she needed to get home. As she walked to the other platform, she remembered how Charlie met her there and remembered the state she was in at the time. She looked at the scar on her hand as she switched platforms for the Glasgow bound train. She stopped and looked at the point where she ran into his arms the last time she came back from Paris. She tried not to think about how Charlie would never meet her again, at a station, or anywhere else. Yet, she

461

stood there for several minutes just imagining he was waiting for her again.

Claire had received a call from the police. They looked into Charlie's phone and could see from the messages that she'd been round to see him that night. They contacted her and went to her flat in the early morning so as not to break the news over the phone. When they got to his flat, they found his next of kin details which he'd left in the event of anything, at which point they'd contacted his parents.

'What about Jess?' she asked.

'We tried to call the number but it rang out, we've left a couple of messages to call back. We were guessing that's his girlfriend?'

'Yeah,' Claire said, 'she's a teacher.' They asked what school, but Claire didn't know.

Jess slept sweetly, full of anticipation for seeing Charlie the next day. She got a call early in the morning but she didn't hear it because she was asleep. She woke up late and had to drive all the way back through from Stirling and get to school. She noticed the missed call was from a Glasgow number and she had a voicemail. She was really pushed for time, so thought she'd listen to it later, perhaps when she arrived at work. It wasn't anyone in her contacts so it was probably just someone trying to sell something.

The traffic was terrible and she got caught out by the M8 in the morning. She had very little experience with the morning commute on that road and completely underestimated the traffic. Usually she only ever had to take the surface streets between her flat and the school. By the time she arrived, the bell was about to ring and she went straight into class. She'd forgotten all about her voicemail.

'I have to go round to his flat.'

'Why Nic? What's it going to do? Anyway…how do you plan to–' Nicola produced his keys and Claire recognised them – the black pear-shaped fob which opened the door from the street and the two big square keys. She still had them from when she stayed with him after the break-in. He'd mostly forgotten about them, but still wanted her to have somewhere to run to if she really needed to. He did have an image of Nicola turning up when Jess was there, but he also knew that would only ever happen if something really serious had happened.

It was only recently that he thought about getting those keys back. After all, he had to give them to Jess. 'I think it's a bad idea.' She could see that Nicola had already made her mind up so Claire just had to decide whether to go with her or not. She thought she ought to. 'But

463

what about Jess? And his family? What if they're there? What will you do?'

'I don't know, but I have to go.'

Nicola drove them both to his building and parked neatly in the visitor parking. They let themselves in and there was nothing spectacular about the place. There was no sign that the man who lived there died the night before trying to help people. There was no indication that the place would now have to be vacated of all of his things. Perhaps most importantly, there was no one else there, only Nicola and Claire. His parents and Jess alike were mourning. The clearing of the flat could wait.

Jess got a visit from the police at school and the Headteacher called her parents to come and collect her. He waited with her until her mum and dad arrived. Her sister arrived later in the evening to help comfort her but they weren't leaving her flat that night. Charlie's parents called his sister and she was travelling up from London, so they were waiting for her to arrive and they wouldn't do any more that evening either.

The lights were all off and the place seemed so inert and vacant. The same views faced them; the hills from one direction and the city from another. The Clyde flowed like normal, the wind blew like normal and the cold nipped like normal. There was nothing to show the huge loss that Nicola and Claire and Jess and his family had suffered. Claire sat on the sofa in tears and Nicola walked around in silence. She touched the surfaces and the walls. She touched one of the large glass panels that led outside and it sucked the heat out of her fingers.

She closed her eyes at some points and remembered him. When her eyes were closed, there was light in the place, she could feel him and his warmth and comfort. She could see the times he'd made her breakfast or dinner, or they'd ordered something in and sat at the dining table to eat and the mornings spent out on the terrace when she stayed in the summer. She loved the place. Not because it was fancy but because it was Charlie's and it was the only place she'd ever felt comfortable and truly herself for as long as she could remember. She made love to him in that room and how she truly regretted it would only ever be the one time.

She looked in his fridge. She wanted to look at the foods he liked to eat. She knew what he liked and what he didn't and could tell the items that belonged to Jess in there. There was a bottle of whisky with a glass next to it sitting on the corner of the kitchen counter. She pulled the top off and the cork squeaked. Claire looked round curious to the sound.

She gushed a few glugs into the glass and lifted it to her nose. The smell meant him. He liked his whisky. He often used it as an escape for the torments in his past but he enjoyed whisky in happy times too. Other than her dad, he was the only person Nicola knew that could drink straight single malt. 'You know, he gave my dad an education on whisky once.' She smiled before taking a sip. It stung her mouth and throat as she gulped it down. It was so strong, it was so intense, it was too much for her to handle. It was so Charlie. She took another sip and the strength and taste didn't diminish. She took a final sip and it was gone. She felt like she could breathe fire as the whisky trickled its way down into her and spread its warmth from within.

Claire watched her as she walked around the flat and wondered what exactly Nicola was trying to achieve, but knew she had to be there with her. She walked over to his computer and there was a small filing cabinet under the desk. She tried the top drawer and it was locked. She tried the bottom drawer somehow expecting a different result, but it was also locked. Noticing the keyhole she thought back, 'I know where this is,' she said to herself. When she stayed with him, she opened the cutlery drawer and took the scissors out to open a packet of coffee. Subsequently, she made a mess by spilling coffee beans over the counter and into the open drawer. She picked up the cutlery insert to collect the escaped beans and noticed two small keys on a split ring. She didn't know what they were for at the time, but now she'd figured it out.

She had no wish to look in the filing cabinet before and she didn't even know that it was locked. So what did he keep in there?

She went to the cutlery drawer, lifted the tray and sure enough, the keys were still there. 'What are you doing, Nicola?'

'I just want to see…'

'See what? That's obviously his private stuff.' There was a combination of exhilaration and trepidation. Was it his work stuff? She dreaded to find something about missions or people he'd killed, but she also wanted to know everything else about him all of a sudden. She still hadn't come to terms with it but something inside compelled her to try and fill herself up with him because now that he was gone, he'd only start to trickle out of her day by day. If he had any more secrets, she wanted to know them all.

The key fitted and turned. She opened the top drawer and went though it, even if only vaguely. There was nothing that seemed to jump out at her. She looked in the bottom drawer. 'Claire,' she lifted a file out, 'look at this…' It was marked *N*. She tentatively placed it on the coffee table and stared at it for a while wondering what might be inside. It looked like the kind of file she imagined someone would get from a private detective, containing a hundred pictures of someone going about their daily life and speaking to people, including information on everyone inside and their relationship with them. Or perhaps she'd just seen too many movies.

'Well, Nic, are you going to open it or not? Isn't it what you wanted?'

She peeled the file open as if it was an unexploded bomb and lifted the first sheet out. "McDonaugh Motors…" it read. "…£1000 deposit paid…Charlie Maxwell." It was signed by him. She showed Claire and she analysed it.

'So it wasn't the dealer who put the first grand in then. It was Charlie all along.' Nicola was gobsmacked, as was Claire. He hadn't even told Claire, he just wanted her to have the car and would do whatever it took. There were printouts from florist's websites, about the sweet pea flowers, including screeds of correspondence about his special request. It was obvious the lengths he had gone to just to obtain those flowers. There was a slip from *Round the Clock Locks* to the value of £235.60, again signed by Charlie. The receipt for her suit was in there. She realised she never did pay him back for it. There were other various things like that: a ticket stub from the play they saw in January and the confirmation of her Eurostar tickets.

There were photos. The first one was of all three of them on her birthday weekend. She had the same one at her desk at work. Then there was one more photo. It was of Nicola when she was staying over.

Charlie tried to show her how to bake bread and she was making a mess with the flour and yeast. 'Okay, smile! This is going to Good Housekeeping,' he joked. Nicola was laughing. Her mouth was open and her smile was genuine and pure. Her hair was tied back in the slick ponytail that he liked, yet a few frisky strands escaped. She wasn't looking directly at him when he took the photo. She wore a plain black jumper and there were puffs of flour on it. That was his favourite and most prized photo of all. She didn't pose for it; she couldn't touch up her hair because her hands were sticky with dough. It was pure and real and natural. It was the Nicola that he wished he had all the time.

He never showed her the photo. It was taken in an instant and nothing was made of it. That was the first time she'd seen it and she was struck down with grief. It used to stay in his bedside unit, but since he started going out with Jess it was grudgingly relegated to the filing cabinet and only looked upon when he was home alone. She fell to the floor clutching the photo and Claire rushed over to cradle her in her arms. Nicola didn't know what she was looking for when she wanted to come over to the flat but either way, she certainly found it.

She looked to her left from where she was bundled on the floor. That's the spot where they made love on the sofa. She remembered how tender he was and how when they were together, it seemed like that was everything in the world and that there was nothing else. She couldn't believe that he was just always there, whenever she needed him and he always gave her everything – as much or as little as she wanted. He loved her and cared for her magnanimously. He made no demands of her or put any pressure on her. He was continually perfect.

Since she arrived at the flat, the fatigue from travelling was finally starting to set in. She got up still clutching the photo and headed through to his bedroom. She picked up the photo of him in his uniform and climbed into his bed with it. She held it close to her chest and pulled the covers over before crying herself to sleep.

# Chapter Twenty-Two

The police drove his car away from the scene and although it spent a night at the station, they returned it to the flat the next day and dropped the keys there for his family to deal with. His mum, dad and sister arrived late in the morning and that had been the first time his sister had ever seen the place. His mum and dad had hardly spent any time there either because he'd usually just go home when he wanted to see them. The only other person who knew the place well other than Charlie was Nicola. Jess was getting to know it too of course, but she'd never actually lived there with him and now she wouldn't ever get that chance.

They went through his things and it took a long time. They went down to the car, opened all the doors and boot to empty it of its contents. They found a whole host of equipment neatly stashed away in cubbyholes. He had an old ammo box filled with various survival items as well as two separate purpose rucksacks, but only he knew the exact load-out and purpose of them. They were secured to the bulkhead on the back seats with a piece of cargo net he'd made himself and bungee cords, secure enough to survive whatever driving style he adopted, yet easily enough deployed in a hurry. That's the way Charlie liked it and he'd always been very fastidious. He particularly liked the set-up he had with that car, *space and pace*, he used to say. His dad looked in the front passenger seat and noticed a letter. It was a plain white envelope with *Charlie* written on it. He pinched it a few times between his fingers and ascertained it was just a letter, perhaps a couple of pages. The writing on the front looked feminine and elegant, so he supposed it must have been Jess's writing.

Jess, her parents and her sister came to his flat whilst his family were all still there. She hadn't yet met Charlie's sister and had only met his parents on a couple of occasions. There was an inherent awkwardness to the situation. She didn't know them well and didn't want to belittle any of the grief they were feeling. He was their baby boy and baby brother, but he was also Jess's. His dad handed her the letter and of course she didn't recognise it. She put it in her bag. She didn't want to read it in front of everyone, whatever it might be.

Snow carpeted the ground at the cemetery. It was where the majority of Charlie's family were buried, in a quiet corner of East Lothian. There was a huge turnout. Charlie's friends and colleagues were there. There was a beautiful Dutch journalist with her husband, former fellow operatives from the UK and Overseas, and former commanding officers. His family were there as well as Jess and her family. Andrew was there with his wife and Oscar as well as the other couple that stopped to help. Rachel was there with her husband and three young children. And then there was Nicola and Claire.

The snow was dry and fell as if in slow motion. Jess stood next to the hole in the ground where Charlie would be laid to rest. She saw Claire and assumed the person standing next to her was Nicola. Jess handled herself very well. She was beautiful, despite the lack of sleep and the obvious dread she'd had about the day. She had to make the effort however because it was the last time she was going to see Charlie. Claire had pointed her out to Nicola, but it was obvious who she was, since everyone rallied round her because she'd just lost the love of her life.

After he was committed to the ground, Jess approached Nicola. Claire saw her coming and was very apprehensive about what might unfold. 'Nicola, I presume?'

'Yes…it's nice to meet you.'

'Likewise. Thanks for coming. I just wish we were meeting over better circumstances.' Nicola didn't know what to say. Jess continued, 'Will you come to the wake?' Nicola was shaken by Jess's strength and felt massively uncomfortable.

'Erm...I think we need to head off back to Glasgow.'

'Okay, well, thanks for coming.'

At the wake, Jess seemed to float around between people. Everyone offered their condolences but she felt like she was having an out-of-body experience. She listened to a conversation Andrew and his wife were having with Charlie's parents. 'We really can't come to terms with this ourselves. He stopped to help us...he got Oscar out...' his wife started to cry and kiss and cradle Oscar, 'The emergency services said that the only reason I didn't sustain any more injury was because he insisted I keep my seatbelt on. He saved my life, and Oscars.' Tears fell from his eyes now. 'If there is anything, and I mean anything we could ever do for you...please let us know.'

Jess floated over to where the older couple were. They were speaking to some of his old colleagues. 'Well, it made perfect sense that he was ex-forces, because...well, he had such a command over the situation. He was calm and told Jan to keep the baby whilst he looked the driver over. And he had me in his hi-vis trying to…' he paused, 'well…I just wish I had–'

'Derek it's not your fault.'

'I just wish I'd done more…'

Jess contributed, 'The truck slipped on the black ice…there wasn't anything you could do about that.'

One of his old colleagues spoke, 'Well, that was just Charlie all over. He had to help people, even if he put himself in harms way. He used to look after all of us, everyone is his old unit used to call him *dad*. And not *just* because he'd look after us, but he'd tell us off if we were misbehaving!' Jess smiled at the sentiment as he continued. 'He only ever wanted to make the world a less cruel place. And the world is slightly darker now losing someone like him.' He addressed Jess, 'You should be very proud of him.'

Jess tried to reply 'I am', but she felt choked. Her lips moved but no words came so she just nodded.


Nicola sat in her car with Claire outside the cemetery thinking about him. They waited for everyone to disappear into their cars and make their way to the wake. She tried to find somewhere that sold sweet pea flowers to put by his grave but she couldn't get them anywhere. She had no idea how he managed to find thirty for her birthday. He really was amazing.

Once the coast was clear, she went back into the cemetery by herself. She didn't go back to the grave, but sat on a bench in the corner where she could see him. She used her gloved hand to clear the light powdering of snow off the wooden slats as it continued to fall over the fields and hills around her, cancelling all the colour out of the countryside with a plain light white. Claire stayed in the car to give her some time.

The snow pirouetted around in the air. It swirled and looped like blossom caught in the spring breeze. It was cold, yet she felt warm. She had the memory of Charlie in her, as she would for the rest of her life.

# Epilogue

Jess went home after being at his flat with both her family and Charlie's family. She went straight into her bedroom and the rest of them were still up, making supper and cups of tea and talking about how to best support her and to watch out for her until she got over things. She knew her life had to go on without him, but she'd never get over his loss – not ever. She was so frightened about losing him to someone else, but to lose him like that was absolutely crippling. She felt so devastated that she hadn't been able to see him again after their argument. Somehow, after his death everything became so clear. She knew deep down that Charlie *did* love her and so what if he'd said someone else's name? Everybody's got a past.

There wasn't much comfort from them making it up on the phone. She hated how stupid she'd been. She hated how she didn't just hold off so they could talk about it properly instead of on the street before work, or for not just forgetting about it completely and taking his word for it. Thankfully, she was also unaware that Charlie would have probably just went straight home if he didn't have the stress of how he'd upset Jess and the guilt about Nicola lingering over him, so he would have never been there on that road at all.

She climbed into bed and peeled open the letter that Charlie's dad had handed her. She had no idea what was inside, but felt she had to open it when she was alone. It was Nicola's letter.

*Charlie,*

*I just really wanted to apologise to you. I'm sorry about how I was at the restaurant, I was really out of order. Things haven't been great for a while between us and I know it's really been down to me. What you did to Patrice was such a shock for me. I never ever saw you as a 'violent' man and just sort of couldn't believe that you'd do that. But now I think I understand and I've never heard from him again. I feel like he's really out of my life and I've got you to thank for that. I'm sorry I called you a dangerous man. You know I don't really think that and I know that you'd never really hurt anyone unless they really deserved it. You were only protecting me.*

*Claire keeps telling me about you and I know that you're with Jess now. I just want to say that I hope you're happy. She tells me that you are and that she means the world to you. I'm glad you had such a great time in New York with her and I hope she treats you the way you ought to be treated, because you deserve nothing but the best.*

*Well, I've started, so I may as well go on and get everything off my chest. I've been so mixed up these past few years and I don't mean to go on about it Charlie, but honestly, you've been like a guardian angel to me, and to Claire, but to me especially. There is no way I could ever, ever repay you for everything you've done for me. I'm really sorry for messing around with you. It's not like I didn't think about you and me, in fact, I thought about it all the time. But it was also the first time in seven years that I'd been free and I suppose I just needed to blow off some steam. But I used you and treated you really badly and as much as I can apologise for that, I don't think I can ever forgive myself for it. You were just always there and so willing to do everything for me so I suppose I just took advantage of that – as shit an excuse as it is.*

*There was a spell, I think you know, where I slept with a lot of guys to try and fill some kind of void, and the void was for someone to treat me well and make me feel good again. Then that's what you always did, but I never realised it at the time. After being downtrodden so badly for so long I think it spoiled the way I view men, but you're not like any other man I've met. I just felt like I had power over them and it was like a false way of building myself up. But you've always made me feel so special and never ever asked for anything in return. You know, I usually never get treated the way I deserve to be, and in a roundabout way I can say the same about you because you treated me so well when I didn't deserve any of it.*

*I think I wanted to be with you, God knows Claire wanted it, but I was so messed up that I felt I couldn't love you the way I should. You're so perfect and I'm far from perfect so I was always scared I'd let you down. When we made love, it was unlike anything I've ever experienced, it was too real and it scared me shitless. It felt like you had control over me, because there is nothing else and no one else that can make me feel like that. I was frightened it would be something that I'd depend on and I didn't want to feel weak and feeble, I just wanted to be myself and not need or crave anyone or anything. With the others, it was always an empty exchange and that was always easier for me, because I knew I could walk away from them at any time. And then I started going out with Tommy, mainly because I'd never hurt him, didn't feel any guilt towards him and wouldn't be reminded about how shit I'd been all the time.*

*I know I'd still be in that bad place I've been the past few years if it hadn't been for your input though. You've broken that unhealthy cycle of Paris/Patrice, running home and running back. I'd never dream of interfering with you and Jess, but it doesn't mean that I can't tell you*

*how much you mean to me and how special a person you are to me.
You've had such a positive effect on my whole life.*

*I hope this letter finds you well and that you can understand how
grateful I am for everything, even though I have a funny way of showing
it. I hope that we can stay good friends, because Claire and I really love
hanging out with you. I know we hardly talk anymore and I really miss
getting your messages all the time, they used to always brighten my day.
But I understand you're concentrating on Jess so that's why I don't
hear from you much. I just hope that you can accept my apology for
everything and that we can just go back to how things were at the start
of the year, because I can't imagine not having you in my life now.
Maybe over time I can at least try to repay you for the kindness that
you've shown me, if you'll give me that chance.*

*I'd really like to meet her some time, just even to tell her to take
good care of you, but I'm sure she does. And just to tell her how lucky
she is to have you, although I'm sure she already knows that too, and
maybe tell her not to blow it like I did.*

*So this is turning into a mammoth letter and I'm sorry if I'm
boring you, but I've got one last confession I suppose. I'm way too
chicken to say it to your face but after everything recently I've come to
realise that I love you Charlie, and the thing is, I always have and I
always will. I destroyed our potential though and I know I've missed my*

*chance with you. I don't mean to tell you this to cause you any trouble or to have you say it back to me. I just wanted you to know.*

*Thank you for giving me my life back, I'll never forget it so long as I live. I understand if you don't want to speak to me anymore but if that's the case then I just want to wish you every happiness in life. But I really hope we can see each other again soon.*


*Nicola xxx*

Printed in Great Britain
by Amazon

54664141R00286